The Children of Opella Book 1

-Tendrils of Nahasmen-

Rebekkah Kniffen

Alonili Press

Cover design by Miblart

Alonili Press

aloniliconnections@gmail.com

ISBN-13: 978-1947517028

ISBN-10: 1947517028

For more information, contact publisher at above email or go to www.alonilipress.com

Printed in the United States of America

To my husband,
without your help I would not have finished this book.

\- and -

To my children,
may you take the tools we gave you and build the weapons you
need to slay your own dragons.

Contents

Prologue 3

Chapter 1 5

Chapter 2 27

Chapter 3 35

Chapter 4 61

Chapter 5 84

Chapter 6 111

Chapter 7 135

Chapter 8 158

Chapter 9 187

Chapter 10 225

Chapter 11 235

Chapter 12 253

Chapter 13 284

Chapter 14 305

Chapter 15 333

Chapter 16 361

Epilogue 389

Prologue

The Fourth Age

As peace ruled in the higher realms, the gods again turned their attentions to Lur. The world which Indar had created was untamed. Descending the bridge and passing the gate, Bakarrik saw that the world was ripe for a lesser being to rule it. Bakarrik was strong, but also wise and noble; and he considered it improper to rule the world himself. However, he knew that the untamed must be ruled, lest chaos increase.

So he created man in his own liking, but he lessened the reflection of his powers. And therefore man was less wise, less noble, and less mighty. But in spite of being lesser, man retained Bakarrik's sense of pride. And so man developed his own jealousies, ambitions, and lusts. Finally, Bakarrik placed within man love and the desire to be loved, and so the struggle within the soul of man began.

Bakarrik, not seeing the developing unsavory qualities in his creation, made many more. They all had different features, colors, sizes, and shapes. He made men and women and gave them the ability and knowledge to procreate.

As men expanded across Lur, the qualities within man developed something Bakarrik could not have predicted, because it had never before existed among the gods — the capacity to develop new power. Man grew stronger and greater, with his eye ever raising himself to the greatness of the god he saw himself to be. Seeing these, Bakarrik blessed his remaining creation by giving man apathy, and thus the driving fire within man was tempered.

To resolve the disputes among men, Bakarrik placed over them kings, judges, and counselors from among their own kind. These he blessed with higher wisdom, for as long as their lives should last.

For a time, there was peace on Lur.

Oracle Li'Viadimeir, The Histories, translated by Kallalia

1

Autumn of 3551 through 11th of Lar Rala, 3552

Meira

I stormed through the trees, leaving a trail of whirlwinds behind me. *Just try to follow me*, I thought. With a final glare over my shoulder, the floor of red and golden leaves erupted into the air. I dropped onto my bed, a burning ember in the crisp evening.

"Dear love, dear love, be peace," the wind sighed.

"Shut up," I demanded.

Meira, Father spoke directly into my mind. *I wasn't done.*

Fine, then talk. It's not like I can't hear you. Unlike the fortunate races, Fae children couldn't escape lectures.

You know that it's not safe.

You've been teaching me diplomacy for the last fifty years. Do you plan to ever let me use it? Just once?

Meira, it's critical that I send someone with substantial experience. The situation is just too volatile. If anything were to go wrong, anything at all, you could be caught in the middle of a bloodbath.

You think Terdangia can fix that? She's a terrible ambassador! You send her all the time. Can you even count the number of complaints you've received after her "negotiations" were finished? If anyone's going to cause a bloodbath....

Meira, the lessons I'm teaching her are different from the ones I'm teaching you.

This was at least the fiftieth time this week he had said that. Father really needed to invent some new sayings. *What, so she's expendable?* I dropped back into my bed.

Rae, I love all of my children.... And I love you.

Oh, don't even start, I thought. His love wasn't in question. His faith in me? Well, to be in question, I would need some evidence that he actually had any.

When, Father? When will I get to go?

When you're ready.

So that's when exactly? Another fifty years? A hundred? You had Corwyn out when he was thirty.

He's a teleporter, Meira, not an...

And Yur... forty.

Meira....

And Elris... even Elris... you sent him at sixty.

Father was silent. Finally. I glared at the branches over my head. Five, four, three...

Meira, my mother interjected. She was quicker to jump in than usual. Perhaps she had been listening in. Under the right conditions my mother could intercept mind speech. It had been a big moment in the lives of each of her children when they discovered that Mother was listening in to their secret conversations. It was almost as disconcerting when we discovered that it was impossible to convincingly lie over mind speech. *Your father really does have your best interests at heart, even if you don't always agree with his actions.*

Mother, could you please convince him to back off, then? I'm getting smothered here. You know I've never actually been anywhere interesting without an escort.

That's not even remotely true.

I'm not counting Killallia, Mother, or T'grivven, or Nor'troth, or anyplace else where the greatest health threat is being trampled by chaperones.

Mother was silent for several seconds before reproaching. *Where is it you would like to go, Meira? What dangerous thing would you like to do?*

I'm not asking to jump right into the middle of some war. Just not be stuck digging up tubers and curing venison.

I will speak with your father again, but you will comply with his decision.

I folded my arms across my chest. Of course I would comply; he was the king, after all. Compliance wasn't exactly optional. If he were just a normal father, I wouldn't have to get berated for "setting a bad example for everyone else." Well. I might be stuck with being the perpetual good example, but I didn't have to be silent about it.

Clearly I wouldn't be assisting the team who was negotiating the release of the last of the nobles out of the goblin prison. The goblins had already killed everyone they didn't consider valuable enough to ransom. Had I gone when I wanted, a month ago, I knew I could have saved more lives. But saving my innocence was the most important thing to Father — or "saving your young eyes from the horrors of Lur," he said often enough. It was as though I were being prepared to ship off to some other planet. The only way to escape the great "horrors of Lur" was to die or to go live with the gods. And they spent their whole time watching the "horrors of Lur" anyway.

The next several months did little to allay my annoyance. Father didn't bother addressing the issue at all. This was what I fully expected; he wouldn't bring it up again until I pushed the topic all the way to the wall. Then mother would go talk to him, and eventually… eventually… he would roll. He couldn't justify keeping me sheltered and naive forever.

But I wasn't interested in waiting that long, not this time. I was nearly ninety-three years old, and I was going to finally do something to prove myself, whether Father sanctioned it or not.

My opportunity came on a dreary spring day when Father and Malachi were clashing their wills against each other… again… like elk battling over a doe. Within a month or two they would be on amicable terms. Over the last several years their relationship had become so strained that many of us feared it would break completely. But ultimately they continued to prove that their love ran much deeper than any of their conflicts could uproot.

As was typical, Father penalized Malachi by assigning him to menial tasks for the next several weeks — a particular frustration for Malachi, since he was overloaded with his own pursuits. But as these were usually the bone of contention, Father was quite satisfied stomping all over them.

Malachi left in a huff to eliminate most of the list quickly, and it was sixteen days before I saw him back in the court to retrieve whatever assignments had collected while he was gone. On his way back out, I quietly joined him as he plodded through a tree portal, tapping his shoulder at the last moment so we would arrive in the same place. While moments ago we were in Nord Flaume, we reappeared in Urlin.

He put his arm around me and gave me a squeeze. "You decided to join me for this one, Firefly?"

I smiled up at him. "Actually..." I hadn't prepared for how I wanted to tell him that I just wanted to take over the entire mission.

"Father doesn't know you're here, does he," he determined.

"No, not really." I paused for a bit while Malachi waited patiently. We would be walking for a few hours anyway. "I... actually, Malachi, I was hoping to handle this one myself. You know, my own assignment."

"I see," he answered. A normal brother would frown or smile or chuckle or shake his head. Malachi did none of these. Emotion and feeling were missing elements for him—too many scars, Mother had explained many decades ago. "It's not exactly an assignment if you're volunteering. It's more like... a volignment." He pondered for a bit. "Do you know what the mission is?"

"Umm, no, actually."

"A few thugs dammed up a stream, and now they're charging the locals for access to the water. The locals don't have anyone else to help them."

"So we just have to blast open a dam?"

"Well, that would be the simple answer, certainly, but it's not very permanent, do you think?" Malachi raised his brow at me.

"No, not really. Once we're gone, they'll just block it up again."

"Right."

I thought about the various things I had been learning over the last several decades. All peoples, I understood, had reasons for what they did. It was simply a matter of determining what would appeal to both sides in order to achieve a lasting peace. Of course, this principle was different for different races. Goblins were typically unreasonable and only responded well to superior force. Dvergr desired security for their children's children's children—especially in the form of great wealth. Centri needed the peace that came from knowing the will of the gods. Pixies only sought trinkets and abandoned fields. Humans, the most complex of races, were diverse and hid their desires in lies; but typically they fell into two groups—those who wanted to dominate their neighbors, and those who wanted only to be left alone.

We found a small village on the nook of a dry stream bed. A water-wheel sat idle. Men were unloading barrels from a cart, while women distributed water from them to their children. One of the women, looking up and seeing us, shouted cheerfully. Several children ran in our direction. Try as we might to blend in, the sight of our brilliant silver and golden skin was unusual for most humans.

"Good Fae," one of the elder men called as we came into range, "thank you for coming. We really didn't expect it."

"Well," Malachi said quietly to me, "a good first impression is always a great place to start. Dazzle them." Then he stepped off the path in another direction, as though suddenly interested in the birds in a tree.

I opened my mouth briefly, searching for my tongue. And before I knew what to say, I repeated a simple phrase that had been drilled into me. "My father sends his greetings, sir. What would you ask of us?"

"It's our water, princess. They took our water, and we're having to sell our livestock and all of our food just to pay for that. We told them that we're already too poor to pay, but they don't care. It's a stream. They shouldn't have a right to take all of it."

"Who has taken your water?"

"Kobolds, ma'am," he answered quickly. "There's a large city of them to the west, and they've never been trouble to us, before."

"Why would..." I started too quickly. I shut my mouth. *Listen first,* I remembered my mother repeating over and over. *Then think. There is time for talk when both of these are well finished.* I breathed. Kobolds were just tricksters, not dangerous. They were interested in enjoyment and the thrill of life. Their humor was reckless and occasionally dangerous. Certainly they had no respect for property, but they couldn't hold a prank for a long period of time. Stealing water to sell it again seemed out of character with their race. "Are you certain that these are kobolds who are doing this?"

"Ma'am, I was just there buying water from them." Several other heads around the elder nodded in agreement. "We've got nothing against them as a people, but these particular folk are bleeding us dry. And we did try getting pushy over it, but they outnumber us. And, you know kobolds are… well, they're not easy to fight."

"Fine, then. Let's go to them." My tone expressed confidence, which was a total lie. I had no idea why they would be doing this. Then again, that's what talking was for. The men offered me a place on their cart, and I did my best to accept it graciously. It was filthy, but they were kind enough to apologize for that. Malachi waved goodbye and walked off, leaving me now completely without assistance. I was both thankful to him and utterly terrified. I had, actually, expected him to at least stand by in case I fell in over my head.

The trip was less than an hour before we stopped at a small lake, though at the pace our horse was dragging along, it was amazing we traveled any distance at all. At the near end of the lake, in the only place where a wagon could be moved to the water, was a large dam of lumber, stone, sod, and pitch. Trees stuck up out of the water, showing that it was a rather recent addition to the landscape. Several squatty kobolds emerged from their resting places to greet us.

Kobolds are invisible while they're resting or sitting around. It's only when they move about that they can be seen. They're masters at creating ambushes. So I couldn't tell how many were here, just that there were four who came to speak to us. I stepped down from the cart and approached them.

"Friends," I began with all the pleasantry I could, "I am Meira, daughter of Matthias, king of the High Fae. I have been asked to speak with you regarding the river that you have blocked."

The kobolds looked at each other unpleasantly, wringing their hands, until another appeared, sliding off a stump. He was slightly smaller, but he bore the arrogance of an aristocrat.

"Who are you to think you can question us?" he demanded in a tiny, shrill voice.

"I am Meira, daughter of Matthias, king of the High Fae," I answered. I was fairly certain I had just said that.

"And who is that to us?" he demanded, strutting up within an inch of my knees until he was staring straight up into my face.

I tried to remember everything I had learned about kobolds. I had never actually met any, and they were never considered significant players in Lur. So I had, reasonably I thought at the time, not paid any attention. Honestly, I had no idea what I was doing, but this little shrimp was unnerving me with his lack of basic personal boundaries and utter disrespect. *Above all, keep calm,* my mother's teachings reminded me. *When you're agitated, you make decisions to avoid agitation, rather than to make things just.* That's what this little bugger was doing. I took another deep breath.

"I am High Fae," I stated with confidence. "My father is the king of all fae—you included. You will speak with me, or you will speak with him." Of course I couldn't enforce this. If he demanded that he speak with my father, I couldn't very well admit that I had been here. Father would kill me, and worse he would find me to be a failure.

"Very well, gangly giantess," the shrill kobold waved his hand, "bring your father, so I can speak with him." This made him the very first being, living or dead, to call me tall. How he managed to enunciate that with such condescension was beyond me.

More importantly, wasn't this exactly the thing I didn't want? I panicked. "You would have him come to you?" I sparred, his contempt getting the better of me. "You pathetic creature, my father does not come at your beck and call."

"Well, I'm not going to him."

This was getting nowhere. We could spat like little children here all afternoon. "Why have you dammed up the stream?" I demanded.

"I don't answer to you, missy," he resolved and walked away.

My anger flared. Negotiation nonsense… just non-sense. I summoned the wind. It sailed along the ground, picked up a tree branch, and balled him over. The imp jumped up, which admittedly was a rather cute little jump, and turned to face me, teeth bared. A dozen more toothy faces became visible from a variety of places around me.

My guides, the reasonable men that they were, pulled out crude weapons and backed away toward the cart. "Come, princess, we're done here," the elder stated.

"No, we're not," I announced. "Kobold, you have stolen from these people, and I am here on behalf of Matthias, son of Malakee, son of Keltus, son of Bakarrik, high god of Lur. You will speak with me!"

"I don't recognize your authority!" the imp spat back.

"Then you will recognize mine," a deeper voice announced. Malachi strode up, sword drawn, eyes dancing with fire.

"Oh, another demander. I guess that changes everything," the kobold mocked.

Malachi, I'm supposed to negotiate. How am I supposed to negotiate with this?

Negotiate what exactly? They don't seem particularly interested in conversation.

"Surrender?" he offered to them a single time.

"Ha ha," the kobold leader laughed. "You pretend you come to talk, but you just want a fight."

"A fighter!" the kobolds cheered, whipping out a variety of knives.

"She came to mediate," Malachi motioned at me, "but I came to win."

The leader shrieked, and the whole lot of them attacked Malachi at the same time—twenty-three to one. He sliced the first across the middle and kicked it into the crowd, scattering the kobolds. Then he half-spun, slicing four on a pass. Their knives were meaningless. Though they were agile, Malachi was cleanly faster. It was, mercifully, a brief fight. As their carcasses lay bleeding on the ground, Malachi announced to the humans, "You should dismantle the dam now. But make sure you do it slowly. Otherwise you'll flood the village."

"I don't understand," I told him, wrinkling my nose at what was a fairly familiar end to negotiations whenever Malachi was involved. "Kobolds aren't supposed to be like this."

"They don't fit the mold of what a whole race is supposed to act like? Imagine that," Malachi remarked. He hopped up onto the dam to help the men. Within moments the stream was trickling back through. They lashed and nailed several logs together to prevent it from pouring out all at once.

I was flustered. I had completely botched this assignment—or volignment, I guess. Malachi put his mud-streaked arm around me again.

"Firefly," he started, "negotiations have their place. Diplomats and ambassadors have their place. And you should be the greatest of them. But there are those who just need a swift kick to the head."

"I wanted to resolve this without anyone getting killed."

"To clarify… I didn't ask them to attack. They did that themselves. And admit it; it's easier to reason with the dead."

"I needed this, Malachi. I needed to show Father that I could actually do this. Now he'll know for certain that it's just too dangerous to let me leave home for anything. I mean, this wasn't exactly a world-threatening dispute."

"Meira, listen to me. First, this was most certainly a world-threatening dispute for the several dozen humans who live in that village. Second, it's almost impossible to know before meeting your opponent if you should win with words or weapons. But once you know, don't beat around the bush about it. Cut right to the point."

"Father's negotiations sometimes take years."

"Occasionally, that's true, especially when the sticking point has been reduced to baseless anger. Usually, though, you'll know within days, even minutes, whether a negotiation can ever be achieved. Everything after that is stalling for an advantage. Besides, didn't you see the way he stood there looking up at you? He was begging for you to fight him."

"That was… weird."

"Well, I suppose you haven't met any kobolds yet. They look up at people the same way tall people look down. You were losing respect every second you didn't drop-kick him into the lake. Now, if you would like, I have a few other assignments that might go a bit more like negotiations. And I suspect you might enjoy them much more than I will."

I smiled at him and agreed.

We bid the locals farewell and took the tree portal to Pagrid. A war had broken out between dvergr and goblins. Typically, the dvergr would call in support from their allies abroad to crush their enemies. But their home was difficult to reach, and early winter storms pounded the seas. It was a brutish four days working out the details between them. But Malachi was right from the on-set; it took but ten minutes talking to each side to determine that peace could eventually be established between these historically hostile races. And while my court graces were amateurish, I was excited to apply them appropriately for the first time — even for goblins.

Next we visited a woodcutter's lodge in Lindisidia. A prominent local had been kidnapped for ransom. We successfully solved the case, handing over the man's son and his secret lover to the local authorities for trial.

Malachi's last assignment was to deliver a package to a young lady in Wellid. This was the most rudimentary of all assignments, and Father had given it to Malachi specifically as final punctuation on his punishment. Any teleporter could have taken the package within minutes, but Father knew it would be a two-day walk for Malachi from the nearest tree portal to the intended destination.

Malachi looked at the package and sighed. To uphold peace, he was willing to do it. But I could tell he had other far more pressing matters to attend to. He always did.

"Um," I offered, "why don't you just let me take it?"

"It's a trip either way."

"Malachi, I fly." I looked up at him, and it was clear and obvious he wanted to ditch this task. So I pressed the issue. "Come on. Risk to life and limb: zero. You have mountains of things to do. I have quite literally nothing else to do."

He handed me the package. "Remember," he said, "anything dangerous or risky happens, Mother is bound to find out."

"I know. She's my mother, too."

One of the great but occasionally annoying aspects of our mother is that she can see events surrounding our lives — usually in the near future, but sometimes deep into the future as well. They are rarely the happy moments. So if we want to keep something reliably secret from her, we have to be careful to avoid anything that can trigger a vision. Delivering a package? She would be totally blind to it.

"Well… thanks, Meira. You're a good sister."

"And you're a good brother," I answered.

"I'm going to be gone for a while," he clarified. "I have to deal with a few problems."

"I know. You always do." I choked. "Come back."

"I will this time… but maybe not the next."

My eyes filled with tears. This was his way of telling me that he was about to do something Father would never approve for a million years. He was going to lay waste to somewhere, to someone, to something. It was going to get dangerous and bloody and brutal. He would very nearly die. Yet… he would come back to me. He promised.

When I was much younger, Malachi simply reminded me that he would always come back. But Father, during one of their arguments, put an end to that. He told Malachi that one of these days he was going to get himself killed, and making a promise to always come back was just filling me with false hope. From that time on, Malachi would only make the promise for one absence at a time. That promise was the only gold given to me—just for this once. Next time he would give me the promise again. So far, he had kept his word.

"Bring my babies to see me next time?" I asked.

"Certainly," he replied. He wrapped his arms around me, making me disappear into his firm grip. I left wet spots on his shoulder. As he walked through the tree portal to some other continent on Lur, the sky darkened.

I filled my lungs and cleared up my emotions as best as I

could. Then I went through the tree portal to deliver this oh-so-important package that required the escort of the most reliable warrior alive.

It was raining in Wellid when I arrived. Normally rain doesn't bother me, but I didn't want the package wet. I spoke softly to the wind, and it cut a path for me through the clouds. Rain fell steadily on both sides of the road. I unfolded my wings and lifted into the sky. Beyond the mountains along the horizon was my destination. Where Malachi would have to climb and wind his way through, I could just fly over them. Halfway to there was a quaint village, set on a knoll beside a river. A pair of cute, ivy-covered towers were set on opposite sides of the village. I've never found human villages to be particularly interesting, since the first thing humans do is chop down all of the pleasant trees.

I hummed along, enjoying the scenery. Had I been more interested in the village, I may have noticed that it was remarkably dead for midday.

"Fae fly!" a deep voice blurted out. An arrow sliced near my ear. My wings whipped it as it passed between them. I stopped in the air and turned around to see him. But he wasn't there. A bit to the left of where I was looking, another arrow zipped from the trees. I reached out my hand to grab it and missed. My heart filled with terror. These were not friendly arrows, and I couldn't see who was firing them.

I charged low to disappear into the canopy.

"Give me cover," I told the air. It replied with cross-cutting winds behind and beside me. Another arrow was snatched by a gust and shoved into a tree. As I passed one of the archers, I caught a glimpse of blue-gray skin around a tree trunk — an ulkra.

My power flared, and I prepared a bounty of response for him. I rushed around the tree and blinded him with a flash of light, then created a violent storm between us, blasting him with debris. He was tossed into the sky above the trees and blown a hundred yards away. His body fell into the merciless branches.

An arm and bow appeared around the trunk of a tree to the left. I concentrated on the tip of the arrow, pushing it aside. The ulkra released his string, misfiring. I charged, catching his eye and his mind.

"Kelton epirian," I commanded. His brain scrambled into that of a small bird. I screeched at him like a hawk, and he flapped his arms wildly, trying to take flight. He panicked and hopped away, flapping.

Another arrow pegged a tree behind me.

I didn't know how many of these enemies were in the trees around me, but I reasoned that the town should be safer. There I would find allies. I zigzagged between the trunks and through the branches to make pursuit difficult. As I emerged into the clearing and over the river, I saw the bodies. All around the streets were the dead — the young and old, men and women. The air was thick with the fresh copper-smell of death.

My mind froze. My emotions surged. There were runes carved into these bodies. This was the work of Nahasmen. The name resonated in my mind as it never had before. The world around me slowed. I felt each beat of my wings. My lungs filled a single time.

Three thousand years of Fae knowledge rushed into my

mind. Three thousand years of purpose and intent filled my bones. It was the experience of a first moment—that moment when you first enter water, when you first taste food, when you first experience breath. My eyes opened, and I received the gift and the duty given to every High Fae.

I dropped to the ground and stood steady, staring down at the empty eyes of a child, a curse drawn on his chest. The cold anger of justice steadily replaced the heat of hatred. My emotions calmed. My mind was steel. Whispers from the past filled my ears.

"Use the blade," they told me. "Listen to your teachings. Destroy Nahasmen."

Meira! My mother cried into my mind. *Meira! Where are you, baby girl?*

I ignored her.

The villain had entered the road fifty feet away, dragging a body out of a house. He looked at me with his unnatural yellow eyes—contempt, cool calculation. Then fear. He ran.

"You are mine," I whispered. I directed the wind at the far houses. A tornado, brought together by a hazia, an elemental spirit of the air, fell from the sky into the street, spinning and splintering houses. It threw walls, doors, bodies, and shards of ice at the villain. He fled the towering spirit of the air and came toward me. I withdrew my dvergr-crafted blade and handled it with care behind my wrist. He would see it only once, and it would be too late.

"Assist me!" the villain yelled, and three enemies came to his aid—an ulkra, a goblin, and a human.

I cursed the ulkra's brain as I had done the other, and he fled on four limbs, shrieking like a terrified pig.

The goblin screamed as he charged, a cleaver swinging wildly over his head. I have little sympathy for goblins. The wind impaled him with two flying limbs and hurled him into the hazia. The man drew his sword, and I drove his mind into sleep. He dropped unconscious to the ground.

"Villain," I decreed, "you are condemned. Part from this life in peace." I tried using my magic to infiltrate his mind, but the tendril of Nahasmen that possessed him blocked it.

He sneered and charged. I flew at him, slamming him with light and wind. The swing of his sword caught the edge of my left arm, slipping through it. Pain seared my brain. I screamed. I called on the wind to strike him from both sides. Gusts caught him at his head from the right and his feet from the left. He twirled midair and slammed into the ground. I pulled my wrist across his neck. A single pass of the enchanted blade severed flesh and throat. I intentionally left his arteries intact, so he wasn't dead, but he was bleeding out quickly. I had little time.

The whispers returned.

"Yes," I responded to them, "I know the ritual."

Meira! my mother's voice repeated, urgent.

I'm fine, Mother, I answered. *The threat is gone.*

I picked up a rope from the debris as the hazia disappeared into the sky. I tied one end to his ankle and the other to the overhang of a building. Then with all of my strength and beating wings, I pulled his dying body until he hung from the building upside down. I slid a barrel under his head to collect as much blood as I could. Then with a nearby shovel I dumped the bloody dirt into the barrel as well. His breath came in short rasps. He tried to reach his ankle with his hands, but he no longer had the strength.

I pulled the stones of condemnation from my pouch and placed them around his hanging body while I sang the ritual song. It was a song every Fae was taught as a child, should the day ever come when we needed it. Today, I applied my will and magical intent behind it. It reverberated with force, crushing and binding the spirit tendril inside the possessed villain, refusing to let it escape at the moment of his death.

As the song approached the final notes, a rock sailed past my head, bouncing off the wall.

"How?" I asked aloud. The human was up again — mostly anyway. He swayed a bit on his feet. I considered a curse, but my magic was busy binding the tendril of the enemy. Using magic now would ruin the ritual. He drew his knife. A few more moments. I continued the song, starting my last pass around the villain. The man stumbled over, lifting his knife to cut down the body.

"No!" I shouted, rushing him. I slammed into him, and he plunged his knife into my side — once, twice, three times. Fresh silver blood spilled out. He was still off-balance from the sleeping spell, so I shoved until he tripped over his own feet. My blood covered my left side, caking my clothes from shoulder to ankle. I stumbled back to my place and finished the binding spell.

I could nearly see the tendril struggling against its bonds. Then, with my blade, I swung once more. The villain's head fell into the barrel, quickly followed by the rest of his blood.

The human was back on his feet, knife in hand.

"Will you please just stay down for a moment longer?" I begged. He came anyway.

I swung the shovel, which drove him back. I needed fire to finish this; I needed to burn the villain's body. Only then would the bound tendril be destroyed. But I was beginning to wane from my wounds.

Meira! my mother called. *Please let me help you!*

I wanted to reach out, to tell her where I was. But if I did, Father would lay every bit of the blame at Malachi's feet. There would be a permanent rift in the family, and the entire kingdom of the Fae could fracture.

I pulled two stones from my bag. They were healing stones, which I desperately needed, but the magic bound within them was sufficient to create the fire I required. I held them together and released their powers before dropping them into the barrel. They grew white hot and ignited. Bodies do not want to burn, and I was only hoping that these would do the trick. Leaving them, I stumbled inside the building, slammed the door shut, and dropped a crossbeam into place. The man pounded against it.

My magic was spent, my body aching and tired, and my mind miserable.

Meira, please Meira, talk to me.

I fell back into a chair and stared blankly at the far wall.

Humans and their taverns. The entire wall was lined with

alcohol of various forms. Kegs filled a whole side of the room. Outside the human had given up trying to come in and was battling the blistering heat coming from the dying healing stones. He was trying to release the body. I doubted he even knew why. The tendril was calling to him to protect itself. Between the slats behind the kegs I could see the white-hot glow was the only thing keeping him from success.

Somewhere in the back of my mind, a little voice told me, "Alcohol burns." I smiled. My entire body screamed in pain, but this was worth every bit of the agony I was about to endure. I stumbled over to the tower of kegs and flew up to push the top off the stack. It fell to the ground and cracked, glugging out its contents. I pushed the next onto the first, nearly spent. The alcohol flowed, filling the ground at my feet and spilling through the cracks in the slatted wall. I peaked through. It flowed down toward the hot barrel. A single spark dropped into the volatile liquid. Fire rippled along the surface of the fluid, filling the ground beneath me with flames.

"No," I muttered. Every one of these barrels, the tavern, and everything around it would be engulfed in seconds.

Corywn… call me! I cried out. *Call me now, Corwyn!*

At home, in the safety of the High Fae court, he heard, closed his eyes, and saw me. Then he summoned me to himself. The world faded around me, and I blinked directly in front of him.

"Meira?" he looked me up and down. "You're injured."

I collapsed.

2

Meira

From time to time, throughout the next several days, I joined and left the waking world. Waking moments were difficult to find, and they were accompanied by soups and tinctures. My mother preferred that I sleep anyway. But during one afternoon she permitted me to sit up. A strong arm behind me lifted my back, while another propped pillows for me to lean against.

"Mother..." I tried. There was little behind it. My father's face appeared on the other side. Nothing but concern etched every aged groove and feature. "Father..." I tried again. I was grateful they both were there, but I was also ashamed. I awoke again deep in the night. They were gone.

I had completely failed, and with it I had ruined my chances for freedom. I'm not sure if I dreaded the fire more or Father's impending restrictions. Once he knew what had occurred, why I had nearly died, he would never let me leave his sight again. My lungs shuddered, which ached horridly, and my tears fell.

"Rae," I heard him say softly. He came and knelt beside me. "Rae." He brushed back my hair with his thick hand. Then he kissed my forehead.

"Father," I tried again. I had nothing to tell him, nothing to admit, nothing I wanted to reveal. No secrets were available to be shared. The most dangerous thing to give him now was the truth. "Father, I'm sorry. There's so much I can't remember."

"It's all well now, Rae. When you have time." He smoothed back my hair again and simply sat.

"Father, you have so many things to do."

"I have nothing else to do," he lied, "but to be here." He stayed with me and conversed for hours about all types of things unrelated to what had happened or where I had been. He stayed through dinner and late into the night, exiting only when Mother dragged him away to address the bags under his eyes.

Deep in the night, as bats and owls danced their deadly circles above the canopy, a dark figure knelt beside me.

"Firefly," Malachi whispered. I could barely make out his features in the dark shadows under my tree.

"Malachi? You're back."

"For a few minutes. I'm setting up an ambush right now."

"Silly, you have to be there to make an ambush work."

"It's okay. If I'm a bit late, they won't know the difference. I needed to come and see you."

"You heard then."

"I do talk with Mother, you know. Something about Nahasmen and you losing half of your blood."

"It wasn't quite that bad."

"No? Had to be pretty bad. You kept several healers busy for a week."

"Felt like fire."

"It's alright. You lived. You're recovering. Can't say that for everyone. At least half the people who fight to the death don't make it. And you… you did them one better. You beat Nahasmen alone. That puts you in a really special category."

"Yeah… really stupid."

"Well, maybe. But a fierce stupid then. Don't think he'll forget you anytime soon. Now, have you been taking those horrible medicines like you're supposed to?"

"Ick, yes."

"Excellent. And those foul-smelling tin.. tinteds… tiny-tins…"

"Tinctures?"

"Yeah, those awful things."

"Using them. I smell like a yak."

"No better way to drive away the suitors. Keep it up." He kissed my forehead. "Sorry I didn't bring the babies. They're working right now, and I didn't have time. I'll be back soon, though. I just have to do this thing."

"Thanks for coming to see me."

"Thanks for not dying." He stood up to leave. "Oh, and Meira… you did well—really well." With that he left, disappearing through a portal to wherever his ambush was set up. I leaned back my head, knowing that his hidden, dark anger would be boiling, and some villain in Lur would be reaping the awful benefits.

Of all of my siblings, only Yur, Malachi, and Corwyn came to see me while I recovered. I knew my place in the family. I just wish the rest of them knew how much I hated it.

It was only a couple days after I was able to stay reliably awake that Mother sat with me late at night.

Meira, she spoke directly into my mind, *we should talk.*

"Alright," I replied quietly.

You need to tell me what happened, before your father presses the subject.

I sighed. I knew this was coming eventually. *Mother, if I do, then everything will fall apart… for everyone.*

You stole an assignment didn't you? She wasn't really asking.

"No," I mumbled aloud.

Tell me directly.

No.

No you didn't, or no you won't tell me?

It was a poor attempt, and I was cornered. I bit my tongue.

Meira, I can either tell your father that you went to Wellid, probably by yourself, or I can leave out that rather pertinent information on your whereabouts. Either way, you need to trust me to not fracture our family. I know your father can be stubborn and bullish. I've known him for a bit longer than you have.

You haven't told him already, then?

He knows that I saw you in danger. I told him you would come home alive. He sweated until you did, nearly telling Corwyn to pull you out sooner. But he waited, because I told him to wait.

You told Father what to do, and he complied?

Oh, Meira, your father trusts me when I tell him what to do, because I never do. You should remember that for when you find your own mate to bond. Reserve your orders for the critical moments when you're certainly right, and you'll be trusted immediately. Now, tell me why you were there.

I needed to get out, to do something else, I skirted.

Meira, you know you're doing something here. You're learning.

I'm not learning anything at all, Mother. I sit and listen and memorize stupid things that don't matter.

No, Meira, they do matter, she sighed. *That's why you were able to resolve the dvergr-goblin feud.*

I sat in stunned silence.

Yes, I know you were there. It seems Malachi trusts me far more than you do. He wanted to verify that your father wouldn't be looking for you for a few days.

I thought… I thought you would have a fit if I went. So Father knows?

Oh Bakarrik, no.

Why did you let me go?

Same reason Malachi did; it was time you learned in the real world. Besides, if Malachi had done it alone, he would have offended the goblins too horribly to create any sort of peace. Not that, I suppose, it would have mattered. He would have just killed them all.

Mother, I've never seen you as one to go behind Father's back.

She pursed her lips and sat back, thinking carefully. *Rarely,* she said at length, *very rarely. It's a terribly dangerous practice — not because he'll get angry, but because it would cut him deeply. Every time I do anything like this, it's a fracture between us. So I do so only very carefully, and only to prevent worse things from occurring.*

It just doesn't seem… well… honest.

Says the daughter who's trying to figure out how to lie to her father to avoid losing her brother.

I breathed deeply. It was, horribly, true. *I shouldn't have to choose.*

No, Meira, you shouldn't, and neither should I. Now, let's consider this carefully. Do you really want to sit there and lie to your father?

No.

Then don't. Let me speak with him, instead. Where he won't listen to you, he'll listen to me.

I was exhausted from the mental anguish I had put myself through. My mother had never failed me. *Alright.*

So tell me, what happened?

I sighed and started into it. *I asked Malachi if I could have his last assignment, since it was just a silly package delivery. He didn't want to, since he knew it would be trouble with Father, but I convinced him. So I took the package. But on the way, several ulkras attacked me. The leader was a tendril of Nahasmen, so I destroyed him.*

So you did it, then. You fought Nahasmen and won.

I looked at her curiously. *I thought winning was the expectation.*

Well, it is, but not alone. And we haven't found a tendril in decades. So, who was the human who stabbed you?

You saw all of it, then?

Most of it, yes.

Why did mothers always have to ask when they already knew?

One of his followers, I answered. *I tried putting him to sleep, but I did something wrong.*

Humans and spells are… well… we'll discuss that later when there's good time. For now you need to tell me, was the tendril destroyed, with certainty?

Yes, I felt it dying as Corwyn pulled me out.

Good. Even though he'll be disappointed that you disobeyed him, your father will still be proud of you for your accomplishment.

That's something, I suppose. But he'll still be angry.

He'll be upset, yes, but you earned that one. Even if you think he's being unfair to you, you did nearly get yourself killed. I would have been there to help you at any moment, but you wanted to keep it a secret and do everything yourself.

I did manage, I claimed. It was technically true.

Meira, you're the most powerful Fae I have ever known, more powerful than your grandmother. Your potential is boundless. But you're not all-powerful. When your magic is busy, you're as vulnerable as any little girl. Now, you stay in bed and sleep. I will speak with your father and see to it that he understands. Then we'll set this event behind us.

She patted my bandaged arm carefully. Then she replaced the healing stones around my bed and gave me another horrible soup to swallow.

The following morning, Mother and Father spoke quietly in private while I pretended to sleep. Father was visibly perturbed, but after the multi-hour conversation, which consisted of them sitting and staring at each other, expressions shifting every several seconds, he left on an excursion to clear his head. As Mother promised, the topic was thereafter dropped as an issue — at least my part in it. For two months, as I recovered from my aching, I cringed whenever he passed by, not out of fear of what he would do, but from the unspoken thoughts that had to be eating at him.

3

24th of Lar Indar, 3552

Meira

Finally, at the waning of spring, I was able to be back in the air, flying amongst the trees. And, with Father's explicit blessing, I left the court to take in this year's surroundings. The forest in Nord Flaume, where we had lived for the past several years, was thick and vast. Humans lived only twenty miles to the east, and there were hundreds of miles of deep, uncultivated forest to the west before running into the sea. My quest was to explore the interesting habits of humans — admittedly the more masculine of the species. After all, I justified to myself, wouldn't I be dealing with them just as often as dvergr, kobolds, ulkras, and goblins?

And that's how I reasoned myself into perching in a tree for hours while several of this larger, non-magical species were sparring with staves in an open field — sometimes beating each other silly.

There was much about the human fighting art that I grew to admire very quickly. First, there was no credit paid to mind games, as magic was not even available to them. While they mocked and jeered, it was to goad the other person into making a foolish emotional mistake, as opposed to eliminating them from combat altogether. Second, while strength was a primary asset, they didn't concentrate solely on superior power. This was a goblin trait, in which they would beat on each other repeatedly until one or the other fell. Instead, the humans used lithe and guile to avoid blows. Fighting, for them, looked more like a dangerous dance, and whoever was the more proficient dancer came out on top.

I took mental notes and returned home to ponder and dream about it. This is what I was missing—that human who attacked me, however he managed repulsing my spell, could easily have been defeated by a skilled human warrior. He was unsteady and sluggish. Were I to learn the human fighting skill, I could master both worlds.

So with this as my new goal, I practiced in secret—first watching how they attacked and parried each other, and then retreating to a secluded place to practice the moves myself. For three weeks this seemed like a reasonable option, but eventually I slapped myself for my silliness. I could never, through self-teaching alone, accomplish what these men were accomplishing. I needed a real teacher.

I held my stave in my hands and harrumphed. Where was I going to find one? A real one?

"What do you think, wind? What about a trainer, eh?"

I glanced over at a squirrel and chirped out the same question to it. The squirrel shrugged his shoulders.

"That's what I thought." I swung the stave in a long arc around and then over my head. I had been trying to get this particular maneuver right, but it wasn't coming. The stave cracked against a branch and dropped a pine cone on my head. The squirrel laughed at me.

"Right, like you would do better."

He stuck out his tongue and snatched a small twig. He was, to be frank and honest, a terrible fighter.

"You have to swing it over your head, too," I chided.

He chirped back his objection that, of course, his arms couldn't actually extend behind his back.

"Well," I corrected, "if you're going to criticize me about it, you need to carry the same burden yourself."

I tried the swing again, with no improvement in the result. I definitely needed help. I sat and talked with with the squirrel for a while. I learned his name was Arthur, and he was, in his own humble opinion, the greatest of his clan. Admittedly, I was never clear on how squirrels defined their own greatness.

The following day I sneaked through a portal to visit Merdinia the Grey. She was a well-known centaur prophetess, one who could give reliable and understandable answers. When I arrived at her campfire, she held her finger to her lips. Her eyes were closed.

"Meira, I've been expecting you. You have a question for me, no?"

"Yes, I do."

"I know, my dear. I've been searching for his name, but it's still a mystery to me. But I needn't anyway, you have already seen him. You've been watching him." Merdinia chuckled to herself. "Beautiful man. So don't ask me for anything else. Go back to where you were yesterday. Let your eyes find what you desire, and there he will be."

"I'm... I'm not looking for a man."

She laughed heartily again. "Honey, we're all looking for a man." She opened an eye at me and laughed again. "Don't starve yourself pretending you're full."

I returned to my perch. One of these humans would teach me what I needed to know. I decided that perhaps the large, yellow-haired one with bright skin and the pale blue shirt was the one Merdinia the Grey intended. He was the most proficient, he provided the best advice to the others, and they all paid deference to him. I watched him closely for the rest of their practice. His arms were thick and well-muscled. The day grew warm and he removed his shirt. Beads of sweat glistened in the sunlight on his broad and strong shoulders.

He clearly gauged his blows for the strength of his opponents; with two in particular he fought hard. It looked to me like he used his full strength to spar with them. Several of the others, however, were not as strong, so he trained them in other ways, making sure to work on their strengths as well as insure that they could defend against their weaknesses. At the end of the day, regrettably, he re-donned his shirt, and they each mounted up on their horses.

"Bring me the blue-shirted one," I told the wind. "Whisper to his horse."

The wind rushed out to meet them, and it tickled the horse's ears. The horse turned his head this way, but his master took control of him quickly. The wind shrugged and tried again, this time whispering into the man's ears. He stopped and turned, looking about. The other men took no heed and traveled along the eastern road.

I dropped to the ground and walked out to the edge of the forest. My heart beat quickly, for no reason that I understood. I was only looking to conduct a business transaction, I explained to myself, but my heart kept reminding me that he was terribly enjoyable to watch.

"Be quiet," I chided myself. For a human, he was certainly attractive. All of the aspects of a human that I was seeking would be naturally attractive. I couldn't escape that, but rationally that didn't mean I needed to be drawn to him as well.

He walked his horse in my direction, eyeing me carefully at the edge of the trees before dismounting.

"Did you call me?" he inquired.

"I did."

He looked about, as though for an ambush. Though a sword hung from his side, he walked easily without touching it. I wasn't fond of blades at the moment, and I had no qualms about removing his.

"You live around here? Traveling?" he continued.

"My name is Meira," I explained, quickly determining that my status was unnecessary for his knowledge. "I am looking for a trainer."

"A trainer… for?"

"I need someone to teach me the human art of fighting."

His eyes grew wide, and he fought to contain the smile that argued with the corners of his mouth.

"You train those humans, no?"

"Those?" he pointed back. "My men? Sure, yeah, I train them. They're among the best."

"If they're among the best, and you train them, then you're the one I'm looking for."

"Alright. Um, I do have to get back. You said your name was..."

"Meira."

"Meira. It's a good name... a pretty name. If you want to spar sometime... I suppose... we could do that." He nodded his head with not a single hint of agreement. "How old are you?"

I stiffened my back and stood at my full four foot two. "My age isn't relevant," I argued.

"Alright. If you want to try it out, we can meet here again tomorrow." He nodded to his own suggestion.

"Tomorrow? Why not now?"

"Well... do you plan to fight in a dress?"

I looked down. I thought I looked fabulous. And this was my replacement for the dress I was wearing when I fought the tendril. Why did it matter?

"Okay, here. Lesson one: You need appropriate fighting clothes — shirt and pants. I'm assuming you have those?"

"Yes, I have those," I answered.

"Great. Tomorrow then?"

"I'll be here."

"Then so will I." He bid me farewell and rode away.

Mardok

I dropped off my horse and stepped inside the residence of Robert Everet, king of West Haulay. He was, as usual, easily located in the kitchen.

"Dinner's in the pantry," Mary, Robert's head chef, declared squarely when I entered. "If'n ye be wontin' sump'ting warm, ye can cook it ye'self."

"Thanks, Mary." I grabbed a hunk of bread and cheese, then hopped on the counter next to Robert.

"Robert," I said quietly.

"I still go by that name, yes."

"I found something new today."

"Is that a good kind of 'new,' or one of those less pleasant 'news'?"

"Well, it looks pleasant enough, but I can't say quite for certain yet."

Robert swiveled his head slowly. "Okay, Mardok, I'll bite. What's her name?"

"Meira."

Robert chuckled. "Mardok, I'm going to win the bet."

"No, not from this one. She's not human."

"You don't say. What is she?"

"I think she's one of those fae-things, but it's hard to say.

Don't they have silver skin?"

"High Fae? Silver, yeah. You found one?"

"Well, maybe. She had gold skin, copper hair."

"Golden skin… not familiar with that. Perhaps bad lighting?"

"No, not the lighting," I disagreed. "I talked to her. Tiny little thing—like a young girl. But she was as snarky as Mary."

"Fae haven't been in West Haulay in… heavens, not since my grandfather. You sure?"

"Pretty sure. I'm going out to meet up with her tomorrow."

Robert started chuckling again, letting it roll into laughter. "Clearly, Mardok, the nonhuman bit doesn't seem to be an impeding factor."

"No, no, no, not to court the little lady. I swear, Robert, she's not but… fourteen, maybe?"

"You try that one, I'll have a new practice dummy."

I rolled my eyes. "Robert, I'm telling you, I'm not trying to court the girl. She wants fighting lessons."

"Alright," Robert summed up. "So you're going out tomorrow to beat up a little girl. Way to start off renewing diplomatic relations with the gods' choice race."

"Really, I'm only going to spar a bit with her. I'm not going to harm her. Remember Ira's little girl? I didn't break her, now, did I?"

"Well, she was six."

"And a mite tougher looking than the twig that's wanting me to teach her. So let me give her a few lessons, then maybe we'll find out why she's here."

"Fair enough. Just do be safe. If the stories merit anything, she could turn you into a newt or something."

I stuffed the rest of the bread and cheese into my mouth. There was a cut of ham on the far counter. "Want some pig?" I asked the king.

"If you're willing to risk your fingers getting it."

I looked around. Mary was out back. I hopped down and took a couple large slices from the beautiful haunch. I threw them onto the nearest pan and put it on the stove. Within moments the wonderful sizzling of glorious goodness caught the attention of our killjoy. Mary sauntered over, hands on her hips.

"Wha do'ya thin' ye doin'?"

"I'm cooking," I replied. "I wanted something warm."

"Not in my kitchen ye ain't. I'n not want'n ye to burn down the whole place."

"Mary, it's a kitchen. It's made of stone."

"If'n I know anyone who could burn stone, it'd be ye. Shoo!"

"But my pork..."

"It not ye pork til I been say'in it's ye pork. Now go!" She hip-bumped me back away from the stove. I looked back to Robert, but he had spirited himself away. Coward.

The following day I gave my men—affectionately labeled the Deadly Dozen—a break from exercises. To be sure, they had earned the title for actually having skill. We had other units of soldiers throughout the kingdom with similarly dangerous names who had yet to earn it. The Viper's Brood was a small crew on the Plateau who spent far more time wandering the countryside in their flashy armor than practicing with it. The Bloodthirsty Rogues were deeply engaged in new safety measures to prevent them from ever bleeding. And the Young Marshals of the Dead were just… well, they were just disappointing.

The Deadly Dozen, though, had all seen combat, dealt with coastal raids, cleared the woods of bandits, mended the wounded, and earned their position through strife and conflict into Robert's court as the elite. Should general war ever ensue in West Haulay, which we had no reason to think would ever occur, the Dozen would lead the combined armies of the Dukes. At least, that was the theory. Anyone who knew court politics knew better.

In the mid afternoon, I mounted my horse and rode out to our practice field. We didn't pick a location so distant from the castle for its convenience, but to give the horses exercise each day. There was also a sizable pasture where they could run, prance, and do all kinds of horsey things.

I found the general area of the place where Meira had appeared the day before and looked cautiously into the trees from a distance. Should it be an ambush of some sort, I wasn't volunteering to be easy pickings. I stepped up carefully to the trees and entered. The sun disappeared quickly overhead, and I walked slowly, waiting for my eyes to adjust. Birds chirped, and wood creaked with the wind. I stepped carefully, keeping the edge of the trees within sight to my left, while trying to ascertain whatever I could for ten minutes or so. Other than a few concerned deer, I could find nothing. Perhaps the little Fae girl wasn't that interested after all. I turned left and retreated to the open field.

Stepping through, I looked back toward the pasture. There she was, the gold-skinned girl, walking cautiously through the grass, her left hand reaching back toward the forest.

"I suppose it would be easier to find each other if we knew exactly where we were meeting," I called out.

Meira turned and strode toward me, her head held high. She was wearing a basic leather outfit as promised, carrying a fresh sparring stave. "Do I pass lesson one?" she asked as she pirouetted.

"Yes, lesson one is good. Do you have any previous fighting experience?"

"Plenty... but not using your methods. That's what I need to learn."

"Alright," I replied. I wasn't sure why such a young girl would have plenty of fighting experience, but given the reputation of her race — fiercely independent, proud, just, individually lethal — perhaps she was not what she appeared to be. If stories were to be trusted, she could conjure a legion of soldiers to fight for any cause she determined would please the gods. So a small mite of my purpose here was to ascertain what she wanted, and another was to keep her appeased. "Let's see what you know then." I held my stave at ready, prepared for a series of rapid, uncoordinated, and weak attacks. The girl did not disappoint.

Thwack, whack, snap, snap. I blocked four shots without effort. All were well-telegraphed and predictable. She swung twice from the left, making a supposed feint to the right. Then she swung down over my head. I parried it down to the ground.

"Stop," I directed. "Now you defend." I worked to judge my swings very carefully. I wanted my hits to sting enough to make her think again about this line of training, but not enough to seriously hurt her. I also had to be careful not to swing so quickly that it might hit her before she could respond. Fortunately, I had taught several children already, so I was somewhat accustomed to this type of training.

"You're insulting me," she announced after the first several swings. "You're being slow and weak for me. How am I going to learn to fight off something real if the training isn't."

I stepped back, accepted the criticism for what it was, and re-approached with a bit of vigor. Within a few seconds she was overwhelmed. I still had to pull back my blows so they wouldn't break her ribs, and I declined aiming for her head entirely. But the beating I put on her stave was enough to force her to drop it and hold her arms in pain. I stabbed one end of my stave into the ground and rested on it. I wanted to say something encouraging, but she didn't look like she was interested in me patronizing her.

"I'm doing something wrong," she surmised the obvious. "What is it?"

"You can't block without getting hurt," I answered. "You lack physical strength and give in your stance. You take the entire blow and absorb it with your wrists. I'll break them just by hitting your stave if you keep doing that."

She popped the stave back into her hands and practiced a bit with her wrists to absorb a blow with her muscles rather than locking them and taking the hit with her bones. It was painful watching her do it. So I assisted and explained how to take hits. Then we tried again.

By the end of the day, when we finished, I was truly surprised. First, her looks belied her age. She clearly was several years older than she appeared. Second, she was a quick learner. And third, she accepted the pain and continued, and I knew she was feeling it heavily in her arms.

"I thank you," she said with a bow. "I will work on what we covered today. Would tomorrow do well to meet again?"

"Tomorrow?" I asked in shock. "No, not tomorrow. You need to heal, or your bones will break from the stress. Besides, I can't neglect my men. I have obligations to them."

"Then when can we meet again?"

"Are you sure you want to do this long-term?" I queried.

"Certainly. Would a week away be acceptable?"

"Well, today is the nineteenth of Lar Eguzki. So meet again on the twenty-sixth?"

"I will be here." She bowed again and walked into the trees.

I waited for her to disappear past the first coverage before running at an angle to follow without being noticed. Inside the forest I kept running, keeping my feet from hitting snags of dry branches. I looked about, but I only heard a humming sound rushing around me. I spun to see it, but it was gone. I kept my eyes peeled. She shouldn't have traveled quickly enough to be out of range already, not walking with those short legs. I stepped lightly forward again several paces.

"If you want to follow me, you'll need to be quieter," she declared behind me.

I turned, embarrassed. "I, umm," I thought quickly. "We never established an actual meeting place."

"I see," she replied, crossing her arms. "You should know that even though I have asked you to teach me to fight your way, I am not defenseless."

"I'm not surprised," I shrugged. "I wasn't trying to hurt you."

"Just in case you needed to know," she concluded. "Now, if you don't mind, there's a nice clearing near here. We can use it as a practice ground." She led me to a small spot with open sky. It was filled with brambles, but she promised to remove them before the week was out. It seemed fair enough, and there was a suitably simple route from the pasture to here so I could find it again.

"One more thing before I go," she stipulated smartly, "if I'm going to fight a man more than once, I really should know his name."

"My name? Sorry. It's Mardok." I could give more, but that seemed sufficient.

"Mildly pretentious," she mused.

"Why? It's a popular name."

"Not among humans."

"I'm working on changing that."

She pondered for a bit before letting it drop. Then she bid me farewell and departed. I took the wiser course of not following her. I had other things to do this evening anyway, like sitting around.

Meira

I watched Mardok leave the forest and ride away, then I flew back home. Father was finishing business with two centri when I arrived. They typically came whenever they had something significant to disclose about where the gods were looking, or what they might have been indicating, or they had some cryptic message that left everyone wondering why they were there. Father and Mother had mastered the art of nodding and looking grim. Occasionally, and only occasionally, their words were deeply impactful. Such was the reason we had moved to Nord Flaume.

I stashed my stave and practice clothes in a secret place so I could arrive home in one of my typical outfits. Then I disappeared to my sleeping area to sit on my bed. I laid back and thought about the different ways Mardok had parried my strikes. I recalled how easily he dealt with each one, as though he knew what my next strike would be. Was I that predictable, that a total stranger knew what I would do before I knew? If this were the case, making opposing attacks should be effective in countering his lazy defense. I slept deeply that night, and I spent the next week perfecting a different set of strikes that were far less intuitive.

Mardok

A week had passed since last sparring with the Fae girl, and I knew that I shouldn't keep her waiting. I rode my horse into the forest and to the training clearing that she had shown me. She sat on a stump into the middle. As she had indicated, all of the brush and debris had been cleared out. It was far too much work for her to do alone. I stepped into the clearing, holding out my arms to reveal my interest in how she did it all.

"I have friends," she replied. That was the last she spoke on the topic. "So, do I get to try again?"

"If you like," I replied. If she held true to form for a rookie, she would have crafted a new technique utilizing the principle of opposing attacks. That is, she would intentionally strike in ways that were the most counter to what she would do naturally to foil me. Again, she met the expectation. I met each strike with ease. Only once did she move to a position I wasn't readily expecting. But her speed was lax, permitting me to counteract without difficulty. After her routine was finished, I turned the tables and put her on her back. Then I sat on the stump.

"What was I doing that made it so obvious?" she asked, clutching her forearms.

"You make predictable attacks," I explained. "You need to vary it on the fly. Don't plan ahead of time exactly what you're going to do. Only plan the immediate attack, and vary it. Otherwise a smart opponent can analyze your attack style."

"You're doing more than that. I did switch, and you blocked me anyway," she remarked.

"Every strike has pre-motions, so your body tells me what you're going to do before you do it. For example," I stood up and posed to demonstrate. "You can tell when I'm going to make an overhead strike from the right; my right shoulder falls back. Coming hard from the right, it drops further. So when you wind up for your attack, I move my stave to block. Even the flicker of your eyes will give me clues, but that's much further along than where we are right now."

"So... you always know where I'm going to attack?"

"Well... yes. If I didn't, I wouldn't be here. Battle is very unforgiving."

"You've been in battle?" She was immediately interested.

"In a much earlier time, when I was a new squire. I fought in a siege in Terga. Don't get the idea that I did anything brave, though. I was ten, and I was just staying alive. Brave men have a powerful habit of dying."

"But your skill kept you alive," she surmised.

"Skill I didn't have; luck saved me. Arrows and lances kill the skilled and unskilled alike. My lord, the Earl Tallwyn, fell that day, and he was exceptionally skilled. Now, if you don't mind hopping back on your feet, it's time you learn how to defend. I would like to walk you through predicting attacks." With slow motions, I demonstrated how to accurately predict an opponent's next strike. She was terrible, which was a bit better than most students on their second lesson. Her stamina was perhaps her greatest asset. While the young boys I typically taught learned disciplined fighting out of obligation, this Fae was dedicated heart and soul, as though her life depended on it.

We passed through two hours before I made her stop. "Maybe you're still feeling fine, but I'm getting winded," I told her. "Honestly, I don't know how you keep going. I'm ready for a break."

"No breaks in battle," she reminded, slinging her stave around pointlessly. She lost her grip and it flew off into the trees.

"No, you're right. That's what rotating troops is for, if you have any at the front who are fortunate enough to still be alive after that long. So I'm aiming to rotate out. But it's been a fabulous session. You have potential."

Potential. The word stung fiercely. Potential. As in, you're nothing. Maybe someday you can accomplish something, but for the foreseeable future, nothing. Potential is how Father saw me. I would not ever, ever be simply potential to this man.

"I have a different idea," I offered. "If I can get my stave and hit your back, you owe me... another hour."

"Seriously?" Mardok inquired. His eyes sized up our features, namely how my legs were only half the length of his. "Bets go both ways. What if I win?"

"Then..." I thought long. I had anything I wanted, but to give it to a human was a problem. He wouldn't care about any non-magical trinket the Fae make, and no magical item would be permissible. Magical items left in non-magical hands had produced unforeseen disasters in the past, and Father was leery about trading them. Besides that, there was no way Mardok could even use most of them. Furthermore, how long did I want to spend trying to find some item to secure this bet? All I had was what was on my person. What would this man, this giant among the land of men...aha!

"A kiss," I declared. Then I clamped my mouth shut. That was a really stupid offer. What if I actually lost? Well, that wasn't happening, so it wasn't a problem.

"A kiss?" he clarified.

I could tell he wasn't expecting this particular direction. Neither were my cheeks. "Yes, a kiss," I repeated. I wouldn't be a liar, and I wasn't going to lose anyway. "I will impart a blessing to you with a kiss. Fae kisses have power." I wasn't entirely making this up, but I couldn't really tell him why.

"Alright then. This is the first time I've ever made a bet for a kiss. But I'm going to have to say that I'm only more dedicated to winning then."

I was offended and flattered.

"Three..." he counted. "Two... one... Go!"

He bolted, and I took flight. In the air I was ten times his speed. Alright, three times, looking back, but still. Finding it was also part of this challenge, and I now had the height advantage. I zigzagged through the trees, scanning the ground. It was here somewhere. I charged deeper and then back. Where was my stave?

"Meira!" he called from a ways back. Oh no, I had gone too far! I zipped back, and he stood there, holding both staves.

"How? No!" I was utterly flummoxed.

"You flew right past it. I saw where it landed." He stood looking at me somewhat awkwardly.

"Cover me," I whispered, and the wind hit him with a flurry of dirt and pine needles. Mardok threw up his arms to cover his face. I took the opportunity and dove in, snatching my stave and wresting it from his hand with all four of my limbs. Then I flew up into a tree.

"Pth, pth," he spit out. "What in the world!? Alright, first you cheat by flying. Seriously, that's no fair. Then you pull some magic whirlwind routine on me."

"That's how I fight."

"Not with me, it's not. Look, I understand that humans are fairly beneath the Fae in power. Only really stupid kings try to cross your people. But if you're wanting to learn our art, you've got to learn on our terms."

"You're angry," I announced. I felt genuinely terrible.

"Only because I've got a pine needle stuck up my nose. It's not pleasant."

"I'll get it out." I descended and walked up to him. I looked up his nose, which should be the first and last time I ever do anything like that. There was the pine needle stuck way up there. I chittered, and Arthur came over. I gave him my directions and picked him up.

"What... are you doing?" Mardok asked.

"Hold still, courageous warrior," I told him. The squirrel looked back at me with distaste.

"Oh, don't wimp out now," I told him. "It's important."

"Are you talking to me or to the rodent?" Mardok wanted to know.

"Hush up. You're moving your face."

Arthur grimaced—but not as much as Mardok—stuck his paw up in the man's nose, and retrieved the needle. Finished, he wiped off his paw on Mardok's shirt, announced his distaste at this disgrace of a job, and ran off to find water to wash up.

Mardok touched his nose tenderly. Then he turned his back to blow it. I'm certain there was a fair quantity of dirt still lodged in there.

"Not to upset you or cause any problem," I murmured, just loud enough for him to hear.

"Yes?" he asked, blowing again.

"Um," I tapped his back lightly with my stave. "I win."

He rotated slowly, his eyelids and lips sagged low. I smiled brightly. He quietly picked up his stave and walked to his horse.

"Um, I...." Great, I had completely blown it. "Mardok, please... stop."

He mounted up and began plodding away. I flew up beside him.

"Please, wait. Talk to me."

"Look, it's fine that you don't want to lose; I get it. I wasn't exactly planning to make you keep up your end of the bet. Look at this face." He pointed at himself. "I've seen this face. I wouldn't want to kiss something that looked like this. I'm certainly not going to make anyone else do it. Seriously, Meira, I'm not the guy to make a girl do that, especially one I've only known for three hours."

I switched to the other side to avoid branches. "A deal's a deal, I announced. I grabbed his forehead and kissed it. He was a bit shocked, but his shock settled out quickly to ease. Then he was recharged. I gave him just a tiny amount of Fae bonding magic. I wasn't supposed to use it for this sort of thing, but it was functional under the circumstances. Besides that, it had the added benefit of improving his immediate attitude toward me.

"That's... honestly, Meira, you didn't need to."

"Yes, I did. I made a bargain."

We traveled along to the edge of the forest together. He stopped just outside the trees.

"I'm not going to pretend for even a moment that I don't appreciate it. Actually, I'm not going to pretend I wouldn't do just about anything for a repeat..." he trailed off and fell silent.

"Mardok, how about if I make you a different bargain? We'll meet regularly, and any time I can't figure out the lesson without explanation, I'll give you one of those kisses."

"Just like that?"

"Just like that."

"Okay. Then how often are you wanting to meet? Bi-weekly?"

"If it's the same to you, I would like to meet every week. I certainly need the practice, no?'

"I'm afraid, my tremendously adorable student, that you certainly do. Weekly..." He mulled this over. "I can manage that. We'll have to skip a few for when I'm otherwise occupied, but I'll let you know ahead of time."

I considered his previous term for me. "Do you think I'll make it past... potential?"

"I wouldn't say you had potential if you were never going to get anywhere with it. That's the whole point of the word; you're going to get better. Fight in ground combat? Let's avoid that. But fend off a thief or attacker? Certainly. You need to agree to a bit more on this deal, though. First, you don't get to use magic. And we'll work in your flying... um... as we can. Honestly, I'm not sure what to do with that yet, but I'm afraid that sticking a stave between your wings would probably knock you down. So I wouldn't count on using them. Instead, you'll learn to use your opponent's height against them."

I nodded definitively.

"It's not that I want to break away from you and go back home to sleep. I just want to break away and go back home to sleep."

"It's alright," I answered. "Enjoy the night." We left for our own places, and I felt just the tiniest part of me leave with him.

4

22nd of Lar Izoztu, 3552, through 6th of Lar Tripta, 3553

Mardok

Over the next half a year, Meira continued as one of my students. Her growth was substantial, although she was severely hampered by her size, strength, and stubbornness. She was also flighty and prone to attempt unconventional and often foolish maneuvers. No matter how many times I see someone try spinning a full circle to make a strike, it's just as terrible of an outcome. Young boys always feet the need to try this move at least three times. Meira? Fifteen and counting. Each time, she was convinced her wings could make all the difference.

That said, she was still progressing faster than nearly any of my other younger students in the past, two particularly gifted young men notwithstanding, both of whom were now in the Dozen. I still wasn't fighting her without limits, but I was growing convinced that one day that would become necessary, even if just to prove to her swelling ego that she would never become truly unbeatable.

As promised, she continued her "payments" each session. I tried to protest the necessity of these payments, but she wouldn't hear it. "Services rendered require payment," she insisted. "I will not be a charity case."

Robert laughed at me, wanting to know just how many times I said, "Oh please, no, don't," before caving.

Alright, to be fair, I protested once on our second session and then managed another protest on the fourth. After that, I worked diligently to earn them each time, and each time the unnatural rush that came over me brought me superior speed, reaction, and endurance. I am certain it was not all in my head. Seth and Burke noticed that I was becoming virtually unbeatable on each day immediately following their days off.

Robert had also noticed. Twice on these days I had saved his life. The first was from a large tusker during a hunt after Robert's horse had thrown him, and the second was from an assassin who had managed to kill four of our men and enter the king's chamber before I stopped him. Neither story ended well for either target, though the former made for a good dinner. Fortunately, Robert was unaware of the connection between the "payments" and my heightened senses, otherwise I would have heard no end to it.

On the other hand, it didn't improve my jousting. What can I say, except that my lance-aiming skill was underdeveloped. Harry, one of the Dozen, did inform me, though, that this improves significantly as you raise children.

After the initial excitement of her kisses faded, I was forced to evaluate another problem — a problem I had not planned, but one into which I tread willingly. No, not willingly — eagerly. What would I be able to say to another lady whom I desired to suitor? That I reveled in the kisses of another woman? I couldn't deny that the connection between Meira and I increased with each kiss she placed on my forehead. Three months and twelve kisses after I first thought about this, ignoring the problem fell apart as I left the forest and found Amos, the oldest of the Dozen, leaning against a tree, smoking his pipe.

"That will kill you, you know," I remarked.

"Not as quickly as you're planning to destroy yourself, I'm afraid." Amos looked at me, his eyes thick with hard-earned wisdom and the wrinkled brow of a concerned father.

I would never, for any reason, level a thought against Amos, much less speak belittling of his insights and, in this case, admonition. I knew I had been found out, and my guilty silence was the only answer I had for him.

"My lord," he continued, "I cannot pretend to tell you how to behave, but I also cannot leave you to sail alone into rocks without fair warning."

"I don't know what you mean," I lied.

"Your lady there. To whom does she belong?"

"She's not a slave, I think, Amos," I answered dishonestly. I knew what he meant, and I knew he wouldn't let me get away with it, even before I said it.

"Is she yours, Mardok? Did you marry her secretly?"

"No, Amos. I think you would be aware of that."

"Well, I wasn't aware of her at all until a month ago."

I looked at him in shock. "You've been following me?" That it took him four months was quite the accomplishment on my part.

"I would like to think, Mardok, that I've become more

than your servant over the last two decades."

"You were my father's only real friend, Amos. I called you uncle until you made me stop. I would never consider you to be my servant."

"Then my friendship demands that I do what's best for you, not merely what's happy. This relationship you have with this lady… what are your intentions?"

"She's my student."

"I've had a few female students as well, Mardok, but kissing them was never part of the training."

I was about to quibble that I wasn't the one doing the kissing, but I was fortunate that my brain sounded the alarm on how idiotic that excuse would sound before it escaped my mouth.

"I'm not going to make you do anything, Mardok. I'm not your father, and I'm not your king. But you do need to resolve this one way or the other. Are you planning to marry this girl? Or just play with her until you've crushed her heart?" He didn't wait for an answer. He just walked off toward the pasture.

I didn't need an oracle to explain where Amos' opinion on this lay. He and my father both asserted that a man's physical attention to a girl should be accompanied by an oath of fidelity.

"Boys kiss and run," my father had told me when I was only twelve. "Men kiss and marry."

But what if I were still uncertain about this? What if this situation wasn't exactly my fault? I didn't actually ask her to kiss me.

My own thoughts on this issue were conflicted, and my father wasn't helping me with it. Again and again his voice came back to me.

"What is a man if he cannot love? And if he can love, then why should he strive for less?" "If she's the right lady, why would you wait to die from old age?" "Girls' feelings aren't toys. But men play with them all the time, only to throw them away when they're broken." "Don't ever do anything you can't explain to your wife."

I sat in front of my parents' sepulcher.

"Alright, dad," I sighed, "how do I deal with this one then?"

I sat for an hour and listened to the wind. It had nothing for me. Memories of my parents rippled through my mind. Unlike most of the couples I knew, my parents were openly infatuated lovers. They hugged and kissed readily and freely. My father made certain I knew everything he could share about relationships and how to love my own future wife. He never doubted for a moment that I would "find the right lady and make her very, very happy... on pain of death." And I believed him; I really had no reason not to.

Until their own deaths.

Things at that point changed. On the day I received the news, I made an oath: I would never be the death of my wife. I struggled for years to not blame him for my mother dying; the fact that they were never apart played into that. And on the day I accepted the role as Robert's bodyguard, I made another oath: I would not die and leave my wife alone to fend for herself. I had seen too much war, known too many wives who had lost their husbands to the sword, left to struggle alone to raise their fatherless children. Reminding them that their husbands and fathers were heroes did nothing to fill their stomachs through the winter.

"The worst curse a man can lay upon his wife is to abandon her," my father explained to me as he paid the debts of a woman whose husband had left for faraway places. But wasn't dying just another way to abandon someone? I was certain that it was.

"I know, dad... the answer seems obvious. 'Just marry the girl.' That's easy for you to say. But if I do... if I wanted to..." I didn't really even want to. "I can't do that, dad. How many years do I have? One of these fool dukes is going to start a war, and it's nearly certain that I'll end up dead. I'm not going to abandon a wife like that. I can't."

Why wouldn't my father just accept that answer? Still, he haunted me, reminding me that "a man's purpose is in the love he shows his family."

"Robert is my family now. He's my brother, and my future is wrapped up in his."

I stood and kissed the cold, mossy stone.

"I miss you, mom. You would have known how to help me figure out what to do."

My sleep that night was terribly restless. As was the next, and the next. I was plagued with the thought that in a few days I would be back in that place with Meira, enjoying every moment together, accepting her kiss, and having nothing for her in return.

"I won't be a charity case," she had said. Yet what was I, if not a lover's charity case?

So naturally, I went to meet with her, felt guilty, and reaped the reward of a job well done. The pleasant energy surged through me as Meira smiled at me and brushed her fingers over my face, and I was revived. And I rode home bitter and self-loathing.

Days passed, weeks passed, and I changed my routine around the castle. Wherever Amos would be during the day, I found a way to avoid him. He never said anything, never asked, but merely his kind smile and laugh was guilt-inducing. His silence on the issue was even more maddening than if he were to throw me into a corner and demand an answer for my insolence.

During our next meeting, Meira kissed me on my cheek. I turned to let my lips brush hers as well. This pleased her, and she glowed pleasantly... quite literally glowed... as she flew away.

"You're toying with her. She's not your plaything," my father's voice chided me.

"Yes, I am. I know. It's exactly what I'm doing. Want to explain to me how to not?" I dug my heels into the flanks of my horse. He took off, and my ears filled with the rushing wind. Eventually I drowned out the remonstrations. Alcohol gave me rest that night.

Winter that year was mild, and it didn't freeze until Lar Izoztu, although the Northern Coast had probably been pounded with hail since Lar Sartzea, two months earlier. Then again, that's why sane people didn't live on the Northern Coast.

Meira and I continued training straight through, even though everyone else took the winter off.

When we met at the beginning of Lar Tripta, though, the temperature had plunged, sapping the heat completely from our fingers. So we just sat together in the clearing, wrapped in a blanket, warming our hands and toes by a small fire. I should have used the opportunity to speak with her about our relationship, whatever it was, just to be on the same page. But I didn't want to make things more awkward. I was concerned that merely discussing it would result in having to address the big question that I wasn't prepared to answer.

"You know," I started off, mostly to avoid discussing anything important, "I've been serving Robert as his bodyguard for nearly a decade. He's a good king—not like most of those kings out there." She sat and listened. I really didn't have anything else to say about that, so I waited for a bit and tried something different. "So I don't know how you folks live. I suppose in houses, or something. Most humans do, anyway. I actually live in Robert's castle, along with about thirty others. It's a pretty big place. Large... and stone... a wall around it."

She sat quietly and leaned her head against my shoulder.

"So... where do you live?" I asked.

"In the forest," she answered quietly.

"Like... in a house or something?"

"Under the trees."

I was taken aback. "What do you do when it rains?"

"If you get wet, you pick a better tree."

"That's sensible, I suppose. Have you ever thought about building a roof, or something?"

"Makes it really hard to see the sky, and the stars... and the birds."

"I would be concerned that the birds would leave unpleasant gifts on my bed."

"You get used to it."

I couldn't imagine I would ever get used to that. We waited another while before she asked a question.

"Mardok, you said that you've been to war, haven't you?"

"Yes, long ago."

"What was it like?"

"It was the thing of nightmares. Men screaming in agony, nobles throwing them into the fray for their own glory. Or maybe they just enjoyed the show." I paused a bit. "We were fighting to defend Terga, our southern neighbor. Robert's father determined it was better to join in the battle than to risk them falling to the invaders. We took a few thousand men. It wasn't the largest army we could have mustered, but it was all we could take for political reasons. When we arrived, the invader — some guy named Simin — had announced we would be the start of his new empire. He had just burned several villages and distributed the women and girls to his troops. Maybe it was some sort of sick payment for their loyalty. Robert's father was furious, and he sent my lord, the Earl Tallwyn, to negotiate for their release. Simin committed treachery during the negotiations. Tallwyn escaped, but most of his men were killed. He didn't make it through the following battle." Without thought, I snapped a twig in my clenched fist. "For half of the day I sat next to his body and blubbered like a little child. I only survived because the king grabbed me by the shirt and dragged me away. We escaped with less than a quarter of our army." The agony of that day was still fresh. I couldn't deal with it yet, so I pushed it back down.

"You lost then."

"We lost. But we won the war. While he was a brilliant tactician, Simin was a foolish politician. He made the people so angry that they started hunting his troops wherever they could find them alone. Four men would go hunting in the forest, and they would simply never return. His brothers were poisoned by a chef while celebrating one of their birthdays. Eventually Simin was caught off-guard and killed, too."

"How?"

"Well... um... he was in the privy, and someone tied a rope around it and burned it to the ground."

"That's pleasant," Meira replied with disgust.

"Not the way I would want to go, but it seemed fitting."

"You were forged during that war, weren't you?" she surmised.

"Well, I learned that I could kill."

"You fought then?"

"No, I tied the rope. I was only twelve; I couldn't really fight a grown man, not without cheating."

"An execution is a valid way of purging evil people from the world."

"That's what Amos said, right before he sent Harry and I to murder... to purge him."

"Why didn't Amos do it himself?"

"He was busy putting a knife into Simin's guards."

"So, not the coward."

"I've never seen a man with more courage." We sat quietly a bit longer. "So we won, I suppose. Obviously the enemy troops were still there. Their general took control and set fire to the capital in retribution for Simin's death. It probably would have been nice to have known that they were related. The king and his family died in the blaze. So Robert's father announced that his cousin Tiller would assume the throne. Tiller was a crass and brash man, but with an amazingly loyal heart. He was, I didn't understand at the time, exactly the right man for the job. He had been in-country for about eight years, so he was able to rally the countrymen and harass the general so horribly that the viper slithered home. At the same time, we sent spies to stir up a contender for Simin's throne. So the general fled for home, only to find someone else had taken over. They had a brief civil war and managed to kill each other. After that, another lunatic came to power. Fortunately, his was the type of lunacy that's normal for kings — mostly interested in amassing wives for himself."

"Rough year," Meira murmured.

"Rough four years," I corrected. "My parents were so relieved when I came home after the first battle, especially since so few of us returned. It nearly crushed them when I went back two years later."

She brushed her fingers through my hair. The sensation tingled straight through me, down to my toes. I closed my eyes and leaned against her.

"You know," I continued quietly, remembering. "Tiller had this tiny gold ring that he had put on a chain around his neck. At one point it broke off, and he had us searching for four days before we found it. When he had it back, that great big warrior sat clasping it, crying. I didn't understand the significance until Amos explained that he had pulled it from the burnt finger of the king of Terga's six-year-old daughter. Tiller had the smithy mount it in the pommel of his sword."

"You're still angry about it," Meira stated factually.

"Yes, I am." We rested quietly together.

I woke several hours later, terribly cold. The fire was long out, and the wind was pulling heat through the fabric of the blanket. Meira was tucked in beside me, seemingly warm.

"Meira," I whispered. She didn't respond. I cautiously kissed her cheek. I needed to know what it was like. I needed to know if I really wanted this to be something... permanent.

The first wasn't entirely conclusive, so I tried the experiment again. Both times magic flowed through me — not the kind of magic that Meira could grant, but the normal human kind, upon which families for a hundred generations had been launched. Yes, I thought, I would be willing to make the journey from who I was to who I would need to be — from the boy who struggled in battle to the man that my mother clung to each evening, so grateful to be forever loved.

I was completely unfit for the job.

Meira

Arthur bounded up to me as Mardok rode away.

"How do you handle this cold?" I asked.

Arthur took a stick and poked at the fire until a few hot embers emerged, then he curled up next to them.

"I see. You don't. Aren't you supposed to be taking your winter sleep?"

He answered that yes, of course he was, but this level of training required dedication. And if I was dedicated, he would be dedicated, too. He hopped to his feet, whipped out his stick, and gave several dancing moves swinging the stick around until he fell over.

"Oh, Arthur, I'm sorry. Fighting with sticks isn't really a job for squirrels. That's why you have claws and teeth."

According to Arthur, though, claws and teeth hadn't fared well in their long struggle against the wolves and owls. Explaining that his stick was far less of a threat than his teeth wasn't helpful. Arthur just couldn't understand that level of complexity. He was carrying a weapon, he reasoned, so he should sufficiently be able to protect his family.

Accepting his error, I packed him up in my cloak and blanket and returned to our court. Several great fires burned brightly, radiating warmth throughout. Because it was winter, there were more taskings than usual. Summer brought war and treachery — much more in the northern hemisphere than the south — but winter brought starvation. And so we spent a great deal of time transporting food from the warmer hemisphere to the colder, prioritizing those localities where unfair calamity had struck, rather than merely laziness.

Father came out to me.

"Meira, there you are. Would you like to go on an errand?"

"If you needed me, why didn't you call to me?" I asked.

"You and the gentleman were having a fond evening. I didn't want to distract."

I was struck cold in the middle. "You watched?"

"I saw, Meira. I try not to spy where unwarranted."

"Did you follow me?"

"Meira, I am your father. Were I to follow you, that would be only appropriate. But no, I asked Telrin if perchance he had seen you. He told me where to find you with a handsome man. Rather than disturb you, I wanted to see this catch for myself. I'll admit, I was rather surprised, even momentarily perturbed. But I asked myself if there was a particular reason this human shouldn't be yours. And other than creating a potential riot among your siblings or turning the heads of the gods, nothing came to mind."

"Father, he's not mine. He's my combat trainer."

"Meira, I have now been alive for nine hundred and seventy-two years. That was, without a doubt, the worst combat training I have ever seen. It looked quite a bit like an evening alone by the fire."

"Well, that's actually what today was, yes. It was too cold

to practice. Honestly, father, we've never done that before."

"I don't see why not, you seem rather fond of each other. Have you considered making this a permanent venture?"

"Bonding with him?" Did he know that I had been giving Mardok the bonding magic? I hoped not. It wasn't always simple to know when father was ignorant or just probing. "Father, I cannot bond with a human."

"Just because it has never been done doesn't mean it can't ever be. Meira, before you were born, we were sent to this place with the understanding that your future lay here. I never understood why that might be the case. This isn't exactly the most exciting of lands — which, incidentally, makes it an excellent place to live. However, if your future is among humans, then so be it. I will not stand in the way of the gods. Should they have chosen to fulfill your future by the re-merging of our races, I will not be the one to oppose them."

"So you're fine with it if the gods are fine with it? How do you know if the gods are fine with it?"

"Because if it weren't the case, we already would have heard from Jov. You know how he views such things. Besides that, no matter how long we have been a pure race of Fae, we're all still half-human. Now, if you like, there's a group leaving shortly to carry food. I would like you to go with them."

"You would like me… your daughter Meira… to go do something? Something important?"

"Yes, Meira, I would like you to go do something important."

"Yes, Father, I would be honored to do so."

"Only because it's your first tasking. Sometime around your three-hundredth, you won't feel so honored."

I gave him a hug and a kiss on the cheek. Then I set off to join Yur and his group preparing to leave.

"Oh, and Meira," my father called out. "If someone attacks you, give them hell."

Mardok

"Alright, Amos, I'll do it."

"Come again?"

"I'll do it," I repeated.

"You'll do what?"

"I'm going to marry her."

He stood and stared at me for a while. Then he pulled his pipe and tin from his coat pocket. "Mardok," he started, pausing for a lengthy time while he filled his pipe and lit it. "Are you telling me or telling yourself?"

Now it was my turn to wait. "I'm telling you," I determined, "so you can remind me if the time comes."

"As surely as I've known you since you were weaned... the time will come soon... and possibly repeatedly."

"I'm going to be better than that. I'm not a child anymore."

He snickered to himself. "You and Robert," he muttered. "Bakarrik bless us for your good hearts, because it isn't for your age."

I gave a disapproving look.

"Look, I have a bag of silver here that says that you don't even know her name."

"Seriously?"

"Mardok, I've never known you to get close to a girl;

merely the thought terrifies you. And I doubt you know much about her, either."

"And you're willing to bet your own silver on that one?"

"No, of course not. I'm confident, not stupid. It's Robert's silver. But I'm willing to bet it. And I'm confident he would be foolish enough to make the bet. So tell me... what's her name?"

"Meira, Amos, her name is Meira."

"Is that all?"

I stood stalk still until he roared in laughter. If only I knew.

"Look, I haven't met her father yet," I tried. "I don't have her lineage names. But obviously I'm not marrying her until after then. But I'm dedicating myself to making this work.

"So, is she poor or moneyed?"

"What does that matter?"

"It will matter a great deal when you try to find her father, and most certainly in how you present yourself to him. Come across as too wealthy, and he'll be too embarrassed to bless the wedding. Then again, maybe she's the daughter of the Fae king. Ever considered that?"

Now it was my turn to laugh. "If she were the Fae king's daughter, that's something I would know."

"I'm trying to make a point here, Mardok. What happens if she would be marrying down? Are you certain that her family would be fine with that? You know far too little to make this decision."

"But..." I wasn't sure what to say.

"But you can't choose the other path," he surmised. "You're not willing to do well by her if you don't marry her."

Yeah, that.

"Mardok, I was young once, back when dirt was first invented. And I knew this young lass named Perella. She was, to understate her beauty, a goddess. Somehow, without a bit of earning it on my part, we became close. But there was a bit of a problem." In his Amos way, he sat and puffed his pipe for several very long moments.

"Going to continue, or is that the end of your story?"

"I just want you to consider the worst case situation here."

"Worst case? She was married."

"Funny you should mention that. How fortunate you are, Mardok, with this particular love trap of yours. Marry her and enjoy your life together. But be very careful not to end up in this situation again. It won't be so easy to resolve a second time." He puffed his pipe again and started walking away.

I had to know.

"Amos... was she married?"

He continued walking.

"Wait... were you? You were married?"

He ignored me.

"It's not fair to start that kind of story and not answer the question."

"Would it make your own life better if you knew?" he queried.

"No, but it's going to drive me mad if you don't."

"Enjoy your madness, Mardok."

Ten minutes later, I hopped up on the kitchen counter next to Robert.

"Say, you know everyone's names." He had just stolen a warm loaf from the oven, which Mary retrieved with various threats of starting a revolution before disappearing outside into the garden.

"Well, I try, anyway. I'm certain there are a few people I haven't met yet."

"Who's Perella?"

"Perella? Wow, I haven't heard that name in a while."

"Not surprising. She would be pretty old by now."

"She's been dead for nigh on to a decade. Actually, it was when she died that Amos stepped down as head of the Dozen. He left to take care of her family for nearly two years, if you recall."

"Well, not surprising, I suppose. He said he was leaving to care for family, didn't he?"

"Well, of course Mardok. Perella was his sister."

I sat there looking stupid.

Robert eyed me keenly. "There's more to this question, isn't there."

"He said… well, now I'm not certain I should say what he said."

"If you know something truly terrible about Amos, do share. I can't stomach not knowing whatever poor scraps roll through the male gossip network."

I snickered. Robert detested gossip.

"He… well, he insinuated, anyway… um… that he was in love with her." Boy, repeating that was terribly awkward.

"What? Wow, have to admit I didn't see that one coming. At least he had good taste, no?"

"No, I don't know."

"I suppose not. You never met the gal. Twenty years our senior and as hot as Mary's oven. Sweetest thing; smile could have lit the whole forest on fire."

"Why would he have had a thing for his sister?"

"Well..." he pulled on his beard. "I don't know."

"Well o' course ye don' know," Mary announced as she sauntered back into the kitchen. "Ye wernt their closest friends now, were ye? They were separated at birth, they were. Somethin' abou' their parents didn't take—divorced they did, the poor souls. Amos and Perella met years later, not knowin' a thing abou' each other. Even decided to marry. I felt terrible when I found out and had to break the news to 'em. Woulda been a cute cake, though. Perella had good taste."

"So, only moderately embarrassing, not full fledged scandal," I offered.

"Sadly, it seems that way," Robert agreed. "Nothing worthy of a public pillary."

"And it probably wouldn't make him any happier with us. You know, there are those funny moments that you never let a guy live down… and then there are those other moments that… you just have to let go."

"Mardok, I have no idea what you're talking about."

"Well, let's say you had courted Sapphira, not realizing she was your sister. Is that something you would want everyone to talk about forever?"

"I have royal blood. People would expect it."

"Alright, fine. Good thing you married her off, then."

"Had to, before someone like you came up with that really rotten idea."

"What about… say you didn't know, but you ended up courting your mother."

"It's been done, Mardok. And honestly, are you trying to churn my stomach? Because it's working."

"Well, fine… then we'll do me. What if it turned out that I had a sister."

"I would never let you forget it, not for a single moment."

"You're not really a very gracious man, you know?"

"Did you notice that Mary left?"

"I'll get the ham."

5

4th of Lar Indar

Meira

"Ooof!" I felt the air rush out of my lungs as my back hit the ground. My vision swam for a moment before I could sit up.

"Would you like me to tell you what you're doing wrong now? I believe this is, what, your sixth try?" Mardok leaned on the end of his stave looking down at me.

"Seventh. And if you manage to knock me flat once more, then I'll ask for your instruction." I gave him my best flirtatious glance, despite the headache forming behind it.

"You're just trying to avoid paying me today. Either that or you're enjoying staring into the sky."

I winked at him. A wry grin was sitting on his face just begging me to knock it off. I stood, shook the butterflies out of my head, and took a deep breath. We squared off on our separate sides, and I planted my feet a shoulder's distance apart. On the stump in the center of the clearing, Arthur was mimicking.

"Ready," I declared firmly. I was prepared for his charge this time. I had been letting him knock me off my feet all afternoon to lure him into dropping his guard just a bit. He charged me the same way as before, and at the last moment I stabbed the end of my stave into the ground and swung around it with my feet together. My aim was true, and I hit him squarely in the back with both feet as he rushed past, his head spinning lazily around to see where I had disappeared to. I could see his hand grasping at empty space as I left it behind. For once, the action had the desired effect. Mardok collided face-first with the ground.

"Pth!" he spit a chunk of grass out of his mouth.

"You're a bit shorter when you're lying down," I announced, placing my own chin on my stave. I had to lean it at an odd angle to do so. "I declare success!"

"That wasn't quite the point of this exercise," he picked himself up out of the dirt. He was clearly amused and impressed, and the left side of his face had taken on an earthier tone.

"I know," I laughed, "but I was successful. You never said I had to remain planted while you hit me. And since I managed to knock you down," I commented rather smugly, given it was the first time I had ever knocked him down without magic, "you owe me my instruction without payment."

The disappointment on his face was immediate and clear, but he masked it with a false smile. "You didn't discover the maneuver I was hoping for, but I will certainly honor our agreement. I congratulate you." He gave a slight bow.

"I thank you for your instruction, sir." I gave him a studious bow in return, reveling in pride at besting him without cheating. "It's getting late. Until next time?"

"I forgot to mention last week," he commented. "We're set

to travel tomorrow and do not expect to return for three weeks." His earlier disappointment became suddenly clear again. "We'll be making our annual trek to the king's older brother's home, and then we have to investigate some strange rumors we've been hearing from one of our settlements in the north."

"You're expecting trouble," I surmised.

"No, my finger aches. It hit a rock when I fell." He shook it out. "And then Arthur jabbed my arm."

Arthur stood with his paws on his hips and stuck out his tongue. Mardok stuck out his tongue back.

"Children..." I chided.

"It's an annual holiday with the nobles — the first half is. I'm sure I've mentioned what we think of them."

I nodded.

"The 8th day of Lar Indar is called Settlement Day, for when our people first arrived here in West Haulay. So, each year we make a short trip around that date — maybe to pretend we're still travelers. In some places it's a really big deal, with people traveling weeks to see their relatives or even just total strangers. After visiting the king's brother, the nobles will return to their own homes. Then the king, the Dozen, and I will travel on alone."

"You have my sympathies, friend. Will you have any time to yourself?"

He stroked his meaty hand through his hack-cut hair, pushing out a few stray blades of grass. Fresh lacerations were visible on his thick forearm where he broke his fall. They were insignificant cuts and would easily heal. Many others over his years of tale-laden service had left their toll on his tanned skin.

"Precious little while we're traveling, I'm afraid. And in the evenings I'll be on duty telling drunk nobles to leave the ladies alone." His eyes brightened as he caught my suggestion. "Would it be possible for you to join us on the journey?"

"I would be only too delighted to accompany you and your king, though I am unsure how well I travel... your way."

"My way? I ride a horse, and I try to keep to the road."

"I'm not unacquainted with horses, I just never ride them. Flying has been so much more convenient for me. More so, I'm hesitant about sleeping along the way. Humans like to sleep in tiny spaces surrounded by large open areas where they can watch their surroundings while still hiding. For Fae, the trees really are our home. They provide us with shelter and safety."

"We do sound pretty strange, the way you say it. But we're not fond of waking up to bears."

"Bears can be so rude."

"Bandits, too."

"I'll admit to never really having those problems. Bandits are terrified of us, as they should be. Even if they aren't, a notice-me-not charm is pretty effective if you have to sleep alone. And bears... they'll wake us up because they want a treat, but they're not really threatening to us."

"There is so much about your kind that I don't understand."

I pressed the tip of my finger to my lips and placed it against his forehead to grant him a small portion of the magic for our lesson. His muscles relaxed under the effects flowing through my brief touch. The anxieties of the coming journey melted away for a few moments, and he was unconcerned with anything outside of our clearing.

"That much will have to last you until our next lesson." I grinned at him as he re-opened his eyes. "What time should I meet you in the morning to leave for the trip?"

"In theory we'll leave right after breakfast, but don't count on it. Who knows, though, we might have a lucky year. Would you meet me at the stable an hour before sunrise?"

I bit the corner of my lower lip in nervousness, "I've never actually been to the castle, and I'm not sure what a stable looks like, much less where it would be."

"I apologize for not thinking more clearly." He shook his head, and I wondered if the fall earlier had rattled him more than expected. "Would you be willing to come back with me this evening and stay at the castle tonight? I won't have the opportunity to come this far out of the way to fetch you in the morning, and I need to get as much rest tonight as possible."

"Are you sure that I would be welcomed there? Some humans do not like fae."

"I have made the king aware of our friendship, and he is looking forward to meeting you. Besides that, he would never object to me housing a guest."

Meeting the king that Mardok spoke of with respect and fondness was something I had thought about many times but had not expected would happen for several more years. It would be nice to meet Mardok's closest friend. I was rapidly approaching the point with Mardok where I would have to explain what was happening to him when I paid him for our lessons. On that day, he would have to make a choice about our relationship. I wanted to have the support of his friend and master in that decision.

"It would be my honor to meet the man of whom you speak so well. If you will wait here a few moments, I will gather my things and we can go to the castle."

Mardok

Meira flashed me a brilliant smile as her translucent, dragonfly-like wings opened and lifted her from the ground, casting rainbows on the forest floor. I watched her body sway as she flew off through the trees.

Now that I had decided on a clear direction with her, my father's words came to mind once more, "If she's the right lady, why would you wait to die from old age?"

"How about because I'm still terrified, Dad?" And, yet, all I wanted to do was to hold her tightly, to absorb her, to make her the better part of me. I sighed. I had no idea how to move forward. I decided to put it out of my mind until we returned from the trip. The distraction of a close relationship, much less an impending marriage, would be problematic until then.

I touched my forehead where she had pressed her kiss against me. The spot still tingled slightly with the sensation. I closed my eyes and breathed in, feeling my heightened senses.

Tomorrow would be an interesting day. Likely little would be required for Meira's visit, except perhaps beating off prying eyes and ears. The citizenry would find her presence and her person to be a thing of novelty and curiosity. Without a barrier or guardian the nobility wouldn't give her a moment's peace.

A rustling in the leaves nearby roused me from my thoughts. I looked over toward the sound expecting to see Meira but found myself instead looking into the silver-skinned face of a Fae I had never seen before. He wore armor with the dents and scars of many battles, and it hadn't been cleaned of ichor since its latest use.

"Short-life," he addressed me with cool ease, "if she comes to any harm while she is away, I will hold you personally responsible." His stone face betrayed no hint of emotion. "She has always been a free spirit, but that does not make her any less one of us. We take care of our own. My sister is valuable to me." He rested his hand lazily on the hilt of his sword, his finger flicking briefly. I recognized the subtle motion as he stated the threat, having done it myself many times.

I swallowed to clear my throat and held his gaze, "Protecting her is a duty and honor that I gladly accept. If it requires my life to keep her safe I will be only too happy to give it." I inclined my head respectfully, but I gripped my blade reflexively.

"It's my duty before yours. It will be your duty when you've earned it." Then he disappeared between two trees. When he vanished neither the limbs nor the leaves moved. I pondered the interchange and decided that I liked him. Moments later I heard the reassuring hum of Meira's wings.

"I am ready," she declared happily. She held only the tiniest of bags in one hand. She had braided her copper hair into a crown around her head with wild roses woven into the tresses, and she wore a light green gown I had never seen on her before. It had many flowing layers, each visible through the other, begging the eyes to see what was just under the next. She was stunning.

I bowed, taking the moment to hide my lack of composure. "That was exceptionally quick."

"Thank you. I saw no reason to keep you waiting."

"Normally braiding hair like that would take hours."

"I'm on good terms with a family of raccoons."

"I knew it wasn't Arthur. He's been sitting here glaring at me the whole time you've been gone."

Meira laughed. It was like the gurgling of a new spring falling over smooth stones.

"Do wild animals typically help you get dressed?"

"Oh, not at all, not since I was young. And it's not like they sing and dance or sew my clothes."

"That's heartening, I suppose. Well, shall we be off then, m'lady?" I offered her my arm.

"M'lady?" she asked quizzically as she took hold of my elbow.

"It is an abbreviated title of respect befitting a member of the court. That is likely how most people will address you, unless you have a preferred title."

"Consider me an Ambassador of the High Fae. That way it will not seem strange that I accompany you on the journey." She paused seemingly to find the right words, "I would not want to cause your king any undue trouble within his court, and inviting a new foreign ambassador to view the sights of the kingdom would not be seen as improper, correct?"

"So you're an ambassador, then?"

"I've been granted that status by my king for this trip, and if all goes well, it could be permanent."

"Okay… alright… I wasn't expecting that."

"What were you expecting then?"

"Well, I don't know. Just being a High Fae would have given you tremendous status and novelty… in the court." I couldn't tell her that I was the one shocked about this. She may have seen it as insulting.

"Is it because you thought I was someone insignificant?" she pried. "It's all right, Mardok. I'm more flattered that you would think well of me as an underling rather than as a member of the court. Though, with your view of the nobility, maybe that would have been the more challenging accomplishment."

"Well, I should have known." I was flummoxed. To cover for it I started babbling. "Typically, our conversations are much more geared toward fighting stances, weaponry, and the occasional squirrel. Actually, I really know very little about you or your people."

"Well then, we'll have to change that." She smiled. "Being an ambassador, now, I can share pretty much anything."

I gleaned from her demeanor that she was referring to more than just information. "I look forward to it."

"The Fae king is most kind to his people, but also very protective. His queen is like a mother to all the Fae. But with so many different races of fae, the politics of court can be very complicated."

"You've mentioned other races before. Here we're only really familiar with goblins and pixies."

"They get around. But there are also dvergr, centri, sphinx, and many others. Most of them are chimera — descendants from gods and creatures. But a few were created by the lesser gods. Technically, we're a chimera race, too, though few people think of us that way. The High Fae are the descendants of the high god Bakarrik and our mother Opella, who was a human. Bakarrik put us in charge of all the fae, not that some of them listen to us. But it's our job to keep them in line, whether they like it or not."

"I see." I shook my head. I didn't see.

"And I'm only familiar with politics because I grew up dealing with it," she said matter-of-factly. "It comes with being the youngest of the royal family."

"You're a princess?" I stopped in my shock. "As in, the king's daughter?"

"Yes, I am, but I'm really not that important."

"I've been beating up on a princess for almost a year?" Worse, I could already hear Amos' laughter in my head. I couldn't wrap my mind around the hundreds of times I tripped, shoved, pummeled, or in other ways behaved so inappropriately to her. Male royalty, sure… but a princess? How was I ever going to live up to whatever standard I now had in front of me? There wasn't any way I could imagine in which her father would be convinced to permit me to marry his daughter.

"Most of my siblings don't even like me," she muttered.

"Is it possible that… oh, I don't know… that you could have mentioned that at some point?"

"I just did. I thought you ought to know about it now, so that you won't be shocked when I introduce myself to your king. Anyway, we should..."

My brain continued imploding; her father was the Fae king.

"...said I should conduct myself as an ambassador from his court. I can't tell you just..."

This wasn't going to work, there was no way I could marry her now. If I had known about it sooner I might have been able to break off the bargain. I was utterly desperate for her.

"…but like I said, once I gained his blessing to go..."

Her brother… was he aware that I was nothing more than a count?

"…and besides all that, he does seem rather fond of you."

Whoa, hold on what? "He's fond of me? Your brother? I mean, you're father? How does he even know who I am? I've never met him."

"Do you really think he would leave me to meet with a man alone for a year and never look in on what we were doing?"

"That's… sensible, I suppose. If I had a daughter I'd definitely be screening the men she came in contact with." I knew I was babbling again. "Oh, just before you came back, I ran into your brother. He was rather insistent that you not die." Her eyebrows creased. "He seemed somewhat concerned that you might come to harm while traveling with me."

"Unfortunately, in my family it's rather hard to say who that might have been. Brothers can be over-protective…" She trailed off. We started walking again at a brisker pace, and she flashed a quick smile at me. "Back to forms of address… 'Meira, Fae Ambassador' will suffice for formal occasions, 'Ambassador Meira' for informal, and you may always call me simply Meira in private. Actually, please don't call me anything more formal than that if you don't have to."

"What is your family name?" Amos' question filtered through my confusion.

"Family name? I don't have one. I'm the king's daughter. I have only one name."

"How… odd." Ha! Amos would owe me something for that. "In my culture the more elevated in rank a person is, the more names he has. I personally have nine names and several titles."

"Truly? So, what is your full name?"

"I don't actually remember them all. I go by Count Mardok Adlar of Adalstienn. I know that one of the middle ones is Kjell, because I thought it sounded funny when I was a kid, but it was still short enough to pronounce."

She stopped and stared at me quizzically. At length she continued walking. "The thing I find odd is that you could have so many names that you can't even remember them all. Amongst Fae, those in the king's immediate family have only one name each. Fae of lower position have more names. Those in high positions are most recognizable and need no explanation; only lower ranking individuals ever need to tell who their parents were, their place of birth, or their position."

It sounded logical and infinitely more memorable. We had reached the edge of the forest when she stopped. I turned and looked at her. Her eyes were distant, her vision wandering.

"We have to keep going to get to the castle," I said gently.

"I know." She paused, seeming to gather her courage. "It is… more difficult to leave than I had expected, because I know I won't be returning quickly. I've seen some of the most desolate places on Lur, but I have never slept outside the forests." She inhaled slowly and let out a long sigh. I didn't understand the unusual impact this was having on her. "The sky is so empty. Even when I was shepherding my sapling forest Oihana, there were still a few big trees to shelter in."

I looked with her out at the rolling hills of wheat, barley, and grass, rows of shrubs and rock walls marking property lines, and ivy-covered houses. Squirrels and birds dotted the country-side, flitting about. It was full of life, not empty.

"Come on, Meira; I hate missing dinner." I urged with a slight tug on her arm. She straightened her shoulders, took a firmer grasp of my arm, and stepped out of the shade of the trees. She looked back, and the wind whistled mournfully behind us as we walked away.

"I will miss you," she whispered. The wind whipped the nearest trees; their branches dipped briefly to the ground and returned to full height again.

As we walked away, a horrible screeching sounded behind us. We turned together. Arthur stood at the edge of the trees, waving his twig. Along with him, five other squirrels were standing in a row, resting their chins on their twigs. Arthur had an odd tuft of yellow moss on his head.

"What, pray tell, is he doing with that on his head?" I asked.

"It's your hair," Meira suggested. She waved back and chittered at them. Then we were on our way.

We walked in silence to the other side of the pasture, where I collected my horse. He leaned down to her for scritches and a treat, which she somehow always had on her person for him. I believe he had grown to like her more than me in the time since I had begun meeting with her. Instead of riding and flying, we continued on foot together for a couple hours to the castle. As we approached, the sun touched the horizon behind us and turned the outer wall a rosy pink. Meira simply stared at the massive structure. It was an old fortress that the king had restored and modified to be his primary residence. It was appropriately impressive and intimidating with its five stories and towering turrets. It stood on a rise on the plane with miles of visibility in all directions save the forest, and no sane army would march through there.

"I never imagined it would be so massive," Meira said with admiration as we neared the walls. Her eyes were filled with wonderment, soaking in each little detail, especially, I suspected, the moss and ivy overrunning the gray stonework.

"It is large. But your forest is much more expansive, and you navigate that extraordinarily well," I said, trying to soothe her anxiety. I steered us through the military gate to avoid the traffic at the main entrance, handing off my horse to a gawking attendee. Frank and George were on gate duty and looked up quizzically at me as we passed. I noted their eyes lingering on my stunning guest.

Within moments the gossip network would be buzzing. I needed to get Meira into the king's audience chamber as quickly as possible to keep it from getting out of hand. We crossed the distance between the gate and the keep in short order, maintaining a normal pace, but as we entered the confines of the building, I turned my focus to haste.

"We are going to move swiftly for a few minutes in darkness," I said as we left the small courtyard and entered the shade of the doorway to the castle proper. "Don't worry about learning the way. I'll teach it to you later; I promise." She nodded her understanding. I pushed open a hidden door set behind a giant urn filled with dead flowers. Meira stared at them in horror as we moved past. Inside she changed her hold from my arm to my shoulder and took flight. I moved just short of running through the unlit passages, more by memory than sight.

"We're nearly there," I told her as we exited an invisible door behind a tapestry and entered the large main hall that led directly to the audience chamber. "It would be better if you walked now."

"I agree. I recall how shaken you were the first time you saw me fly." She gave me that stunning smile again.

"You stuck a pine needle up my nose."

Her bubbling laugh echoed in the hall as she folded her wings back and they blended almost seamlessly into the back of her gown. Very practical, I thought. I offered her my arm once again, and we walked to the doors of the audience chamber. I nodded to the guards, Harry and Amos, and they opened the doors for us without comment, though Amos raised a brow at me as I passed.

"It's Meira. Just Meira, no family name," I whispered at him as we passed. "You owe me."

He quietly slipped a small bag into my hand. "Well done,"

he said.

"Your Majesty," my voice boomed across the echoing walls, "I have met a visiting dignitary who wishes an introduction."

"Yes, I was just informed of her arrival by Lord Gifford. She is most welcome." He gestured for us to approach. I bowed as my position required and we walked past the gaping nobles to the dais.

"Lord Gifford?" I queried.

"Yes, and he heard it from…" he raised an eyebrow to the lord.

"Madeline, my daughter, Sire."

"There, see?" Robert smiled broadly back at me. In a perfect rescue of my confusion, Meira stepped forward.

"Majesty," she began with deference and grace, "I am Meira, youngest princess of the High Fae." She paused to allow the murmuring to soften. "My father sends me as an ambassador of goodwill to your court. He also sends this gift." She opened the tiny bag I noticed earlier and extracted an even smaller box. She handed it to me, and I carried it to Robert. "The box holds one of my mother's most finely crafted pendants. I can hardly describe its value in terms of goods."

The king took the pendant from the box and held it up by its chain to inspect more closely. It was formed of intertwined gold and silver, shaped like a leaf, perhaps of elm or cherry. It was covered in intricate lettering that, from a distance, was the leaf's veining.

"We have never seen its equal. The gift is most heartily accepted along with the goodwill of your people. We are most honored to have you in our court. As a return gesture, is there anything of value to the ancient and noble High Fae which exists among men?"

"From men we request nothing, noble lord, but the welcome of a peaceful neighbor."

"To be sure, we were unaware until a year ago that you were our neighbor. My father's father had cleared the land of goblins, and we have not seen High Fae in these lands since that time."

"We have only returned to the nearby forest within the past ten years. But we have always moved about the forests of Lur freely."

"Such is your right, as the gods have decreed. We acknowledge your right to the trees and your stewardship of all living things."

This caught me by surprise, and I knew my face reflected it. But I also knew that many in the court would immediately resent this particular acknowledgment. They rejected the authority of the gods and, therefore, the Fae. Robert had, without consulting the Counsel of Dukes, declared that most of his kingdom now belonged to the Fae. A wise man would have pointed out that it always had.

"We are pleased to find that the ways of old are accepted here." I would have to brief her on her poor assumption about this later.

"If there is anything at all that the High Fae should need or find in short supply, we welcome their request and will do whatever we can to provide it."

"We thank you for your generosity, gracious king of men." She tilted her head slightly in thanks.

Watching as they continued the conversation was like watching an elaborate dance. They were both masters of the craft of courtly performance. And while very real negotiations were being conducted, I knew the pretexts of formality were for the benefit of the audience of nobility—not all of whom were happy with the results. Among other things, Meira's presence was to be a semi-permanent feature, along with the potential presence of armed Fae. Also, the Fae would start conducting pixie removal, who typically were not a major problem in West Haulay, but humans were restricted in their unscheduled movements within the forest to within a mile of the edges as long as the Fae remained. This was for the protection of the people, who occasionally did not return, but I knew that the nobles would be most upset about now having to speak to the Fae before organizing an impromptu hunt.

"Would you care to join us for a private dinner?" Robert asked finally. He could see his nobles getting restless and knew as well as I did that they would swarm Meira, given the chance. "Please pardon our informality, but we are afraid you caught us at a poor time for entertaining as we are preparing to leave for a journey in the morning."

"I would be honored to join His Majesty for dinner," she answered, perhaps a touch too quickly for propriety. I could see that her otherwise steely nerves were starting to fail her. "My escort took the liberty of informing me of His Majesty's impending travels, so there is no offense to forgive." She inclined her head in respect.

"We will adjourn our audiences early today," Robert announced to the assembly. "We must finalize preparations for our holiday." The nobles knew a dismissal when they heard one, even if they were reluctant to leave with so little information about the strange new ambassador of the magical and mysterious fairy people.

"Come," he gestured to us. We left the audience chamber and followed Robert's private passage to his suite. Meira kept up her official façade until we were in his sitting room and he had dismissed the other guards.

Meira

It was excruciating to perform the rituals of court again, but I knew that it was necessary for me to be able to travel with Mardok. Once we were alone in the king's rooms, however, I relaxed and dropped my formal manners.

"Robert, it is a pleasure to finally meet you. My friend here has told me much about you." Robert took my hand and bowed graciously.

"The pleasure is all mine, Ambassador."

"Please, just call me Meira."

"Meira, then. Your name is as beautiful as you are." I widened my eyes at his openly flirtatious statement. "Don't get excited," he said quickly. "It's my only line, and I say it to every girl. Mardok has spoken only wonderfully of you. Please tell me that what he said about me was positive as well." He had an easy smile.

"Most of it. Although, he did recount to me one or two episodes of mischief from your childhood together." I glanced at Mardok; he was staring at me with wide eyes and a slightly tilted head. It was an expression with which I was unfamiliar. Was he wanting me to tell more? To stop talking? "Perhaps we can discuss that sometime later," I said. "I would like to make an official request to join your traveling party. I am reluctant to have to give up my lessons for so long and would very much like to see your country."

"I would be delighted for you to join us!" He appeared genuine. "It will give me a chance to disavow any knowledge of the events Mardok has told you about. As for your lodgings tonight, I'm afraid I don't have an ambassador's suite available. The housekeeper is quite busy helping the various nobles prepare for the morning. She will no doubt have something appropriate available for you to use at any time once we have returned."

"If I may be so bold, since I know no one else in the castle, I would feel most comfortable if I were able to stay with Mardok." The surprise was easily readable on both of their faces. "Is that an unusual request?"

"Well..." Robert's voice trailed off.

"It is a bit, yes," Mardok finished. "It's much more typical for the unmarried men and women to sleep in separate sections of the building... or separate rooms, at least."

"And separate beds," Robert added.

"I'm not sure what you —"

"I know nothing of the sleeping arrangements of the Fae," Robert interjected.

I looked from Robert to Mardok, perplexed. "If being separate is required..." I began again.

"Not required, understand," Robert explained. "Except for the beds. That's required. Is there a particular reason you're asking to stay with him?"

"I have never slept inside a building before, and I am not certain how well I will adjust to it," I said.

Both men nodded, pretending to understand.

"Well," Robert said, "Mardok's personal rooms were

originally an extension of my suite…"

"I won them fair and square."

"… and… no, Mardok, you cheated. Anyway, I believe there is an extra room available between the two of us if that will suit."

I looked at Mardok for his input. He nodded his assent.

"As long as there is a window it should be fine," I said.

"Where are your things? I'll have them brought up."

"I brought them with me," I replied, smiling at the generous if unnecessary consideration.

"You did?" Robert inquired, leaning over and peering around behind me. I pulled out my bag.

"Yes, right here," I showed him. The two men stood staring at the bag as if it were a simple pouch. I rolled my eyes; this naivety was going to take getting used to.

"Shall I call for supper then?" the king asked, clearly not convinced.

"Certainly." I took a seat on the couch nearest the fireplace. Mardok sat next to me, and Robert flopped down in a large chair across from us and threw his leg over the arm. He tossed his crown on a pile of socks on the floor. We kept the conversation light and inconsequential as dinner was served. Mardok watched Robert and I chat for a few moments before he joined in. He looked relieved that we were getting along so well.

Once the servants had finished bringing in the dinner

trays and left the room, I moved on to the more serious business that I needed to explain. "I have two important pieces of information regarding my presence that I feel you need to be aware of." I paused to find the right words before continuing. "The first is regarding the pendant that I gave to you earlier. It is no ordinary piece of jewelry. It is a maoim beatha. If at any time I am in danger you are to hold the maoim beatha in your right hand and ask for help. My father will send his emissaries to assist you in returning me to safety. Second, if I am injured in a dangerous situation in your presence and you haven't used the maoim beatha, when the first drop of my blood touches the ground an army of fae will appear on that spot and they will kill anyone nearby, friend or foe. I am my father's favorite daughter and he takes my safety very seriously."

Robert turned somewhat green. "If I had a family of my own, I'm sure I would feel the same way." He forced a smile. We will do our best to prevent the need for such measures."

"I know. I just needed to make you aware of what could happen. Now that all of that is out of the way, let's enjoy our dinner." Dinner consisted of vegetables and fish. The three of us chatted easily for the rest of the meal and then for a dessert of fresh berries and apples afterward. It was nearly midnight when Robert yawned.

"Oh, I've kept you from your rest!" I exclaimed.

"Nonsense," the men replied in unison.

"No, I have. You were both planning on going to bed early to be ready for the morning."

"Well, it was a pleasant diversion from the schedule," Robert said. "Besides, I'm a king. I don't need sleep. I have servants who sleep for me. And in the morning, nobody can leave without me. I practically own the place."

"I'll show you to your room." Mardok offered me his hand. "It's definitely past the king's bedtime."

"Good night, my new friend," Robert yawned again. "Rest well, for the morning shall come sooner than should be allowed."

"Pleasant sleep to you as well, Robert." I let Mardok guide me out of the king's sitting room and into a narrow hallway. We passed one closed door and he opened the next one for me.

"These are my rooms," he said huskily, trying to stifle a yawn.

I arched one quizzical brow at him.

"Sorry, I'm more tired than I realized. I can have fresh water brought up at any time if you need it." He gestured to a basin resting on a table near the window on the wall opposite the door. "I usually eat breakfast in the kitchen before most of the castle is awake. You may pick either of the two rooms on that side." He motioned to my left. "My room is through that door on the right, closest to Robert's rooms."

"Thank you, my friend. I know you are tired, so go ahead and get some sleep. I need less than you do." I fluttered up and kissed him lightly on the forehead. I granted him only the tiniest bit of magic with it, for fear he would fall asleep where he stood.

"Good night," his voice was husky again when he spoke. He seemed almost reluctant to let go of my hand that he had been holding since we left the king. He kissed my knuckles gently and went into his room. The skin on the back of my hand felt warm for several minutes after. It was the first time that Mardok had shown me any deliberate physical affection.

I felt guilty for robbing Robert and Mardok of their much-needed rest, so before I looked into the bedrooms, I quietly went back into the narrow hall and stood between the closed door we passed earlier and the door to the king's room. Peaceful sleep is one of the earliest spells a Fae learns, so I began to sing the lullaby to help my friends rest. I am by no means the most talented singer in my father's court, but I have some measure of skill, and the area surrounding the king's suite quickly became still and quiet. Confident that they would rest more effectively, I returned to Mardok's rooms.

I surveyed the two rooms that he had offered me and found that one not only had a window but also a small balcony where I could stand and see the edge of my forest. I knew I would sleep nowhere else. I stepped out onto the balcony and let down my plaited hair and the flowers that mother insisted I wear. The dress was too fine for me to wear all the time, so I removed it and opened my bag. I started digging through it as the breeze licked at my legs. I giggled at it and told the wind to go play with the flags instead. It took a quick nip at my stomach and drew out my hair as it left.

I felt the moon and looked out at my forest. It seemed so much smaller from the castle. I gazed across the yard and noticed several of the night guards staring up at me, their mouths open. How friendly these humans were, even though I was a complete stranger to them. I smiled and waved.

It took a while to find the garment I was looking for, since I had packed it so hurriedly. The bag had been a gift from my great grandmother and no matter how much you put in it, it always had room for more, and never changed shape or weight. However, unless you were careful with how you put things in, they were often difficult to find. After a bit of searching and not a little repacking, I found my normal dress. I pulled it over my head, folded the more formal dress, and packed it carefully away.

I whispered my night blessing to the trees and tittered as the breeze brought me its new toy, a standard it had torn from its pole. I waved, and the wind took it away to the forest, where my heart resides. As I sank onto the ledge, listening to the sounds of the trees, pleasant sleep overcame me, and I dreamt of the uncertain future.

6

5th of Lar Indar

Mardok

I woke the next morning renewed and refreshed and in plenty of time for breakfast. There were only a few things left to ready for the trip. I saw with pleasure that Meira had chosen the balcony room and knocked on her door. I didn't have long to wait; she opened it almost before my hand had finished knocking.

"Good morning," she said cheerily.

"Good morning to you. Did you rest well?"

"It was different than what I expected." She paused. "But not unpleasant. And yourself?"

"I feel strangely invigorated." I ran my fingers through my hair to put it back in place for the day.

Meira smiled again, obviously not saying something.

"Shall we get some breakfast?" I suggested. "I need to prepare my horse before sunrise."

"Of course."

We laughed easily. We were too early to the kitchen to

have any of the morning bread, and I didn't have time to wait for it. I grabbed a pair of hard rolls from the previous day. Meira experimented with a small portion of it but chose to have mostly nuts and berries for her meal. I explained the concept of having a specific location to keep all of our work animals to keep them safe and easily cared for, but she was so used to the forest life that she didn't understand until I showed her.

She stood with her mouth agape for a few moments. Several of the animals she had never seen before, like the dairy cows and the egg-laying chickens. They had been imported from the plains, so she had no experience with them. My horse was happy to see her again and leaned his head down for her to scratch between his ears.

"This is an amazing place. I am astonished that you are able to keep so many animals together in such a small area."

"It's a rare treat to have such an appreciative visitor in my stable," a tawny-haired, clean shaven older man said as he walked up behind us.

"Good morning, Master Thomas. Ambassador Meira, allow me to introduce the stable master. Master Thomas, this is the High Fae Ambassador Meira." A thought occurred to me. "Tom, are you busy at the moment?"

"No, sir. The horses and oxen are fed and ready. The last-minute things have to wait until the last minute, and my apprentices can take care of most of them. Is there something I can do for you?"

"Ambassador Meira has never seen a stable before and is most curious about it. I thought that you might give her a tour while I ready my horse and gear, since you would be the most knowledgeable person to guide her."

"It would be my pleasure, sir." He bowed. "Please call me Tom, m'lady Ambassador, I only make obnoxious people call me Master Thomas."

I whispered to Meira, "He's a good man. You can trust him." She nodded and accepted the arm that he offered her.

Meira

I was surprised that Mardok introduced the stable master to me with such a high amount of respect. He was the first person that I had met at the castle other than the king. Tom and I walked down the rows of stalls, and he told me about all of the different animals that we passed — where they came from, what they were used for, and what their names were. He showed me a wild black horse that had just been brought in from the plains.

"Here's the most recent addition to the stable. I haven't had time to tame him yet, but he's awfully purty, don't ya think?"

"He is beautiful." I agreed. "He's not happy in such a confined space, though."

"Yeah, he kicked down the barrier between two stalls when he first got here. So, we put him here where there's at least a bit more room for him to pace." I held my hand out to the beast. "Ye may not want to be doing that, m'lady. He bites." I just smiled at Tom and whistled softly to the horse. He looked up and came trotting over to me. Once he was close I could see how large of an animal he really was. He bent his head down lower than his shoulders so that I could reach his cheek and leaned into my hand so that I could scratch him better.

"Does he have a name?" I asked Tom, who was staring at me slack-jawed.

"Er, no. We don't usually name them until they're tamed."

"He should be called Dusk," I said. Tom reached his hand

up to pet him as well, and Dusk turned his head and snapped at it. "No, Dusk." I pulled his head back to look at me. "Master Tom is very nice. You should not try to hurt him. He does not want to hurt you." I reached over and took Tom's hand and placed it on Dusk's forehead. Dusk whuffed uncertainly and almost tried to pull away, but I kept my other hand firmly pressed against his cheek. Dusk's ears flicked back and forth for a few moments before he finally accepted Tom's attentions. I dropped my hands back to my side and Tom kept rubbing the horse's head.

"I've never seen anything like that before." Tom gave the horse an apple from his belt pouch, and we started walking again. "No one has been able to touch him without getting bitten or kicked since he was brought in."

"Animals like me. It is a gift of mine." I shrugged.

"I should say so." We walked along quietly for a few moments until we came to a stall that had several brown furry beasts in it that were yapping like wolf pups. In many ways they were wolves, but their hair was short, their ears were floppy, and their noses were thicker.

"What are those?"

"Those would be dogs, Ambassador. His Majesty's best hunting hounds, bred and trained them all m'self." He practically swelled with pride. "They're getting itchy for the hunting season and don't appreciate having to stay cooped up in here too often." He reached out to the nearest one and showed me how they liked to be scratched behind the ears. This was nice; grown wolves don't like being touched. Just then one of the stable hands came up and asked Tom a question. "Could you excuse me for a moment, Ambassador?"

"Take your time." The dogs drooped their tales as he walked away.

"So, you're dogs," I remarked to them. "I've heard about you before. It's good to finally meet you." They seemed so sad, so I decided to climb into the stall with them to cheer them up.

Mardok

I heard the barking from down the hall. It sounded rather frenzied. I looked down the stable to the dog pen and caught a glimpse of Meira as she stepped off the fence and into the swarming and excited mass of dogs. They immediately jumped on her and took her down.

"NO!" I yelled. She hadn't even been with me a full day, and already her brother was going to kill me. Just one… drop… of blood… I ran down the hall in a panic. When I got there, I couldn't even see her underneath all of the dogs.

"MEIRA, are you okay?" She didn't answer, but even over the din of the excited swirling mass of wagging tails I could hear her laughter, like a burst of bubbling water. I caught a glimpse of copper hair and then she sat up in the middle of the pack. She had the biggest smile I had ever seen. I sighed in relief.

"I'm fine. These dogs wouldn't hurt me. They were just a bit enthusiastic in their greetings. And one of them was licking my foot. It tickled." She actually physically glowed with happiness.

"Is she alright, sir?" Master Thomas came running over after hearing the commotion. "I only left her for a moment. Had to deal with a duke, sir. I didn't think she would climb in there with them."

"A duke got up early?"

"Surprised us all, sir."

"Well, she's fine, fortunately. *My* heart stopped, but she's having fun with your dogs."

"Oh, Tom, I'm glad you're back. Does this one have a name?" Meira indicated one of the many she was petting.

"That'd be Rei. She's a sweet one and right smart, too."

"She's also recently in the 'motherly way'. That tall one," she pointed to a sleek brown spotted hound, "is the father, and it will be a large litter."

"How do ya be knowing all of that, m'lady?" Tom slid into his country drawl, clearly as confused as I was.

"She told me." Meira said it so pragmatically that neither of us could come up with anything to say in response. "Mardok, could you give me a hand, please?" She reached out her hand for me to help her out of the pen. When I pulled her over the fence, she paused at my ear and whispered, "I have nothing to fear from any animal. Not even the most vicious beast alive would dare hurt me. So, do not concern yourself with keeping me safe from them. It is the race of men that causes my father to worry for me."

I nodded and fought the rush of blood that her breath against my ear caused.

Master Thomas looked at her with concern. "Are your wings okay, m'lady?" Meira and I both stared at him, bewildered. "Well, I know it's a secret, since you're hiding them. But I'm not ignorant about the fairy folk. I happen to be a master at the art of breeding." We were still amazed. "Your gait, m'lady. You walk as though you prefer to fly."

"Do I really?" she asked me.

"Yeah, actually… come to think of it."

"They're fine, Master Thomas. They're quite sturdy."

"If it's not out of line, m'lady, I would love the privilege of seeing them sometime."

Meira smiled, "Of course, good sir. After we return. Perhaps I can show you how we Fae keep our animals."

Only when his sons were born had I seen Tom happier.

Meira came back with me to watch me finish saddling my horse so the stable master could resume his work. I showed her how to smooth the under-blanket so that there were no wrinkles and how to tighten the saddle belt so that it would remain secure for the entire ride.

Once my saddlebags were packed and ready, Meira and I led my horse out into the main courtyard. One of the pages was waiting to take him to my post, where he would be tied until everyone was ready to leave. We saw one of the stable hands leading Robert's horse to his post while we were headed back to the main building.

"There are likely to be many more people up now. Do you want to go back through the main doors, or should we go through the servants' entrance?"

"I will have to meet them sooner or later, and most will be preoccupied with their travel preparations and will be too busy to bother us long."

"As you wish, Ambassador Meira." I bowed slightly and held my arm out to escort her inside.

The inner court was bustling with nobles commanding

their servants with their trunks and barking other self-serving orders. The smart ones had the majority of their things loaded onto the carriages last night and only had small bags to add this morning. So naturally, many of them had to load all their luggage now and they were loudly obnoxious about it.

"Ah, Ambassador Meira, I was hoping to have the pleasure of meeting you this morning." A black-mustasioed, rotund man with slicked-back hair tied with a velvet ribbon approached us and bowed with masterful precision, defying his physique. "I am Baron Thaddeus Mark Kinsley of Saltwood. Have you broken your fast, yet? I would be honored if you would join me as I was just about to go to the dining hall." His smile was calculating, and his teeth gleamed as if by their own light.

"It is indeed a pleasure to meet you, sir. However, I fear that I have already eaten and still have a few preparations of my own to complete before it is time to leave."

"Oh, so you will be going on holiday with us then?"

"The king has graciously offered to show me his kingdom, and this morning's journey was conveniently planned already. I look forward to making your better acquaintance along the way."

The man made the appropriate bows and returned to loading his meager belongings. I felt Meira shudder on my arm. "Do not ever leave me alone in his company," she said softly, so as to be out of earshot. There was a tremor of cold fear in her voice.

I placed my hand over hers. "I won't. I wouldn't trust him with… well… Let's just say I wouldn't trust him. Especially

with my—" What exactly was she to me? There wasn't a word
that described a charming lady whom I really liked and hoped
someday to be my bride, but whose father I had not yet talked
to, and who was way out of my league, and who I was doomed
to lose for being merely a human. Without an apt word, I
simply added, "dear friend." A quick change of topic was in
order.

"Come and meet a better man, Meira. This is the Duke
Terkins." I extended my arm and took Terkin's shoulder.
"Terkins, this is Ambassador Meira of the High Fae."

"Ambassador, a wonderful pleasure to meet you. I saw
you come in yesterday, and I must say that you put the castle
in a tizzy. This is my wife, Emmalyne."

"Good day to you." Emmalyne offered her hand and
Meira took it.

"If ever you have trouble, they're safe," I explained.

"Thank you, Mardok," Terkins replied. "We try to not
make ourselves completely impossible. And while I agree with
the negotiations in general, I gave the king my best impression
of a growl when he mentioned I would need to get prior
approval before hunting."

"We've had issues with people shooting at Fae thinking
they were deer," Meira replied.

"I understand the problem," he answered. "I've had a few
people I wished were deer so that I could shoot them."

"Haven't we all," I said. "Perhaps the same people?"

"Pringe won't be coming, Mardok, so no luck making that

mistake this trip. I did note, though, that a few other people have decided to come since the Ambassador arrived yesterday." He inclined toward Emmalyne.

"Yes," Emmalyne said. "A young count, along with two attendants who had 'mysterious maladies' — suddenly cured."

"We suspected the Ambassador might cause a bit of a kerfuffle," I commented.

"I'm sorry," Meira replied. "I wasn't intending to create trouble."

"Not at all, dear." Emmalyne touched her arm gently. "So far you've only caused people to inadvertently express honesty. And for this group, that's a breath of fresh air." We expressed final greetings and moved on our way.

Other nobles paused to greet Meira as we crossed the courtyard, but as she predicted they were busy and didn't stop us for long.

We walked up to Robert's suite. Meira wanted to wash up after her incident with the dogs in the stable, so I led her back to my rooms and went to check in with Robert. Servants scurried in and out of his rooms with bags and trunks.

"Are we going for an entire year, Your Majesty?" I teased.

"It's easy for you. You get to wear your uniform for official events. I have to bring an entire wardrobe just to appear presentable. I'm still going to be holding almost daily audiences with the locals while we're on the way to Gavin's house."

"I know. We've been over your schedule a hundred

times."

"But now we have an ambassador attending. She is delightful, by the way."

"She won't be a bother. Once the novelty wears off, the nobles will calm back down, and they will see her for her position only. I will be keeping a closer eye on our favorite baron, though."

"What happened?"

"He introduced himself to her when we came back from the stable. He wanted her to join him for breakfast and was delighted to know that she was accompanying us for the trip."

"So, in other words, he did nothing overt, and was the most polite gentleman, which usually means he wants something."

"Exactly. He looked her over like some sort of commodity, and she felt it, too."

"She is a smart girl. I'm glad to hear she's wary of him as well."

"She actually shuddered after he left us."

Robert sighed with me. We were both lost in our own thoughts for a few moments.

"So how did Ambassador Meira find the stables?" he asked, finally.

"Completely fascinating. And she informed Master Thomas and me that your favorite hunting hound is going to be a mother. The smart bay you got from Greyplain is apparently the father."

"How could she know all that?"

"She said that Rei told her."

"She spoke to the dog?" he was incredulous.

"No, Robert, the dog spoke to her. This is a thing with her. She has seemingly intelligent conversations with animals on a regular basis."

"Hmm," he thought for a moment. "I know that she doesn't have any luggage, but have you asked how she will be most comfortable traveling? Does she want to ride in a carriage or on horseback, or should we expect something more... exotic?"

"I've been so busy getting other things ready, I neglected to ask." I nearly smacked my own forehead for my lack of consideration. "If you'll excuse me, I'll go find out immediately." I rushed back to my rooms. I didn't think to knock on the door, but burst right in.

Meira was standing at the basin, ringing the water out of her dress in her hands. Her skin was golden and flawless. The morning light glistened off the veins in her wings and the water droplets slid down her arms. She turned to the door and it seemed that her whole body brightened to a shade of rose-gold when she noticed me. I realized that I had been staring and quickly turned to examine the wall.

"Forgive me, Meira. I'm not used to knocking on my own door. It didn't occur to me that you might not be ready for company." I could feel the heat in my own face as I stammered.

"I'm sorry. I didn't realize this would be a problem. Next time I'll take the bowl into my room and wash there, if that's more suiting."

"Um, yes, it would be. Not that I don't appreciate… I mean…." I wanted to punch myself. "Yes, it would be."

I heard the rustling of fabric. "I am clothed now." Sadly. I turned back to her but couldn't bring myself to look her in the eye.

"I'm sorry for any embarrassment I caused," I croaked out.

"I wasn't embarrassed, just… surprised." She shuffled a bit. "You seemed rather in a hurry when you came in; was there something the matter?"

The water from Meira's dress pooled under her feet.

"Yes! Er, no, not really, except neither Robert nor I know how you would be most comfortable traveling. Both of us neglected to ask if you would need a carriage or a mount of some kind. I didn't mention that you could fly, since we had already discussed keeping that secret for now… not that Tom didn't already figure it out on his own." I was babbling again.

"I, too, had not thought of it. I would not be happy in a carriage like the ones we saw this morning, because I will not be able to see much of the country as we pass. And since I've never ridden a horse…"

"We can fix that," I offered.

"I'm certain, but I'm afraid I would be…" her voice trailed off and she stared thoughtfully. "I have a solution. Do not worry yourself for my comfort. I will take care of it immediately."

"But I rather like worrying about your comfort," I muttered under my breath.

She flashed me one of her brilliant smiles and disappeared into her room.

Meira

I leaned against the cold door fearing that if I moved I would be unable to stand. I still felt the warmth of his gaze on my skin. I realized in that moment that I needed to tell him about the bond much sooner than I had originally thought. My body's reaction was a definite sign that the bond was becoming stronger than it should have been so soon. I thought that I had at least a few more years before Mardok would have to make his choice, but it felt to me like I only had a few more days.

I shook my head to return to the task at hand. I needed a mount to ride. I stepped onto the balcony and out to the edge. The wind swirled cheerily around the corner of the castle, and it carried the smells of the forest. Then it whipped through the layers of my dress, pulling out the water that remained.

I breathed deeply and began the Song of Summoning. I informed my subject to meet me a mile down the road from the castle and received a satisfactory response. I grinned as I thought about how Mardok and Robert would be quite surprised.

I returned to Mardok's sitting room. "If you would be so kind as to allow me to ride with you for one mile, I have made arrangements for a mount to meet us there. I am afraid that he would not feel comfortable coming too close to the castle for fear of causing accidental harm."

"Your song was lovely. I would be happy for you to ride with me for as long as you need." He looked positively enchanted.

"How far do you expect we will travel today?"

"It depends on how soon the nobles finish loading. We're already a bit past our officially scheduled departure time, but truth be told neither Robert nor I ever expected to leave for at least another hour." He grinned.

"Will we have time for a lesson after we set up camp tonight?"

"Not likely, unless it's very late. I've been thinking about how we could manage a lesson with so many other people nearby, and I believe I may have come up with a solution. Robert plans to hold daily audiences with the locals, so his tent will be divided into two halves. One will be his sleeping quarters and private receiving room, and the other will be entirely open and free of obstacles. I will ask Robert if we can use that space after everyone else has gone to their tents for the night."

"That sounds suitable, if he agrees."

"Let's go and ask him." He offered me his arm and I took it as was becoming habit, even though it wasn't precisely necessary. I would have preferred to have held his hand, as we did last night. And from his intermittent and secretive glances at my body, I believe he preferred the same. We walked to Robert's room, and he greeted us with a wave while he finished talking to his steward.

"Did we get the travel accommodations straightened out?" he asked when he was able to break away and join us sitting at the fireplace.

"Everything has been taken care of. I have arranged for a mount to meet us a mile down the road and Mardok has graciously agreed to share his until then."

"I'm sure he has," he answered. Robert was clearly amused.

"We actually have a request for you."

"If it is within my power to offer..."

Mardok explained his thoughts about the audience area of Robert's tent and our need for a practice space away from spying eyes.

"You may have the space on one condition."

"What is that, most esteemed and glorious majesty?" Mardok asked with a flourish of his hand.

"That I might occasionally be allowed to watch the two of you spar. I will admit to having a long-standing curiosity about your lessons, and I promise to stay out of the way."

I smiled at the king. "If you have no other engagement at the time, your presence would be welcomed for nearly all of our lessons."

"It is a bargain. Let us strike hands on it." Robert shook my hand firmly and I added the customary magical bind to it. "What was that?" he asked as he drew his hand back looking at it cautiously.

"When a bargain is made between Fae, we bind it with magic so that neither party will be able to forget the deal. It does not prevent the breaking of the bargain, but it prevents a party from breaking it without conscious choice. It is so much of a habit for me that I forgot to explain. Please, forgive me." I felt chagrined.

"No, what a marvelous concept!" Robert cried. "To know

that someone could not break faith by accident."

"But sire, that's the dukes' most cherished pass-time," Mardok said. "What would become of the kingdom if they couldn't pretend that they simply didn't remember their commitments? Come to think of it, don't ever let Mary know about this."

"Pardon me, Majesty, but I believe that the nobles are nearly ready to depart," Robert's steward announced from the doorway. "Is everything prepared to your satisfaction?"

"Thank you, Steven. There is very little left in here that we could possibly take along." The steward did not smile at the king's joke, and Robert let out a little sigh. "We will come down momentarily." Steven left to pass along the message. "Few of the servants appreciate my sense of humor. They are either afraid to laugh, or they think I am trying to play favorites."

"Or they understand how truly horrible your jokes are," Mardok muttered.

"I am scandalized!" Robert recoiled in mock horror. "The king's humor is the most refined in the entire country." He leapt up on the seat of his chair and pointed to the ceiling to punctuate his statement. "And he'll have your head if you disagree." He threw an imaginary cape over his shoulder. I covered my grin with my hand to keep from laughing.

"What, pray tell, would you do with an extra head?" Mardok jumped onto his own chair as if on cue.

"Why, if it were your head, I would set it up over the gate to scare away my enemies."

"Oh, sire, your head is certainly as fright-inducing as mine."

"Well, then, how convenient that we have two gates!"

"Your citizens will be forever safe…"

"And free from taxes."

I couldn't hold in my laughter any longer. The scene was obviously well-rehearsed as if they had done it many times, but it was so ridiculous that I couldn't help myself.

"Enough! I yield. Please, no more!" I said between fits of laughter. The two men hopped down from their seats and took a bow.

"I do believe she likes it," Robert said to Mardok.

"What a very odd reaction. No one has ever *liked* it before."

"Indeed, what ever shall we do with her? If it gets out that someone actually likes our jests, our reputations would be ruined." Robert and Mardok stroked their imaginary beards. "I have it!" Robert declared so suddenly that Mardok jumped a bit. "We shall have to make her our friend, so that if she were to tell anyone, her own reputation would be at stake." He crossed his arms definitively.

Mardok's grin was positively wicked. "What a marvelous idea."

They each offered me a hand to stand up, and when I took them both they tucked my hands into their elbows and escorted me to the door. We marched all the way down to the courtyard arm in arm in arm, laughing and teasing the whole way. It must have been quite a sight because the servants who were still in the halls either openly gaped at us or scurried out of the way as we walked. We stayed arm locked until we reached Mardok's horse, where the two men had a mock fight to see who would be allowed to help me up. They were making quite the scene, but only a few nobles took more than a passing notice of the affair. Suddenly Mardok threw a shiny silver coin, and while Robert pretended to be distracted by it, Mardok jumped up on the horse and pulled me up behind him.

"You win this round, sir, but I will gain the advantage over you next time!" Robert cackled as he mounted his own horse backwards. By this time I was holding my side from laughing so hard.

"Peace, I beg you, or I will not live until the next time. Ow." I wrapped my arms around my stomach and bent over.

"Shall we be off then?" Mardok asked in a completely serious tone that belied his previous antics.

"Indubitably," Robert answered, mirroring his friend's inflection. He looked down at his horse's rump with a frown, then swung his legs around to face the proper direction. Then he turned his horse to face the assembly.

"That would have been simpler, sire, if you had stayed in one place and just turned the horse around," Terkins commented. Robert opened his mouth to comment back but thought better of it. Instead he addressed the crowd.

"Our most noble lords and ladies, good morrow to you all." He held his hand up in greeting and waited for the noise to die down a bit before he continued. "We have a last-minute announcement to make. The newest arrival to our court has agreed to join us for a tour of our wonderful country. We hope that you will make her feel welcomed among our people. Some of her ways will seem foreign to us as some of ours will be to her, so be courteous even if something feels like an offense. It is likely only a misunderstanding.

"Without further ado, let us be off!" He spurred his horse into motion with Mardok only a half-step behind. I felt the horse lurch and grabbed onto Mardok's chest for dear life. Eleven mounted soldiers joined us as we sped out the gates. We galloped for about a hundred yards before the men reigned in their mounts to a much slower walk.

"You can loosen your grip now, Meira," Mardok remarked. "I do still need to breathe."

"How long do you think until they catch up?" Robert turned to watch the first of the carriages roll through the gate.

"A bit faster than the last time I would suspect. They were much closer to being ready when we left today."

"And only two hours late this time," Robert noted.

"At least it wasn't like last spring," Mardok said grinning. Robert rolled his eyes. "I distinctly remember unpacking the tents before we left the gate."

"Blasted self-important, entitlement-driven, inconsiderate, lazy, intolerable nobles," Robert muttered. "By the way, Meira, sorry about not talking to you first about my speech back there, but I felt that they should know that I would be on your side if a dispute arose. It helps to preempt some of the machinations if I declare my positions outright."

"Not at all. I rather appreciate the support. I'm afraid that

I will likely offend someone—if only in ignorance."

By the time we had traveled the mile to meet my
summoned mount, the rest of the party had caught up with us.
Robert called a halt for his personal guard. I had mixed feelings
about the timing. The train of carriages would be passing by
and allowing people to stare right as I met my ride. Mardok
looked at me. As he lifted me off of his horse, his hands
lingered on my waist a moment longer than necessary. I smiled
at him and turned to call my friend.

7

5th of Lar Indar

Mardok

My hands were still warm from helping Meira down when she let out a piercing whistle. The entire entourage whipped their heads toward the sound. A pile of rocks beside the road began to move. It rose up to the height of a man before she spoke to it in a garbled-sounding language. The rock pile became fuzzy and out of focus until it rearranged itself into the shape of a bull elk. Meira reached for my hand to help her up, and I belatedly responded to assist her.

"I hope you don't mind, Mardok, but I placed my pouch inside your right saddlebag. I would not want it to fall from my hand while riding." I could only nod at her. I climbed back up on my horse and Robert called out the march. Meira's elk came up and walked in step between Robert and me.

"Since I know you are wondering, this is a terriculum. They have no name in the common tongue. They are a race of fae who are very loyal and smart, but not any more intelligent than a fox or a wolf. I have known this one since I was a babe. The rock-form is their most natural shape, but I felt this would be less intimidating and more comfortable. It took me a while to decide on the most appropriate form. Tomorrow I might have him be a horse to help alleviate some of the novelty."

"Could you not have asked him to be a horse today?" Robert's face was filled with child-like curiosity.

"Oh, no. He's never seen a horse before. He's lived deep in the forest until now. If he watches the horses carefully today, then tomorrow he'll be able to make a reasonable impression of one."

"Fascinating."

We rode in comfortable silence for several miles. Robert or I occasionally pointed out interesting landmarks to Meira.

The party did not stop for midday meal. Instead, pages carried travel foods up to everyone from the kitchen wagon in the rear of the line. I noticed that Meira only picked delicately at her food.

"Is something the matter with your bread?"

"Is that what it's called? I've never really eaten it before, other than that one I attempted this morning. From what kind of plant do you pick it?"

Robert and I laughed once before I answered. "It's not a plant. It's made from grains that have been ground up into a powder and mixed with water, eggs, sugar, yeast, and oil. Then it's baked in a hot oven until it comes out like this."

"Oh." The confusion was still clear on her face.

"Have you tried a bite?"

"It is very hard. I was concerned that it might break my teeth."

"Only the outside is hard. Here, let me break the crust for

you." I took her bread and broke it into two halves. "Now pull a bit out of the center and try it."

She cautiously did as I instructed and placed a tiny piece of bread in her mouth. She closed her eyes to study the flavor and then opened them wide. "It's good! Many forces have lent themselves to its creation and they flow together instead of competing for dominance."

I didn't understand her description, but at least I knew she liked it and that she wouldn't starve eating our foods.

One of the pages asked Meira if she would go back toward the carriages where the Countess Amelia Rosen wished to visit with her. I encouraged her to go, because the countess was one of the few single noblewomen in the country. She was also the youngest with standing and had few friends of her own.

"Good idea, that one," Robert said after Meira was out of ear shot.

"Which one. I want to take full credit?"

"Manipulating the two most eligible women in the country to become friends."

"I'd never thought of Meira as eligible, er, that is, it wasn't my intention to manipulate anyone." Robert smiled at my fluster.

"You like her, eh?"

"Who, the countess?"

"No, you idiot, Meira. And unless I'm entirely off base, she likes you, too."

"Yes, I do, terribly. I was making plans toward that end. But, then I found out that she's a princess," I explained.

"Well aren't you the snob. Don't let a few inconsequential details stop you from being happy." He paused. "As my father would say, 'The opportunity won't come around often.'" Robert's expression darkened.

His father had died unexpectedly when Robert was only seventeen, and he had to take up the mantle as king immediately since his older brother had become politically ineligible for the crown. The nobles in his father's court had mostly accepted his rule, but there were a few who fought and questioned his every decision for the last twelve years. One duke openly defied his right to reign until Robert had him stripped of his titles and imprisoned him for treason for masterminding a failed coup.

We continued on the road with Meira alternating between riding with us and visiting with various nobles until almost suppertime. Robert called the halt near a valley where we stopped every year. There was a crowd of at least a hundred peasants and merchants waiting for us, eager to provide their hands or goods for a little extra income.

Meira pulled a soft green tent from her tiny bag and set it up without assistance before anyone else. Robert's tent took the longest as it was by far the largest structure. Both my and Meira's tents were set near the private entrance of his. The cooks didn't wait for a tent to be erected to start cooking dinner, and most of the nobles started their drinking earlier this year.

"It appears that we may be able to have our lesson sooner than I originally thought." I whispered to Meira as we stood watching Robert's tent going up.

"Why do you say that?" She fidgeted with the hem of her sleeve.

"The drinking has started, so it will be loud at dinner, but they'll go to sleep much sooner afterward. Alcohol relaxes people and can make them drowsy."

"I'm familiar with alcohol, though we favor sweeter flavors than humans typically do."

"By the way, that's a cute little tent you have. I thought you said Fae sleep in the open air."

"Yes, we do. This is my brother Corwyn's tent, for when he's traveling. I borrowed it."

"The symbols all over it. Is that your language?"

"Yes, it is."

"What does it say?"

"It says, 'Corwyn's tent,' about a thousand times."

"Either he's arrogant, or a character."

"Mardok, may I ask a favor of you?" Her expression darkened a bit.

"Of course."

"I know that we promised Robert that he could join us for my lessons, but would you mind if I asked him not to, just for tonight? He can attend the next one." Her eyes bored into mine searching, and there was an edge of desperation in her voice.

"I don't mind. Was there some reason in particular?"

"There is, but I will have to explain it to you later."

"He *should* be supervising the camp layout about now. But knowing him, I would be willing to bet he's ignoring that and watching the horses eat their supper. He often likes to do that."

"Thank you, Mardok. I will find you again after dinner." She squeezed my hand and then walked away, leaving me at a loss. Without further explanation from her, I feared that she had some kind of terrible news.

I had no idea how I was going to manage it, but I knew I had to tell him about the bond tonight. I walked quickly to the horse corral to talk to Robert.

"Majesty, may I have a quick word with you?" I called out before I had reached the pens. He stopped chatting with a stable hand and one of the soldiers who rode with us earlier and waved me over.

"Let's take a walk," he said softly. "We're less likely to be overheard that way, and I can pretend to be doing my supervisory duties, as if they're really necessary." The soldier nodded at a glance from Robert and followed us at a respectful distance.

"Good idea." I waited until we were a bit away from the corral and tents before I said anything else. The evening was still warm, and the sun had not yet touched the horizon, so we strolled in comfort for a few moments. "I have to ask that you not join Mardok and me for tonight's lesson," I said abruptly.

"May I ask why?" He stopped mid-stride and turned to look at me.

"I have to talk with him. If it were not so very important I wouldn't ask."

"Is something wrong?" His brow furrowed in concern.

"No. And yes… maybe."

"You don't sound very certain."

"I would like to explain it to you, but the information is

deeply personal. So, I would need to bind you to secrecy."

"Of course." He nodded and looked at me with curiosity.

I held my hand up, palm facing him. "Give me your hand." He put his hand on mine. "You will not be able to speak of this with anyone that does not already have the knowledge."

"But how will I know?"

"The magic will not allow you to speak of it if the person does not." I spoke the word to form the secret bond. I let his hand drop and took a deep breath. "First, I need you to know that I made a huge mistake and miscalculated my timing. Once again, I have failed to take into account how much more quickly the magic would work with a human involved than it does with only Fae. I was certain that I would have at least a couple more years before my relationship with him would approach the point where any decision would need to be made.

"My people have a magic that is part of who we are that allows us to choose to be bound to one other soul. I have only ever personally observed this bond between two High Fae, but I have heard it is possible between High Fae and other races. The bond is developed by sharing a specific type of magical touch with another individual over an extended amount of time. The touch is exhilarating and can sustain and energize a person for several days."

"The payments," he said, realization dawning in his eyes.

"Yes," I answered quietly, examining the dirt near my feet as I explained. "When I first met Mardok and we began the lessons, I gave him the bond magic as payment, because I had never shared that kind of magic with anyone, and I was curious to know how it felt. I was overly confident that I knew enough about the process to avoid any problems. I didn't count on how much we would both enjoy it and always be anxious for the next time. The more I got to know him, the more I wanted to know about him. The more often we met for lessons the more I wanted to meet with him and spend time with him." I paused to breathe and make my heart slow down again. I could feel tears stinging the back of my eyes, but I forced myself to continue.

"Now I am out of time. I cannot give him another payment unless he chooses to fully accept the bond. And I am afraid that I waited too long to say anything. If he rejects the bond at this point I will likely not recover from it." I couldn't hold the tears back any longer, and they began to trickle down my cheeks.

"My tent is finally finished being set up, and it's beginning to rain. Let's finish this conversation in a more comfortable location." Robert handed me a small cloth and led me to his private receiving room.

"I appreciate your kindness." He poured me a glass of water and we sat down on the ample cushions that were spread on the floor.

"I feel that it is a small repayment considering you were responsible for helping Mardok save my skin last year."

"Were you in danger? I'm sorry; I didn't know."

"Mardok claims twice. But the one, with the boar..."

"I'm happy to have been of assistance, but that doesn't solve my problem now."

"What will happen to Mardok if he refuses you?" Robert

looked thoughtful.

"Mostly nothing. Because the magic is not naturally a part of him, he will feel a temporary loss from the sudden cessation of its influence. But it would be easier than withdrawal from too much pain numbing tea. And it will lessen quickly over time."

"And if he were to accept it?" His eyes twinkled, but his face was still thoughtful.

"We would continue to grow closer and be bonded for the rest of our lives. The bond would strengthen over many years until we would be excessively uncomfortable separated from each other for any real length of time."

"So, in our culture you would have to marry."

"I suppose that would be the most appropriate route. To not have a human marriage would be seen as scandalous, yes?"

He nodded.

"I don't want to be a part of undermining his reputation."

"What about your family? Surely they have something to say about this."

"My father has already given Mardok his blessing, although Mardok doesn't know it yet. And if my mother objected, she would have told me, probably before I met him."

Robert looked thoughtful for a few minutes. "Tonight, when the nobles have retired to their tents, you and Mardok may use the audience partition as agreed. I promise not to attend. Just be sure to arrive first and wear the gown that you wore when we were introduced yesterday. I could tell that he liked it. I honestly don't think you have anything to worry about. I know that he cares for you."

"The friendship you have shown me will never be taken for granted. Thank you."

"I'm becoming fond of your company as well. Now go get yourself some supper, and remember to arrive first." He winked and shooed me out the door.

I meandered around the camp until I found myself at the kitchen tent. I took the bowl that the cook offered me and looked skeptically at its contents.

"What is it?" I blurted without pretense.

"Venison stew," the cook replied with equal frankness.

"Oh, venison. I didn't have to prepare it this time. I'm sorry, but could you tell me what else is in it?" I picked up a few of the unknown vegetables with my spoon, examining them.

"Ye be knowin' venison then, like'n a good respec'able lady. Tha vegetables 'r taters 'n carrots 'n onions. An' there be spices fer flavor. It's me own secret blend." She winked at me.

"What are 'taters' and 'carrots?'"

"They be fat roots from tha earth. One be brown wiv white insides, 'n tha other's orange clear through."

"Are they tubers?"

"Th' 'taters 'r m' dear."

"Oh, I see. My people have something very similar that we

eat. Thank you for your kind explanation. Is there also any of the 'bread' leftover from our lunch meal? I found it delicious and would love to have more."

"I was afeared tha' ye didna like it when ye didna eat any o' it at breakfast this morn'."

I met her gaze in surprise.

"Don' ye be thinkin' I forgot about ye, Miss." She shook her stirring spoon at me.

"I wasn't sure what it was when I ate breakfast, but, fortunately, I had someone to explain it to me at lunch."

"Well, Ambassador Meira," she labored over the title, "I heared before tha sky was warm this morn' that ye be joinin' us for tha trip. Me name is Mary and I be the king's head cook. If'n there e'er be a meal that ye want ta know abou', feel free ta come back 'n aks me. If'n I'm not around, aks one o' tha girls ta fetch me 'n I'll be mighty 'appy ta come 'n talk with ye. N' if there be somethin' that ye miss from home, tell me abou' it, 'n I'll try 'n make it fer ye." Her eyes sparkled at the thought of a challenge.

"I'll be sure to do that; thank you again." She handed me a small parcel with two of the rolls from lunch and went back to her work. I turned around to return to my tent and nearly ran straight into Baron Thaddeus. "I beg your pardon, Baron; I was not paying attention to where I was going."

He smiled an oily grin and replied, "Not at all. I was hoping to run into you again, Ambassador." He chuckled at his own joke. "Since I see that you have not yet eaten, perhaps you would consider joining me for supper."

"I would be only too happy to," I lied, "but I was just on my way to join Countess Amelia for the evening meal. Permit me to sup with you another time."

"I could join the both of you, then."

"That seems rather presumptuous, don't you think? I wouldn't dare bring along a guest without prior invitation."

The baron hesitated. "Well, perhaps another time, then, when proper invitations have been extended."

"I look forward to it immensely." He bowed perfectly and went to retrieve his own meal. I shuddered inwardly. Fearing that he might follow me to be sure that I was indeed going to visit Amelia, I walked straight to her tent.

"Countess Amelia?" I spoke uncertainly at her door.

"Yes?" She poked her head out of the tent. Her hair was sticking out in all directions as if she had scrubbed it and not brushed it out. I was struck speechless at the sight. "Oh, it's you, Ambassador. Please come in! And don't mind my appearance; my maids are trying to get the dust out of my hair with little success."

"Thank you. I was hoping to…" My courtly manners couldn't stay intact while looking at her struggle with her unruly tresses. "May I be candid with you?"

"Please do or I'll have no dignity left at all." She smiled.

"I needed an excuse to avoid dining with Baron Thaddeus, and your name was the first one that came to mind."

"In that case I'm more than happy to be of service. No woman, especially an attractive and single one, or one that's still breathing, should be forced to be in his company alone. His last wife died under suspicious circumstances and he's been on the prowl ever since."

"Thank you, again."

"Go ahead, sit and eat, so you'll not have lied." I sat on the cushions she indicated. "It's difficult to be single in this court. The married women think you're after their husbands and so do not trust you, and the men think that unmarried women have nothing of substance to say. I have so little company, so I'm truly glad that you've come to court. Though, it doesn't seem that you suffer from the same lack of conversation partners. You talk so easily with His Majesty and Count Mardok, the two most eligible bachelors in the country…" Her statement was obviously leading.

"I have known Mardok for nearly a year. As he has been friends with King Robert since they were children, it was very easy for me to become friends with him as well." I tried to smile encouragingly.

"Oh." She sounded crestfallen. She sat silently as her maids finished struggling with her hair. I finished my stew and one of the rolls. Then I had a flash of inspiration.

"Amelia, would you allow me to borrow one of your lady's maids for a short while? I have a meeting to attend later and need some help to prepare for it."

She perked up, "What kind of meeting?"

"Forgive me, but I can't tell you now." She started to droop again, so I added quickly, "But I promise to ride near you tomorrow and tell you all about it!"

"I will hold you to that. You had better get going unless your meeting is going to be *very* late indeed."

"Thank you! I will send her back soon." The maid followed me as we hurried back to my tent. I saw Mardok coming out of Robert's door as we reached mine. "I'll see you later," I whispered to him as the maid and I passed under my tent flap.

I dug quickly through my bag to pull out my gown. I shook it out to be sure that there were no wrinkles. The maid helped me change and then began the task of combing out my braid. I usually wore my hair tied in a long plait down my back. Tonight I wanted to have it loose and flowing. It took the two of us a quarter of an hour to comb the entirety of it.

"Might I say that m'lady has lovely hair?" the older maid ventured at length.

"Thank you. And thanks also,… what is your name?"

"Helga, m'lady."

"Helga, you have my sincerest gratitude for helping me prepare. I would not be ready in time without you. Please, tell your mistress that I will not forget my promise to her." I sent her off. I cast a 'notice-me-not' charm on myself so that I could slip around to the entrance of the audience tent undetected. I hoped that I would be first like Robert had instructed.

I entered the tent without incident and found the interior empty save for a large blanket on the floor with cushions and two trays. One held a bottle and two goblets; the other had fruit and some other things that looked edible. There were also candles lit around the exterior walls of the tent. "Thank you, Robert," I breathed. He had done more than I could have asked to aid my nerves. I stepped over to the blanket and felt its softness under my bare toes. I closed my eyes to enjoy the sensation.

"Good evening, Meira," Mardok said as he entered, startling me from my thoughts.

Mardok

Meira stood on the edge of the blanket as if she barely touched the ground. She looked absolutely breathtaking. Her long copper hair was loose in ringlets down her back and a few had fallen forward over her shoulders. Her emerald eyes sparkled in the candlelight. I was glad now that I had taken the time to brush the dust from my uniform before I came.

"Good evening, Mardok. Would you join me?" She motioned toward the cushions. I sat in a lounging position, uncertain what to expect. "I have something very important to tell you, and I need you to hear me out before you respond."

I nodded my agreement, although my heart had ceased beating waiting to know.

She continued, "I have done you a disservice. I did not trust you soon enough to give you the proper time to consider things before you have to make a decision. I must apologize. I must own my mistake."

Her mistake? I most certainly had made mistakes, but I couldn't remember anything she had done to hurt me. Was she talking about our obvious mismatch in status?

She paused to take a deep breath before she went on. "I have to dissolve our agreement about the lessons."

I sat up, and my eyes lost their ability to focus.

"I can no longer offer you the payment we agreed upon. In the beginning I offered it because I had never shared that kind of magic with anyone and I wanted to know what it was like. I felt that my knowledge was complete enough to ensure that it would not cause a problem for either of us."

By now I wanted to cry out, to insist upon keeping what was slipping away. After nearly a year, with all of the wavering back and forth between whether I should or should not marry Meira, the very idea that it might not occur, stated here and now, instantly solidified my resolve. No, I wasn't interested in this slipping away. I couldn't stomach the idea of losing her. I would not, could not, let this precious angel slip out of my life. Yet what was I to do? I couldn't change all of the rules and customs of Lur. I was neither king nor prince.

"I was wrong. In Fae culture the magic I shared with you is usually shared between courting couples. It forms a bond that will tie their souls together."

Indeed, we were tied together already, but what did it matter? I couldn't imagine that it was due only to Fae magic, but even so, magic wouldn't be enough to resolve this. I was a fool from day one, knowingly throwing myself again and again into this trap. And now I would be cast from this relationship.

"The bond usually takes a great deal of time to form, decades even, and if one or the other of the two wishes to change their mind, there is time to do so before either one will be permanently injured. It has become clear to me in the past two days that I have exceeded that time."

I could hear it coming; she was going to relegate me to the status of "friend."

"I have to ask you to choose now whether you want me to stay with you as your bond-mate, or if you want me to return to my people."

My ears repeated her words several times, reprocessing

them so I could understand. Had she just said the opposite of what I was anticipating? Or did I just not hear correctly? I leaned in to understand further. Stay? Bond? This was actually a question?

"If you choose for me to leave I will do so immediately, and I will trouble you no more. If you choose for me to stay, which would make me very happy, we will need to be married soon to avoid any scandal among your people."

She finished speaking and sat staring at her hands in her lap waiting patiently for my response. I didn't keep her waiting. I had so many questions, but how could I possibly walk out of this tent away from her, knowing the damage it would do to her, knowing that I would never see her again? This wasn't a matter of whether I wanted to have the occasional magical kiss because of the pleasure it induced, which obviously I did. I wanted the kiss because it was hers, from her lips, from her soul. And certainly yesterday I was unbalanced, uncertain, and frankly insane. But now I had clarity. My father wasn't joking when he clarified the responsibilities and duties of a loving man. Certainly our lives would come with risk, with pain, and with loss. Certainly there loomed the threat of death. But to avoid these, I would have to become the worst of all men—the man who abandons the lady to suffer alone. If I wanted to avoid that, I missed that opportunity a year ago.

I barely felt myself reach over to hold her face in my hands. A tear escaped from her eyes and I wiped it away with my thumb. Her lips were trembling, so I covered them with my own. Meira clung to me as we kissed. The thought of how she looked this morning came unbidden to my mind. I had to struggle against the urge to react to it. Meira had used two kinds of magic on me, one was not intentional and not strictly magic, but certainly effective.

"I could never leave you," I said finally.

She released the breath that she had been holding. She kissed me this time, and I felt the warmth of her body against me.

I gently pushed her back to catch my breath. "Let's save that for a bit, or we'll have to be married tonight."

"That's a fine idea, I think," she replied.

"Weddings are a bit slower than that. Let's explore the refreshments, shall we? I'm going to assume Robert knew something about this before I did."

"I needed to tell someone, and he knows you best," Meira replied, looking a bit at the ground. "He arranged for the tent to be set up this way and told me to arrive here first."

"He does enjoy playing matchmaker on occasion." I took her hand in mine. She moved to sit next to me. "Although it does look like I'll lose the bet… but I think I still win," I said with glee.

"The bet?"

"Yes, the bet," I replied. "Robert and I had a bet regarding who would be married first. We made it back when girls were still the enemy."

She looked at me quizzically.

"When we were only ten or twelve years old."

She nodded her understanding, then furrowed her brow

and shook her head. "What's the bottle?" she asked curiously, deftly changing the subject.

"It's a very fine wine," I answered. I gaped as I looked at the label, a bit shocked that Robert had brought this particular bottle with him. "Would you like to try some?" I gestured to the goblets.

"Just a taste for now." She smiled at me again. I popped the cork and poured a small measure in her glass and a full one in my own.

"Just a sip is fine. Actually, a single sip of this probably costs more than I get paid in a year."

She lifted the goblet and inhaled deeply. "Sun, earth, and fire," she marveled before allowing the liquid to pass her lips. She closed her eyes and held the sip in her mouth for a moment, then swallowed. "Delicious," she commented at length. "It reminds me of a drink that is served in father's court on special occasions. But that is made from honey and tastes more of the wind and earth, less of the sun and fire."

"I think I understand earth and the fire, but how can something taste like the wind or sun?"

"First you tell me what it tastes like," she directed.

I shrugged and took a sip and let the flavors swish around in my mouth for a moment. "It has the flavor of a well-aged wine that was pressed at the end of the season when the last of the wildflowers were blooming."

"When they have seen a good number of days in the sun," she prompted.

"It also reminds me of my days as a miscreant youth. Robert and I got caught stealing a bottle of this vintage from his father's cellar when we were boys. He was most put out."

"So it sparks a memory."

"Yes, particularly of scrubbing walls and mucking stables." I swallowed another sip. "I believe we were on dishes duty for four weeks before his father gave up trying to find it." I looked again at the label and wondered... was it possible?

"I also speak of memories when I say something tastes like the wind. The wind carries smells and sounds from wherever it has been and can pass along messages if asked correctly. The wind is a wild and untamable force, but it can be gentle and comforting at the same time. Honey tastes like wind to me because it is made by the wild and gentle bees." The sound of her voice was hypnotic as she recalled the impressions.

We stayed up for quite some time comparing the tastes in the foods that Robert had left for us. When she finally yawned her exhaustion, it was very late indeed. I couldn't help yawning as well.

"We should be in bed. The morning will come early for us," she announced with a start.

"It will, but I'm reluctant to leave you for tonight." I was rewarded with a smile.

"It is the same for me. But you still have duties to perform tomorrow, and Robert will want a report on this evening's events, I am sure."

"I'll be surprised if he didn't try to listen through the canvas, but you are right."

I stood and held out my hand to help her up. She took it and used her upward momentum to pull herself up to my mouth. I felt the magic flowing through the kiss stronger than ever before.

She pulled away and whispered, "So you won't be as tired tomorrow."

I escorted her back to her tent and then returned by sheer force of will to my own. There was no way I would be able to sleep now.

I was unconscious before my head hit the pillow.

8

6th of Lar Indar

Meira

I held the flap of my tent open to watch him until he disappeared into his own. I wanted to dance and shout at the top of my lungs. I plaited my hair but left a few curls hanging forward over my shoulders, because he liked them, and changed into my regular dress. I couldn't help fluttering around my tent as I packed my things. Sleep would not find me this night, so I decided to be productive reorganizing the contents of my bag. I found a pair of shoes my mother had been missing for several hundred years. By the time the first of the sun's rays started to warm my tent I was ready to take it down. I had it packed away when Mardok exited his.

"Good morning." His voice was warm and welcoming, his eyes bright and alert.

I turned and found that he was putting his bags outside his tent. Two bleary-eyed servants were already working on dismantling it. "Good morning. I see you didn't get much sleep as well." I couldn't hold back my smile any longer.

"I found that I was curiously energized early this morning, and I decided to prepare my things for the day. I was just about to go and fetch myself some breakfast. Would you care to join me?"

"I would be delighted." I took his arm and we walked
through the maze of tents and dodged many servants and
attendants rushing to get things re-packed for the day. The
kitchen tent was being packed as well, except for the breakfast
foods that were laid out on a long table.

"Good morning, deary. I see that ye found y'self a
respectable escort this mornin'." Mary gave me a wink. "Let
me know if'n ye want me to tell ye abou' any of tha foods. Th'
s'mornin' tis mostly fruit and sweet breads. It helps with them
what overindulged in their ale last eve. I've things to get done,
but call me if ye have a question!" She was all bustle and hurry
as she swept around her cart motivating her help to get on with
their tasks.

"What did she mean about a respectable escort?" Mardok
arched a brow.

"When I came to get supper last night, I ran into Baron
Thaddeus....",

"No further explanation needed. Were you able to get
away?"

"Yes, I made up an excuse to leave. Amelia told me more
about him. I agree with her that no woman should be left alone
with him. That reminds me, I promised to ride with her for a
while this morning." His expression drooped. "I will rejoin you
as soon as I can." I reached up and cupped my hand around
his cheek and was rewarded with a smile.

"Och, ther' be none of that. Least not until the bands have
been read." Mary was wagging her finger at us.

I blushed. "I'm sorry. I didn't mean to…"

"Don't mind us, m'darlin'. We don' miss anything. We already know."

I was speechless.

"M'dear, who da ye think put tha food in tha king's tent fer ye last night? An' you'll find that we keep better secrets than anybody else." She winked boldly and sashayed back to her tasks.

We departed together, eating our breakfast. At the corral, I instructed the terriculum to imitate a horse for the day. Mardok watched in fascination and amusement as it shifted its form to be somewhat accurate, and then readjusted several times to correct itself.

"All noble marriages have to be approved by His Majesty." Mardok said suddenly. "For us to be officially engaged, we need to ask his permission." He had a devilish grin.

"All right." I said warily. "Are you sure that the king is even awake?"

"I sure hope not. Let's go ask him." He pulled me along.

My eyes widened as we approached Robert's tent. Mardok waived the guards out of the way claiming an urgent matter of state.

"Sure it is, Mardok. Fill us in later, will ya?" one of them teased as he pulled back the flap.

He used the same excuse to shoo the other servants out of the receiving area. Then he pulled the canvas down that separated it from the king's sleeping room. Robert was in his dressing gown with one leg, midair, stretching through his trousers. He started with a playful squeak of alarm, but then seeing Meira raised his brows completely.

"Majesty!" Mardok bowed deeply and began boisterously. "An urgent matter has come to my notice that needs your immediate attention."

Robert recognized the game. "Rise, Sir Mardok, and tell me of this emergency that could not wait until I had my pants on."

Mardok stood at attention and reported, "There is a noble couple who wishes to be wed, and they have not yet received Your Majesty's permission."

"This is a very grave matter indeed," he asserted, while hopping around trying to find the second hole to his trousers. I tried to stifle my laughter, but I was less than successful. "And who are the horribly imprudent offenders?"

Mardok dropped his pretense and grabbed my hand. "We are!" He looked deep into my eyes and I felt as if my legs would melt out from under me.

"CONGRATULATIONS!!!!" Robert jumped over the cushions, tripped in his pants, and crashed into a table, reducing it to firewood while spilling his breakfast across the tent. Were it not for his laughter, I would have been concerned for his health.

One of the guards entered. "Sire, if thy table offends thee, I could have it arrested for attacking you. Perhaps we could have it hung, drawn and quartered, or even belegged." He eyed the table more closely. "But it appears you've already accomplished that much."

Robert recovered quickly, finished pulling up his pants, and rejoined us in a more suitable standing position. "Ira, good, yes. Personally I was thinking a simple lashing would do. However, I'm rather busy certifying an official request of international importance."

His grin stretched beyond the limits of his face as he crushed us together in a hug.

"I take it you approve." I said softly.

"Heartily. Nothing could make me happier than to see the two of you together, except perhaps seeing you together after I'm dressed. How soon should we start planning? Do we need to make special accommodations for your family, Meira? We'll have to remodel Mardok's quarters to make them more comfortable when we get back. Or perhaps, Meira, you could convince him to give them back to me. Mardok, you'll have to make sure to have the secondary guard well prepared before you go on your honeymoon." Robert didn't wait for any responses from us. He was having a conversation with himself.

We took the opportunity to slip out of the tent while he continued rambling to the far wall. Mardok squeezed my hand and reached into his pocket.

"Now that it has been approved, I can give you this." He pulled out an old cloth and placed it in my hand. It was wrapped around something. "I had planned to ask you to marry me after we came back from the trip. And then I thought, I don't know, maybe I'll ask you on the way back. There are a couple of really beautiful places that I think you'll enjoy. Then, after you told me that you were your father's daughter, I gave up, since there was no way you could marry me, not with me being a lesser. But I guess I was pretty fortunate that I forgot to pull this back out of my luggage." He let go, and I opened it while he continued. "Our custom says that an engaged woman should wear a piece of jewelry that belongs to the man. This once belonged to my grandmother and to my mother. It's the symbol of my family, and the matriarch of the family wears it. And I want you to wear it." I pulled out a large sapphire pendant on a long silver chain. The morning sunlight sparkled in the depth of the stone. The face of the stone was completely smooth, and it was nearly flawless.

"I would be honored to wear something so dear." He lifted it from my hands, looped the chain over my head and pulled my braid through it so that the stone rested between my breasts. I placed my hands over it for a moment and then tucked it under my dress. "For safety," I said. "I wouldn't want to lose it."

Mardok

It took until mid-morning to get everyone packed and re-loaded and moving on the road.

Meira rode with Amelia in her carriage, where Amelia spent a good portion of time squealing so gleefully that the entire caravan could hear. I tried to maneuver close enough to listen in, but she shooed me away, claiming her god-given right to private conversation. Eventually, Meira convinced her to come join us on horseback.

"What does it take for a gentleman to move aside and let a lady join him?" Meira called out from behind us.

"I supposed there would have to be a gentleman present to accommodate such a thing," Robert replied.

"As well as a lady to request it, and I see no such persons present," I added.

Meira pushed her mount between us and punched my arm. She motioned for Amelia to come up next to her so that the two ladies were riding betwixt Robert and me. Then she winked at me and whispered, "I have a secret to tell you later." She rode on as if nothing were different than the day before.

Feeling impish, I leaned back and whispered, "It's a pity I didn't get to see you washing this morning."

"Give it time," she whispered back.

"If our companions are going to whisper secrets and not share with us, we should do the same and come up with something wicked to do to them," Robert announced to Amelia loud enough for Meira and me to hear. I noticed that Amelia's ears turned slightly pink as he leaned over to whisper to her.

"A truce!" I declared, holding up my hands.

"Then you will tell us what you were whispering about?" Robert grinned.

"I was saying something appropriately scandalous to make my new fiancé blush." I looked at my bride-to-be, who rode upright and proud. "Ineffectively, I might add."

"Are you saying that you need help?" Robert queried. "It would be a shame if you needed mine."

"Sire, you're never a help," I declared.

"I would recommend, Majesty," Amelia offered, eyes sparkling with mirth, "that we provide him with plenty of help. Surely we can come up with something to create a blush."

Robert's eyes flashed wickedly, "What a wonderful idea, Countess. But please, if we are going to be in conspiracy together, call me Robert."

Amelia's grin was positively radiant. She turned her face to study the mane of her horse, and she tilted her head so her hair covered her cheeks. She softly replied, "Thank you, Robert; please, call me Amelia."

Robert leaned over to her to whisper, and the two spoke for several minutes.

Meira inclined toward me. "That is my secret," she pointed her head toward our riding companions. "She was worried that I had come to court to ally with Robert. When I told her of our engagement, she was so relieved that she confided in me her long-term affection for him."

I grinned. Robert, the matchmaker, finally had someone to compete with.

"Hey, now. You aren't allowed to say anything to him yet," Amelia interjected, as she pulled Meira away and whispered in her ear.

Meira's body turned maroon. "I could never..." she said barely loud enough for me to hear as Amelia kept whispering.

Robert's gaze was shock and curiosity. He caught my eye and mouthed the words, "I have no idea."

Amelia and Meira settled into other conversation, with Robert and I sidling up occasionally to add in an unimportant phrase or comment here and there.

"As I said before," Meira continued, "I am the youngest of the royal family. I have eighty-nine older siblings." We each gave her competing looks of disbelief.

"How is that possible?" Amelia gasped.

"Father is nine hundred and seventy-two years old. Mother is a bit older, and they bonded at a very young age," she stated simply.

"Meira, dearest, how old are you?" I asked as calmly as I could.

"I'm only ninety-four, but I'm still old enough to bond," she replied in a sour tone. I froze in my seat. Amos turned in his saddle from his position ahead of us and looked me in the eye before turning back. I knew I would owe him for this one.

"Ha ha!" Robert laughed aloud. "And you were afraid that you were robbing the cradle, old friend!"

"I don't understand the expression." Meira looked confused and hurt.

"It means Mardok thought that he was too old for you," Amelia explained kindly. "By human standards you look very young, but in years, you're old enough to be my great-grandmother."

Meira's mouth formed an 'O' and she sat silently on her horse for a few moments. "Well, I'm barely over the age of majority for a Fae…"

"At least the kingdom's older than you," Robert laughed. "I think my great-grandfather was born about the time you were."

"I'm really not that old," Meira objected, shifting in her seat.

Suddenly there was a piercing whistle from the trees. Meira's head whipped left, and she jumped from her seated position, twisted in the air, and plucked an arrow from seemingly nowhere. Alighting on the mount's back with her feet, she continued to ride standing as she displayed her catch.

"I caught it this time!" she announced with a grin. "Last time it took me three weeks to get feeling back in my left pinkie!"

The arrow was wrapped in a sheet of translucent parchment. She slid it off and read it aloud, although the language was incomprehensible. She dropped back onto her mount, whispered into its ear, and gripped its neck. The terriculum morphed into an oversize cougar, and it carried Meira down the road much more rapidly than anything I had ever seen.

The horses pulled away sharply and bucked.

"What was that all about?" Robert asked, as he reigned in his and Amelia's mounts.

"I don't know." I couldn't fathom what possessed her to bolt like that. I felt a pressure inside my head. *Come,* it said. I waved for Ira to take my place and dug my heels into my horse's flank. I couldn't imagine where I was going, but the voice was Meira's, and I couldn't ignore her.

After several miles of furious riding, I came across a stand of trees near the road. The terriculum was waiting outside of it. Had I not previously seen it in its rock state, I would have ridden past. I dismounted and tied my horse to a protruding portion of the terriculum, knowing it would not leave without Meira. Then I cautiously entered the trees.

As my eyes adjusted to the lower light I saw Meira hugging a tall male Fae with dark hair and silver skin so pale it was nearly white. He was smiling at her, and I could see the hint of wrinkles around his eyes.

Meira

"Papa!" I threw my arms around his neck when I saw him. "I'm not gone from home for two whole days, and you miss me so much you have to come find me?"

"How could I stay away from my favorite daughter?" he asked laughing. "A passing breeze told me that I needed to come hear a bit of news."

Mardok stepped through the trees. "Mardok, come meet my father." I let go of Father to grab Mardok's hand.

"Then it is true," he sighed. "I have been replaced in my daughter's heart. I hope you will endeavor to be worthy of her."

Mardok bowed and answered, "I can aspire to nothing else, Your Majesty. We were hoping to be wed when the party returns home. I would be most honored if you and your family would attend."

"I would be pleased to stand for my daughter. Meira knows how to send me the details. And it might be a good idea for you to arrange an introduction for me with this human king before the blessed event, Meira. You are, after all, my ambassador, and I feel that it would be inappropriate to wait until the wedding to meet him."

"I am sure that Robert would be happy to meet you, Father." I couldn't stop smiling.

"Good. I'm sure that your companions are overflowing with curiosity about your sudden departure, so you should go back to them, my little Rae." He paused to tousle my hair before I left. "Mardok, could I speak with you a moment before you go?" I knew a dismissal from Father. Squeezing Mardok's hand in encouragement, I stepped back out of the grove. Mardok's horse seemed happily oblivious that it was tied to my mount, although I would have to talk to Mardok later about tying his horse to my terriculum's nose. I dawdled as much as I could, waiting nervously for him to rejoin me. I could only imagine what Father was saying to him. I tried listening; clearly Father was speaking directly into his mind.

After a few minutes, Mardok emerged from the trees looking rather shaken. I rushed back to him. "Are you okay?" I asked worriedly.

"I will be," he answered stiffly. He took his horse's reins. "He showed me memories of your people. All the things that you have left to be with me. Your great-grandfather… Keltus? And how he grew up, raised by Bakarrik. You really are a descendant of the gods. I mean, I knew it was so… but it was never… real." His expression was blank. "I'm just… just a man."

I was lost at how little these humans seemed to know. I had grown up with it. I had lived and breathed it my entire life. I had even met a few of the gods. Father and some of my siblings had met many of them, and Malachi had even been to the realm of the gods.

"But you were made by Bakarrik!" I emphasized to him. "Mankind is the only race that was designed by the high god, created by him. Everyone else just simply happened. The High Fae are descendants of Bakarrik and Opella, a human woman."

"I know; you've told me that. I've seen it now," Mardok answered. He stood dumbfounded. "I just never really… it just never really sank in that the world is so… so much bigger." Several minutes passed while I waited for him to process this new information. Father must have revealed much to him.

His lips quivered again slightly, and he held out his left hand, palm up. "Then he gave me this." A blue eight-pointed star was still fading. I knew the mark; it would be silver and permanent when the magic was complete.

"He marked you as a friend of the Fae," I explained. "It's a great honor that he gives to his closest friends."

"Yes, he said that. And then he told me exactly what he would personally do to me if I ever hurt you." He added quietly, "I didn't know some of those things were possible."

I huffed.

"And then he gave me this." He showed me a ring on his left hand. "He said to never take it off."

"That's one of his rings," I commented. "He wears it often."

Mother, was giving him the shield ring your idea?

All will be well, Meira. If it weren't so, I would have given him something else.

He'll be in danger then.

He's always in danger. Now have a little trust. She paused. *Oh, and Meira, your father would like it back when you're done with it.*

I looked him in the eye. "Don't take it off—ever."

"Alright then."

"Let's get back. I'm sure that they're worried about us by now, and I'm hungry for lunch." I hugged him tightly before I climbed up on my mount. It seemed to shake him out of his thoughts.

"By the way, where did you learn to catch an arrow like that?" he asked as the animals began walking back to the rest of the party.

I laughed. "If you had as many older brothers as I do, you might have learned it, too." He laughed along with me, his good humor returning. It didn't take us long to rejoin the group.

"Welcome back." Robert looked at us quizzically.

"I apologize for my sudden departure. Family business," I explained.

"Understandable with current circumstances." He nodded. "Although that method of sending you a message gave the soldiers quite a start. I wish they would respond to a drill with the same haste. Maybe you missed it, but we had thirty archers with arrows nocked in record time."

Mardok dismissed the secondary guards back to the rest of the caravan. "Are we too late for lunch?" he asked casually.

"It should be passed out soon. Did you two work up an appetite while you were gone?" Amelia raised her eyebrows suggestively.

"Are you insinuating that we acted improperly?" I asked in mock scandal.

"Well, you did say that it was 'family business.' Starting

one is the most basic family business I know of."

I stared intently at my mount's ears. "Actually…" I heard my voice crack. "We met up with my father to share our good news. I'm assuming he's a suitable chaperone." I cast a glance at Amelia. "And he wishes to set up a time to meet you before the wedding, Robert."

"I am at his disposal, though it might be better to wait until we've reached my brother's house and are not on the road every day."

"I thought as much, but I didn't feel comfortable speaking for you. I will send him a message later."

"If you need a bow, I'll have one available for you." Robert winked at me. I smiled back. "On a more serious note, I hope your father knows that I'm not quite as skilled at catching messages. I would hate for him to send me one that way."

"That's okay. It only came that way because my brother Lari sent it. We do have safer methods of delivery."

"Perhaps just walking up and saying 'hi,'" he suggested.

I chuckled. "That's generally preferred."

We fell into our previous riding formation. It was comfortable riding with Mardok, and Amelia was clearly relaxed exchanging hushed thoughts with Robert.

I could smell lunch several minutes before it arrived. By the time we started eating I was salivating.

"Mary's outdoing herself on this trip. Don't you think, Amelia?" Robert commented after he bit into his stuffed roll.

"Perhaps she knows that she has an appreciative audience," she observed. I then noticed that all three of my companions were watching me eat.

"The food is really wonderful. I've never had anything like it before," I said between bites, "and I've learned so much about your foods and where they come from. It's really fascinating. You put so much effort into it. We usually just pick things and eat them." They chuckled at my enthusiasm.

The rest of the afternoon went by quickly as we chatted contentedly. Before we stopped for the day, Robert persuaded Amelia to ride with us for the rest of the journey. It really wasn't difficult.

The camp hummed with noise. The gossips had already spread the news of my engagement to Mardok around every tent. Like Amelia, most were surprised that it was Mardok and not Robert to whom I was betrothed. They had assumed that I had been sent to forge an alliance by marriage to the king. They clearly didn't understand Fae politics, which is just as well since few Fae understand it either. I wished I didn't. When we walked to the kitchen to get our supper, we received many congratulatory remarks.

"I be knowin' ye'd find one 'ventually!" Mary said as she slapped Mardok on the back, nearly causing him to choke and cough on the bite he had taken. "I'd wager th' cravin's 'll start b'fur a month i' o'er." Mardok had recovered from his initial coughing fit only to begin anew.

I looked at him worriedly. "Are you okay?"

"Water," he croaked. I handed him a pitcher. "Thanks," he managed to say after downing nearly half the contents.

"What did she mean about cravings?" I asked, trying to puzzle it out.

"Human women often crave unusual foods when they're expecting a child," he mumbled.

"Oh," I thought aloud. "Interesting. That doesn't happen to Fae."

Mary stopped and came back over to me. "No cravin's for tha Fae?" She leaned back and stared at me with disapproval. "Pity."

Mardok

"We won't be traveling tomorrow. There's a large village near here, and the king has audiences to handle while we're so close. I won't be able to spend much time alone with you. However, as an ambassador to the court, you'll be welcome to sit in. So at least I'll be able to be near you." I grinned hopefully.

"I would not choose to be away from you, now that you have chosen to have me."

I rose from the table and offered her my arm. We walked out of the meal tent and traversed the camp to see if the nobles were settled enough for us to have a lesson this evening.

"You know," she began softly, "it is perhaps fortuitous that Robert has chosen to watch our lessons."

"And why is that?" I was confused at her tone.

"Well, if people are this suggestive of our possible impropriety when we're so newly promised, imagine what they might say if they noticed that we were spending large amounts of time together unchaperoned."

"Is Mary's comment bothering you that much? She knows me well enough that she likes to tease. She meant no harm in it."

"I know there was no malice in what she said. She has been nothing if not kind to me thus far. But she is not the only one to make similar comments. And many of the others were not teasing." Her eyes darkened and her brow furrowed.

"Who has been talking that way?" I demanded. The court was bound to gossip, but Robert had made it clear in the past that rumors and speculations were to remain firmly behind closed doors.

"I don't know everyone's name to place blame, but I should mention that they obviously don't know that I can hear them."

"Ah. I think I understand. It is in the nature of this court to gossip about any and everything that happens. Robert tried to quash it a few years back, but he found that it caused more problems than it solved. The younger nobles have adopted his attitude somewhat, but the older ones have such ingrained habits. As long as they don't say anything outside of their own quarters it's generally overlooked."

"But some of what I've heard this evening is so hurtful. Even if it were said inside their tent, how am I supposed to ignore it?"

"Exactly how much do you hear?"

"I can hear every conversation happening in this camp. I can hear all the songs of the birds in this field. I can hear the mice and rabbits burrowing below the grasses. I can hear the whispers of my forest carried on the wind."

"You hear all of that?"

"When I focus, yes. But I generally only hear what's nearby or when people speak my name, or about me… and now you."

"It's the worst right now," I offered, "since they're all drinking."

"I… have never heard the kind of… lascivious things that

are being said about me." Her skin glowed with brooding anger. "Do all humans gossip like this?"

"Sadly, many do," I confirmed.

"Excuse me, Mardok. I'm sorry, but I have to take a walk."

"Where are you..." But she was marching off through the camp. She glowed like a torch in the evening light. I followed several steps behind her, since she didn't seem particularly interested in waiting for me.

She stopped in front of a tent and whipped her head around toward it.

"Urpin," she barked. There was silence, some shuffling, and a tent flap opened. A slightly cross-eyed man looked out at her. "No matter how many different synonyms you use for the word 'tramp,' not one of them describes me. And no, I'm not pregnant, Mardok isn't buying off my father, and your king isn't my secret lover. However, I know everything about Margret, if you would like me to fill in the camp." He stared up at her flashing eyes in horror, his jaw agape. "That's what I thought." Then she stomped off to the next tent.

"Meira... umm..." I tried. She ignored me.

"Janice!" she snapped at a woman sitting near a fire. "One more lying, slanderous word about me, and I'll fill in the camp about your daughter's... condition."

"Wha..." she shook her head fiercely.

"And you, Harria, you... you don't understand a thing about magic. Stop pretending you know anything about it. I did not ensorcell Mardok into marrying me. Just think about how silly that is, just for a single moment. That's not even possible to do. I can, however, turn you into a deer; I've done it before. Ask Mardok how that turned out. Hope the leaves look yummy."

By now there were all kinds of people stirring about, running out of her way. Chattering was at its height. Heads were sticking out of every tent.

"Blenish… where are you, Blenish? What kind of name is that, anyway? Your mother must really hate… ah, there you are!" A man was hiding behind several girthy women. "You think I don't know your loud mouth? I can hear everything you say, every single word, no matter who you say it to, no matter how quietly. I know what you're planning. Want the secrets out?"

"No, no, m'lady, please no."

"Then tighten those teeth around a bit and keep your silence." She glared around in a circle at dozens of rather frightened and uptight nobles and servants. "You have accusations to make? Make them to me. Present your evidence. Otherwise, hammer a nail in your lips." She fumed at them. "And the next nasty thing I hear about my betrothed… I'll set your tent on fire." Then she stomped off to her tent and disappeared.

"A bit of a demon in that angel," Robert mused, standing behind me.

"Robert… I love that woman."

Meira

Mother, I called out with my mind.

Yes, darling.

You were right. Humans can be petty and nasty.

What happened?

They whisper to each other, constantly, making up all kinds of vile things about Mardok and me. She was quietly listening. *Are you sure… what you said earlier?*

Yes, I am. You'll be fine. I know it's frustrating, but you will get used to it.

I slumped onto the floor and fiddled with a pair of beetles in my fingers.

He really loves me, you know?

Yes, I know. I've seen it.

The mark on his hand… your idea, wasn't it.

Yes, darling. He will need it very soon. Be at peace, though. You both will be fine.

What happens?

The future's been foggy, dear, I don't really know. Rest lightly; I see you together long from today.

I introduced the beetles to each other. They weren't particularly interested in each other, though.

I love you, Mother.

I love you, too, Meira.

I sighed and took the beetles outside so they could fly away. Robert and Mardok were both waiting for me.

"I would like to apologize on behalf of my people," Robert started.

"Why? If they were anything like you they wouldn't talk like that," I quipped.

"But I am responsible for them."

"Oh, Robert, don't take on yourself the guilt of people you cannot control. They wouldn't listen to you if you told them it was morning."

"Actually, sire, she's right. They don't listen when you tell them that," Mardok confirmed. Robert rolled his eyes.

"So, Mardok, are you ready for my lesson? The camp is settled for the night, and I am not ready yet for sleep."

"Are you sure that you're up for it?" Another worry line creased his forehead. "I wouldn't want to push you after…"

"You wish to renege on our bargain? My arms are itching to smash something."

"That's only a bit… frightening." He shifted slowly. We walked toward the audience tent.

"Are we good for me to join this evening?" Robert asked.

"Yes, Robert, certainly," I clarified.

Mardok had put our practice staves into the room after the tent had been set up. We went through our warm-ups and spent the late evening practicing the move he had taught me at the end of the last lesson. That had been our pattern for as long as he had been teaching me. Test the skill to see if I could discover it without instruction; give instruction and payment if it were necessary; and then practice the technique. This time was different only in the fact that we had an audience, and Robert actually gave out pointers as I perfected the move. Before long Mardok was winded and slightly bruised.

"I don't think I want you watching anymore, Robert," Mardok said, still breathing heavily.

"Why is that, *old* friend?" Robert was grinning.

"She doesn't need your help to learn the maneuver by the end of a normal practice session. With it, she has a distinct advantage much sooner." He grinned as well.

"Shall we end this lesson early?" I asked in my best innocent voice.

"Honestly, I don't think I could handle much more tonight. I didn't earn a full payment last time, so I'm not quite able to keep up." He winked at me.

"Should have stayed on your feet, then." I grinned saucily, and Robert let out a laugh.

"Mardok," he jeered, "did you just admit that you need magic to beat a girl?"

Mardok glared at him through one eye and offered Robert his stave.

"Sadly, my elbow just isn't feeling well... and my knee... definitely my knee."

"And your hip?"

"Yes, that table this morning. It was dreadful."

"Hmm, I see. So you get to laugh at me, because I was bested by a girl. Sire, I believe that you were bested by a table." Robert rolled in laughter and took the stave.

"Fine, Mardok, I'll earn your pay for you." Four rapid strikes later, I was on my back.

We put the staves away.

"Now, Meira, pay up," Robert said. "Course, I know what that kiss does; better give it to him." He looked rather disappointed.

I slipped inside of Mardok's outstretched arm and took the opportunity to kiss his forehead. The magic transfer took less than a second, but I felt as if the whole world moved beneath me. The bond had begun its final stage and the power involved overwhelmed me.

The room began to swim, and for a few brief moments I could actually see the magical bonds that held us together. They stretched in nameless colors through our bodies, binding our souls.

Mardok

Meira almost stumbled as she stepped back from the kiss. The room seemed to spin in front of me. "I do not think it would be wise for me to do that again until we are wed." The words sounded forced. Her breaths were rapid and shallow. I looked her in the eyes. I opened my mouth to say something, but no words came out, so I closed it.

"A-hem." Robert cleared his throat suddenly and we both jumped a bit. "Would you two like to be alone for a while?" He looked back and forth between the two of us and changed his mind. "On second thought...."

"Ah, I-I believe it is time for me to retire for the night," Meira stammered. She recovered a bit of her composure.

"Allow me to escort you to your tent." I offered my arm, and she took it cautiously. I looked to Robert for dismissal, but he gave me our private sign to return quickly. I groaned inwardly. He didn't want me to linger in saying goodnight to her. We walked the ten feet to her tent in silence. She squeezed my arm gently before she let go and disappeared inside. I stood outside for a moment staring at the flap, then sighed and turned back to Robert's tent.

"She's a remarkable creature," he said when I re-entered.

"You'll get no argument from me." My brain was swimming in ruminations of her.

"Do you think that she would be willing to travel with us after we leave Gavin's?" He carefully avoided mentioning the end of the lesson.

"I doubt you could convince her not to, in all honesty. Why?"

"I hoped as much. If her hearing is as acute as it was this eve, she could be a great asset to us there. But it may be prudent to invent a ruse to make it seem like she has returned with her father, just to make sure that the gossip doesn't explode again when we return to the castle."

"We could let it be known that she has preparations to make with her family for the wedding," I suggested.

"Excellent idea. That would be well within the realm of what they would expect." He looked thoughtful for a few moments, then seemed to shake it off. "I wanted you to know that our schedule for tomorrow has changed somewhat. I will only need the morning for audiences. I received a message from the mayor during dinner, and he says that the majority of the issues have resolved themselves one way or another. However, he does still need me to pass judgment on the criminal we knew about before, and apparently they found new evidence that adds to his list of crimes and makes the ones that were already known more gruesome."

"Ugh. Simply murdering a whole family isn't enough?"

"I guess not for him. The mayor has also requested that should the sentence be execution, which he strongly encourages, that it be performed before we leave so I can stand witness.

"I see. You'll want the rest of the day to recover then before we move on anyway."

"I'm afraid so. I hate executions, but I understand why I'm wanted at this one. The extended family needs to see me there." Robert sighed.

"I suggest that we get some rest. Tomorrow will be a difficult day for us both."

"Just make sure you end up in the right tent tonight, my friend." He grinned while expressing all due seriousness. I just nodded in return and went to my tent. Sleep that night was particularly difficult to come by.

9

7th of Lar Indar

Meira

I slept past the false dawn the next morning for the first time since I had recovered from being attacked. It was hard to believe how much had changed in thirteen months. The events of the previous day had left me both drained and exhilarated, so my sleep had been interrupted several times during the night when I started awake for no obvious reason. I knew that if I did nothing to change it I would be short tempered and sharp for the rest of the day.

I cast a quick notice-me-not charm on myself and slipped away from the camp. When I felt that I was far enough to be out of earshot I began to set my power circle. I placed stones at each of the primary and secondary directions, one in the position of my birth star, one in the direction of my forest, and a new one pointing back to the camp where Mardok was. I smiled to myself that I could finally add this last stone.

I stood in the center of the circle and called the wind. It came at first strong and angry in response to my agitation. Then gradually it softened until it was a merry breeze that played with my hair. I opened my senses and heard all the messages that had been sent in it. I smelled all the flowers it had passed. I reveled in its delight at my newly formed attachment and sent a message in its soft swirls to my father to join us when we arrived to meet the king's brother. Reluctantly, I sent the wind on its way. The sun was beginning to warm the dew on the grasses of the plain. I sang my greetings to it. I picked up each rock as I finished the Sun Song, which my mother had learned from the dawn pixies, and built a cairn of remembrance with them where I had stood in the center.

By the time I returned to camp I felt much lighter. The ritual had served its purpose. But Mardok was pacing outside of my tent looking worried.

"Good morrow."

He stopped mid-stride when I spoke.

"Where were you? Is something wrong?" He reached out and took both of my hands in his as he asked.

"I was greeting the wind and the sun and sending my father a message. I'm fine," I tried to reassure him.

"I thought maybe you had become ill, or maybe something was wrong. I sent a maid in to check on you, but you weren't there. So I checked with the guards, but no one saw you come or go."

"I'm sorry to have given you a cause for concern, my love. If we have time later, I'll show you how to use our bond to find me so that it doesn't happen again."

"That would make me…" he trailed off, "wait, what?"

"Well, I wouldn't want you to be worried. I can show you how to use our bond to find me."

"How do you mean 'use our bond?'"

"Our bond… the magic that flows between us. You can use it like a compass."

"That's magic, Meira. Humans can't use magic."

"Well, now, aren't you the expert."

"Okay, fine," he sighed in defeat. "Obviously, I'm not the expert here."

"It's okay. I'll show you. Magic just isn't inherent to humans, but you can use mine."

"Huh."

I beamed at him. "So, what are you going to pay me for teaching you how to use magic?" I gave him a flirtatious smile.

"Are you hungry?" His voice cracked as he changed the subject. "I haven't been to get my breakfast yet, and we need to hurry before the villagers arrive for audience this morning."

I laughed.

"Let's go see what Mary has prepared, then." He kept one of my hands in his as we walked through the camp. He seemed almost afraid to let it go for me to get my food. Mary noticed his fidgeting and chose not to tease us again, but she winked as she handed us our breakfast. After we finished the meal, he took my hand again, and we walked to the public entrance of the audience tent. Servants were arranging cushions around the edges with aisles for walking between. Robert had an actual chair which was as yet empty and the only one in the room.

"What a rather… interesting piece of furniture," I whispered to Mardok.

"Yes, that. You should have seen him when he found out that protocol required him to bring it. His steward had to hunt the castle for it, since Robert and I had hidden it inside the bell tower."

"Why did he bring it then?"

"Some sort of tradition. It was hewn from a tree that someone had given someone, and someone else had cut it down for some reason that no one can really remember."

I snickered. "Poor tree." I bit my food. "It's bad enough to be chopped down, but to be turned into that." I ate with Mardok for a bit before addressing the obvious. "So why have we stopped here? It has you worried."

"No, I'm disgusted. Robert's business this morning is particularly unpleasant, and it will end in an execution near lunch time. He has been called to approve the judgment of guilt, pass sentence, and witness the punishment. While executions are never pleasant, this one will be a relief for the whole village. The man butchered several people, including two children. The written record of evidence and witnesses was received at dawn, and it has everyone a bit shaken."

I was at a loss for what to do for him, and I didn't quite understand why he was so caught up by a simple execution. I could not share any more of the bond magic for fear of being overcome and unable to control it. So I just stood there letting him hold onto my hand, sure that any further intimacy would be unfitting. Robert came in to the audience room from his receiving area. As he stepped through the divide in the wall I noted that Amelia and two of Robert's advisers were remaining behind. His face was somewhat pale, but his features looked determined.

He was wearing a blue tunic with a silver-maille sash. On the tunic was a finely embroidered emblem of a pair of scales hung across an axe, a sprouted seed in one pan and a skull in the other.

"The prison escort will be here momentarily. The accused has been tightly bound and gagged because he has already injured three of the regular guards. Meira, if you wish to remain present I ask that you stay up here next to Mardok and myself. The last thing I need is an army of Fae to come in here with swords blazing." He gave me a half grin and a forced snicker. The twinkle was gone from his eyes.

"Majesty, the nobles you requested are ready to be seated." A page bowed low to deliver his message.

"Show them in. It would be better if they were settled before the prisoner arrives." Robert placed the braided circlet he had been holding on top of his head and looked distastefully at his chair before taking his seat. He shifted uncomfortably for an excessive length of time.

"My grandfather always said that you should never be comfortable sitting in judgment over other men. I hate that he took things so literally. I've got a knot under my left cheek."

Mardok led me to a place on Robert's right, and he took position on his left. He placed a hand on the hilt of his sword. The stone-faced expression he wore staring into the room had been long practiced. Two of his fellow soldiers took their places on either side of us.

I watched the handful of selected members of court find their places along the sides of the room, leaving plenty of space in front of the door flap. The last of them was barely seated before the local guards led in the prisoner.

Mardok

The prisoner's eyes were yellow, and they darted around the room menacingly until they landed on Meira, then they narrowed and would not leave her face. She seemed surprised at first, and then met his glare with equal threat.

I tightened my grip on my sword and drew it an inch. The stare-down between them remained. The hatred that flowed was obvious, and I was nervous at having the king separating myself and this man's clear target. Seth and Harry, on either side of us, had also noticed, each toeing combat stances.

The room nearly crackled as the last of the guards and the mayor entered. It was the mayor's unpleasant task to read the list of charges to the assembled court members.

"Your Royal Majesty, Honored Ambassador, Lords and Ladies of the court," he began. Someone had been thoughtful enough to mention Meira's presence to him before he arrived. "The accused, George Fergisson, did knowingly and intentionally murder eight residents of Maeville. He was discovered standing over one of the bodies wielding a knife with which he was carving symbols and an unknown language into the victim. The bodies of the other victims, including two young children, were found in similar condition during a search of his property after the accused had been arrested." Then he proceeded to recount the horrific findings in gruesome detail.

A couple of the nobles looked like they wanted to retch. He continued.

"When questioned about the crimes, the accused showed no remorse and even a measure of pride as he described how he enjoyed torturing the individuals before he allowed them to die. When asked what had motivated him to commit such horrifying acts the accused laughed and only answered, "Tisks errend."

"This writ has been signed by all of the town elders including myself." The mayor finished reading and looked up to meet Robert's eyes. His complexion was a bit green. "Majesty, we request that this man be parted from his life that he may not be allowed to inflict such pain on others." The mayor bowed.

Robert paused to allow the mayor's statements to settle in everyone's minds before announcing his judgment.

"We have seen the statements of the witnesses against this man. The crimes are so gruesome that we have never seen the like. We feel that the sentence is indeed both just and necessary to protect our other subjects. Let this man be executed by hanging as soon as possible." There were nods of agreement from the court members.

"Your pardon, Majesty." Meira spoke up suddenly in a stiff and formal tone; her voice was cold. "This individual, I can hardly call him a man, is not just a simple criminal. The deaths that have been described are not simply murders. They are sacrifices," she paused as the audience murmured, "to a dark spirit called T'xerren Nahasmen. He has willingly allowed this evil sway over his actions and has reveled in the power it gave him. You cannot execute him in the manner stated and expect the evil to die with him."

The prisoner began to twitch against his bonds.

"It has become powerful enough to move to a new host

once this one is dead," she explained. "It will choose a witness to his host's death to inhabit and the murders will continue."

He started struggling in earnest now and working his jaw against the gag as the guards held more tightly to his restraints.

"Since you have experience in this matter we will yield to your knowledge, good Ambassador. How are we to rid ourselves of this evil?" Even though his face did not betray it, I could tell that Robert was as surprised as everyone else and that he clearly wanted an explanation.

"The dark spirit maintains his presence through blood, and so we must bind them together. This spirit's servant must be hung upside down and have his head removed. Then you must drain all of the blood from his body and collect it. The blood must be burned along with the head." Meira's eyes were steel. A couple of the nobles were staring at her as though she had gone crazy.

Robert addressed the assembly, "Let it be done as the Ambassador of the High Fae has said." He turned to Meira again, "Ambassador, would you know of an individual who may perform this binding you spoke of?" He maintained marvelous composure. I knew that his insides were churning.

"I have the knowledge and experience necessary to accomplish it. I would be only too willing to lend my services to aid in ridding the world of this evil." Even though she spoke to Robert, her eyes had remained locked on the prisoner. He was fighting so violently now that Seth and Harry had joined the troops to control him. She turned her attention to the guards. "And be careful. Do not let him kill himself. He will try."

"Return the prisoner to his cell until the preparations have been made," Robert ordered. The guards and soldiers lashed his feet together and carried him out of the tent. "Is there any other business which needs our attention, good mayor?"

"No, Majesty. I cannot fully express my gratitude for your relief in this matter. The entire village will be relieved when we have finished with it. I find it most fortuitous that your Majesty came to court with a High Fae in attendance. It would have served poorly if this 'dark spirit' had taken hold of you, instead."

"Yes, most fortuitous. We shall adjourn until the preparations are complete. Marcus," he looked to his treasurer, "disperse reparations to the families at twice the customary rate, and reimburse the town for any expenses associated." The mayor stared at the king in amazement. Robert turned his attention again to the court. "We shall not require any of the court to be present for the execution, should they desire to be elsewhere. However, an announcement will be made ten minutes before it begins for those who feel the need to bear witness to it."

Robert gave me a look that said we needed to talk and reached over to offer his arm to Meira before we stepped into his quarters. He listened at the flap to the audience room to make sure that the nobles were indeed leaving before he turned to Meira.

"I need you to tell me everything you can about this. I apologize for not bringing you into our confidence and sharing the written testimonies and evidence before the audience. I had thought to shield you from it."

"You do not need to shield me from the evils of this

world," she stated softly. "My family fights it daily. There is nothing that has been done that we have not seen." She sighed. She seemed resolute, but tired. "How long do you think it will take for the townspeople to prepare for the execution?"

"They have already expressed a desire to have it accomplished at noon. I don't believe they will need more time than that."

"Good, then I have time to give you little more of the history. The recitation will also help me to prepare for my part in this." She took her hand from Robert's arm and settled herself cross-legged on a cushion. "Make yourselves comfortable." Robert and I did as she requested. Amelia, Amos, and Ira were still present and were already seated. Robert had a page bring two pitchers of water and six glasses before clearing out of the room. Meira brought her hands together, touched her fingertips to her lips, and then touched us each lightly between our brows. She closed her eyes, and suddenly I could hear her voice in my head.

Meira

First, I apologize for not taking the time to explain this method of communication before beginning. With evil such as we are facing I felt the need for both speed and secrecy. I forced my emotions behind my mental wall and gathered my thoughts to put everything I knew into weaving the tale. I wanted them to feel the story as well as to hear it. So I put into their minds the sights, the smells, the tastes of the places and the people I was describing, as it had been shown to me by my father. As it had been given to him by his father.

Long ago, when the world was new and the gods still interfered directly with its inhabitants, there was a human woman named Opella who was beloved of Jainko Marduk-Bakarrik, the most powerful of the gods. She gave birth to a son, and the first race of Fae was born. The high god was pleased with his son and bestowed several of his powers on him and his descendants. Other gods and mortals begat the other races of fae and each of them were also gifted by their immortal parents with the abilities that now defines each race of their descendants.

One of the lesser gods, who was known for his pride but not for his intelligence, was not so fortunate as to be loved by the mortal he had chosen to bear his child. When it was nearly time for her to deliver, she hid herself from him and bore the babe in secret. She hid the child for several years before the lesser god could forgo his pride and ask his brethren for help in finding her. By that time she had tainted the child with tales of horror about his father. When the lesser god attempted to bestow his gifts of power on the child, the boy cursed him, and the gifts were twisted and lost.

Having lost the measure of power that he had tried to give to his son, the lesser god left the world and returned to the heavens to mourn his loss. Bakarrik witnessed these events and knew that they would eventually cause trouble for his own offspring, so he planted the knowledge of how to resolve it in his son's bloodline to be passed on to his children and his children's children.

The powers that had been twisted remained lost in hiding for many hundreds of years, without the soul of a living being to temper them. By the time the gods had returned to the heavens the powers had developed a personality and will of their own. Afflicted by the pride of their creator and tainted by the curse and rejection that had left them to wander the world alone, they sought out souls that would welcome them and their influence.

Not all races of the fae are inherently good. There are some races that use their parent-gifts to gain power and possessions. These are the ones who were first to fall under the influence of this dark spirit of chaos, this T'xerren Nahasmen.

Nahasmen encouraged and gained power from the wars that raged internally amongst these fae for many centuries. Then they spilled over and began to affect the peaceful races. Many good fae were infected before the problem was realized. The other races did not know how to bind Nahasmen to the blood of his pawns. Scores of good fae were overcome simply because they had been present when what they thought was just an evil individual had been killed. It is a time that my family still grieves over.

Bakarrik's first child, Keltus, was King of the Fae at the time, and he witnessed a nymph sacrificing a victim, in the same manner you heard described today. The knowledge that his father had granted woke suddenly within him and his brethren. They worked as one to bind the tendril of Nahasmen and execute the murderer. They spread the news to all of our family, and our whole people went to war. We shared the knowledge with those who had the power to use it, and eventually we contained Nahasmen to a single entity on an island far across the sea. My people did not have the ability to remove it from the world completely, as it does not need a body to survive, but we have fought many battles throughout the rest of our history to keep it contained. Whenever there is an outbreak we immediately hasten to quash it. The duty requires constant vigilance.

However, I now believe that Nahasmen is changing its strategy. It has never before shown particular interest in the race of men. I will help you remove this pawn, and then we will need to contact my father and seek his counsel. This change does not bode well for the race of men, and your people will need the assistance of mine.

I opened my eyes far less anxious than I had been when I started the tale. I had never told the story by myself before — instead of being part of a chorus — and sharing it brought a sense of relief. It was several minutes before anyone spoke.

"That was very real," Robert started. "I could feel my own hands in battle. The sweat, the taste of blood, the fear."

"These are the memories of Keltus, the first Fae King, my great grandfather, and several others who fought with him."

"I could actually feel their grief," Amelia added.

"We all feel it. This is how Fae never forget."

"I have lived through both war and peace," Amos offered quietly. "At times the latter was more threatening than the former." He stopped to draw in from his pipe. "But at some point fear left me behind. For many years I reminded myself that the sword could take me any day. I found that the way to live is accepting my eventual death as a comforting reality. It permits me to remember that I don't have to fight these fights forever." He leaned back and looked at the top of the tent. Then he turned his attention to Meira. "My young lady… and I mean no disrespect to the years you have lived far beyond me… I am again awash in fear. This doesn't seem the enemy that kills bodies. It comes for your very soul. Is that true?"

"It leaves nothing inside a man undefiled," I explained. "But understand… there are those who embrace it, to their own eternal demise. And there are those who struggle against it. But eventually it breaks them as well."

"I was figuring that might be the case." Amos paused momentarily. "This ceremony… have you ever performed it before?"

"Only once, just over a year ago. I was on my way to deliver a package when I was attacked by a group of bandits. Their leader was a willing pawn of Nahasmen. The band followed him out of fear that he would take one of them for sacrifice if they could not find him a substitute. By the time I found them, the leader had sacrificed an entire village. Once I killed the villain, though, his followers didn't matter anymore."

"You did that alone?" Robert sounded incredulous.

"Yes. His band was made up mostly of various fae, and my magic was very effective against them. My only difficulty came from the one human who was following him. I had not calculated for that, and it very nearly cost me my life."

"I'm afraid I don't understand," Robert said, clearly confused. "Men can't use magic."

"About that…" Mardok began.

"Very few do," Meira interrupted. "Fae magic works differently on fae than it does on humans. It is my limited understanding of how much different it is that caused my miscalculation then, and again with our bargain, Mardok. Fae take longer to enchant and recover more slowly from enchantments, because magic is part of who we are. I can, with effort, magically convince a fae and a human that they are deer, for instance. I do not actually change them into deer, I merely convince their minds for a time that they are deer and have always been that way. Under the normal spell, the fae would think that he was a deer for an entire day. The human's mind processes the conflicting sensory information so quickly that he remembers he is a human within a half-hour and immediately begins to wonder why he ever thought differently. He will also go looking for the source of his confusion." I paused to cover my embarrassment. "I barely managed to fend off his attack until the fire had destroyed the tendril of Nahasmen bound in the head and blood. By then I had lost so much blood from the wounds he had inflicted that I had to have my brother pull me away. It took me weeks to recover. It was then I decided to go in search of someone to teach me to defend myself without magic."

"But why couldn't you just bespell him again when he attacked you?" Mardok asked.

"Binding the possessed takes *all* of my magical focus. If I had used it for anything else, Nahasmen would have been loosed to inhabit me. I don't have to keep all of my attention on the spell for it to work, but I cannot use my magic for anything else until the rite is finished. And remember, I was alone. I had to create a collection container for the blood and build the fire myself. That's why it took long enough for the first spell to wear off." There were a few nods of understanding.

"I ought to warn you as well that I will seem distant and unresponsive during most of the ritual. This will pass as the danger does, but I don't want to worry you. If anything goes wrong, Robert, I want you to have my maoim beatha in your hand for the entire ordeal. If I make a mistake and Nahasmen is loosed, I will be its target, and everyone in this camp and the village will be in grave danger."

"But..." several voices interrupted at the same time.

"*If* I make a mistake my own death is a small price to keep this evil at bay. My father will understand. He will not like it, but he will understand. He will not take the loss of my life out on any of you or your people, and I am sure that he will help rid your people of the evil regardless of whether I succeed or fail today."

"Could we not wait until he can be reached to take care of this one?" Robert found his voice first, but Mardok clearly had similar thoughts.

I could contact Mother right now, but I didn't want Father's interference. I didn't want him to take over so that I could return to being the spoiled little princess.

"Unfortunately, no," I lied, "haste is required. It wouldn't be the first time someone under the control of Nahasmen killed himself in order to switch bodies."

"He's bound head to toe."

"Unless you can force him to keep breathing, there's nothing you can do to keep him alive. If we wait even another day, he may build up the determination to suffocate himself. Besides, I don't know where Father is, so getting a message to him could take time. His affairs extend all over the world." Obviously, I could actually get a message to him within moments, but they didn't know that. I wanted to prove to them, and a little to myself, that I was fully capable of handling this problem.

"What can we do to help?" Amos asked.

"Guard me. He might have followers amongst the townspeople, since it took so long to discover him. If there are, they will probably try to attack me during the binding. Mardok, if the attackers are fae, hold your hand to them and show them the mark. It is binding even for those under Nahasmen's control. They won't obey you, but they cannot hurt you. If they are not fae, just do what you do best." I tried to make my smile encouraging.

"We have a few more minutes before we need to leave. Is there anything else we can do?" Robert was sitting back on his cushion processing all of the new data I had given him. Amelia was eyeing Robert. Ira was cleaning his nails with his knife and watching Mardok's face for cues out of the corner of his eye.

"I would not be opposed to an early meal. It will take a lot of energy to finish this." I was tired already. Ira went out to call a page to fetch us lunch. Mardok shifted from his cushion to sit next to me. He placed his arm around my back and pulled me to lean against him. "I am glad that I don't have to manage it alone this time," I whispered to him.

Mardok

Meira nestled in my arm.

It was hard to mesh together the soft, innocent, naive girl that I held beside me with the cold gaze of hatred she had leveled at the unfortunate victim of that ghostly monster. Well… she had leveled it at the monster, I thought. But maybe it was the man… She had said he was willing. But was the man really so much a monster already that he knew what he was getting himself into?

Her judgment against him was instant and severe—no consideration, no hesitation, no consultation. His level of intended participation wasn't apparently on her mind.

The pragmatic side of me understood this, of course… especially considering the vision she had given to each of us. But the idealistic side of me railed against it. If a man is merely a pawn of gods and ghosts, what hope does he have?

This side of Meira… this is the side of Meira I needed to understand more. How deep did this go? This violent side, this darkness, this… what exactly, I did not know.

Amos was right, as typical, I had not felt such abrupt fear of anything since I was a boy at war. And yet, while now the fear had passed, I knew that the monster we faced was greater than anything we had ever imagined.

Who was unreasonable then? Meira, for rushing into the fray to exterminate the enemy in front of her? Or me, for considering how I might spare it? Perhaps Meira was more pragmatic than I.

My father would have pointed out that typically you learn these things sometime before you ask a girl to marry you. But then again, I hadn't asked… she had. And, of course, he had managed to make it all the way to my birth before he had met my mother's parents. So I had that on him.

Meira twisted a bit to get more comfortable. That put her even deeper against my chest, her head on my shoulder. I liked that she found me comfortable. All I had to do was figure out how to keep her alive.

When we finished eating it was nearly noon. Robert, Meira, and I left the camp followed by a squad of guards and only three nobles, whose names I had forgotten. We reached the village square and Meira took charge of the situation. The prisoner was already tied hanging upside down from a pole. I don't think the town guards bothered returning him to the cell. His face was puffed beet red and eyes swollen as though he had been hanging that way the entire time. The heap for the bonfire had been built to a surprisingly large size, and all the wood was smeared with pitch.

"Interesting," Frank noted to me, "ol' Fatteous isn't anywhere to be found. He usually enjoys a good execution."

Meira started moving stones around the hanging prisoner. As curious as I was about what she was doing, I forced my attentions to other people in the square. The mayor was there as well as the guards from the prison who were doing all the prep work. There was a group of men and women who looked like they could be the town elders. There were very few citizens out, though, which eased my mind. If there were to be an attack it would be easier to see them coming, and it was less likely there would be incidental casualties. I stood as close to Meira as I could without getting in her way.

Once the stones in the square were arranged to her liking, Meira closed her eyes and began to sing. The words were unintelligible, but the melody was mournful and haunting. Everyone listening held their breath so as not to disturb the music. She walked around the prisoner three times holding her bag in both hands as she sang.

On the second pass, an eerie whistle came over the wind, repeating the notes as she sang them.

At the end of the third pass she withdrew a wicked-looking knife. Without even changing the tone of the song she nimbly removed the man's head in one swift motion and placed the knife gently on a square of leather and set them on the ground. His blood poured into the waiting bucket, and she placed the head deliberately on the pile of wood. Meira kept singing until the stream of blood had stopped.

An oppressive silence followed the end of the music. She waved for two of the guards to lift the bucket onto the center of the pile, and they obeyed without hesitation. Meira pulled out a flint and steel from her bag and struck it once. The bonfire roared to life immediately. She turned her back to it and picked up her knife again.

She used it to cut down the now headless body and remove his ties, after which she crossed his arms so that he looked as peaceful as he could. Then she took an oiled cloth from her bag and began cleaning her knife.

"Is it over?" I asked quietly.

"Yes," She said as she bent to examine the blade more closely. "We were fortunate. The people of this village are good folk. They were not tempted by the power as he was." She finished her examination and cleaning. Then she wrapped the clean side of the cloth around the blade and put it back in her bag. "They do not need my help to bury the body. I would like to return to the camp so I can rest."

The pitch-soaked wood was burning hot and fast, so larger logs were being added to keep the fire going. I gave Meira my arm and looked for Robert, but he was missing.

I walked with her to the corral. Robert was petting the mounts as he fed them carrots.

"My king..." I began.

"I was there," he answered. "I was required to be there, and I was there."

I could see the remnant streaks of tears in his left eye. If history served well, the left eye generally gave way after the right, but he had that hidden with his body against a tree.

"Anything..." I started again. But what was there to say? I shut up.

Meira, however, smiled sweetly. She withdrew from my arm and reached out to him. Taking his hand, she lifted it up and gently ungripped the white-knuckled fingers around the maoim beatha.

"The danger is past," she noted.

He turned on her. "How do you walk in and out of that without so much as a quiver in your voice?"

Looking up into his eyes, she answered simply, "I have lived but a short time. Even so, I have seen more men dead than you have seen alive."

Robert was silenced and stepped back.

"Please," she begged, "don't let this come between us. We are friends and family."

"I will speak with the mayor and meet up with you later," Robert concluded. Then he wandered off. I escorted Meira to her tent. She still seemed distant.

"Will Robert cut me off?" she asked plainly.

"No, he won't." I sighed. "Don't worry about him. He'll recover with time and humor. He always does. He's not a stranger to death, either, you know."

"I know. Merely to making it. And it makes him uneasy that I make death as readily as I keep life."

"Well… that's not… human… typically."

"You need to meet more humans," she replied. After a bit she continued. "You think that, too — that I don't behave humanly."

"I would be lying to claim otherwise."

"My best friend," she answered, "I am not, nor have I ever been, human. The purpose of man is to reign in the chaos of Lur and tame its wilds. The purpose of High Fae is to serve as judges. Men are typically suited for their role. High Fae are exceptional at theirs." She looked into my eyes imploring, "I hope this does not come between us."

"Never," I stated resolutely. Whatever this might mean for the two of us, I knew we could work through it in time. "Is there anything I can do for you now?"

"What I need now is rest. Do not worry for me. By dinner I will be myself again."

I took her hand and kissed it gently before she disappeared into her tent.

Then I went in search of Robert again. The sneaky king had circled back to the corral. I joined him, and we watched them in silence.

"Did you know that Meira tamed that black stallion that we received two weeks ago?" he said at length.

"The one that was trying to kick down the stables?" I asked surprised.

"That's the one. I was talking with one of the hands here on the trip, and he said that the horse came right up to her and wanted her to pet him. After a few seconds he was tame."

"She has some sort of connection with animals. You know she has a squirrel friend who's learning the stave?"

Robert tilted his head each way.

"Seriously, we would be doing our lessons, and this silly little squirrel—Arthur was his name—would be copying her moves with this itty bitty little twig." I tried to explain with my hands.

"So she's got a pet squirrel… named Arthur…"

"She didn't name him, actually. That was just his name. Not sure where he got it from. But yeah, he skipped sleeping through the winter just to practice with us. One time he was mad at me, or something, and he poked me in the head with his twig."

"I'm trying to envision this."

"Don't bother. I saw it, and I still can't believe it."

"He any good?"

I laughed.

"Well, maybe he could replace you when you retire."

I laughed again. "That'll be the day."

Robert didn't laugh. He looked at me seriously. "Mardok, we do need to come up with a few candidates for your replacement."

My stomach hit the ground. "Why?"

"I can't ask you to try to protect both Meira and me. She's going to be your bride, and today's events have made it clear to me that she has some very real dangers to face. She's going to need you to be free to watch out for her without you having the added worry of whether or not I'm safe."

I opened my mouth to interrupt him, but he cut me off.

"Don't try to argue. I've already thought this through. You'll still be the leader of the Dozen. They wouldn't willingly follow anyone else anyway — except, perhaps Arthur. And you're a Count in your own right, so your position in court won't be harmed. I'll officially name you my Chief Counselor. Not that it will surprise anyone, but it'll confirm your status. As an allied ambassador, Meira's already counted among my counsel, and as a foreign princess she carries her own significant status in the court." He paused to take a breath. "I'll still need your advice and company. You're my best friend. I'll always need your counsel. But Meira is the one who will need your protection."

"I concede your point," I agreed reluctantly, "though I don't know if I agree with it entirely. Did you see that knife she used today?"

"I did, but you were much closer. Was it really as big and ugly as it looked?"

"Yes, and it had tiny spikes all over the hilt. I couldn't have held it like she did without my hand coming away bloody. But she wielded it like an artisan's brush. And the care she took in cleaning it wasn't amateur."

"Not exactly the butcher's preferred weapon."

"But effective. Perhaps we're paying the wrong smiths to sharpen our swords."

We shifted to talking about the horses that were shoving to get our attention and only noticed the passage of time when we could smell dinner.

We walked together to check on Meira and found that she had already left her tent and was visiting with Amelia. We caught up with them at the entrance to the dining tent.

Meira

Supper was pleasant. Mardok was more attentive to my needs than ever, but the tone of our jokes and teasing was unchanged. Word had spread around camp about the day's events, and the rest of the party was somber and drank heavily of their ale and wine.

Amelia seemed reluctant to return to her tent for the evening, so I asked Mardok and Robert if we could let her join our confidence and watch the lesson. They agreed, and I gave her a short explanation of our routine.

When we arrived in the audience tent, it had not been cleared from the morning's business. We worked together to move most of the cushions out of the way, leaving two for Robert and Amelia to sit on. This was accomplished mostly by throwing them at each other.

Mardok took Robert's chair back into his private receiving room, though Robert recommended the bonfire. By the time the room was ready, the noises from camp had begun to soften.

"Meira," Mardok asked as we finished, "why did you ask me to be your teacher when we met?"

"What do you mean? I told you the story of why I needed a teacher," I responded.

"No, I mean, why me? Your father has troops, the dvrger have warriors who could have taught you, and I know that some of your siblings are well-versed in hand-to-hand combat. Any of them would have made as good of a teacher as I am. Why me?"

I paused before answering. "I didn't want them to treat me like the spoiled little princess who wants to play war. They would have pacified my request; but at the end of the meager training they would have given me, I would have been no better off in skill. As to why specifically you, I cheated."

"Meaning?"

"I couldn't ask Mother for where to look, because she would have given me a teacher who was approved by Father. Instead, I went to a centaur who also has the gift of future sight and asked her who my teacher would be. She was expecting my arrival and knew my question, but she wasn't able to tell me who. Instead, she told me where I would meet him, er... you. So I went there and watched for you." I stopped and Mardok considered this in silence.

"How long did you wait for me?" he asked finally, very quietly.

"Honestly? About three minutes."

"New lesson," he chuckled as he took up his stave and tossed me mine. I caught it and nodded. "No comments or help from the peanut gallery." He glared meaningfully at Robert.

"We're just sitting here to enjoy the show," he replied innocently.

"Make sure it stays that way," Mardok nearly growled. He faced me again. "We've covered all of the basics for this weapon. You have the advantage in speed and agility, and I have it in size, strength, and experience. I want you to use everything you've learned up to today. We pull our head-shots, but everything else should be full force. Understand?"

I nodded. He grew suddenly more serious than he had ever been during a lesson. I took my stance and waited. Mardok whipped his stave around his back and out to strike at my left. I dodged the swing and danced forward to tap his wrist.

"That's not enough force to do you any good," he said as he switched the stave to his other hand to swipe at my exposed back. I ducked under it and rolled out of the way. Since I was already crouching, I aimed my swing for his shins. He avoided it with one leg and stomped down on it with the other, pinning my hands under the end of it for a second before I pulled them free. He picked up my stave and started swinging at me with both of them. I was able to dodge them for quite a while until I misread his feint and he landed a blow on my arm. I heard Amelia gasp aloud. It stung terribly. I caught his next swing and flipped over it, using the full weight of my body to twist the stave out of his hand. His swings became faster and more furious, and I was having a hard time blocking or dodging them all. I jumped up, using only a single stroke of my wings for lift, flipped in the air over his head and landed two solid blows to the pressure points on his back before my feet touched the ground again.

"Better," he grunted and turned to face me again. His moves were stiffer after that, but he did not stop the assault. The next volley of swings was easier to dodge, and I jumped over his head again. But instead of landing behind him, I opened my wings and fluttered over his head. It was a good move, since he stabbed his stave behind him and followed it immediately with a crushing swing.

My absence confused him for a moment. I landed with my knees on his shoulders and pulled my stave up under his chin.

"Do you yield?" I punctuated my question by pulling the stave tighter. But he clenched his jaw and smacked both arms down on the stave, popping it out of my weaker hands. Then he grabbed me off his shoulders and pinned me with my face to the dirt. "I yield!" I cried. He pulled his knee off me and helped me up. "So, what was the point of that?" I asked.

"You needed to practice defending against an actual attacker. No one on a battlefield is going to slow down for you. You won't get the opportunity for a second swing if your first isn't hard enough." He wasn't even winded from the exertion. "And you didn't actually start to fight back until I landed the blow on your arm. In a confrontation you can't just let your opponent have an opening like that and expect to survive the encounter. If I had been wielding a sword that blow would have taken off your arm and cut halfway through your chest before your blood touched the ground and the army of Fae came to your aid. The promise of an army doesn't prevent you from dying before they can arrive." He pulled two of the cushions off the pile and put them down next to Robert and Amelia. "Come on, let's take a break."

We sat next to the other couple and let my heart rate return to normal.

"So," Robert began hesitantly, "you have wings."

"Oh, yeah. I had forgotten that you'd never seen me fly. Mardok and I decided that we would keep it secret to help avoid some of the shock factor."

"I can see how they could cause a bit of commotion," Amelia added.

Mardok

I felt guilty for pushing so hard during the lesson. If I had been thinking clearly I would have begged off for the evening and let myself unwind before I sparred with Meira. Robert sent me castigating looks during the friendly conversation that followed, so I knew that he thought so as well. But I was facing the impossible problem of how to teach her real combat without risking her harm. That simply wasn't possible. She would never accept it if I didn't push her to her limits, and Robert would never accept it if I did. And try as I might, she was simply tiny and physically weak. She would need to be much, much faster to handle a real fight.

"It is truly getting late now," Amelia yawned.

"It is, and I for one would like to put as much distance between myself and this village as we can tomorrow." Robert rose and helped Amelia to her feet.

I followed suit more stiffly as my back was still tense from Meira's well-scored strikes. She may not have muscle, but her aim was deadly. "Oooh," I groaned involuntarily as one of the muscles spasmed.

"Would you like me to fix it?" Meira asked.

"Fix what?"

"Your back, where I hit you. Would you like me to fix it?"

"Sure, I suppose. Another skill of yours?" She walked around behind me and began to sing. Robert and Amelia turned to watch her. She didn't touch me, but I could feel the warmth from her hands as they hovered near my skin. The song was a short one, but when she was finished I stretched and all the soreness was gone. "Amazing. I thought I was going to be stuck feeling those for days."

"Would have served you right if she had let you alone," Robert muttered under his breath. Meira heard it as well. I needed to make amends with her before he would forgive me.

"By the way, Robert, you should know that my father will be joining us on the road tomorrow. His message is what woke me from my rest this afternoon, but I forgot to mention it to you earlier. He wants to hear everything there is to know about the circumstances that led to today's execution."

"I'll make sure that I pack the witness' statements with us so that he can read them for himself." Robert held the tent flap open for the two ladies but let it go so that it hit me in the face.

"I'm sure that he would appreciate it. Good night, friends." She waved to them as Robert escorted Amelia back to her tent. *We need to talk,* she said firmly into my brain.

"I'm sorry…" I started aloud.

No, not out loud, and not here. Let's go for a walk, and I'll show you how to talk my way. I was more than happy to oblige.

"First, do you know how the bond feels when we kiss?"

"Ehh… yes, yes I do. Assuming it's what I'm thinking it's supposed to… um… maybe?"

She looked quizzically at me.

"Well… I know what it feels like to me. But does it feel the same to me as it would to another Fae? I don't know that."

"Fair enough." She paused. "Do you feel tingling in the back of your head? Right above your neck."

"Well… um…" I looked at her sheepishly.

"You can't remember?"

"Well, I was a little focused on other… things." My face flushed. "Like, you know… oh never mind."

She rolled her eyes and gave me a quick kiss.

"Now?" she asked.

"Yes, there was tingling in the back of my head." And other places. In fact, the whole world spun for a bit.

"Good. You need to reside there in your mind when you want to share your thoughts. Imagine sitting there and bringing the thoughts that you want to share into that place with you."

I breathed deeply, figuring that might help, and closed my eyes. Somewhere in the back of my mind I saw myself sitting on a nice little bench. It was spring, and the birds were singing.

"You're not there yet," she whispered. "Go further back."

I breathed deeper. The spring was warm, and the birds were staring at me, as though expecting something to occur.

"Why are you thinking about birds?" she asked.

I popped my eyes open. "It worked!"

She laughed. "Well, almost. I saw the birds, but you weren't there."

I concentrated again. It took several iterations before she was able to find me there as well. When we did connect, a thrilling chill ran through my brain and down my spine. I stepped back in shock.

Meira merely smiled.

"I… I think I touched you…" I stammered.

"And I you," she answered.

"But… how? How can I be doing magic?"

"You're not using your own magic." She reached out her hand and touched my face. "You're using mine."

"It's… it's… wow. It's… really something."

"You're welcome to use it anytime."

"Can I use it to do all those other things you do?"

"Well… no, I don't think so. Maybe we'll leave that conversation for my father some other time."

"I'm not sure he would approve of a human using magic."

"Not typically, no. He's obviously fond of you, though."

"Only because of you."

She shrugged.

"Now try it again. Tell me something," she instructed.

I concentrated again, as hard as I could, thinking about the phrase, *I love you.* I tried to put it where the birds had been.

She shrieked and wrapped her fingers around her head.

"Not so loud!"

"Loud? I didn't yell."

She burst out laughing.

"What?"

"Just… back off a bit. Think quieter. Focusing doesn't make you clearer. It just makes you louder. Breath, calm your mind, and try again."

I inhaled and exhaled slowly. Then I looked into the back of my mind and said there, *I'm sorry. I hope this is better.*

Much, she replied.

We bid each other goodnight to have our more important conversation the magical way, not that I was looking forward to the topic.

Thank you for taking me seriously, she said after we had each entered our own tents. *That was the best lesson we've had yet.*

I don't know how to teach you without hurting you. I hate doing it.

Mardok, I'm glad you push me. I'll never learn otherwise. Please don't stop.

My mind was blank. I had no idea what I was trying to do… train her to fight demons with a stick? *I'm so sorry. I train warriors, and I fight enemies that bleed real blood. It's all I know how to do. I don't know how to fight against magic or gods or….*

I can teach you, but it will take much longer than it did for me to learn the stave. Teaching a human to use magic is a difficult and dangerous task, she warned. *Please don't worry, my love. If you're facing that kind of opponent, I'll fight for you.*

I don't want you to have to fight for me.

You fight what you're good at fighting. I'll fight what I'm good at fighting. Then we both come out alive. Fair? I felt her encouraging smile. I nodded. Even through my mind, I could feel her eyes on me, looking inside of me. *There's more. What's bothering you?*

It's nothing, really.

One more thing about talking through minds. Lies are obvious. Tell me.

I sighed. Was this a secret I could tell her about myself? I considered her and her desire to uphold me. Yes, this was safe with her.

Robert has decided that I won't be his bodyguard anymore, and I'm to find a replacement for him. I shared with her the conversation Robert and I had earlier. *He doesn't want me protecting him, because I need to protect you. But I can't protect you!*

There is more to living than just protecting people, she objected.

It's all I know. It's what my lineage is about. One of my names is Adalward. It means protector of Adal. Adal was the king who established this kingdom and drove out the goblins. I am Count of Adalstienn. My great-great grandfather received the lands as reward for service in saving Adal's life in battle. And he died from it. I rubbed my forehead in frustration, trying to figure out how to explain it better. *I told you earlier how I went to war and how hard that was on my parents. My mother had sworn that she would never let me out of her sight again. But two years after it was over, when I was fifteen, a plague broke out in Adalstienn. My parents made me stay at Robert's castle and refused to let me come home. They chose to go back and help our people, because that's what my family does. My mother swore to me that she would be back for me. My father... before they left, he gave me a hug. I remember the tears in his eyes. He said,* "Mardok... it doesn't look good. If we don't make it..." I stopped and choked. I paused to get a grip on myself. "If we don't make it, become the man I never was. Be better." I never really understood what he was talking about, since he was just about as perfect as a man could be.

I was so angry when they left. I blamed my father for fooling my mother into thinking everything was going to be fine. But I was just lying to myself. She knew, but she was always the optimist.

I never heard from them again, but I did hear about them. They managed to save an untold number of lives before it took them. Robert's father kept me as his own. Robert has been my brother in nearly every way since they day. Protecting him is my job. I owe it to Robert's father to protect his son as he did me. And I owe it to my parents and my entire lineage to give no less than they did.

She paused for a few moments. *Never before have I understood the weight of the burden you carry.* I heard a cricket chirp outside the tent. *As his counselor you would be in a position to protect him from different kinds of threats, much larger threats. You would be able to step in if the nobles try to align against him, and you can watch for perils that are not as overt as the ones you have dealt with in the past.*

The overt threats are so much easier to spot and divert.

I know, but I can help. I have sixty-five years of experience on you.

Ouch. I lay in my bed and pondered this for a while. I really was marrying a woman older than my grandfather. I chuckled. *Will you forgive me for hurting you earlier?*

I already did.

I worked to phrase my next thought with care. *Are you allowed to tell me about the knife you used today? It was an impressive piece of weaponry.*

I wondered how long it would take for you to ask about it. I felt her grin again. *Because we High Fae are the race most equipped to deal with Nahasmen, the dvergr make one of those knives for each newborn. We are taught to wield them alongside our reading and writing lessons. You have a knife that you use as a tool for many things, but my knife is truly a weapon designed for killing. Fortunately, I have only had to use it twice.*

I yawned sleepily.

I heard that. Do you find my conversation so tedious, then?

Never, dearest. It has simply been a very long day.

Then I will let you sleep. Pleasant dreams. Even though she wasn't near me, I could feel her lips on my forehead where she had so often kissed me after our lessons.

I don't have a choice, now. I heard a muffled bubbling sound that I knew was her laugh. I shifted to get comfortable and fell asleep almost instantly.

10

8th of Lar Indar

Meira

I heard the last of the owls hoot as he flew back to his perch. Finally, I thought. It had been a long night. I rubbed my forehead and groaned. My eyes hurt to keep open, but when I closed them I saw him coming after me, his yellow eyes boring into me, sword swinging. I pushed my eyes back open. It was the man we executed yesterday, but he was in Wellid. And the boy he had killed was talking to me, telling me that I would be next.

I leaned against the center pole. I tried to meditate, to push everything from my mind, but the boy wouldn't go. He reached his hand out to me. When I couldn't take it, he knifed me.

My eyes popped open again.

I stood up and walked out of the tent. It was still dark; not even the false dawn disturbed the stars. I stretched my tender arm, looking it over, giving myself something else to think about. I didn't have any clothes with sleeves long enough to cover the bruise, so I knew I was going to have to heal it. Healing others had always been easier for me than healing myself.

I sighed and walked a circuit around the camp, quietly greeting the guards on night shift. They each smiled and spoke well in return. When I had completed the circuit, I returned to my tent. With a bit of energy expended, I was awake enough to avoid slipping back into the dream, but still I didn't dare lay down.

I packed up everything inside my tent and made sure that the floor was clear. Then I looked through my bag until I found my new healing stones. These stones were actually seven different crystals that had been worked until they were round and smooth. The smallest one was the size of my palm, and the largest was double that. The inside of my tent was only just wide enough to set the power circle. I stood in the center of the room waiting for the first of the sun's rays to touch the horizon outside. I closed my eyes and dug my toes into the dirt. I felt the sun break over the edge of the sky and began my song. I could feel the power flowing up from the earth through my toes. The wind found its way into my tent and whipped my hair around carelessly. The muscles in my arm relaxed and the bruise faded, but it did not disappear completely. I sang more forcefully, trying to coax the last bit of the discoloration to vanish, but the wind stilled, and the power flow ebbed.

Disappointed, I picked up my stones and packed them away. My arm didn't look bad, and it was unlikely that most people would notice the faint mark that was left. I shrugged off my chagrin and disassembled my tent.

"I enjoyed the wake-up call," Robert said as he walked up behind me.

"Thank you. That was not its purpose, but I appreciate the compliment." I smiled as brightly as I could manage.

"I want to apologize for Mardok's behavior last night..." he began.

"That is not necessary. He and I had a chance to talk things over. I asked to be taught the way a man would be taught, and not the way a princess would be taught. He respected my wish. He also knows that you're still upset with him about it. I want you to know that you need not worry on my account, but he is taking your request that he find a replacement very hard."

Robert looked shocked. "I thought he understood why I did it."

"He does understand, but that understanding doesn't make the task easier. He wants to be certain that you're safe, and he still feels that he is the most capable to do the job."

"I know. Is your arm okay?"

"I'll recover. Try not to be cross with him today." I smiled again.

"Something's wrong. If it's not your arm..." Robert inquired.

"It's nothing, really."

"I'm not going to insist," he said, "at least, not in an official capacity. But, as a friend... I insist."

I let out a large sigh and leaned my head into his arm. He was a bit surprised but took it well.

"I am so tired." I wanted to cry. "I barely slept, and it was horrible. I'll be fine, really."

"I'm afraid," he said, awkwardly patting my head, "that you're a terrible judge of how well you're doing. Why didn't you sleep? Does it have something to do with Mardok?"

"No," I shook my head and his arm together.

"It was the execution then."

I lifted my head and looked up at him. I'm sure I was the sight to behold. "Yesterday, I told you about the first time. It was far more traumatic than I let on. It was a miracle that I survived. If it weren't for my brother, I would have bled out in a tavern that was on fire."

He gave me a hug. "Well, that certainly puts an exciting spin on that story."

"It's been just over a year. And while my wounds have healed, it feels like… it feels like they're still there. It feels like they would be somehow less painful if they just bled."

"Hello," Mardok's voice came softly behind me.

I reached out my hand to take his arm, then dragged him into a fierce hug. He held me tight.

"That seems less… more… well, less awkward. That." Robert concluded.

I hid my smile. He was such a nice and silly man.

"Where have you been?" I asked Mardok.

"My fault," Robert volunteered. "I sent him to fetch breakfast for the three of us while you were still singing. Figured it served him right for beating you up yesterday." He gestured for us to join him in his receiving room. We settled on the cushions, and Mardok handed out sweet rolls.

"I'm afraid your roll may have accidentally fallen in the dirt on the way back, Robert, but I blew the dust off and picked out most of the rocks, so it should be okay to eat." I couldn't tell whether he was joking or serious.

Robert examined his bread. "I call truce," he said finally and threw the roll back at Mardok. Mardok pulled another roll out of the basket and gave it to Robert. "Are you sure you want to marry this oaf, Meira? He fights dirty."

"I am sure." I paused. "You haven't seen me fight with magic. I can hold my own when I'm not concerned about casualties." I concentrated on the rolls. I had a flash vision of an ulkra aiming his arrow at me, but I repressed the memory. This type of magic was not natural to me, so it was difficult for me to learn and required several years of practice. I floated the rolls out of both their hands up to the ceiling of the tent. I sat comfortably and ate my breakfast while the bread raced around the room, occasionally smacking them in the head, but always keeping out of reach. Robert laughed easily, but I noticed that Mardok took more effort. He gave me a disagreeable look, so I used the magic to toss the bread basket onto his head. His half-mirthful look when he pulled it back off told me I had been successful. "Never think you can win a prank war with a girl who has more than fifty older brothers," I said in fake menace as I stood up and left the tent. The bread fell back to the cushions as soon as the flap closed behind me.

The journey that morning was pleasant after we reassured Amelia that everyone was better. Father met up with us at lunch time. After the briefest of introductions, he stayed only long enough to have Robert and Mardok recount the previous morning's events and take the witness papers to study before he rushed off.

"That was... well, I don't know how to say what that was." Amelia looked to see if Meira would take offense.

"That, dear friends, was my father. He's a bit like a tornado, here and gone again, and Bakarrik help you if you try to stand against him. This is how I remember him for most of my life. He's always king first, and father... sometime later. One does eventually get used to it after forty or fifty years..." Meira said with humor to ease Amelia's discomfort.

"A feat worthy of the undertaking, I'm sure," Robert said.

"Only if you're related to him." Meira looked at me meaningfully. "There are many members of the Fae court who feel, even after ruling for nearly five-and-a-half centuries, that he is unnecessarily brusque. But it is simply the way he approaches things that they find unpleasant. He wishes to get the distasteful business completed as quickly as possible so that he may spend his time on happier pursuits."

"I agree with his motives," Robert said matter-of-factly.

"And someday," Meira pondered aloud, "someday he might actually get to them." She forced a grin. "Have we long to travel today?"

"I thought you were close," Robert said. "He seems really fond of you."

"He's fond of me, and he loves me. But I've spent more time talking to him during this week than I have in the last two months. My oldest brother was always more of a father figure to me than he was."

"I'm sorry to hear that."

"Please, let's carry on. The only thing I hate worse than mourning over my upbringing is having a crowd help me do it."

"Fair enough. Today's journey is going to be the hardest of all. We have to travel until after sunset in order to reach the next stop. Most of the servants will be riding in the wagons and carriages today so that they may be rested enough to get camp set so late."

"Oh." She sounded disappointed.

"We will, however, be riding through what I consider to be the most beautiful view our little country has to offer. There is a point where a canyon falls away from the road and, on a clear day anyway, you can see a beautiful blue bay extending off the ocean. Unfortunately we won't be there at sunrise, but if you ever get the opportunity, you have to take it.

"What is ocean? I have never heard that word before." Meira looked puzzled.

"You don't know what an ocean is? It's like a lake, but much, much larger. And you can sail on it for months."

"Ah, thank you. We call them *rians*, although I'm sure my siblings would know your word for it. Certainly my brother H'gorian does. The spirits of the water are his friends, and they obey him. He is wonderful and kind and giving… just never home. It's hard to find trees in the water, you know." She paused and looked at me like I should know what she was talking about. I shrugged, so she continued, "There is a race of lesser fae called the mer who live in the rians who have the tails of fish and the torsos of humans. They are mischievous, yet cantankerous."

"The mer?" Robert eyed. "Yes, we're familiar with them. They're excellent trading partners. That's why that ocean is called the Mersea." Meria's eyes brightened.

"What is it, Meira?" Amelia asked.

"I didn't know we were next to the Mersea. I probably should pay more attention to geography. I lived many years near the Mersea, in my forest, Oihana. I never did get to see it though."

"Don't you know where you are in the world, Meira?" Amelia gawked.

"This continent one year, that continent the next. I go where I'm told. I asked Father once; I didn't bother to do that again."

"He was upset?"

"No, he gave me a hundred maps and told me to study them. I hate maps. When I want to see something around the world I take the trees, or Corwyn takes me."

"Corwyn?" Mardok inquired. "Your brother who gave you the tent?"

"Yeah, that's him. He and I are the youngest. He's still unbound, so when he's not working for Father he has plenty of time on his hands. Though he's been a lot busier, off doing his own things, the last few years."

"So," Robert remarked carefully, "you grew up you don't know where, and you currently live you don't know where."

"Might be the same place. You'd never know," Amelia added.

Meira giggled. "Yeah, that would be pretty funny."

The afternoon passed quickly. The sun had begun to dip toward the horizon when we reached the lip of the canyon. Robert looked absolutely crestfallen when he saw that there was a heavy fog bank in the valleys on the other side. He started to turn to lead the caravan on its way when Meira jumped off her mount.

"The wind is my friend," she announced before she strode to the edge of the crevasse. She dug her toes into the earth between the giant rocks and began to sing. The music was ethereal and lilting. The wind began to whirl around the caravan. It gathered around her, blowing harder and faster, though it merely tousled her hair like a gentle breeze. Then the tone of her song changed, and the wind flew down the canyon to the valleys beyond. It left with such violence I was afraid that Meira would be blown away with it, but she seemed wholly unaffected by its passing. Within a matter of moments the fog bank was ripped to shreds. The evening in the land beyond the mountains was at once clear and crisp. "I have never seen the Mersea, and I wished to know its wonder," she said simply as she slipped back onto her mount. "The wind will return the fog to its place once we have passed so as not to disturb the natural way of things too significantly."

"The words she uses are familiar, but the meaning she gives them feels very foreign," Robert told me as Meira and Amelia's mounts walked ahead for a moment.

"You get used to it after a while."

11

9th through 11th of Lar Indar

Meira

The few days following were long and uneventful. The party would stop at night near a village or town and set up camp. My nightmares kept interrupting my sleep, but I managed to get enough rest to continue functioning. Every morning Robert would hold court, hear any grievances that needed his attention, and offer his blessings on events that required royal permission. By lunchtime each day, the camp would be packed up and ready to move on.

By sitting in on the audiences, I learned a great deal about how West Haulay worked. Overall, the kingdom ran with simplicity and efficiency. The mayors and magistrates handled most of the day-to-day issues and only involved the nobility and the king when there was either a problem that was outside of their experience or one that affected more than their area of governance.

After the third day of this routine, Mardok informed me that the next day we would arrive at Robert's brother's. A rainstorm throughout the last night muddied the roads and made travel slow and difficult. The entire party was journey-weary and caked in mud by the time we reached our destination. Robert was the only one who seemed to have any energy, and it increased in intensity the closer we came to his brother's house.

"Did you meet Gavin when he was at court last?" he asked Amelia, who had kept her promise to ride with us for the rest of the journey.

"I was away during his last visit." Her horse stepped in a large puddle and splashed mud onto her skirt. "But I've met him before. Truth be told, he was my first love." She tried vainly to shake off the filthy water.

"Oh?" Robert asked. "You had a thing for my brother?"

"He was so charming and kind. And I was a single six-year-old." Amelia gave up on her dress and batted her eyes at Robert.

Mardok rolled in laughter. He lifted his drinking horn and announced, "Here's to the chaos of our youth!"

"Here here!" Robert and several of the guards shouted.

"You probably don't know," she explained to me as the men continued to yell random exhortations at each other, "but I spent a great deal of time with Robert and Mardok when we were younger. My parents were scholars, and they worked for the king. We spent quite a bit of time there."

"So all of you grew up together," I surmised.

"For a while," she explained. "Then there was a giant accident — magic gone awry, I was told — and the king, my father, many others… they were all killed. My mother was so shaken, she lost her mind. We moved in with her sister, and that was the end of it. I've lived there ever since."

"Well, I'm glad you decided to come for the journey," I encouraged.

"I desperately needed to get away. And my aunt is desperate to marry me off. So it works out well for everyone."

"Are you not interested, then?"

"Oh certainly I am, but I won't admit it to her. Honestly, Meira, I'm scared. I don't want to become just a feature in someone's family tree. I want a man who will love me."

"Amelia… I think you're going to be fine. Robert…"

"I'm not going to get my hopes up," she interrupted. "If he's interested…"

"Amelia," I interrupted back, "I know what he and Mardok whisper to each other. He is definitely interested."

"Then why doesn't he say something?" she asked.

"Because… because…" I stumbled through my thoughts. "I don't know. He's a man."

She laughed.

"Just be patient. You've already stolen his heart. I wish I had better advice for you."

"And if he waits forever?"

"Then you get him drunk and ask him yourself." I winked.

"That's so… manipulative," she scolded. "I like it."

Amelia's about to burst, I told Mardok. *She's desperate for Robert to ask her for permission to court her.*

Good news, he answered. *He's just working on the wording. He's got six different speeches in his saddlebag. Can't figure out quite how to say it. Oh, and he's insisting on making it a poem, so it's going to be awful.*

She'll love it, even if it's terrible. It's nice that we won't be the only engaged couple.

Gavin's home was set deep into the trees near Styn, one of the largest cities in West Haulay and the hub of his dukedom. An impressive iron gate marked the turn from the main road to the path that had been cut through it. The gate was standing open, and there were a handful of guards watching for our entourage.

"Greetings, Your Majesty!" The head guard shouted as we came near. "My lord offers his hearty welcome to you and your party." He bowed deeply.

"We accept. We would like a messenger to let our brother know that we had a last-minute addition to our party. This is Ambassador Meira, princess of the High Fae. She is recently betrothed to Count Mardok and wished to join us for a tour of our kingdom."

"Ah, yes, Your Majesty. This message was already brought to his attention by another party."

"Whom? All the court gossips are traveling with us!"

"It was the Ambassador's parents."

"Well, that's excellent." Robert glanced at me questioningly. "I'm looking forward to spending time with them."

"Ambassador, I was also informed to pass along a message to you from your father."

"What is it?"

He indicated that I should dismount, so he could tell me quietly. "I apologize, but the message was not intended for the entire party to hear," he said after I was standing.

"I understand."

"He wishes me to inform you that your entire immediate family will be staying here in the forest until you depart from this place," he whispered. My mother could, of course, have just told me herself, but Father made an effort to make everyone feel useful, even if just to deliver a message.

"I thank you for your diligent performance of your duty, sir. I will take the message into advisement." My friends were staring at me waiting for me to explain, but I just smiled at them as we rode onward to Gavin's home.

When we were finally able to see the mansion, I was awestruck by its loveliness. It was nothing like the imposing fortress where Robert lived. It had an intentional beauty that spoke of many years of care. The gardens surrounding the main structure blended the deliberate plantings naturally into the forest at its border. The whole party seemed to relax as we approached the main door.

"Robert, I am so glad to see you!" a fair man, who could only have been Gavin by his informal address, shouted from the steps of the house. "And Mardok, old friend, I hear you've finally decided to settle down. I can't tell you how happy this makes me. Soon you can commiserate with me about the woes of married life." He smiled easily and clasped hands with both

Robert and Mardok as they dismounted. Robert shook his head at his brother's constant stream of conversation and moved to help Amelia down. Gavin kept up his cheerful chatter without allowing anyone else time to comment. "And this lovely creature must be your betrothed. Allow me to introduce myself. I am Gavin, Robert's unimportant and forgotten older brother." He lent me his hand to climb off my mount. Then he placed my hand on his arm and began to lead us inside. "We poor, irrelevant siblings must stick together, or no one would ever give us any notice." His grin was infectious.

"I wholeheartedly agree, Gavin. And I am Meira, youngest daughter of the Fae king. Did I hear correctly from the guard at your gate that my parents are both here?"

"That is correct. They have been here since last eve. My wife and I have been enjoying their company immensely, though I don't know that I can say the same of some of my servants. They are not used to such remarkable visitors."

"I can understand. I was wondering when I could see them. I have not, as yet, had the chance to introduce Mardok to my mother." We passed through the large entry hall and into what appeared to be a sunny sitting room. Robert, Mardok, and Amelia followed closely behind.

"I sent someone to fetch them when you rode up, so they should be here momentarily." He turned to the others. "My steward, Perseus, should be taking care of getting the rest of the party settled in the guest wing. If you will excuse me for a moment I will have refreshments brought for you and bring my wife in to greet you." He lifted my hand from his arm and kissed it genteelly before he left the room. The quality of the light seemed to dim a bit as he exited.

"My brother's energy is almost overwhelming when you're near him, and when he leaves you almost always feel exhausted," Robert said as he sank unceremoniously into a well-padded chair. Amelia smiled in agreement and sat in the chair nearest to him. Mardok moved next to me to take my hand and we sat on a couch opposite them. A page knocked on the door and brought in the promised refreshments. The water was chilled, and the pastries were sweet, and we enjoyed the repast in silence as we unwound from the ride.

"Meira." I heard my mother's familiar voice before I even knew she was in the room. I looked up and smiled at her. At once I was hugging her and she was smoothing my hair. *You're not well, sweetling. Has the journey been that difficult for you?*

No, I've been having nightmares for the past several days. Restful sleep has been hard to find.

We can talk about them later, so that you may have relief. "Would you like to introduce me to your friends?" she asked aloud. Her voice was as soft and sweet as it had been since I could remember.

"Of course, Mother." I pulled her gently away from the door and over to where my friends now stood, having risen from their seats while I was greeting her.

"This is my mother, Lilliana, Queen of the Fae. Mother, this is King Robert Everet, Countess Amelia Rosen, and my betrothed, Sir Mardok Adlar." I knew that my protocol was flawed in the introductions, but I didn't care. This was my mother, after all. "Where's Father? I thought he would come down with you."

"He was in the middle of his meditations when you

arrived. He will come when he has finished." There was a slight tone of worry in her voice as she said this, but it passed before the others noticed. I made a note to myself to ask her about it later.

"It is an honor to make your acquaintance, Majesty," Robert began.

"Please, call me Lilliana. You are friends of my daughter and mine by extension."

"Lilliana, then, I wanted to tell you how much of a pleasure it has been getting to know your daughter." Robert and Amelia stood together and talked with my mother. I looked at Mardok, who seemed to be trying to come up with something to say. I knew that Mother would wait to address him until he approached her. I moved over to his side and squeezed his hand.

"I would like to have your blessing on our marriage," he blurted suddenly, interrupting Robert's description of the muddy road conditions that slowed us. Mother arched her eyebrow at him.

"You have already been marked as Fae friend by my husband and received his permission; why do you ask this of me?" She held his gaze.

"Meira has two parents. She would not be the woman she is, the woman I love, without your influence. I know that I do not *need* your permission to wed her, but I would like to have your blessing to proceed." She looked into his eyes, searching to be certain he was speaking truth.

Did you ask him to speak thus, Meira? she asked privately.

I would not dishonor him or you by doing so. He is intelligent and has excellent instincts. His words are his own.

"You have my blessing, and since you were respectful enough to ask for it, I will grant you a boon." Her eyes became unfocused. "There will soon come a time when you seek someone and will have no way to find him. Set your feet to the evening sun, and look for the city of the horse." Mother's eyes refocused. "Let us sit and wait for our host." Robert and Amelia reclaimed their previous seats, and my mother joined Mardok and me on the couch. I worried over her boon for a bit before I pushed it to the back of my mind. We chatted lightly over the remaining refreshments while Robert nagged Mardok until he wrote down Mother's words.

A page opened the door and held it while Gavin pushed a pretty young woman in a wheeled chair into the room. "Thank you for your patience, friends. Ambassador, Countess, I would like to introduce my wife, Julia." He pushed the chair over to where we were sitting. He slid a pair of sphinx-marked books onto a shelf and drew up a chair of his own to sit next to his wife.

"I am so pleased to have you visit." Julia's smile was genuine. "Amelia, I regret that I have not been able to make your acquaintance previously. My health has not permitted me to travel to court since Robert's coronation, though I do have vague memories of you when we were little. Meira, I cannot tell you how much I have enjoyed getting to know your mother. I understand that you have captured Mardok's heart—a difficult task that one." Her conversation was just as bubbly as her husband's.

"You managed to capture it when we were children, as I recall." Robert teased.

"Yes, and yours as well," Mardok took up the game. "I remember we used to fight for her notice, but then your impertinent older brother stole her attention from us, and we were callously left to grieve for her."

"Well," Robert replied, "now you have someone of your own to console you, and I'm still left to envy my brat of a brother."

"Then why do you not ask Amelia to help assuage your wound," I challenged. "I dare say she could do the job affably." Amelia stared intently at her clasped hands as her cheeks turned pink.

"Ho-ho!" Gavin burst out laughing. "I do believe that Meira can hold her own in your and Robert's games, eh Mardok?"

"I suspected it all along." He winked at me. "Did you know, Gavin, she actually laughs at our jokes?" Amelia was attempting to regain her composure, sneaking glances at Robert to gauge his reaction.

"No," Julia responded in mock horror. "What would people say? If it got out that someone thinks you're funny it would ruin you."

"We thought of that," Robert said. "We decided that we had to make her our friend, so no one would think anything of it. And Amelia's recently joined in our fun as well, and I dare say her jokes were..." he looked at Amelia and rethought, "mature?"

"Robert, I'm sure they were only off-color after they passed from your ear to your mouth," Gavin clarified.

"No," I assured him, "no, it's all her." The men all shut up and looked around the room.

"Silencing the males is a wonderful act of kindness," Mother commented.

"With this many conspirators," Julia said to Robert and Mardok, "we could actually end up with some pleasant company instead of the repetitive litany that you two scoundrels have regaled us with for years."

"Our reputation has truly been sullied. Should we eschew their company?" Mardok asked Robert, emphasizing the word 'eschew.'

"I believe it is too late for that, chum. Perhaps we should stick around and try to convince them that we are still as terrible as we know we are."

"I yield to your wisdom, oh wise and fearless leader, without whom I would be at a loss for direction." Julia and Gavin rolled their eyes, Amelia covered her mouth with her hand, I tried to suppress my laughter, and my mother was smiling.

"Of course you would be at a loss. My own brother was lost for six years until I was born. Now we must be certain that we firmly establish our lack of talent for Meira's parents before they leave, otherwise they will lead the nation of Fae to believe that we are actually *famusing*."

"Famusing?" Julia inquired.

"Yes," Robert replied. "It's 'funny' and 'amusing' together—the worst of both worlds."

"Sensible. Continue," she waved her hand and sipped her tea.

"Naturally," Robert continued. "We did a very poor job demonstrating our famusement for Meira, so we must work extra hard to de-famuse her parents."

Mardok turned to look at me. "I know he smiles at you, since you're his little girl, but can you imagine what would happen if your father actually laughed?"

"His face would crack," my mother said it in such a serious tone that everyone turned to look at her. She sat looking very proper with her hands folded in her lap. Then she started to laugh. I love to hear her laugh. It's like millions of bells are tinkling at once.

Mardok

We were still laughing when the door burst open and Meira's father walked in. His curious expression caused everyone to laugh harder for a few moments until we could manage to regain control of ourselves.

"Come in, dear, and meet King Robert and Countess Amelia. We have been getting acquainted while you were meditating." Lilliana gestured for him to sit in the last open chair next to her.

"Robert I have met briefly. Amelia, I am pleased to meet you. Please call me Matthias. I wish to extend an invitation to all of you present to join my family for our evening meal. Gavin and his lovely wife have graciously allowed the family to stay in the forest surrounding his home, and we have prepared it for a celebration. After all, we have a great deal to celebrate, do we not?" Matthias' expression and smile were well-practiced.

"It would be our great pleasure to join you. When should we be ready?" Robert spoke for everyone.

"I will meet you at sunset at the door to the back garden. Meira, fetch your bag and go ahead with your mother. She needs your help." Meira's look as she nodded to his command was confused, but she did as her father said.

"Well, then," Gavin said as Meira and Lilliana left, "we don't have much time. I'm sure that the travelers will want a quick bath before we leave to wash away the dust and grime of the road. I'll show you to your room, Amelia; Robert and Mardok already know where they need to go."

"Thank you," Amelia replied, as Gavin led her out into the hall.

"Robert, could you take me back to my room so I can freshen up?" Julia asked sweetly.

"Of course, dear sister." They left as well.

It occurred to me at that moment that the exodus had been orchestrated.

"We need to talk, Mardok, and you need to prepare for this evening. Come with me." Matthias' tone was both commanding and compelling. "Meira has explained the Fae bond to you, I know," he began as we walked to my room. "However, I do not believe that she has explained our bonding ceremony. It is very simple; do not worry. You will stand together in front of your friends and her family, and she will share the last of the bonding magic with you. You will both immediately be so overwhelmed by the bond that you will not be aware of anything else for the rest of the night. Your relationship will be consummated while you are overwhelmed, so as soon as the bond is made, the two of you will be transported to a place that has been prepared for you where you can be alone." I remained calm with a serious expression while I attempted to gauge which of us was more uncomfortable with this particular conversation. Clearly it was me. Perhaps this was because he had given this speech many, many, many times before.

"Why are you explaining this to me now? We were planning on having the wedding when we returned to Robert's castle."

"Meira doesn't have that long." His voice was grave.

"I'm sorry, sir, but I honestly don't understand." I shook my head in confusion.

"The bond has already begun its last stage. Do not ask me how I know; just trust me. Once the last stage is begun there is a limited amount of time before it must be completed, or it will be utterly destroyed. Even amongst solely Fae pairings that time is short."

"So, since she has chosen me the time is even shorter."

"Exactly. She does not have the experience to judge the timing for these things yet. And although she is learning from her mistakes, this is one that I cannot allow her to make. It would destroy her. So the celebration tonight is your bonding ceremony. I hope you're supportive of spontaneous life-changing experiences. And if you're not… well, it's a little late for that. You can still have a human wedding for the sake of appearances when you return home, and my beloved and I will participate in it to uphold your reputation amongst your people. But in reality your life with my daughter will begin tonight."

I was in a haze while Matthias helped me prepare. I wondered, briefly, what my father would have said about the unconventional methods of the Fae. He likely would have approved of the expedience. My thoughts returned to the conversation I had with Amos right before I chose to pursue a life with Meira.

"Amos!" I said suddenly.

"What was that?" Matthias stopped as he was handing me a green tunic of the same material as the dress that Meira wore the night I accepted her bond.

"Amos needs to be there. He is the closest person I have to
a father, since my own parents died when I was young. He
should be there."

"I'll see to it that he is present," Matthias said patiently as
he continued with the preparations.

Once I was cleaned and clothed we hurried to meet the
others at the garden entrance. When we joined them Matthias
spoke softly to Julia and Gavin for a few moments while
Perseus and Amos stood stoically behind them.

"Would you like to fill me in on what's going on?" Robert
whispered to me. He was holding Amelia on his arm and the
two of them looked like they had dressed to match
intentionally.

"We're going to a party," I answered.

"All ready?" Matthias asked. Nods answered him. "Here
we go." He pulled a short, carved stick from a pouch on his
belt and tossed it onto the ground. The stick flashed with light,
and the world seemed to bend around us for a few moments.
When it stopped we were in the forest amongst hundreds of
Fae.

My head was reeling. I felt as though I had just been
thrown from a horse, stuck for several seconds in that
disorienting moment right before hitting the ground. Were it
not for a pair of hands to catch me, I likely would have fallen.
Four Fae were standing around us, each stabilizing myself,
Amos, Amelia, and Robert. Apparently Gavin and Perseus
needed no such assistance, and certainly Julia wasn't falling
down anytime soon.

"Smashing fun, isn't it, Robert?" Gavin announced before

my eyes had refocused. "He doesn't even need a wand to do that. Some of the Fae can do it whenever they want."

The majority of the Fae resembled Meira's parents with dark hair and eyes and pale skin. About one in ten had wings like Meira. There were a few whose hair was a very fine gold, but only one had Meira's copper curls and gold skin.

"Mardok," Matthias continued, "let me introduce you to Meira's grandmother, my mother, Galianna."

I bowed low. "I am honored to meet you. I can see that Meira favors your line."

"It is my joy that she does. Anyone present would happily claim her relation, but I am the only one who does not have to say it for it to be known." She seemed genuinely pleased that I had commented on it.

"I apologize, Mother, but Mardok must get to his place." Matthias rushed me past several dozen Fae to a clearing in the trees. It was large enough that the sky could be seen overhead. The sun was setting, and the early stars were already visible. There were lanterns hanging from the trees surrounding the clearing. Robert, Amelia, Gavin, Julia, Perseus, and Amos had already been ushered to a place between two of the trees. Amos wore a smug grin that told me he was genuinely pleased with this outcome of events. The spaces between the other trees and even branches of the trees themselves were filled with the Fae who were there to witness the bonding.

The assembly grew quiet. The trunk of the largest tree on the edge of the clearing split open. Meira stepped out of it and it closed behind her as if it had never moved. She was wearing a layered golden dress that glowed as she did in the lantern light. As she stepped forward, her eyes fixed on mine. She was in every aspect a goddess. I saw nothing else around, as just the image of her filled my entire vision. In a single moment my mind processed every detail and then held on to it for an eternity.

Meira's eyes were accented with tiny jewels. Her ears held intricate gold jewelry. About her neck was a torque of silver and colored metals. Her dress was layer upon layer of lace and a sheer material I could not identify. Merely the lace would have taken a year to create, and it appeared to be actual gold thread.

We met in the center of the clearing, and I took both of her hands in mine. Meira opened her wings, spilling the red and yellow light of the torches in wavering patterns across the ground. Then she kissed me. I thought for a brief moment that the kiss was supposed to be at the end of the ceremony, but such petty details were quickly drowned out of my mind. I closed my eyes and held her close. Moments later, I could feel the magic surge through me, overwhelming what few other senses remained. Then, like stepping into a waterfall, I disappeared into the embrace of our bond, and everything except Meira fell away.

12

12th of Lar Indar

Meira

It went as my mother had said. When I kissed him we were both so overwhelmed by the magic that nothing else mattered. And while later I was glad that we had been transported, out of the consideration for the humans attending the celebration, at the time the urgency of our passion was so great it would not have mattered if we had stayed in the midst of our friends and family.

We held on to each other as we passed through the waves of urgent and wild passion till they ebbed and became gentle and tender. Our souls rose up and crashed together until they could no longer be differentiated.

When the sun rose the next morning, we lay wrapped in each other's arms. Neither of us had slept, but the exhilaration of the bonding kept us from being tired.

"I wonder if Robert and Amelia enjoyed the festivities," I pondered aloud, only now caring to think of something beyond our bond.

"Why wouldn't they?" Mardok asked in a playful banter.

"Oh, no reason. The drink served at these occasions is like

wine, but it's made from honey and laced with a weak love potion." I chuckled.

"You're making them fall in love? I didn't think they needed the help. Besides, manipulating Robert usually isn't a good idea."

"No, that isn't what it's made for. It merely amplifies feelings that already exist. Many a bonding relationship has begun at a bonding ceremony. For my people the results of last night will take several years to come to fruition, but Robert and Amelia's relationship could begin very soon. Mother promised that she would explain these things to them and provide an alternative drink should they choose not to partake."

"Ah, I see." He put a hand behind his head and stared at the sky for a moment. "I wonder if they did."

I stared along with him for several long moments, allowing the concept of Robert's potential future to sink into his mind and begin to trace a smirk across his cheek.

"We'd better get back to Gavin's house," I interrupted. "We have to keep up the façade that nothing has changed for another day, at least until the nobles leave for home. We need them to believe that I'm leaving with my parents to prepare for our wedding."

"I don't know if I have the strength to pretend that I'm the same man I was yesterday," he groaned. He tried grabbing me to convince me to stay longer. I pretended to give in and moved to kiss him, but as soon as he relaxed I flew out of reach. "You're a cruel woman, Meira."

I laughed. "I promise I'll make it up to you tonight after the nobles leave, but things won't go well for us if we're seen coming from the forest together so early."

"Or the way we're dressed." He pulled his tunic on over his trousers. He carelessly tossed me a caterpillar from his shoulder. "One of your friends, I believe?"

"Too young," I responded, looking into the caterpillar's pleasant face. "He's gorgeous, Mardok, but he won't be speaking until he..." He wrapped his arm around my waist and kissed my neck.

"No, my lover," I flashed my best smile at him while disentangling myself from his grasp. Rising further into the trees I placed the caterpillar on a fat green leaf. "We have to do that later."

"Oh, I certainly intend to," he batted back at me.

"My family's still here. They can help teleport you to your room in the manor. I can be seen walking in alone since I was seen leaving with my mother last night, but we still need to hurry. Come on." I pulled him from our small, sheltered clearing. I couldn't help skipping and humming as we moved through the forest.

"You're far too happy for so early in the morning, dear sister." A head appeared, hanging upside down from the tree to my immediate right.

"Good morning to you as well, Corwyn. I was hoping to find you."

He swung down from his perch. "I think you're just trying to disturb my sleep."

"Yes, my first thought on the morning after my bonding

was how I could most annoy my brother." I stood with my arms crossed.

"They say that admission is the first step to recovery. So, what's the plan for the day?"

"We need your help. Could you blink Mardok back into his room in the manor?"

"Having a secret affair with your new mate? Don't tell Father."

"We have to keep it secret from the humans. Their marriage rituals are very different, and they require at least several weeks of publicly known engagement."

"Humans are funny like that. Well, if it's intrigue you're seeking, I'm in."

"By the way, Mardok, this is Corwyn. He's only four years older that I am. We used to get into trouble together since we are the youngest two." Corwyn stuck his tongue out at me but held his hand out to Mardok.

"You'll have to tell me about it sometime, brother." Mardok smiled and shook Corwyn's hand. "So this is the owner of the tent?"

I shot Mardok a look of panic.

"Tent?" Corwyn stared at me. "You're the one who stole my tent? I blamed Hlen since he took it last time. But it was you all along!"

I grinned sheepishly at him.

"You're gonna owe me big time for that, LITTLE sister. I

was stuck sleeping out in the rain last week, because of you." He finished scolding me by wagging his finger in front of my nose. Then he was over it. He turned to Mardok, "Good to meet you, Brother. In all honesty, you're unlike any sibling I've ever had. And a bit..." He lifted his hand up to the top of Mardok's head. "… quite a bit taller."

"It wasn't intentional, honestly," Mardok answered.

"I think you grew up that tall just to show us up. So, you need a quick way into your room. I assume that Meira has spoken into your mind, yes?"

Mardok nodded.

"Great, that makes the process easier, and far less likely to put various parts of you in different places. Now picture your room in your mind, the more details you recall, the better. I'm going to look into your thoughts to see what you see. It'll feel different than when Meira does it, but the effect is similar." Corwyn's eyes closed, and I could tell they were talking about the contents of Mardok's room. When the two of them blinked out of the path, I turned to fly to the edge of the forest.

I had not realized how much I had missed flying on the trip here. I fluttered in the vague direction of Gavin's house, taking as long as I could, and still the trees ended too quickly. I landed on the edge of the garden where the manicured shrubs were still tall enough to hide me from the house and walked through the maze of flower beds toward the manor. When I reached the door, I took directions to the kitchen from a passing maid.

By the time I arrived Mary and Gavin's head cook were busy making preparations for the noon meal, and breakfast was laid out in trays for the servants to take up to the guests. Mary waved me over.

"Ye've already 'ad everything 'ere, except'n th' sausage. Ah won't be describin' zactly how tis made because it isn't very appetizing, but tis pork with pepper. Ah put a small portion on ye tray ov'r here. And th' king has asked that ye join 'im and 'is brother and a few others for breakfast in th' solarium. Tasha 'ere was about ta 'ead ov'r there with th' trays; she c'n show ye th' way." Mary was more hurried than usual, but I knew that the luncheon was supposed to be a grand affair in the great hall, and she had a mountain of work to do.

I followed Tasha as she pushed the cart of breakfast trays through the maze of hallways and into a room full of windows. Robert, Gavin, and Julia were already there sitting around a square table. I thanked Tasha for her help, took my tray to the table, and sat down next to Julia.

"Good morning," I said, as Tasha set out the other trays around the table. "Who else are we waiting for?" I asked Robert.

"Mardok was still changing when I knocked a few minutes ago, Amelia's maid said she was almost ready, and I sent an invitation to your parents, but I haven't heard back as to whether or not they'll be coming."

"You likely will not. They will either come or not, but they won't send word."

"Well then, let's not wait so the breads don't get cold." Robert and Gavin began eating with gusto, whereas Julia picked delicately at her fruit.

"Julia," I began softly, "might I ask the nature of your

illness?"

"Certainly. It's no secret; people just don't often talk about it anymore. Do you know the story of how Robert's father died?" I shook my head no. "I'll start back farther, then.

"I lived at court when I was young. Robert, Gavin, their sister Sapphira, and Mardok were my playmates. I was always a little frail and took ill easily. The king and my parents had long planned for me to marry one of the princes. They weren't particular which one; they just wanted to have a binding alliance between our two families. My constant illnesses worried them, so they began to look for doctors and healers who might have some idea how to make me healthier. I was confined to my rooms, I was moved to different rooms, my diet was changed, I had to have lots of exercise, I was restricted to bed rest. There was so much conflicting advice that they gave up listening for a while. It was a reprieve for me, but it didn't last very long."

Mardok and Amelia entered the solarium together. Just the sight of him brought a great wash of tingling over me. He helped her to her seat next to Robert and then sat himself beside me.

"About six months after the doctors stopped coming," Julia continued, "a woman showed up at the castle. She requested an audience with the king on the premise that she had miraculous healing abilities. My parents and Amelia's were summoned; Amelia's father was a scholar, and the king wanted him to hear the woman's story to verify it. They all listened to the woman explain how she woke up one day with healing powers and that she only had a desire to help. Since she didn't want to try to change my habits or environment again, and perhaps because she didn't ask for money, they decided to let her try.

"It did not go well. When she was in the middle of the healing ceremony, there was an earthquake. Several large beams fell from the ceiling and landed on all of us. My father-in-law, my parents, and Amelia's father were killed, along with many others. I was fortunate to have survived, but one of the beams fractured my spine. My legs have been paralyzed ever since."

"I'm truly sorry for your losses." I said to my friends. Amelia was silent for a few moments, lost in memories of sadness. Gavin placed his hand on his wife's shoulder, and Robert intentionally ignored the conversation.

"But, that's enough sad talk for the morning." Julia said abruptly and cheerfully. "I want to talk about last night."

Mardok

"I agree. That party was amazing." Robert took up the subject with enthusiasm. I have to say, Meira, you and Mardok missed the best parts."

"No, we didn't." I said quietly as I took hold of Meira's hand. *No, you didn't,* she repeated into my mind, her knee touching mine. Knowing glances and smirks were passed around the room.

"The drink was phenomenal. Don't you think so, Robert?" Gavin slapped Robert on the back, causing his head to bob back and forth.

"It was… unique." He tossed a piece of sausage into his mouth and continued while chewing it. "It was surprising, but not unpleasant."

"'Not unpleasant', is that all?" Amelia said with a fake pout, but her eyes were twinkling.

"So, have you made it official, yet?" I asked.

"No, but I'll make the courtship announcement at today's luncheon," Robert answered. For Robert to make this announcement was no small matter. He would not be permitted to back out unless a serious flaw were found in Amelia. Knowing her for as long as I had, I knew that no such flaw existed.

"I have to say, Meira, I didn't actually believe you when you told us that you had eighty-nine siblings. I can't remember how many times a Fae was introduced as a brother or sister of yours," Robert remarked.

"You should be happy that the forest here is not large enough to hold all of my cousins," Meira replied. Thankfully, several of them are on Ehiza right now."

"Ehiza?" I asked.

"Yes, it's a Fae hunt. Each year every High Fae goes on Ehiza. Basically, it's a way to demonstrate your skill luring a predator into a magical trap."

"That sounds rather entertaining," Robert said. "You don't capture prey… just predators?"

"Well, not exclusively. Anything dangerous is acceptable, but wild fae predators are preferred. There are certain rules about what you can and can't hunt, of course. Sentient creatures aren't permitted, for example, only wild creatures and fae. Father had to release more than one satyr or centaur that an over-zealous hunter captured."

"Is that to keep down the predator population then?" Amelia inquired.

"I don't think so." Meira pondered. "You know, I really don't know. We've just always done it. We do keep track of who captures the most dreadful things. The winner used to get to keep the Summoning Jewel until the next year."

"Used to… but not anymore?" Amelia asked.

"Nope. A pixie stole it."

Robert chucked. "Wow… gotta looooooove those pixies."

Meira smiled. "Well, they do play, too."

"Really?"

"Sure. When they see that someone has a trap open, they try to trigger it without being caught, so we don't get anything. The thing is, you're only allowed to set the trap once per year. So if a pixie gets to it first, you're out."

"Not exactly like regular hunting."

"Oh, no, not at all."

"So, my dearest princess, what's the most dreadful thing you've ever caught?"

"I caught a yuyu when I was fifteen. But no one liked that I didn't have to work to get it. So I've basically been banned from playing, unless someone else gets in over their head."

"A yuyu?"

"Yeah."

Robert waited patiently until Meira caught on that he had no idea what she was talking about.

"It's a giant sea monster. Lots of teeth and a large tail with a stinger."

"Wow…"

"It wasn't hard. I just asked it to come into the ring of stones."

I snickered. Only my lover could capture a sea monster with a simple request.

"Well what do you do with them when you catch them?" Robert's fascination was growing.

"They're put into the Kaiola, where they sleep."

"Until?" I asked.

"We don't ever let them go that I'm aware. I just know that they're perfectly okay."

"Interesting," Robert stated. "Hunting without the feast or the trophy."

"Or the poor dead animal," she quipped, giving him the your-hunting-hurts-my-friends look.

"Fair enough," he replied sheepishly.

"Not to change the subject," Amelia remarked. We all laughed quietly. "Some of your family members were definitely more memorable than others."

"Terdangia…." Robert mused.

"Oldest sister," Meira waved.

"If you go by her own assessment," Robert chuckled, "she should be in charge of the Fae."

"If you go by her assessment," she corrected, "she should be in charge of the gods." Robert and Amelia nodded their consensus. *Remind me not to tell you about her.*

"Kigera was…. unique," Robert added.

"She didn't, did she?" Meira asked.

"Bring her cats?" Amelia ventured.

"Oh dear." Meira hid her face in her hand.

Amelia and Robert began laughing.

Cat lady? I inquired of Meira.

Classic, but her story is a sad one, she replied.

"It was completely hilarious," Robert began, "She spent the entire evening distraught with one of your brothers about her missing cat. We thought perhaps she had lost it in the woods until we found out it was a tiger."

I glanced at Meira in disbelief.

"Kigera and her kitties," Meira shrugged.

"Her brother insisted it wasn't his fault," Amelia continued, "that his precious pet wouldn't have harmed her cat unless her cat started it."

"I need to meet this Bubbles," Robert grinned.

Meira bolted upright. I could hear her mind babbling excitedly, but I wasn't able to make out anything she was saying.

"Malachi's here? And he brought Bubbles and Fluffy?!?!?" She nearly tossed the table on us in her enthusiasm. "I haven't seen Malachi in over a year! And he hasn't brought Bubbles and Fluffy in forever!" I held out my arm to hold her in one place to prevent her from bouncing her way off her chair.

I got a fuzzy mental picture of her playfully dancing, tossing around a furry creature of some sort. I tried to focus on it, but the static coming from her mind was impossible for me to penetrate.

"You'll have to introduce us sometime, then," Robert interjected, picking up his cup and wiping up the tea that had spilled all over his arm. Meira nodded a thousand times.

Care to enlighten me? I asked her, finally able to make way through to her mind.

You'll see. Her response was joyful.

We passed the morning with the other two couples telling us various excerpts from the night's festivities. Apparently, after the first toast that happened when we were teleported (most fortuitous bit of magic, that), Robert leaned over and kissed Amelia full on the mouth. And with Gavin and Julia as witnesses he asked her permission to begin courtship, even though it was a little out of order. Shortly before lunch, when Meira's parents and Corwyn joined us, they again congratulated Robert on his tremendous good fortune in a bride-to-be.

We strolled the grounds and took part in the perfunctory mingling that is mandatory when nobility congregate. I am convinced that every single one of them hated it as much as we did, but no one was willing to suggest that they didn't find it utterly fascinating. My evidence was in every sour face.

On a happier note, I observed that Baron Thaddeus had met his match in espionage. While he was slinking about, maintaining a rather bumbling surveillance on us, Perseus was keeping a far shrewder and less conspicuous eye on him.

There is a reason that newly bonded couples tend to withdraw from public for a time, Meira mentioned, as a large group of servants bustled down the hall we were walking. They had lunch preparations and forced us to stand apart briefly until they had all passed. *I really would rather just spend the rest of the day alone with you.*

Me too. At least we get to be together for the journey home. I covered her hand with mine as she re-took my arm.

We'll still have plenty of company.

Well, sure — Robert and my men. But they all already know, so our spending time together won't bother them. And, since Corwyn will be wanting his tent back, it would be ungentlemanly for me not to offer you the use of mine. I was grinning like a love-sick idiot, and I knew it. We entered the dining hall.

"Has Robert explained the seating arrangements for the luncheon?" I asked Meira's parents.

"He did. It is as I expected. Rules of court for humans and High Fae are somewhat universal," Matthias explained. "Some of the other races can be difficult to accommodate. Formal politeness with the sphinx actually involves licking each others' hair. Meira, dear, you'll need to untangle your arm from his to sit with us for the duration of the meal." He said in a low voice, "I've been talking with several of the nobles, and I can't say I find many of them to be particularly trustworthy."

"They're nobles, Matthias," I answered. "Deception and backstabbing is what they do best."

"I've never understood the human propensity for kings to maintain such figures as their subordinates."

"I don't know for other kingdoms, but in Robert's case he didn't get to select the dukes or most of the counts. They were in power first, and a good number of them don't like him at all."

"Then be certain he watches his back."

"I've been watching it for him for many years."

I had to relinquish Meira to sit with her parents while I sat at my customary place on Robert's right. The court members couldn't decide what was more interesting to talk about—Meira's family, or the fact that Amelia was seated to Robert's left. Since court protocol was different with the presence of two ruling kings, two long tables had been placed on the raised portion of the dining room to face each other. Robert and his highest-ranking court members and chosen others sat at one table, and Matthias and the few family members that chose to come into the house sat at the other. I ended up having to look diagonally down the tables to catch Meira's eye as she was seated to the right of her father. The other nobles, who were not so lucky as to have a seat at one of the head tables, had to suffice with eating in the lower dining area around the room.

Once everyone was seated in their proper places, the servants began bringing out the vegetable course, the first of many that were planned. Numerous hushed questions were directed by the Fae into the ears of the servants as each course was served. Meira seemed busy interpreting the various items that she was familiar with, and as the main dish was placed in front of them Meira's gentle voice entered my mind. *Father would like to know that the animals of the forest were prepared properly.* I nodded visibly and whispered clarification to Robert, who raised an eyebrow. Apparently, the information Matthias sought met with approval, and the Fae ate heartily.

After clearing off the main course and before the servants brought out desserts, Robert rose and made his official greetings and announcement of peaceful accord to the Fae. He reiterated the offer to give the Fae basically whatever they wanted, to which Matthias stood and accepted his promise of goodwill with gratitude. Matthias also pronounced his blessing on Meira's and my engagement and his intentions to attend the wedding upon our return to Robert's home. Robert made his formal request of Amelia to begin courting her and was accepted amid the applause of the entire room, the servants more enthusiastic than most.

Baron Thaddeus, who had been intentionally relegated to an unpleasant corner, looked rather upset by the news that Amelia was now spoken for, as noted by his single obligatory clap. I also noticed that he spent a great deal of time openly observing Meira's family. He studied each member carefully as if searching for someone in particular. I didn't see any recognition in his expression, so whomever he was looking for may not have been present at the table. When the affairs of state were concluded, Thaddeus politely excused himself.

Lunch was excellent, and I enjoyed it immensely. And from the thoughts coming from my parents and siblings, they clearly did as well. After lunch the royal parties took a constitutional through the garden. Amelia strolled lightly with Robert, enjoying the security of his arm, while I clung as tightly as permissible to my Mardok.

Ahead of me I could see Corwyn, standing near the entrance to the forest. Behind him several personnel from Gavin's house were installing posts. On the ground lay a freshly painted sign with the words, "Forest of Lilliana, Fay Goddess."

Corwyn, tell me this wasn't your idea.

Me? He was incredulous. *You know what Mother would think of that.*

As if on cue, Mother stepped out of the house with Father at her side. All the background murmuring I could hear with my mind ceased instantly. Every Fae eye turned to see her. Several humans, noticing their Fae companions, also turned to look. Mother was busy laughing and bantering with Julia but quieted as she noticed everyone was staring at her.

What? she asked openly. Not one of her children dared respond or meet her eye.

My new husband, not being as skilled in the art of deflecting a direct question from my mother, answered, *Good Mother, I believe they are concerned with the text of the sign being hung over the path to the forest.*

I could feel the communal trepidation over what was coming. Three of my less courageous siblings blinked away.

Mother scanned over Gavin's workers who were just picking up the sign with the offending words. First, her eyes grew large; then they narrowed. Her skin tone grew pink with perturbation. So deep her reaction, she began to look human.

She parted her lips as if to speak but was interrupted by Father, who channeled her intent as usual during moments such as these.

"Hold it still," he spoke softly, directing his command into the workers minds. Then he lifted his finger toward the sign and began cutting. A flame burned slowly through the words "of Lilliana, Fay Goddess." Pleased with his edit, Father smiled toward his wife.

She stared in silence, her skin calming back to silver. Then producing a mild pout, she tilted her head. Father rolled his eyes and unburned the words "of Lilliana." Mother's smile returned, and she picked up her conversation with Julia as though nothing had happened.

Ambassador, Father spoke to me, *please relay to the king the proper spelling of our people.*

Of course. Mother, please know that they meant well. To them the term "goddess" is actually a compliment.

I do, dear. Don't fret over it. I smiled once again, confident that the matter was settled.

We all walked through the gate, where I saw that Malachi was waiting for us just inside the tree line. He was fresh from some adventure of his, as his various layers of armor were battered and broken, with strips hanging in tatters. Even a few magical pieces, contrived by Father's personal masters of the forge, were broken. I ran to him and hugged him tightly around his chest. He stiffened as he always does in response to physical affection, but after only a moment he attempted a smile and patted me on the head. I grinned.

"Robert, Amelia, Gavin, Julia, and Mardok, this is my oldest brother Malachi, most virtuous and honorable of all Fae." I untangled my hand from one of Malachi's loose armor lacings. "Malachi, this is His Majesty Robert Everet, his intended Amelia, his brother Gavin, Gavin's wife Julia and my new mate, Mardok."

As I was making the simple introductions, I spied Baron Thaddeus. He was leaning his head around a bush in the garden. When he saw Malachi step from the trees to join us, he turned on his heel and ran back toward the house, tripping over a short hedge and nearly barreling over a noble woman in the process. He hopped on one foot through the door and out of sight.

What's with the little fat man?

That's Baron Thaddeus. He's a creep.

Duly noted. So, why's he running?

I don't know, brother; you seem to have that effect on creeps of all kinds.

Thanks... I think.

I paused, growing more impatient by the moment.

So?

So what?

So where are they?

Malachi looked into my eyes, and I put on the best pleading show I could manage—eyes, lashes, pouty lip, tilted neck, the works. I learned it from Mother. Three, two, and there was the smile. I knew my Malachi.

Fine, Firefly, your darling pets are waiting inside for you. I told them you would be coming.

I jumped in excitement and bolted through the gate into the forest. First, to find a treat for each of them.

Mardok

The moment Meira left the view of the garden, she jumped into the air and flew away.

"Well… It's good to meet you again, Brother."

"Indeed."

"You've met?" Robert inquired.

"Yes. The day Meira came to the castle for the first time, this rather imposing figure threatened me with tremendous bodily harm should I take poor care of his sister."

"I haven't reneged on our agreement."

"You know, I have one of those super star marks on my hand now."

"That won't protect you from me."

"I was afraid of that. If it helps, I'm rather fond of her."

"As long as she stays fond of you, I will be, too."

"I was thinking about following her and meeting these pets you brought."

"Please do."

It took a while to find her. Meira was holding two rabbits, snuggling them. She grinned at me.

"Fluffy and Bubbles?"

Meira smiled and nodded, poking her nose between the rabbits again. I couldn't imagine how it would be possible for rabbits to take on the likes of …. Kigera.

"Are they fire breathing or something?"

"Of course!" Meira chirped, flipping their ears.

She had to be kidding of course. But then again, I had seen stranger things among her family.

"Mardok," Robert's voice called from behind me.

"Over here, sire!" I called back, whipping around to find him. Meira strolled off while I walked back to Robert, who was just entering the clearing, along with Amelia, Corwyn, and Malachi. Gavin and Julia, I noticed, did not attempt to follow Meira's sudden flight through the trees, but Perseus had decided to join us as well.

"Robert," I said, drawing within normal earshot. "I have solved the mystery of Fluffy and Bubbles."

"Oh really," he responded.

"Yes, they appear to be fire-breathing rabbits."

Corwyn, who had been tossing nuts and berries into his mouth, choked on one. He began coughing violently.

"Are you okay, friend?" Robert asked, smacking him on the back soundly several times. Amelia appeared concerned.

"Yes, quite fine, thank you," Corwyn said as he recovered.

Robert, sensing the obvious timing of his cough, probed further.

"Fire-breathing rabbits, Corwyn?"

"Oh yes, sir, definitely fire breathing."

"Why do I sense there's more to this?"

Corwyn feigned innocence. Malachi's expression was completely blank. It was difficult to tell if Malachi was even aware we were standing there.

"Robert," I ventured, "Corwyn is as rotten a jester as either of us. He's clearly hiding something."

"It will be obvious soon enough," Corwyn barely managed a straight face.

"We could torture it out of him," Amelia suggested.

"Yes, I suppose we could," Robert agreed. "Did I mention she's going to make a great queen?"

"I don't know, Robert," I challenged, "Meira might be most put out. She seems to like him for some reason."

"Depending on the method, she might actually help," Robert countered.

"She would definitely help," Malachi stated blandly. And after a pause, "and so would I." Corwyn appeared a little green. I believe he was legitimately nervous.

Meira walked back, still carrying the rabbits. Meira and Corwyn locked eyes for several moments. She pointed at the rabbits and started giggling.

Care to share the joke? I asked her.

You'll see. She flitted back and forth just inches from the ground, as happy as could be.

I leaned over to Robert and whispered, "Perhaps they really are fire-breathing."

Suddenly, the sky above the clearing went dark and there was a roaring wind as though a violent storm were dropping in on our heads. I immediately stepped close to Robert and Amelia to provide them cover. Amelia was ducking under Robert's arm. I turned my head to assess the situation.

Two giant reptiles descended through the branches above our heads, their enormous wings pounding the air underneath them. Each was larger than a small house. The trees were blown out of their way so none of the boughs fell on us. I could only crouch like a stupid schoolboy, open-mouthed while their talons bit into the earth beneath them. By the time I regained enough composure to come up with something to say, Meira ran up in front of them and tossed the rabbits she had been carrying toward the beasts' gaping mouths. Each one neatly plucked his own rabbit from the air, flashing their razor-like teeth in the process. The poor critters went down their throats alive.

*Meira.... * I thought hesitantly. *Dearest.... what in the world are those?*

"This lovely green fellow is Fluffy. And the greedy blue little girl over there sniffing about for more rabbits is Bubbles. They're dragons, and it is quite safe for us to be here."

I had never seen such enormous and dangerous beasts—tough scales encircling their bodies, folded wings with clawed fingers the length of my forearm, and whip-like tails extending at least twenty feet behind them. Then again, I suppose dogs and chickens were new to Meira.

Malachi and Corwyn had moved behind Robert and Amelia.

My brothers are prepared to catch them if necessary. The sight of my lovelies is sometimes the cause of unconsciousness.

Thanks for not having anyone to catch me.

Oh come now, dear. You'll be fine.

Perseus, oddly, seemed completely unconcerned and even smirked a bit.

With bright eyes, Meira chirped lightly to the green monstrosity. It snorted and crawled across the ground to her, leaving several troughs in the dirt behind it. The last three feet of its tail twitched in the air.

She reached out her hand for the dragon to sniff, any sense of apprehension completely devoid from her countenance. When the beast dropped its head beneath hers, she gave it a tight hug and nuzzled it.

"Husband, come meet Fluffy." She reached out, grabbed my shirt, and pulled me to join her.

"P-pleased to meet you," I said at length as Meira held out my hand for Fluffy to sniff—or eat. She was humming a peculiar tune as she did so.

Bubbles, seemingly jealous of the affection, lumbered over to join. She pushed hard against Fluffy, shoving him over several feet.

In my non-existent experience dealing with creatures capable of felling entire armies, I could find no reason not to grab my bride and flee. Meira filled the air with the sound of her laughter, while Fluffy and Bubbles snapped at each other for a better snuggling position.

I was trying to calm my heart and trust that Meira knew how to avoid being crushed under their weight, or perhaps being whipped by their wicked tails. Looking about for some back-up I found her father and mother a distance away chatting with other Fae. They were watching with apparent amusement.

They like you.

I turned back to Meira again. The brilliant blue head of Bubbles was approaching my torso, her sharp eyes examining my features in detail.

That's what concerns me. I may be somewhat tasty. Meira laughed again.

"They don't eat people they like, silly. And they would never harm one of my friends... would they," she glared into Bubbles' eye. Bubbles looked chastised and retreated a short distance.

I'm certain that after this, nothing will surprise me ever again.

Amelia found her voice, "So, they are actually the fire breathers?"

"Naturally," Corwyn responded with a flourish and a grin. "Are you familiar with the writings of Li'Viadimeir?"

"Li whodawhatsit?" Robert asked, an eyebrow in his hairline.

"Oh, how naive the world of men. The story of their origin is absolutely thrilling and terrifying, but it really should be saved for after dinner. It's more dramatic by firelight—which, of course, they can provide!"

Malachi rolled his eyes. "Rude, Corwyn."

"That's not rude. It wasn't rude when Father gave Gavin the Histories, was it?"

"Father has tact."

Meira hovered over the dragons to stay out of their way while they jockeyed for position. At length, they managed to work themselves into a place where she was perched on both of their necks and using her hands to scratch an eye ridge on each. The beasts in unison sighed their contentment and settled down onto the forest floor.

"So, you named a pair of dragons Bubbles and Fluffy?" Robert asked Malachi.

"Who says *I* named them?"

"Well, they're yours, aren't they?" I asked him.

"They had quite suitable names when I first met them. However, I had an annoying four-year old sister who insisted on renaming them."

"I see," Amelia smiled, clearly pretending there weren't man-eating creatures only twenty feet away. Her white-knuckled hand had to be cutting off all of the blood to Robert's arm, but I was impressed with her outward composure.

"Out of curiosity, what were their names?" I inquired.

Bubbles suddenly leapt into the air with Meira on her neck. Meira's arms were outstretched; and her squeal sounded like a waterfall, piercing the whirlwind of the creature's wings. Within moments they were so high that the canopy made it nearly impossible to spot them. Even in my mind I could barely hear her clamoring on and on about how great it was to be free in the wind again.

As they flew away, I could see that Bubbles' tail was significantly shorter than Fluffy's. The back end of it looked like it had been severed or chewed off, and there were several vicious marks on what remained.

They flew about in the air while we stood around watching Meira enjoy herself.

"Thirsty?" Perseus asked Malachi, offering him a small silver flask.

"Not really, why?"

"You seemed it. Please keep it until you need it." He handed Malachi the flask and nonchalantly wandered away.

He looked at it with curiosity, but a commotion with Matthias and Lilliana distracted him.

"Malachi!" his father called. Malachi strode over to have conversation with him. They spoke between themselves for a time. Matthias was highly displeased and argued with him.

"Not our business?" Robert queried me.

"I'm afraid not."

"Good. I really don't want to know."

Malachi came back and spoke to Corwyn.

"It is sooner than I expected. I must leave." He made a piercing whistle and Bubbles descended rapidly back to the forest floor.

"I was having fun!" Meira whined and pouted, as Bubbles settled herself.

"I'm truly sorry, sister. There are matters that I must attend to." She sighed deeply, as if she had heard that phrase too many times.

"This better not be capturing something for Ehiza."

"It's not."

Then she slid off Bubble's neck and hugged Malachi again. Her mood was much more subdued.

"Will you come back this time?"

"This time, yes, but maybe not the next." They spoke the lines as if they were rehearsed, but there was a note of genuine sadness in them.

"It was a pleasure to meet you again, Brother. I wish you speedy success in your task." I held out my hand to him and was genuinely pleased that he took it. "Can I aid you in any way?"

"Not this time. But in the future, your assistance, and the assistance of all men, will be required. You will take care of my sister, not because you're under threat of personal harm, but because you love her. I know this."

I nodded. He firmly clasped my hand with a squeeze that nearly crushed it. He gave Robert a half nod, leapt onto Fluffy's neck, and the three took off into the sky.

Meira's eyes filled with tears, and I took her into my arms. The sky darkened, and soft rain began to fall.

13

17th of Lar Indar

Meira

It is said that the most glorious sight on any long journey is the sun spilling its noonday light over your destination. At least, that's what my mate and Robert thought. I watched their eyes brighten from their previously wearied state. In fact, all of the soldiers who accompanied us perked up as well.

Only Corwyn and I didn't find the view particularly inspiring.

What do you think? I inquired of him.

Grey. Drab. He paused. *Looks like any other castle.*

I have to agree with you, I returned. *At least there's a cute little village near the river and a forest not too far away on the other side to alleviate the monotony.*

I don't believe the terms "village" and "cute" can be used together, dear sister. Girls, yes. Villages? Not so much.

I laughed aloud. *Well, the landscape does seem somewhat familiar.*

Something humorous? Mardok inquired into my mind.

Oh, nothing.

Mardok looked dejected. A few moments passed, and he suddenly smiled.

What? I asked him.

Oh, nothing.

Now I knew something was up. I reached into my pocket, pulled out a pebble, and tossed it over my shoulder. It landed squarely on Corwyn's head.

"Ouch!" he cried out. "I'm innocent!"

"Of what?" I asked.

Mardok was laughing. Robert was confused. He seemed to spend a lot of time like that, now that Mardok was communicating more often by using his mind.

"Planning to fill me in?" he asked his bodyguard and friend.

"Corwyn gave me a glimpse of Meira as a little girl."

"Well that sounds rather sweet."

Mardok began chuckling. I considered interrupting, but I was honestly rather curious myself which moment Corwyn had chosen to share.

"Well, picture this — a charming little golden girl running into her father's court with mud, twigs, and leaves smeared all through her hair."

That's all you need to tell him, I said quickly to Mardok. I knew where this was going.

The king wants to know, darling.

He'll be happy with that description.

He seemed to consider it for several seconds, then turned to Robert.

"She was absolutely adorable," he finished. I love him.

"Is that all you saw?" Corwyn asked. "I thought you saw the rest of it."

No, Corwyn, don't, I begged.

It is my job as your brother to embarrass you.

I snatched up a pebble, twirled, and plinked him in the side of the head.

"Ouch!"

"Do we have to separate you two?" Robert chimed in.

Ira pulled his shield from his back and handed it to Corwyn. "My lord, you may be requiring this."

"Honestly, it's a good story," Corwyn argued, waving the shield around. "It's not like you did anything wrong."

"I hate being left out," Robert mused, "but it seems Meira isn't interested in the story being shared."

"No, Sire, she would like to avoid that very much," Mardok confirmed. Every soul in earshot was now desperately curious. I buried my head in my hands.

You might as well tell them, I told Mardok. *It's not going to drop until it's out.*

Your story is your story, he answered. *No one else has a right to it.*

Really, it's better to just blab it. Mardok sighed and waited for me to change my mind before telling.

"Well, Sire," Mardok intoned all due seriousness, "it seems that the young Meira, only a tiny thing mind you, decided to use her new-found friendship with the wind to blast the mess out of her hair, all over everyone in the court." Robert's eyes grew. He wanted to laugh, but he clearly was concerned about how upset I was with it.

Feeling the urge to get back at my brother just one more time, I whispered into the wind. A small gust hurried out and returned as a blast, hitting Corwyn hard. It lifted him from his horse and threw him over the side, Ira's shield acting as a sail. He fell toward the ground and vanished with it before landing.

HA! I thought. Goodness knows where he was thinking about when he blinked.

My lady, Mardok started, *you're really angry.*

No, I'm not.

You're starting to glow.

I'm only embarrassed, my husband.

By that little incident as a kid?

I shamed my father. It may be cute now, but he was extremely angry.

I put in his mind the images of my father's response. *There was no laughter in the court that day. I spent the rest of it cleaning the mess out of all the clothing and off the tables. I didn't know until many, many years later that Father was mediating an accord of peace. Two tribes were on the verge of slaughtering each other. A forest had already been burned, so Father was upset with them. He nearly turned over negotiations to Malachi.*

Quite the temper he has.

I share that trait with him. I apologize for whenever you see it.

Mardok leaned over to Robert and explained the incident. They discussed it for a while, and then other things, and then things which had nothing to do with anything. Finally we fell back to silence as we drew closer to the castle.

From several miles out, I could see the details of the walls and gate. To me it appeared that the castle was poorly kept. The gate was battered and worn. The walls were broken down in several places. One of the towers had been recently repaired with wood where stone should have been. At least there were watchmen present.

I took that moment to land on Corwyn's horse and rest my wings. I had been flying most of the time since we left Gavin's. My terriculum was traveling underground, following us until I had need of him. Conveniently, Corwyn didn't need his horse as we approached the castle.

Mardok selected Warner and Burke to ride ahead of the group to announce the king's arrival and to get an idea of what we were facing. They were the two lightest men, both with swift steeds, and were accustomed to this task. Warner lifted the king's banner in the air, and they galloped ahead. We watched as they made it nearly to the gate before a group of archers appeared on the wall, each placing arrow to bow, but not yet drawing them. From this distance I could not make out what they were discussing.

"Bring me their conversation, my friend," I hummed lightly into the air. It circled and danced around me before rushing toward them.

Warner and Burke turned back and made clear of the wall by over an arrow's shot. Mardok and Robert, as well as the other men, looked about confused.

"Good King," I offered, "can you not see what is happening?"

"My eyes are good, Meira, but not that good. I can see that my men have retreated from the castle, and there appears to be a group of men on the wall." So I filled him in on the details.

"Ride with haste and caution, men," Mardok told everyone, "They disdain the king's honor."

Would you like my help, husband? I inquired.

Can you teleport us like you did Corwyn back there? And by the way, where did you send that rascal?

I didn't send him; he left on his own. Wherever he is, he'll be back when he feels like it.

At that moment, the wind returned to me and whistled, "Speak well of the pleasantries. Please love, please love. We're riders of the night, when the moon fails to bring gladness."

"Yes, I know," I hummed back. "What have you heard of the stone workings of men?"

"Chisels are resting, and saws are swaying. The men

speak of fruits and meats and water for their parched mouths. Sad mouths, pitiful mouths. They rasp my air and curse me. The little runners, they laugh and sing, but not today. Today they are silent, eyes weeping or fingers twirling the dust."

"Did the archers speak?"

"Those who whistle through the sky? They offered that the king should come and die before they trust him to not steal what remains in their walls."

"Do they not trust the king?"

"They no longer trust any friend, for all have become foe before them."

Shortly, we arrived at the place where Warner and Burke were waiting. Mardok and Robert could now clearly see the archers watching and the gate shut.

"Sire," Warner began, "the governor has given orders that all are to be barred entrance to the castle until further notice, with no exceptions to clergy or king."

"Was he informed that the actual king was here and not simply a figure of speech?"

"They have gone to inform him, Sire, but they said that it would take some time for him to respond."

"Sire," Mardok began, "it would be inappropriate to permit a governor to keep you waiting while he decides if you're worthy enough to see. If you would like, there are tactical options available."

"I'm not really interested in attacking, Mardok, if I can handle it."

"Robert," I said, "they are stricken with fear. They're weak and hungry."

"How do you know this?" he asked, expressing curiosity rather than distrust. His demeanor grew more serious by the moment.

"The wind told me."

"Sire, why would they be holed up in the castle with no army around when they have a fishing village nearby?" Raeburn asked. He was one of the Dozen I had only met in passing. "If they're hungry, they should be gathering food from the fields and the forest."

"Do you know how many men they have inside?" Robert asked me.

"Too few," said a voice behind us. Corwyn had appeared again.

"Where did you go to?" Robert asked.

"As it turns out, I just happened to be thinking about this beautiful lavatory I had seen at Gavin's homestead. Fortunately, I was thinking about it in general terms and in the context of that castle we've come to see. Hmm, I pondered, I wonder what kind of lavatory the governor has?"

Even with the tension, I had to laugh. It's not the worst place he had ever disappeared to suddenly, but was certainly worth the story.

"So, when my sister had her friend so kindly remove me from my seat, there I appeared in Governor Mephitic's lavatory, my dear King Robert. After my burden was lifted, which is the reason I was thinking about it in the first place..."

"I thought the governor's name was Craddok."

"Shh, Edgar." Robert was amused.

"... I exited the rather small closet and stepped directly into the governor's chamber. I dare say that he was more surprised to see me than I him."

"Why Mephitic, Brother?" I asked Corwyn.

"Well, apparently the governor and his men are rationing on beans, and they have been none too kind to their digestion."

No one had any idea how to respond to any of this, so Corwyn continued.

"So while he sat in stupid silence, I decided to announce that we were arriving, though for what purpose I wasn't quite clear. By the way... why exactly are we here?"

Mardok opened his mouth to answer.

"Oh, never mind that," Corwyn continued. "At that point he started examining his lavatory, pushing against the walls, tapping on the floor. He was a very odd man."

"I'm sure he's not used to people walking out of his lavatory without first walking in," Robert pointed out.

Corwyn blinked a couple times and repeated, "He was a very odd man. Anyway, a messenger banged on the door and announced that you had arrived. The governor told them that he would be out, but not to trust you on your word. I told him that certainly you were who you said, and I happened to be holding Ira's shield to prove it. This didn't please the governor.

He declared that magic was at work, which I thought was painfully obvious, and nothing could be trusted without much more contemplation. Curious about this, I asked him what the concern was. He had very little to offer and instead asked me to leave by whichever means I had come. So I honored his request and returned to you. Speaking of which, I believe this is your shield?"

Ira chuckled and took it back.

At this point shouting came from the wall, and shortly thereafter the governor appeared on it.

"My King," he called out. It was difficult for Robert to hear him.

"Warner, Burke, go tell that scoundrel to either let us in or come out to us. I can't afford tolerating a rebellion, even if it's a misunderstanding." Then, looking at me, "Starving or not."

Warner and Burke cut the distance in half and shouted out the king's command.

"I regret that I cannot trust that you are who you say. I have been fooled twice, and a third would have my head," the governor shouted back. Burke relayed the message to Robert.

Robert sat in silence. He really was uncertain what to do.

"He's not a bad man, Sire," Harry offered. "I've spent many a holiday in his house."

"I wasn't aware that you knew him that well," Robert observed.

"Master Thomas and Harold are actually brothers," I explained to Meira and Corwyn. "They have another brother—

Richard — and ten sisters. Richard's a horse trader. Got these beauts from him." I patted my horse's neck.

"Horses run in your family, it seems," Corwyn noted to Harry.

"You have no idea," Harry answered.

"This is all very entertaining, but it doesn't solve our problem," Ira interrupted. "We need to find a way to verify that Robert is, in fact, the king. I'm not happy that we're sitting out here with something that obviously has the governor terrified. Personally, I would very much like to have walls between us and it... or them."

"It's going to be hard to verify your identity without putting you in range of their archers," Harry added. "I would be happy, Sire, to go speak to him. He should remember me."

"Your kingliness," Corwyn piped in, "do we really need to go speak to him? Wouldn't it be easier if he came here?"

"I doubt he's intending to leave that wall."

"I wasn't going to ask." And with that, Corwyn blinked away and back a second later, bringing the governor with him. For a very brief moment he appeared confident, then confused, then horror spread over his face. This gave time for Robert and the men to adjust to his sudden arrival.

"Well, then," Robert started. "Governor Craddok, so happy you could join us."

Watch, sister, he's going to stand there like a statue, without speaking, for the next ten minutes.

Sure enough, the governor stood slack-jawed while Robert

talked to him, trying to figure out what was happening that had him so terrified.

"Good King, if I may," Corwyn jumped in. "Governor Timorous, if you would be so kind as to discuss the issue with your king, so I won't feel compelled to transport you somewhere unpleasant." The governor stared at Corwyn, caught the idea of the word "unpleasant" and looked back over his shoulder — not toward the castle, but toward the forest.

"Yes, governor, the forest," Corwyn finished.

The governor started mumbling incoherently at first. Then after a moment his brain caught up with his mouth, and from that point we couldn't get him to shut up. Corwyn beamed.

I take great pleasure in my work, he smiled into my head.

Amongst the ramblings, we learned several important things. First, it seemed that a group of well-organized bandits had been raiding farms and the village, taking the food and anything of value, as well as the adults, leaving all of the children behind. The governor's castle was filled with them, but they were essentially out of food. Twice the castle had been attacked directly after the governor believed that the persons at the gate were still friends. Any alliance or friendship prior to the beginning of this nightmare had become meaningless. Both men and women were subject to radical betrayal.

The governor was desperate for help and more desperate for the food still growing in the fields. But he couldn't trust anyone, not even the king, lest he open the gate and find him a betrayer, too.

"Children first," the king ordered, as we entered the castle. "They must be fed, clothed, and taken to safety."

Inside the walls, well over two hundred children peered from every nook and corner. Some were whimpering, and some were complaining of hunger pains. Worry and fear were universal.

"Give me the job, good king," Corwyn nearly ordered, a catch in his throat. And again he vanished.

"Very good, you do... that?" Robert shook his head. "Does he ever wait for permission?"

Meira snorted. "What, Robert, and give you the opportunity to say no? Just ask my mother how often he waits for permission. Show him a hurting child and he'll move all of Lur to protect him. Show him this," she spread her arms to the swarm of staring eyes. "The situation will be remedied."

"So be it. I will consider the problem resolved. Second, we need bread and meat. Troops are useless on empty stomachs. Governor Craddok, you have a fishing village right here, do you not? It's high time we put it to use."

"We can't afford the risk, Sire. Each time we've tried, a raiding party has come from the forest and made off with the food and all of the people we sent. There was never even a fight. This foe is beyond our understanding, much less our capability to defend against. Sire, I believe they use magic."

"You let me deal with the magic. Collect the food." My wife could appear deadly serious when needed.

"My men will guard your fishers. Bring your best," the king ordered.

"Sire," Governor Craddok objected, "your men will be taken as well."

Meira's skin flashed red, her wings pounded, and she lifted several feet off her mount. The sky darkened, and the wind whipped about her, making her hair flow out behind her. Her white traveling tunic blazed of its own light. She was a beautiful terror. More so, she was convincing. Craddok had fallen to the ground, his arms covering his face.

"Send your men. I will protect them myself!" Her voice boomed and echoed through the wind.

"Every able body to the river!" the governor shouted. "Go now!" Men scurried to comply, more out of fear of Meira than their crumpled leader.

"Robert, the maoim beatha, do you have it?" I inquired discretely. He nodded, opening his right hand.

My love, I think you've made your point and have terrified him sufficiently.

You think perhaps?

Yes.

Good.

Love the flashy clothes. You didn't tell me that they could do that.

Oh certainly.

Very useful for traveling at night.

She landed back on the horse and the elements of her terror passed.

"She is... friend?" the governor begged before the king.

"She is. I'm supposing you will be leading our little fishing expedition?"

The governor nodded, "Yes, Sire, certainly, of course," and he ran off, throwing random orders this way and that, generally making things more chaotic than they had been before.

Hours passed, and as the sun cast shadows over the land, the governor had gathered what men were available at the gate—about thirty. All of them, soldier and peasant alike, were helmed and armed. Carts of fishing nets and supplies had been filled and parked, and what few horses they had were fastened to them.

The governor bowed with his little remaining dignity to the king. "Sire, we are ready."

"Good. Then tonight you shall have good fishing. Begin."

"Open the gate," Craddok ordered, and they began their march to the village. The entourage was flanked by our men on horseback, eyes peeled. Meira and I rode with Robert at the head of the train. Meira had given up Corwyn's horse, as brilliant a war steed as he was, even though he wasn't there to need it. Instead she rode her terriculum, who was doing a fabulous job of displaying all the aspects of a real horse—such that neither the governor nor his men knew otherwise.

We reached the village without incident, and the men went about mounting the piers and casting their nets. The village here didn't have boats, but rather it used a pier system that extended most of the way across the river. Nets were dropped from the surface to the bottom to catch almost every fish as it passed with the flow of the water.

"Great Overlord!" Clearly Corwyn had returned. He stood with three others, all cloaked in the robes of the royal Fae, their brilliant silver skin glistening from the light of the moon.

"Good to see all of you," Robert said. I could tell that he was still holding the maoim beatha, stroking it mindlessly with his thumb.

"We have come for the children. Your brother Gavin has volunteered his home and his table for all of them... under one condition."

"Yes?"

"You forbid the nobles from returning to his house for at least a year."

Robert smiled. "How will you get them there?"

"These with me are the best teleporters among the Fae — gifted from birth and recognized as the most likely to get away with pranks of every kind."

"And the most likely to be blamed when anything goes wrong," one of the others chipped in.

"I'll bet tomorrow Father will be blaming us for hiding his socks in the silver mines."

"But you did hide them," another of them added.

"Well, yes, but he doesn't have to assume it's us first."

"Why do I get the impression it's usually you," I asked them.

"Because it is," Meira confirmed.

Robert chuckled. It was a good diversion for the night. "Are you certain, Corwyn, that these brothers of yours will not lose any of the children?"

Remembering how I had to think clearly about my room to get there, I added, "The children have never been to Lord Gavin's castle before. How will you teleport them there?"

"We have all been there, and together we can overwhelm the children's dreams while they sleep. So when they teleport, they will go where we wish them to. We'll take them to the garden, because it will be the most pleasant place for them to reappear. I doubt, under the circumstances, that the children will be interested in waking in a forest."

"I concur," Robert approved. "Take them quickly."

"Throughout the night." Then each of them vanished.

"I suppose, Sire, that we don't need as much food if the children won't be staying." I ventured.

"Governor Craddok!" Robert called out. The whimpering coward ran over, his finger over his mouth, shushing his king. "The children are leaving to safety tonight and will not need food. Gather only what is needed for the men and women."

Excited by the news, he ran off and spread the word.

The air remained still for another hour or two with us

watching, waiting for whatever was supposed to happen. Finally, the men had gathered up everything into the carts, and we started the trip back to the castle. The men were tired, and beyond that terribly hungry. They didn't even arm themselves. Most of them had tossed their weapons into the carts. From a tactical perspective, these men were begging to be captured.

Meira held up her hand, halting the entourage. Fear itself should have spurred the men to grab their weapons, but instead they appeared more lax than before. Several of them looked around them on the ground, as though wanting to sit down. Even our Dozen was appearing somewhat lethargic.

Hold to my mind, husband. Hold to mine, so I don't have to think about holding to yours.

What's happening?

It's an old spell, easy to cast and difficult to defeat. It takes concentration, but your men are untrained for it. I have Robert's mind clear but not the rest.

"Greetings honorable warriors," a voice spoke softly from everywhere — several voices, actually. Many.

Meira lit up her tunic. Between ourselves and the castle stood a large group of people. It was difficult to tell if they were armed.

"A Fae, we see. This is different," the voices spoke softly together. It sounded as if they were nearby, from several shifting directions. I looked around to see where they might be.

"A thousand Fae, wretched creature," Meira announced. "I hold command over a legion and will dispatch you without remorse. Your petty magic is worthless against us. Clear the road."

Laughter surrounded us, chuckling. "We will consider your request. Come near and discuss it with us."

My thoughts grew foggy, and I concentrated as hard as possible on Meira's mind.

"Meira, there are only a handful of them," Robert pointed out. "Go through them. Men, draw your arms!" Robert leveled his blade straight at the opposing force and urged his horse forward. I drew mine to follow him, but only a few of our men followed suit. The remaining were nearly asleep in their saddles.

"These are merely peasants, Robert," Meira called out to him. "Running them through would gain you nothing."

"Then clear them from the road, or we'll have to."

Meira's eyes flashed, and she sang eerily into the air. Her tones were punctuated with claps of lightening. The wind whistled through the trees and grass to her tune. A blast of wind cut across the path before us. Several of our opponents fell outright, thrown to the ground. A few fled. Again my bride sang, deep and gurgling, making sounds I had never heard or ever thought possible. Responding, the wind gathered water from the river and blasted the blockade. Drenched and freezing, nearly all of them fled back toward the forest. Two remained, uniformed soldiers wearing the garb of the governor's men.

"Good enough!" Robert cried, "Charge!" And we did. Apparently fear of our horses pounding over their flesh was terrifying enough, and they ran out of our way.

"Move your lazy carcasses, governor!" the king demanded.

Begrudgingly, the people began moving again. The horses, unaffected by the magic, did their duty well, carrying the valuable cargo to the gates.

"Corwyn!" I yelled through the walls. Immediately he appeared. "There are men sleeping in the field behind us, under a spell." And he vanished.

We entered the gates, and immediately the spirits of the men picked up. They seemed vibrant again.

"What was that back there?" the governor demanded.

"A slumber spell, governor," Meira answered. "It makes you susceptible to suggestion and unwilling to fight. It's why your people never fought back and simply disappeared into the forest." She fluttered into the air to see over the wall. "The one who casts it is watching, for he cannot cast it or maintain it against persons he cannot see."

Corwyn reappeared. "There were four left behind. They're in their beds now."

"Which men? Where are their beds?" Craddok blurted.

"Not in the castle, but not in the field. That's as far as I can move them tonight until the spell wears off."

"It's worn off us completely."

"You're still awake, but they have succumbed."

"Why didn't you bring them here?"

"I can only teleport people to where they are thinking about. These were grown men, not children whose sleeping minds are more malleable. They wanted only to sleep in their beds, so to their beds they went. Now if you would please excuse my departure, I have children who are dreaming of places far better than here." Again he was gone.

The night was terribly busy, but all for the better. First, the children were sent to safety, with the exception of two older boys who refused to leave. Second, the people who had been living this nightmare began to hope again—not that things would be restored, but that at least they might make it out alive. Third, every belly was filled as men sat and rested around a bonfire.

By morning, most of them had dozed into rest-filled sleep.

As the sky began to lighten, Meira and I found a spot on the wall. She wanted to be where the wind could alert her to danger, and it afforded us a place we could exchange secretive kisses.

14

18th of Lar Indar

Meira

I woke mid-morning; thankfully exhaustion had staved off any nightmares. My muscles were sore from the cramped sleeping position I had during the night. I stretched gingerly to test how badly they fared and decided they were not well.

My husband lay beside me on the stone behind one of the battlements overlooking the gate. Below us, carts were already gathered, and soldiers were quietly working. I sang a soft lullaby to keep Mardok's sleep peaceful and then rose to find a place suitable for the day greeting. Sore muscles rarely survived through it. The partially repaired south tower had a flat roof that was just wide enough for my circle, so I flew discreetly up to the top and landed neatly in the center without anyone other than Frank seeing me. He nodded and smiled at me as he went about his guard shift. The wind was happy to find me awake and up so high where it could play with my hair.

"The morning is happy, so happy, our love.

The night is now over. Our dear one's above!"

I had to laugh aloud. The breezes could be so silly. I fished in my bag for the stones and set the circle properly all while the wind played with my curls. Then I began the song. I sang not just for myself but also drawing out the melody lengthily for all the humans sheltering in the castle. There would be much work today, and they would be tired from all they had accomplished last night. I wanted to help them be prepared for the probability of another attack.

My friends flitted around me in a whirlwind, then spun round the castle whispering past all the lives it contained. The aches of yesterday were largely forgotten, and hope was strong as they each began their day. I breathed deeply as my friends surrounded me once again, finished the song, and collected my stones. Stepping off the tower, I fluttered back down to where my husband had been sleeping.

"I could happily wake to that for the rest of my life," he said, smiling at me as I landed. His eyes were still closed, and he looked as peaceful and pleasant as an infant.

"You can rest longer if you like. I was just going to check to see what the supply situation is like after last night's efforts." He nodded at me sleepily. I bent down to kiss his cheek, then descended the creaky wooden steps.

"Governor Craddok?" I inquired of a soldier lacing the bindings on his jerkin.

"Awake, m'lady," he replied, "but only just. He will be inspecting the food supplies."

I nodded and strode across the courtyard. I found the governor and I had similar plans this morning. He was counting barrels and bags and tallying figures.

"I am grateful," he started, not looking up. "We were dead,

and you spared us." I listened quietly. "Not only from the enemy, but from starvation. With the children, we only had food left for a few days. We now have only a fraction of our previous number. Our ration reserves can last us two weeks, if need be."

"It isn't enough for the winter," I reminded him.

"No, it isn't." He stopped and looked into my face. His eyes were tearing. "I laughed last night. I haven't laughed in over a month."

"Laughter will fill your soul again, governor."

He dropped his tally on a small table and walked out of the open-air storehouse. "I wonder sometimes," he trailed along, "if I have this completely wrong." He looked back and verified I was listening. "What if I'm on the wrong side?"

"How is that?"

"You saw them last night. They were fed, not starving. They have everything in the forest at their disposal. I had mourned the loss of Ernst, Tilda, Horris, Graham, Cornin, and Sallis. Countless others. But they're not lost, they were right there! Between us and them, who should be mourning whom?" He sighed.

"You're wondering if it would have been better for everyone if you all walked into the forest to join them."

He nodded.

"Then what of the children?" Silence. "They were torn away from their parents unwillingly. The parents were kept, but the children were sent away. How would they have lived if you hadn't taken them in?"

"The children," he mumbled. "They would have left them for dead."

"And had you all been taken, what then?" More silence. "Don't reject yourself yet, governor. Your brain may be hurting from hunger, but your heart is still worthy of song."

"A song," he said dryly. "That'll be the day."

We walked together to the gate where the men were preparing the wagons again.

"Another trip to the river planned, I see, governor."

"To the fields, Ambassador, if you please. As long as you and the king are here, we need to take the opportunity to collect the harvest, before it rots in the fields."

His actions were more coherent this morning; his sleep last night had afforded him some measure of actual rest and temporary relief from his worries. He joined the men in preparations. I watched until I heard Robert yawn in his upstairs room. I went inside to speak with him, but by the time I had arrived outside his room, he had already mostly finished dressing and was walking down the hall to the kitchen.

"There is no food yet prepared this morning. Everyone who didn't join us in gathering the food was up all night preserving the fish."

"Meira, good to see you this morning. Not even a crust of bread, I suppose."

"Nothing. Governor Craddok is preparing his men to harvest the fields."

"Grown a spine, has he? I doubt our enemy will be allowing him to collect it in peace."

"I am anticipating he will not." I helped Robert with his cloak. "I have been considering who our enemy may be and what knowledge of magic he may possess. I wish Malachi were here. And, I hate to admit it, but I need Corwyn. He can better anticipate things like this. I have had a rather sheltered upbringing. He has more experience than I with the rest of the world."

"Ooh, are you talking about me, dear sister?" Corwyn was now trotting up behind us.

"As a matter of fact, I was talking about Malachi." I stuck my tongue out at him.

"Malachi's still dealing with the priests of Satyriasis."

"Actually, I've been doing a bit of thinking," Robert began, as if Corwyn had been part of the conversation from the beginning.

"I would really like to know more about this enemy, and I want to send a scouting team into the forest to see what can be learned about them. The excursion to the wheat fields would be a perfect diversion to keep the enemy focused elsewhere," he finished.

"I agree," Corwyn answered, "but one of us will need to go with the scouts and the other will need to stay with the governor's people to ensure everyone comes back." I could see the wheels spinning in Corwyn's mind. "I would be more useful in the field with the people."

Robert and I both stopped walking in surprise.

"Well, I would! I have more experience protecting large groups, and I can blink Meira instantly to me if I need back up."

"It's true. He can," I said in answer to Robert's arched brow. "I'm close enough to him that he doesn't have to touch me to teleport me."

"Father gets most put out when I do it to him without permission." Corwyn grinned.

"Then Meira, I'll send you with Mardok, Frank, and George. They know what kind of information we will find most valuable." I nodded my agreement to Robert.

"Another problem, though," Robert queried, "There's no way to get from here to the forest without being spotted. The fields of wheat would provide sufficient cover for as far as they extend. But even the dullest lookouts would notice you for the mile or so between the fields and the trees. Blinking… is that what you call it?"

"Notice-me-not would be better," Corwyn answered easily. "The magic user may have a trap or alarm designed to deal with teleportation or tree portalling—especially since he knows we're here now."

"Notice-me-not isn't perfect," I corrected. "The lookout would probably be looking specifically for something like this, too. The magic wouldn't fool him."

"What if Robert and I were creating a big enough distraction with the harvest?"

"If you could make the harvest party more interesting to see than four people running across a field, my charm would protect us."

"Consider it done," Robert promised. Corwyn gave a wicked smile.

We had reached the courtyard and Corwyn bounced away to talk to the governor. "I'm not sure how to ask this, Meira, but I feel compelled to anyway," Robert said hesitantly.

"Please don't be shy," I encouraged.

"If you have any other skills or gifts or friends that could help us out with this, I would be more than grateful. This enemy is so far beyond anything I have ever seen or heard of... I'm really trying not to flounder here, not when my people need me so much, but it's hard. And distractions and blowing wind is nice..." Robert trailed off. Worry and concern set deep marks into his brow.

"Your people are Mardok's people, and therefore mine as well. And I am my father's daughter, and he is a very powerful king. And we have allies who owe us great debts. I can assure you that should Jov himself come against us, there would be armies at our disposal."

"You're prepared even to fight the gods, eh?"

"There's a first time for everything."

Mardok

Having a full stomach was wonderful, even for those who weren't particularly fond of trout, but following it up with no breakfast or any real hope for lunch wasn't quite as pleasant. And judging from my conversations with the troops, they all held the same opinion.

Mark and Edgar were particularly vocal about the issue. I realized that the two of them had taken the bulk of the watch duties overnight, and I sent them to the stores to take an extra meal's ration without alerting the others.

I made certain that my men were assisting the governor with his preparations, and we assigned several of the women to keep watch on the walls. Not a few of these were very proficient with the bow, and all of them were much more pleasant to the eye than the fearfully unattractive men.

By late morning we had the carts packed and the people ready to make for the fields. One of the boys ran to fetch the king, and he came out with Meira in tow.

"Your Majesty," Craddok approached him, "my deepest apologies for my completely inappropriate behavior yesterday." He bowed low to the ground.

"Impress me today, Craddok, and all will be forgiven."

"Yes, Sire. We are ready to leave."

"Good start. Mardok, are your men ready?"

"Yes, Sire."

"Good, split off Frank and George to go with you and

Meira to the forest. You're going to scout out the enemy's position. And don't blame me, it was Meira's idea."

"It's nearly two miles to the trees," I replied. "We would most certainly be spotted."

"I intend to employ magic, Mardok," Robert responded, as though it would be his own. I believe he was beginning to enjoy having a couple Fae around.

The governor's non-existent eyebrows arched deep into his forehead. Given how magic had been his enemy for so long, his hesitation was sensible.

"You have an objection, Governor?" Meira asked. He stammered a bit and declined to comment. "It's good to see you have faith in the king's war counsel."

"Well, I, um… er, I do, actually. I'm just not used to 'magic' being a valid tactic."

"Today it is."

I couldn't tell if Meira was mildly chiding him or simply enjoying keeping him off-balance and impressed.

The women opened the gates with surprising deftness, and we all departed together. Robert, Corwyn, and the rest made a grand and obvious procession to the fields to the north. They were clearly visible from the forest. For good measure, Robert had Ira prance about with his royal banner and silver trumpet, blasting incoherent commands to nobody in particular.

Meira, Frank, George, and I exited last. A rather familiar pile of rocks was waiting for us. Meira spoke briefly to the rock pile, and it slipped underneath the ground, kicking up a short spurt of dust.

As we rounded the northwest corner of the castle and stepped into the sunlight, we could see the forest stretching out over the great swaths of grain. From our current position we were obviously noticeable. But that was about to change.

Meira breathed in deeply and began to whisper with her eyes closed. A light gust of wind zipped past us.

"And hasten our way!" she finished aloud. Then she tossed a few glittering sands from her pocket into the sky over our heads and declared, "We're not here. Pay no heed."

"Are we good?" Frank asked.

"Generally, yes," she replied. "We're not invisible, but we will be very difficult to notice. Someone looking for us would find us, but only if he were not distracted. Between Robert's silly procession and the clattering of the trees, I think we'll be fine."

Indeed, it became readily obvious in which trees the enemy's scouts had positioned themselves. Four particular trees, and those immediately surrounding them, developed a sudden and consistent series of gusts and gales. It appeared as though the trees were sneezing.

"Just enough to keep them busy," Meira commented. "Nothing too dangerous."

We used the northern fields as cover while we had them. But in less than a third of a mile we were in open pastureland.

"Ambassador," George whispered, as we slid silently

between the rows of heavily-laden wheat. "how do you know where the terry cucumber, is, or even if it's still with us?"

"The terry cucumber? You mean the terriculum?"

"Yes, that."

"Try to hit me, and you'll see."

"I'll decline."

"It won't kill you or hurt you, but it will protect me. Terriculi were created by Ataraxia to commune with nature in perfect peace. They are immortal and invulnerable, as long as they refrain from killing any significant creature — whether animal, fae, or man. They cannot kill directly or indirectly. They are forbidden from killing by accident, lest mortality should fall upon them."

"If they're immortal, then there should be an endless number of them."

"They cannot reproduce. In the beginning Ataraxia made two thousand eight hundred forty-two of them and dispersed them throughout Lur. Today there are two thousand eight hundred thirty-nine. Three, through various means, accidentally caused death and were made mortal."

"Are they intelligent?"

"We can speak with them, and we call them fae, but they are not sentient. It is similar to talking with one of his majesty's dogs and a little easier than talking to one of the horses."

"What is Corwyn doing?" Frank asked. We all turned to look.

Corwyn, his garb clearly distinguishable, was apparently entertaining the workers. We watched as he appeared in mid-air, high above the field and fell, performing flips and cartwheels to the boisterous taunts of the governor. Then, just before hitting the ground, he disappeared and reappeared high in the air to do it all over again.

"Is he... yelling?" I asked.

"Singing," Meira replied. "Drinking songs. Dirty ones." She shook her head.

"You have to admit," George commented to her. "That's a seriously potent distraction."

"Let's not waste it then," I said. It was still over half an hour before we reached the cover of the trees at the slow pace Meira demanded to keep up the charm. Once there, we angled to the northeast and continued walking for several minutes before setting our path east. It was slow going, as we kept our eyes and ears open for any movement.

It was a good hour, picking our way along, before Meira stopped abruptly. It was so sudden that Frank and George bumped into me from behind and caused us all to stumble around for a moment to keep balance.

"I know this place," she whispered.

"What do you mean?" Frank asked.

"I was caretaker here many years ago. This is MY forest. This is Oihana." She breathed in the air deeply. "This is the forest that was burned that Mardok mentioned yesterday. Two tribes fought here, and they both lost. Regrowing it was part of my training. My grandmother was in charge of its regrowth, but she simply started it and left me to care for it..." Meira trailed off for a moment, then motioned to a stand of trees that looked too uniformly planted to be random growth. "See here, these trees, how they form a spiral? I did that. I planted several groups of trees in interesting formations and placed huge rocks to give shelter to the animals. I brought herds of deer to settle here and the wolves to keep them healthy and strong. I lived among these woods for over thirty-five years. I know this place in a way that few others could even imagine."

I shook my head again at our age disparity.

"Why didn't you recognize the area before?" Frank inquired.

"I have never really seen it from the outside, and it has grown tremendously over the past fifty-five years."

"Can you tell us where they're hiding?" George asked hopefully.

"I don't understand the tactics of men. I can tell you what a fae with specific abilities would look for in a hiding place, I can tell you where I would hide if need be, but I still do not know enough about humans to tell you where they would be."

I thought you could tell a forest by its scent.

I can. Something has changed it. The wolves; they're gone. The deer, the rabbits, the birds, even the hawks and the scavengers — they're all in hiding. Fear is everywhere; it's disorienting. It smells richly of unwashed men.

Can you hear them?

I can hear them on the wind, but there are too many voices and not from any one direction. I'm sorry.

For what? Why are you sorry? I think we can use your knowledge of the forest to our advantage.

I fear putting you at risk. Without being able to hear them clearly, I can't be certain that I'm not leading you into an ambush.

You have a terriculum.

Meira smiled. "I have three terriculi."

"Three?" George replied. "Frank and I are missing half of this conversation. I can tell."

"There were two living here when I left. Unlike the animals, they have no reason to leave. They also would have no reason to make themselves known to the interlopers."

She spoke into the ground in the garbled language she had used several times before.

"Now we wait."

But waiting didn't take long. Half an hour later, three rock structures emerged from the ground. One of them, which looked the most familiar, sat in place, while the other two moved around Meira like a pair of self-contained avalanches. She whispered excited greetings to them until they settled.

Meira

"These are my friends, Mumbles and Fliddlehene."

"Mumbles and Fliddlehene?" George raised his eyebrow.

Frank answered, "This is the same girl, George, that named a scaled dragon Fluffy."

"I was three," I defended.

Mardok cleared his throat. "So, my darling, what's the name of the one that you've been riding?"

"Huascaran. It means 'Avalanche' in the ancient tongue."

"What's Fliddlehene mean?" George muttered.

I smiled and scratched his ear. George and Frank watched me as if I were scratching a plain rock. I suppose that's what it looked like, but I knew Fliddlehene appreciated it.

"Aged and blessed lords of the earth," I spoke in their language, "we implore you to help us. There are men in these woods who have killed many, and they are trying to kill us. We are looking for them. We are not asking you to endanger your spirits by breaking the mandate placed upon you. Would you guide us to them by a path and route that they do not take or do not know?"

A small pit opened in the ground.

"Place your weapons in the hole," I told the men. "We are under the protection of the terriculi and will not require them. They do not want to answer to their maker for assisting us in causing death." The three of them looked at me unbelieving.

"They will not fail us. Your weapons will not be damaged, or aged, or scuffed.... or even dulled." I rolled my eyes as they reluctantly hid their oft-polished blades in the dirt. The pit closed and completely disappeared.

We followed the terriculi as they wound their way through the trees. The going was difficult and filled with brush and branches. We stumbled along for several miles, doing our best to avoid making a commotion. At long last, we reached the edge of the enemy camp.

I recognized the structures. The enemy had encamped in my once-beloved home, and they had utterly defiled it. It was at times like this that I wished I had the ability to rend flesh from sinew at thought.

Meira, you're going to give away our position.

I looked down and saw the flame within my skin. I concentrated and brought it back under control. It took every lesson in self-control my father made me take as a child to calm down.

We watched and waited.

The camp moved slowly. Most of the people just seemed to stand around, as though staring at trees, purposeless. A few walked here and there, carrying or preparing food. There was no fire in the pit; a few men were eating meat raw and unseasoned. They did so with cold eyes, seemingly dead.

George, Frank, and Mardok made whispered comments to each other, pointing out tactical positions and counting opponents and supplies. I held my silence, seeking one individual, or evidence of him. Perhaps it was possible that he had left to attack Robert and the harvest. If this were so we would be able to walk among them by simply recasting the notice-me-not charm.

"Where is the spell-caster who leads them?" I asked my terriculum. Mumbles formed a hand and pointed at the large center structure, confirming my suspicions.

It was a building my grandmother had made out of living trees. Seven mighty oaks wound together from the base, where they grew from solid stone. At the branches they folded like hands to seal out the rain. When I lived here, the trees were filled with birds and all sorts of creatures. Sleep at night was pleasant with the constant sounds of busy life overhead.

But now the trees barely held leaves, sick and dying.

Meira, please contain yourself.

I concentrated again to quell the anger that this stirred inside me.

"We have what we came for," Mardok told me. "Let's go."

"We can't leave yet. The spell-caster is inside, and I have to see him. I have to see what he is, and I have to see his eyes."

"He may stay in there for hours, maybe until tomorrow."

I thought carefully, and then I discussed my predicament softly with the wind.

The trees rustled on the far side of the camp. Branches swayed and creaked, and the brush moved sporadically. Only a few men in camp seemed to notice.

"Chief, movement in the brush!"

His chief came out, a jewel-studded club leading the way. His eyes bulged from his head, sickeningly yellow, and his beak was as crimson as the mash of blood-drenched leather he wore on his head.

Satisfied, I turned and left. The others joined me quickly.

"What was that thing?" Mardok asked, a distance between us and the camp.

"It's a foreigner to this land. They are blood-born and serve those who have given themselves over to conquest. It's the leader here, but it reports to someone far more dangerous. It cannot lead itself."

"Is it the spell-caster?"

"Yes. They are magical in birth, but they are not particularly strong. I would fear his arm more than his spells. It's taking everything he has in him just to control the people here."

"Then why don't we kill him and set these people free?" George asked.

"We cannot," I replied, "The terriculi led us here, and they would prevent you from killing him as quickly as they would prevent him from killing you. It is their gift and their burden. They do not get to distinguish between good and evil in this way."

"Can they capture him?"

"They know as you do that you would execute him later. We can leave and rejoin Robert and share the information. I lived here; I can return any time by ways I am sure they don't know. We need to be careful not to kill those he has entranced, if possible; they don't have any control over themselves. They won't even remember anything they have done."

"A single arrow," George advised.

"He's possessed, as with the man we executed before. He must be captured and executed properly, or the spirit in him will possess one of us."

"So he's basically a prisoner, too."

"Oh, no, he definitely deserves it. He's evil by nature, and this does nothing to change that. The possession has merely made him more powerful. He would have happily served Nahasmen without possession, and I'm sure he did at one time. Possession just amplifies his abilities. This is something familiar to my father. He fought against them in the Great War, and they were barely worth remembering."

We returned to the pit of weapons. As promised, they were in perfect condition, perhaps even a little better. This morning there had been a bit of rust on the hilt of George's knife.

We retraced our steps west and then south to the forest edge. After a moment's deliberation we decided to join Robert and the others in the fields before returning to the castle.

There were no disturbances for the remainder of the day.

Mardok

The door opened to Craddok's office, and the smell hit us before Mark was able to step in. "Fresh bread, gentlemen, ambassador."

Our stomachs were pained, waiting for this glorious moment.

"Mark," Robert started with his customary inquiry.

"Yes, Sire," he preempted, "everyone else has been fed."

We each sighed our relief. The scent of hot, rising loaves had been wafting through the castle since we returned from the fields. When the first cart had returned, the women had wasted no time in threshing and sifting the grain, cracking it, and making small hard loaves by the dozens.

Mark passed the precious bread around to everyone before taking his seat near the table that we had re-purposed and moved into the room.

"Governor Craddok, I don't believe we've had time yet for you to make proper acquaintance with my men." Robert inclined his hand toward us.

"Mardok you know. He is my personal champion and responsible for the training and discipline of all the troops. I am also informed that you have had prior acquaintance with Harry, when he was younger. Beside him are Frank, George, Mark, Amos, Burke, Edgar, Ira, Raeburn, Seth, and Warner. This forms the core of my war counsel. Ambassador Meira and her brother Corwyn we have included for obvious reasons. Could you please introduce your companion?"

"Sire, this is Jardin, my steward. Anything that happens in this castle, he knows."

"Very well. Ambassador, could you please tell us what you found out about the enemy."

"Robert, we found the enemy camp and their leader—a powrie who has been possessed by Nahasmen—the same dark spirit that possessed the murderer we executed many days ago. Nahasmen has given him increased magical skill, including the ability to influence and control well over a hundred humans."

"Excuse me, Ambassador," Craddok interjected, "what is a powrie?"

"It's a lesser fae, a blood-borne creature created by Emnonmedea to punish the world for the atrocities of bloodshed and war. Even calling it 'fae' is an insult to fae everywhere"

"I'm not certain what you mean by 'blood-borne'."

"It rises out of the blood of those slain, and it takes as its personality all the vengeance and hatred of the men who had contributed to its formation. They are not normally found in our part of the world. It's either come here on accident…" her voice trailed off.

"Or someone summoned it," Corwyn ventured.

"Hæmomancy." Meira bit her lip.

"Excuse me?" Robert placed his hands on the table. "I know I'm rather new to the world of magic, but…"

"Hæmomancy, King," Corwyn explained, "is blood magic. It's very old. It sources from the power of Emnonmedea. It's usually not any more dangerous than any other magic, because few practitioners are any good at it."

Meira looked at Corwyn, "T'xerren Nahasmen is a hæmomancer, but it has no body."

"Had no body," Corwyn corrected. "We haven't seen it in a while."

"Why is a body required?" I asked.

"Without your own blood, you can't control blood," Corwyn answered, simply enough. "Regardless, as long as there is not a hæmomancer within your realm, then it's not a problem we would need to address."

"But if there is?"

"Then that would be a serious problem. But at the moment it doesn't appear that way. A powrie here could simply mean someone sent one from over the sea or through the mountains. Priests of Emnonmedea abound in the world. Many of them are knowledgeable of the magic, although they usually avoid it in deference to their god."

"And, Robert, Corwyn's right about Nahasmen. He may have taken a body," Meira stated.

"Won't Father be thrilled," Corwyn noted.

"This problem's getting out of control," Robert looked around at everyone, seeking opinions.

"The problem for the moment, my king," Amos injected, "is the problem before us."

"Amos is right, Sire," I confirmed. Several others nodded

their agreement. "Let's deal with what we have. Destroy the pest first." A few ayes were heard around the table.

"Fair enough. Ambassador, what sort of magical ability can we expect it to possess?" Robert asked.

"Little. The creature was already at the extent of his power when he was attempting to ensorcell us last evening. Powrie are good at only a few things, and spells are not among them."

"Can we kill it?" Ira asked.

"Absolutely, but we must employ the ritual that we used at the execution on the way to Gavin's residence."

"Again?" Robert asked. "It wasn't pleasant the first time; I'm not thrilled with the idea of making this a habit."

"I'm afraid, Robert, that it may become somewhat common for a while, at least until this enemy is again defeated," she replied.

"What about the men and women that were taken?" Jardin asked.

"With the creature destroyed, most of them should return to normal as though waking from a nightmare. There will be those who do not, and they cannot be saved. From what we observed, these should be few."

"We've already lost and buried over three hundred souls to this beastly thing. I would hate to lose more," Jardin lamented.

"Corwyn," Robert motioned to him, "can you blink into the enemy camp and capture him?"

"King, I doubt I could do either. He would not choose to come here, and he likely has charmed the forest around him to repel that kind of entry. It's a simple charm, but a strong one."

"Can you lead a group of men back to their camp, then?"

"Sire," I answered for my wife, "do you remember the childhood story Corwyn related as we arrived here?" Robert nodded. "The armies had fought over this area, and they burned this particular forest. Matthias sent Meira to rebuild it. The enemy — the powrie — has taken up residence in the tree-home she lived in during those years.

This revelation drew several eyes.

"I would call that a divine coincidence," Harry said for everyone.

"Is there any reason to avoid a direct assault?" Edgar asked. "We seem to have knowledge of the terrain, and we certainly have surprise."

"Powrie are tremendously skilled and quick in combat," Meira answered. "He could kill several of our men before any chance of harm came to him."

"Battle, my lady," Ira clarified, "is what we do. If we die to rid the land of this filth, then that is the end we face. It is, after all, the reason we wear the armor."

The men nodded and grimaced.

"But the knowledge of his speed shouldn't be lost on anyone," I clarified. "Expect that any strike will be parried and returned immediately. It's best if we never get caught fighting it one on one."

"And keep your pretty faces behind your shields," Amos added.

"The question, though," Robert stopped them, "is will we beat it? I'm not a fan of combat in general, and I really hate losing men for nothing."

"I…" Meira hesitated. "Yes. Between you and they and us… he can't beat us all."

"Then we step into battle as we would any other time," Warner remarked. "I, for one, am ready to risk my life to defeat this enemy." The others chorused the sentiment.

"Especially if we live," Mark added, raising his cup.

"Hear, hear!" the Dozen roared.

"Then it is agreed. We will engage the enemy tomorrow. Kill none if you can possibly avoid it. Mardok will lead the strike against the powrie, at least six swords against it at all times. Craddok, divide up your men and assign them to report to mine."

"Yes, Sire," Craddok agreed.

"Sire," Amos interjected, "if we're going into combat tomorrow, it would be nice to maintain our element of surprise. If we go marching through the fields without a good distraction, the enemy will know of our coming."

"Ambassador, you have power over the weather, don't you?" Mark asked.

"The wind is my friend, yes, but I don't command the weather."

"Oh, I was thinking a good thick fog would do the trick. It's not unusual to see that along the northern coast, is it?"

"No, that's fairly normal around here, though a bit late in the season," Jardin concurred.

"A fog I can handle," Meira answered.

"Excellent. Men, this is a shield-heavy battle. We don't need to turn any more of those children into orphans. And I would rather not have to find replacements for you, either. Dismissed."

Meira

Preparations drew late into the evening.

Sister, come see what I've made, Corwyn called to me. I flew into the air and over to the forge, where the men were collecting and inspecting their weapons and armor. Grim faces were all around; none wanted to attack an enemy that consisted primarily of their friends, neighbors, and siblings.

Corwyn was standing proudly in front of his creation, a carpenter beside him—clearly the one actually responsible for any success in this endeavor.

It's... interesting. It looks like a mobile gallows.

It is. We can take it with us to dispatch the powrie on-site. I don't want to try to bring him back here, and I'm not really interested in giving him time to figure out how to escape.

Corwyn, or I should say the carpenter, had affixed an upright and crossbeam to a cart. He had filled the cart with dried brush and chaff. It was far too short to effectively hang a human, but it wasn't a human for whom it was intended.

If you set the stones and enchant the cart, it will suit the purpose. I'd do it, but I seem to have misplaced my stones.

I rolled my eyes but had to agree with his plan. I withdrew the stones for execution and placed them properly on the cart. The carpenter used a charcoal stick to draw around each one's position as I set them down.

"We need to make sure the stones don't move," I told Corwyn. "This cart seems a bit rickety."

"I'll see to that, m'lady," the carpenter replied. "And I'll be making sure there is more than enough fuel to make the fire plenty hot enough to burn the remains."

"Are you sure you want to set fire to an entire cart? I understand they are quite a commodity."

"Not this one, m'lady." He gestured at it offhandedly. "It was a manure cart that belonged to my late brother. I couldn't think of a more fitting way to retire it and honor his name than to dispose of the disgusting filth that killed him." He was pleased with himself.

I nodded my agreement and left them to their work.

15

19th of Lar Indar

Mardok

The following day could not have come soon enough. Even as I woke, my head was filled with apprehension of combat, but my heart ached for justice.

I walked with my father through the house of a lowly widow who had been ravaged and left for dead. His investigation would be short, since she was able to tell us the name of the villain. But the king, unwilling to punish anyone without sufficient evidence gave my father the task of confirming the story. It was, in his estimation, readily obvious what had occurred — from the torn clothing, the blood on a table corner, and the scattered belongings.

"The world is filled with evil," he said. "It's our job — your job — to do something about it. Some days it's a less pleasant task than others, but you don't get to take a day off from protecting the innocent."

After corroborating the woman's story with a neighbor who had heard the struggle and another man who had seen the man traversing one way and then the other, my father delivered his report to the king. The man vehemently denied what he had done, even smirking when he saw the woman alive. The king pronounced him guilty, and my father took him into the courtyard and ran him through.

- - -

Meira was already up and flitting around the sky over the castle, casting her eagle's gaze over the forest and river. Some of the men were up as well, making first preparations with their armor. To ensure silent passage through the trees, we had decided to leave the horses behind, so two men would be pulling Corwyn's cart into the forest by hand.

Cooks passed around bread and fish, and the men ate in somber reflection.

Robert and Craddok emerged from the residence—each arrayed in full armor. Robert's armor certainly out-shined the governor's, but he held his own for appearance, even if the fit of his breastplate spoke of days when there had been more food to go around. We held conversation openly with each other and the troops while they finished waking and preparing. There was no particular rush, so we made no call to arms. By mid-morning, everyone was dressed and ready for battle.

Robert jogged up the steps of the wall to address us. We were a small crowd—his Dozen, Meira and Corwyn, the governor, and twenty-seven others who were fit enough to carry sword and shield. Beyond the group of us, the rest of the people protected by these walls looked on. Hope was in their eyes, but no one smiled yet.

"Men!" the king called. "Today we engage the enemy. But this is not an enemy that is familiar to us. This enemy is a foe as ancient as the world. Even so, it is as mortal as you or I. You know the difficulty we face. The troops we will meet in combat will be your own families. They'll be brothers and sisters, mothers and fathers. The enemy knows you can't kill them without cutting out your own souls, but we won't have to. Once we kill the enemy who has enslaved their minds, they will be free.

"I'm not saying this is going to be an easy fight. It won't. But it will be victory."

He descended the steps and gave orders to open the gates. He passed between the troops, meeting each set of eyes—some terrified, others sorrowful, others angry. At each he stopped and asked the name of one person they knew who had been taken.

"For Julian," he would say, "for Benson," "for Davian," "for your wife, Hannah."

After passing the last man, he turned around to address them again.

"Quietly," he instructed. "Remember to go quietly." Then he led the troops through the fields toward the forest.

After an hour and a half of walking through the thick fog Meira's 'friends' had laid all through the night, we entered the edge of the woods. We stopped briefly to eat a quick bite and regroup and then moved on toward our target. Meira took the lead as we headed into the heart of the forest. She led us on winding trails and twice up into the trees themselves where the old growth trunks and intertwining branches were unnaturally wide enough for the wagon to pass along the top. It felt as if the forest was encouraging us on our way. Mid-afternoon found us outside the edge of the enemy camp.

I noted the governor and his men looking at each of the people standing or wandering through the clearing. As each person under the thrall was recognized, the governor's men mouthed names to each other. Everyone from the castle knew several of these people. Near the edge of the clearing, sitting on a chopped log outside the treehouse, was the unnatural creature — the powrie — staring into a small fire.

"He's fire-gazing," Corwyn whispered to Robert. "It's a way to communicate with someone over a distance or to see into the future."

"Which is he doing?"

"Even among the gods, only a select few can peer into the future."

The fire dimmed, and the powrie leaned back. He adjusted his headpiece, allowing fresh blood to stream down over his face. It hit his mouth, and he licked it up.

Tell Robert that I'm going to push the powrie back into the house, Meira told me. *Then he should attack.*

Where did you go? I asked Meira.

To get a better vantage. Do not worry, my husband, I will be safe.

"Sire, Meira is about to knock that creature on his backside. Are you ready for us to attack?"

"Yes, signal the men."

I passed the order along. Each of them pulled shield to nose and waited.

We had lined one side of the camp, from the same vantage as the day before, although further back to disguise forty-three people. Our plan was simple — create a wedge of shields and push directly into the center of the camp to plug the entrance to the tree house.

The air drew deathly still. The powrie's smile faded. He opened his eyes wide as they darted about. He jumped to his feet and pulled in his breath to shout, but too late. A blast of air came hurtling from the trees ahead of him, limbs snapped, and leaves billowed and pounded him. He flew off his feet, tumbled in mid-air, and landed on his back several feet from the house.

Then the blistering light that was Meira tore into the clearing, her arms outstretched, her mouth open in silent song. The air circled around the downed fae. He looked into her face and snarled.

"Magic won't protect you from me, witch!" he screamed, diving into the tree house.

"Now!" Robert shouted. Nearly four dozen lungs screamed together as we charged into the camp. Only two of the people in the camp responded aggressively. Both were eliminated swiftly — one with a knife thrown by Corwyn and the other with a devastating upward slash by Frank. The remaining looked up at us confused and bedazzled.

The powrie reemerged, brandishing his club.

"Attack them! Kill them!" he screamed.

Raeburn, Seth, and Warner slammed into him with their shields, forcing him back inside. He laughed at them and began his attack. He swung his jewel-studded club with mind-numbing speed, trying to collapse or move their shields to the side.

Lunging between them I brought down my sword against his arm. He took it with the butt of his club and slung my weapon easily to the side. Then he hammed my shield rapidly. It seemed like a futile tactic until the jewel studs began splintering the wooden body of the shield.

Edgar swung in from the back, promptly taking a beating himself, before the powrie saw an opening and dropped a crushing blow into Warner's shoulder.

By now the wretched thing was hemmed in, but this didn't seem to faze it. Moments later Edgar took a crack to the shin and Mark was bleeding from an unseen injury to his sword arm.

I pressed the attack while Craddok's men behind us retained their shield wall in a pushing match against their mind-numbed friends and family.

Three swords at once we hacked at the powrie. Then he directed his focus back on my shield, hooked it through the middle, and ripped half of it from my arm.

I tried to reposition my sword, but the powrie leapt and brought his club down. I threw up my empty left hand to block the hit.

As the club struck my hand, the ring Matthias had given me flashed and popped, and the club disintegrated, splintering into a thousand fragments. My hand, though, was unaffected. It felt nothing.

The powrie howled from the stun taken by his arms. Off-balance he fell into the wall, but only for a moment. He was up again and sneered, the nub of his club pointed threateningly at me.

"Man-slug!" he screeched, "you expect to take me?" He grabbed a bowl of blood and spilled it on the ground. Then he dove into it as into a deep pool and disappeared.

"Where did he go?" I screamed.

Corwyn appeared in the middle of the room. "Yup, he messed up," he announced.

"What do you mean? He's gone!" Outside the men were pushing back against the crowd with their shields.

"He had to dispel the charm to teleport, even through blood. Tricky little fiend. I told the men to bring the wagon." And he blinked.

"He's out here!" Ira cried out. I ran back out of the house as the powrie was plunging his club handle into the back of one of Craddok's troops. He ducked and rolled aside as Frank's blade zipped across where his head should have been. Another of the governor's men fell to the club handle. A wall of shields began to move around him, and he slid back into the ground, reappearing several yards away where another body lay bleeding.

Meira, who was hanging in the sky blasting air about to keep the innocents at bay, fired a shot at the powrie. It knocked him backwards, and he disappeared into the earth, back inside the tree house where he had started.

Warner, fortunately, was on his guard and held his ground against the raging onslaught of repeated blows. I pushed my way inside to help him.

Make him teleport again, Corwyn pushed into my mind. He gave me an image of a fresh pool of blood with a rope around it.

I understood.

I charged at the powrie, blade swinging wildly. He slid back into the pool he was standing in.

"HA!" Corwyn cried aloud. I whipped around and saw Corwyn toss a rope to Meira. She flew high, towing the powrie, dangling by his foot. She flew over the wagon and secured him in place. Her knife was already in her hand. The air curled with the familiar and haunting song she had sung nearly two weeks previous. It was different this time, since Corwyn was singing it, too. Their voices blended in a perfectly sickening harmony. It was wrong in all ways possible, yet still enchanting.

Robert had reformed the line of troops around the wagon to protect it. Men stood arm to arm, shield to shield, grim-faced against their ensorcelled friends. With the wind dying away, most stood up again and began lumbering toward the wagon and their leader, who was thrashing about, trying to strike people with the stick he held. Unable to reach them, he curled up to free himself.

"Hold his arms, Harry!" Robert ordered. Harry fought with the fae and took a grip of his wrists. Robert swung his sword high and slashed down, severing the fiend's elbows.

The powrie let out a soul-piercing wail, and he struggled harder, slinging his free foot about. Meira ignored his struggle as she sang and flew purposefully about him.

"Kill them! Kill them!" he shrieked. The crowd pushed mindlessly against the soldiers. Only the strength of their sheer numbers was any real threat now. Their leader was losing control of them, and they were losing the will to fight for him.

On Meira's third pass, Robert grabbed the powrie's hair and pulled its head back. The thing uselessly beat on Robert's polished armor with his stumps. As Meira dispatched him, Robert deposited his head in a tar barrel on the cart. We allowed the rest of his blood to pour into it as well.

The people stopped pressing and stood in place to watch, expressionless. And as Meira set fire to the barrel, they stumbled around and fell into each other until each in turn collapsed on the ground and fell asleep.

"Secure the area," Robert ordered. "Bring them back to the castle. Let the cart burn."

Meira

The celebration was, to be sure, much more subdued than it should have been. Most of the participants simply slept through it. The release of stress and emotional strain left several grown men sitting about the courtyard, crying bitterly to themselves, with their wives, parents, and friends finally resting peacefully at their feet.

There were burials as well. I found it hard to express sympathy to the humans concerning death. There hadn't been a death in my family since I was born, and until I met Mardok, all of my friends were family. Several cast looks at me.

"It must be nice, being immortal," said one man, while he looked upon the face of his father one last time.

"Can you bring them back?" asked one of the older boys who had stayed. "Can you heal death?"

"I'm sorry. I'm not that powerful."

I flew up to the top of the north tower where Mardok was keeping watch. His eyes and jaw were set.

"My love," I began. *The battle is won.*

"Something has changed, and I can't place my finger on what it is," he replied. He was gazing over the tops of the trees. Although the river was not visible from here, we could see the gap where it laced its way through the forest before bubbling peacefully between the fields.

"Something," he continued. "A tree. There was a tree. I remember seeing it yesterday and marveling at how large it was and how it glimmered in the sunset."

"A tree… are you sure?"

"It wasn't your ordinary tree."

"From you, that's saying something. Where was it?"

"Several miles away." He pointed into the distance. "I figured it was at the mouth of the river."

"Trees don't knock themselves down, and they don't disappear," Frank said as he trudged up the steps. He stepped onto the balcony and looked over the landscape. "Nor do good watchmen ignore approaching silver faces," he finished, pointing toward the southeast.

We both looked at him and then down the wall. A lone Fae was sprinting toward the castle. His clothes were soaked, and his hair was pulled tightly to his scalp. He wore a tight tunic and pants.

"H'gorian," I replied. "He brings bad news."

"Well, he doesn't look like he's running for fun," Frank mused.

Corwyn, H'gorian approaches.

He's in Niffaria, dealing with a feud between Mer peoples.

Not anymore.

Corwyn appeared beside me.

He examined H'gorian. "Cancel the celebration."

I stepped off the balcony and flew quickly toward my much older brother.

"H'gorian," I asked, "what's wrong?"

"Enemy on the river!" he cried out as he ran.

"How far out?" Robert demanded as we entered the castle gate. Mardok and several others were on his heel.

H'gorian worked for his breath. A soldier handed him water and he drank quickly, grunting a quick thanks. "A few miles," he worked out. "Hard to say. Ships, many of them. Landed at the river mouth."

"Why didn't the wind tell me of this?" I asked.

"Your friend. Ask it, not me." He paused long enough to settle his lungs. "The beat of the sea is oppressive, and the river is confused. It isn't answering me."

"Why won't the water answer?" Corwyn asked.

"What kind of ships?" Robert added.

"I don't know, Corwyn," H'gorian answered him. "The rhythm of the water… it's become dissonant."

"Excuse me," Robert tried again, "but what kind of ships?"

"So something on the water… in the boats, you mean…" Corwyn began.

"Something, for certain… but what?" Meira tossed in.

"I really hate to interrupt, but what kind of ships?" Robert tried again.

"Have you tried calling the txipiori to inquire of it?" Corwyn suggested.

"I have. No reply… nothing."

"But the txipiori are yours to control," Corwyn pointed out.

"Hey!" Robert shouted. Several pairs of shocked eyes turned on him. "Human here… occasionally known to be king in these parts. If you wouldn't mind… what did the ships look like?"

"They were Hinter-class sea galleys, dual-sailed, forty paces long, with Yahm figureheads. Not from the Mersea, in case you're wondering."

"Actually yes, I was wondering."

"I only saw several dozen, but I am certain there were more."

"Just out of curiosity, were these Hinter-north or Hinter-south?"

H'gorian stared back at him blankly before answering. "I honestly do not know. Does it matter?"

"Hinter-north have three decks; Hinter-south have two."

"I tip my hat, young king. You know more than I was expecting."

"It was an obsession of mine as a child."

"They had two decks. So Hinter-south."

"Low in the water?"

"Yes, young king, they were full. But no flag flew to indicate whom. I understand your concern, but there is a far more worrisome issue here—why has the water gone silent?"

"I would think the arrival of ten thousand men on our shores might be worrisome."

"Men can be overcome; mere patience achieves that. But the arrival of a being capable of silencing the water…"

"H'gorian," Corwyn interrupted, "it might be worth noting that for the humans standing here, patience is a poor strategy. They only have so many years, and they prefer not to expend all of them running for their lives."

"Well… not for more than a few weeks at a time," Robert corrected. "And when we plant crops, we tend to want to harvest them."

"With my apology, young king, I have spent my life with the Mer. Their culture and yours share little in common with each other."

"You're telling me, though, that there are other creatures on those ships that are powerful enough to ruin your ability to control the water and, apparently, the air."

"Robert," I stepped in, "what we're saying is that we really have no idea what's on those ships."

"It is not merely a bunch of men," H'gorian added.

"Didn't you say that little imp in the forest was a servant to a greater master?" Governor Craddock queried.

"What imp?" H'gorian asked.

"A powrie," I replied. "If that's the powrie's master en route…"

"There was a powrie here?" H'gorian demanded. "Meira, there is trouble coming. Powrie are not generated from simple bloodshed or common killing."

"We're aware," Corwyn sided.

"How long," Robert asked, "until they arrive?"

"I'll find out," I answered. I flew out of the castle and toward the south-east. I weaved in and out of the trees, balancing speed with visibility. After three miles or so, the wind rushed past me down through the limbs, so I followed it.

There were columns of men working their way along the trails, trampling the undergrowth and chopping fallen limbs to clear a way for supply carts to follow.

An arrow swished near me, and then another. I skittered to the left behind thicker trunks. Several more arrows came flying in. I retreated quickly up into the clear sky. Two more arrows, but these fell short. Then a blast of fire. It thundered harmlessly to my right several yards away.

I turned and looked. A rogue Fae? I dove back into the canopy for a quick peek. No, it was a human. He swung about his staff, hurling several more bolts of fire in my direction.

A Mage! I screamed in my mind for my brothers and Mardok to hear. *They have a filthy wizard!*

My vision swirled, and I appeared back over the castle, near enough to a tower to collide, had I not expected Corwyn to blink me back to him.

"We leave," Corwyn told Robert. "King, I cannot order you or your men to go. But we will not and cannot stay and fight a mage."

"Certainly not one powerful enough to dampen the air and water," H'gorian added.

I turned to H'gorian. "I still find it incredible that he could garner that much power over the water, though. Air is fickle and gets confused easily. Water though...."

"Nice chit-chat; we'll discuss it later," Corwyn interrupted. "King?"

Robert looked like he had been punched. I landed and stood silently along with the other men while Robert considered. He didn't ask Mardok for counsel, or any of the others. Pain crept over his face, and he appeared as though he wished he had permission to shed tears.

"We leave," he resigned. "Gather everyone together. Corwyn, you have become the master of evacuations. Do what you can, and use whoever you need; take these people to join their children."

"Without hesitation."

"The enemy's too close, Sire," Craddok objected. The people are still recovering from the effects of magic. They can't move quickly."

"Anyone," Robert looked around the group, "what do we have besides blood to slow them down?"

"We have big, monstrous rock creatures," Mark suggested.

"We do indeed," Mardok inclined his head toward the young warrior.

"I will bring them, Sire, but remember…" I started.

"They will not kill," he finished. "We need them to prevent killing. And one other thing…" He looked me in the eye, a momentary twinkle returning to his. "The castle needs remodeling anyway. I would hate to give the enemy a perfectly good fortress."

I smiled. They were going to enjoy this.

Mardok

Meira knelt down and spoke her garbled tone into the earth. She continued for quite a while, not simply summoning the terriculi to her as she had before. For a while it seemed as though she were arguing or imploring. But in due course she raised her head, satisfied.

"The trees!" a soldier cried from the north tower. "The trees are falling!"

I looked at my wife who, while still smiling, was crying. Her shoulders and wings slumped, and she whispered sadly into the still air.

I ran up the steps with several others to see what was unfolding.

At the edge of the forest, dozens of trees had been uprooted and cast on their sides. The ground was heaving and jutting here and there, throwing rocks and trees this way and that. All of the routes into or out of the forest were being cut off.

"Okay men, that's enough. Let's get the people packed." I led the remaining men from the walls and into the courtyard.

Corwyn already had everything organized, with Craddok barking at the people to keep them moving. Those still in deep sleep were being moved into carts. The remaining were gathering at the gate. Supplies were hastily loaded and horses hitched. It was a marvel to behold.

"I think," Robert commented, walking up beside me, "that Corwyn is in charge of the caravan of nobles next year."

"Sire," I replied, "not all the magic in the world can

resolve that particular mess."

The soldiers pushed open the gate, and the people began filing out, Craddok again at their head.

"Move quickly," Craddok called out to them.

CRACK!

The thunderous sound echoed across the landscape, coming from the forest where the enemy was traveling.

"Run!" Craddok urged them on. They turned hard to the right outside the gate to keep the retreat of the people hidden. A half mile away they would plunge back into the southern woods. Craddok's few troops held the rear, mounted upon the horses we had brought with us.

CRACK!

"Bar the gates!" Robert ordered, as the last one stepped through it. He was mounting the steps to the wall two per stride.

All that remained inside were the Dozen, Robert, Meira, Corwyn, and H'gorian. We gathered on the wall to see what had caused the commotion.

Two great trees that had been freshly laid on the ground had been cleaved, their centers splintered.

CRACK!

One of the halves was flung into the air in two more large pieces, with smaller sections flying in hundreds of different directions.

CRACK!

Another went flying with the same results. This time, a large opening was left between the forest and the fields. In the opening stood a man clad entirely in yellow, a glistening shaft of metal taller than he in his hand. He spun it thrice and dropped it against the third tree section.

CRACK!

It went flying away in pieces.

Three more spins, and CRACK went the remaining section of tree.

Now a large pathway was open into the trees.

"Men, it's time to go." The terriculi had arrived in the castle—four of them. And if I could guess anything about animated stones, they seemed rather excited to be there.

We watched as they began the process of disintegrating the residence. It was a horrible and thrilling sight. Ancient stonework was being reduced to rubble. The terriculi crumbled the stones as they slowly passed through them, leaving behind rock shards and sand.

"Are we all ready?" Corwyn asked.

"I would hate to find out how close that Mage needs to be to kill us," Robert offered.

"What are those?" Mark asked, pointing to a pair of creatures flying high over the castle. They were orange and difficult to see but for their erratic flapping, then they folded their wings and dove toward us.

"They're trouble," Corwyn replied. "Quickly everyone, hold hands. We're leaving." We grabbed onto each other as the creatures let out a scream that pierced our skulls. "To the king's courtroom," Corwyn shouted over the din. I slammed my eyes shut and concentrated.

And then… nothing happened.

"Now would be a good time, Corwyn," Robert demanded.

"It's not working! The bats have blocked it!"

"Blast this," Burke cursed. He pulled back from the group and whipped out his bow. The creatures continued their scream, spiraling around each other as they closed in on us. Burke placed an arrow into one of their heads. It dropped like a rock. The other peeled off and flew back toward the forest, where the mage's army was pouring out of the trees into the fields. Burke nocked a second arrow, but the bat was out of range.

"Try again?" Robert asked.

"Sorry, but the dispulsion will last until the other one is dead or gone."

"Those weren't normal bats," I told him.

"No, they're hebetates—censor bats. They silence and dampen magic. And today they've chosen to dampen our ability to leave."

"What about the rest of your magic?"

"Only one hebetate means only one type of magic can be dampened," H'gorian answered. "If it chooses to dampen something else, it risks us escaping."

"Fine, then we'll do this the other way," Robert announced. He pulled the maoim beatha from around his neck and spoke into it. "Matthias, we need your help. Now." There was silence for a moment, and he asked again. Then again.

"King," Corwyn addressed him, "I've spoken with my mother. They know we need help, but the hebetate is blocking them from coming, just as it's blocking us from leaving."

"Well, then now I have a creature I hate more than pixies. Nice shot, Burke. If it gets in range again…" Robert nodded. Burke nodded back.

We stared at the mage's army as it filed out of the trees—over twelve hundred men, with another hundred on horseback. Along with them, there were several hundred hideously gray and green creatures I knew about but had never actually seen—goblins.

"What are they doing here?" Robert asked no one in particular.

"Other than acting as wonderful meat shields," H'gorian explained, "goblins survive well in desolate areas. Mages tend to like them for that reason."

"I don't follow."

"Mages destroy things. Everything. It's how they use their magic. They may leave well enough alone as long as people obey them. But when there's a fight, they suck the life from everything around them to utilize their magic."

"The fae don't kill things to perform magic," I interrupted.

"No, brother, they don't," Corwyn concurred. "But mages

aren't fae. They're human. They ravage magic like a catamite. This venery creates a price that must be appeased with blood."

"That's a distasteful depiction," Seth muttered.

"They're phenakists of the worst kind," Corwyn continued. "And Mister Steatopygia out there…"

"You're such a Witzelsucht," H'gorian announced, rolling his eyes.

"Have you ever seen the Mage Wastes, King?" Corwyn inquired, pretending not to notice.

"No, I've never heard of them."

"I've seen the memories of them,"Corwyn began.

"I've been there," Meira interrupted. "Grandmother took me to see them in person, so that I would understand just how heavy the cost was for the world. She showed me her memory of what they were before the Reiving. They were jungles, lush and wild and free. Filled with life."

"It's the reason the mages chose that ground," H'gorian explained. "It gave them power. Something to feed upon."

"They were laid completely to waste. Nothing grows. Nothing breathes. Nothing moves. Only the wind and the sand, and even they are dead there." Meira's eyes reflected utter sorrow.

"What can we do against such a foe?" Raeburn asked.

"Our only chance, Sire," Amos counseled, "is to make for the southern forest, the same route the governor took. Otherwise we die here." I looked at the men. They were shaken.

Courageous, yes; willing to die, yes. But certainly it wasn't what they had planned for the day.

"We can't follow them. Their cavalry would overtake us and then follow our lead toward the governor's people." Robert turned and faced everyone, looking each of us over carefully. "You all know that I would do anything humanly possible to get us out of this mess. But unless our friends here," he motioned to the Fae, "have some other unexpected tricks, then today may be our day."

"If it's all the same to you, my King," Edgar ventured, "I would personally like to turn twenty-two at some point."

"I know. It's a shame," George countered, "you're so young. Not much life to suck out of you."

Frank looked at George, who was only twenty-two himself, and snickered.

Meira and Corwyn were staring at each other.

"What?" I asked.

"Well," Corwyn answered, "you're all... so..."

"Young," Meira finished, kissing my cheek lightly. "Now, I don't think it's a good plan to fight this enemy without some help. Shall we round up an army?" Meria shot up to the tower, where she perched herself precariously on four limbs. Then she cast up her head into the air and let out an awful cry—the howl of a lone she-wolf. Then she made all kinds of strange noises, blowing them all into the air. Chirps and mumbles and yips and noises I didn't know existed.

Meira

In short order, howls returned from the hills around the trees — far more than in the trees themselves, but far fewer than I had hoped. I could hear, as well, that the birds on the wind had heard my cry. Mumbles appeared out of the stonework beside me, having received the request to stop grinding the castle while we still needed it. I'm glad I told him so soon, too, since they had finished turning the residence to sand and powder. I smiled at the piles of wooden beams, old tapestries, and kitchen utensils that remained. Fliddlehene had left to erase Craddok's escape route, so that no evidence of it remained.

Over the course of the next hour, while the enemy continued to gather their forces, my friends arrived and collected outside the wall. I floated down to them. Several pushed their way to me for attention, but I yipped impatiently and asked to speak to the alpha. He walked forward proudly, nipping at some of the younger wolves as he passed by them. When he was in reach I put my hand on his nose, resting my fingers between his eyes.

His thoughts were contained in images and smells, so it took quite a while for me to express what I required of him. He grimaced and acknowledged that though he was unhappy with the task, he would obey — even to the last wolf.

Only briefly did I maintain my conversation with the alpha, but in doing so I learned of the losses the pack had already suffered at the hands of the hunters under the powrie. After showing the alpha that the powrie was now dead and sharing with him the stench of his blood, he expressed his gratitude, and his gaze steeled with firm resolve.

He barked and growled, rousing his followers to obey their last instructions in this world. At first they whimpered. Then as pack fever overtook them, they howled, barked, and leapt about, growling and baring their teeth.

I left them to their frenzy, returning to a rather comical sight on the wall.

"My dear wife, it's good to see you again. What do we do with all of these?" Mardok waved about to several hundred birds who had answered me. A couple had landed on Mardok, and he absentmindedly petted one.

"I mean, the eagles yes, I understand. But… well… sparrows."

"Have you ever had your eyes plucked out by a sparrow?" Robert asked Mardok as he handed a cooing dove to Ira.

"No, I can't say that you have either."

"Let's not provoke them. They could get angry."

"Personally, I would prefer a manticore or two," Seth said. "I don't suppose you have one available."

"No," H'gorian answered, "where do you humans get your silly ideas for what kind of creatures inhabit this world?"

"That's too bad. Have you seen what the enemy has been waiting on?"

We all looked where his hand was pointing. Lumbering out of the trees were creatures I had been told only lived near Bakarrik's Mountains. Two mountain trolls, both with flush white skin and light armor, carried massive hammers over their shoulders while they looked about very stupidly. The mage, their lord, flashed a light before them and commanded orders. I couldn't hear at this distance, but I didn't need a message from the wind to know what they planned. Their target was the wall's only barred gate.

"Arrows are useless against them, Robert," H'gorian explained, "their skin is too thick for arrow heads to penetrate, and their eyes are completely obscured."

"I'm not inclined to let them knock down our gate," the king replied. "How do we kill them?"

"The dvergr rely on axes to their legs."

"I could handle that," Warner offered. "Lemme at 'em."

"You would have to reach them, first, and while I know you're skilled, a thousand men and goblins are a bit much to cut through," Robert remarked.

Warner grimaced, but Robert was clearly right.

"H'gorian could call in a million goldfish to fight for him," Corwyn pondered allowed. H'gorian answered with a slap to the back of his head.

"Sometimes, in battle," Amos counseled, "you have to just cut out the fodder and deal with the big guys last. If the trolls are the only enemy still standing, they won't be a problem."

"Then let us hope, Meira," Robert looked into my eyes, "that your animal army is up to the task."

"Meira," Corwyn asked, "do you remember that trick Uncle Y'argin pulled several decades ago."

"No, I don't."

"He found that he could order the bees. Do you think…"

"I know." I concentrated, listened to the beating of my heart and the stillness of the air, even though it wasn't still. I heard the tiny inflections of the wings of the insects who flitted about. I heard them, understood them, translated them, and spoke back.

16

19th of Lar Indar

Mardok

While I had seen Meira do strange things, this was definitely among the most odd. She flitted back and forth, concentrating her sight on a wasp only inches from her nose. Then she zipped up into the sky and displayed an odd arcing dance.

I suspected the results she received were intentional. For other than making a few hundred birds rather curious, thick clouds lifted up over the forests, over the water, and all throughout the fields.

"I'm not really a fan of plagues, Meira," Robert tapped her ankle.

"They won't be either," Meira smiled as she lit her skin. The glow was not intense, but the insects were drawn to it.

H'gorian stepped to the edge of the wall. "Now it's my turn." He held out his hands and formed a glowing ball.

"Not just a trick for the kids anymore, I see," Corwyn nodded.

"Not this time." And H'gorian hurled the ball several

thousand yards, deep into the ranks of the enemy. It landed squarely between the trolls, who the mage was still attempting to urge toward the castle. The ball stuck to the ground, and the millions of insects who had answered Meira's call were drawn to it. They bombarded the enemy, who for all purposes appeared incapable of fighting this nuisance.

"Onward, my friends!" Meira cried. The walls erupted with wings as every bird took to flight. The raptors screamed as they leapt into the sky. The wolves went silent and charged on padded feet. Few of the human enemy, distracted by the biting and stinging of their first foes, saw them coming, and their first ranks fell quickly.

The bloodshed was swift and grotesque. Beasts fight with what they have, with talon and beak and tooth. The plague gave them cover for a time, and they took great advantage of it. Hundreds of humans fell in minutes, although the toll on the wolves was great. The goblins, for their part, fared well. Being used to swarms of insects, they generally ignored them. But neither did they come to the aid of the humans, as the birds harassed them with impunity. Goblin axes, clubs, and spears were worthless against them.

But the onslaught had to end. With his staff, the mage emitted a thunderous roar. Sparks of lightning jumped from it to anything nearby, killing friend and foe alike. Then he twirled his staff over his head and thrust it into the earth. Black smoke boiled from the ground, and then a new enemy entered the field of battle.

It arose from the water, like a waterfall spilling into the sky and splashing against nothing in the air. Steadily streams of water split apart, forming several arms, legs, and a few heads, which came and went quite fluidly. Giant sprays of water flew from the creature, covering the troops with rain and drenching the plague of insects.

H'gorian gripped the wall as though ready to jump over. "Traitor!" he screamed at the being from the wall. "One touch. Just give me one touch," he fumed.

But while the insects were no longer a threat, and the wolves were being dispatched, the birds themselves were making tremendous gain with blinding their foes. The screams of agony from the enemy troops chilled our blood. It was a callous way to cripple an army. My heart complained that there was no honor in it.

Meira settled beside me. "The terriculi have left to deal with the txipiroi."

"The what?"

"The txipiroi. The water spirit. The terriculi will challenge and fight it."

"I thought that was against their moral code."

"Txipiroi can't be harmed, only dispelled."

"So we have an enemy that can't be harmed? This gets better and better."

"Well, it's not even technically alive." She looked around. "Where's H'gorian?"

"He was just…" but he wasn't. The gate was open, and H'gorian was running across the fields toward the water spirit. Frank and George were on his tail, but there was no way they would catch him. At least they were armed.

"Re-bar that gate!" Robert ordered. "The fools!" He returned his gaze to over the wall. "How are our friends fairing? Do we have the edge yet?"

"Perhaps," I answered. "Our wolves are almost gone, but the birds are still haranguing the enemy. In a few minutes, we might be able to handle them with swords."

"Only that beastly bat, two trolls, a mage, and a giant water… thing… to deal with," Robert said. "I still don't like our odds."

"Sire, if you like, I can handle the bat if you want the trolls," Burke replied.

"My love," I asked Meira, "do we have a chance against that mage?"

"No."

"Well, that's a way to encourage the troops," the king intoned.

"You would have me lie?"

As H'gorian and our two men charged off into fate, we were relegated to observe as our hopes for victory came and went again.

"Is there anyone else we can call?" Mark asked.

Birds and wolves littered the ground. The enemy troops were still slapping at insects that, though no longer flying, were stinging and biting every inch of skin they could penetrate. In war, morale is a major ally, and the enemy no longer had any. Hundreds of enemy soldiers stumbled about or sat, hands over their bleeding eyes, never again to see the light of day. Their cavalry were completely decimated. The battlefield was utter chaos.

The terriculi reached the txipiroi long before H'gorian, and the fight they began was like nothing I had ever imagined. Pillars of stone shot into the air, landing all around the spirit, crashing into the water with giant splashes. They sprayed thick clouds of dust and debris, turning the sprays of water to mud, which fell far short of the field of combat.

"Do they even know what they're doing?" I asked Meira.

"They're not experienced with fighting. This is completely unfamiliar to them."

"They don't seem to have a tactic." They were presently building a giant stone wall between the spirit and the armies. The txipiroi drew up an enormous ball of water and blasted the wall several times before putting a hole through it. At least they now had its attention. Unfortunately, they had acquired the attention of the mage as well.

He and H'gorian reached the water's edge at the same time. The mage fired several blasts of fire, which H'gorian deftly dodged before plunging into the river, swimming at unthinkable speed toward the txipiroi.

"Just reach him, brother," Corwyn quietly begged, his fists clenched.

Lightning began to spark from the mage's staff. He twirled it and brought it down in an arc toward the water. But at that moment, two things occurred.

First, a terriculum emerged from the ground in front of the mage, thrusting up a pillar into the air, catching the sparking staff and driving it far out of the mage's reach. Second, H'gorian's hand flew up from the water, followed shortly thereafter by his bared teeth, and caught the mage by the throat. His other hand held a knife. They hit the ground in a death struggle.

Frank and George charged in, swords at the ready, but the txipiroi blasted them with water, sending them backward. Several dozen goblins also closed on the area. Frank and George jumped back to their feet and turned to face the enemy.

H'gorian and the mage continued to roll about, but H'gorian was clearly the better fighter. The terriculi, not able to involve themselves with a fight between mortals, tried to busy the txipiroi again, but to no particular affect.

"Friends," Meira whispered into the stone wall, her hands pressed against it. She mumbled deeply. Seconds passed, and the terriculi vanished into the earth.

"Where did they go?" Robert asked her.

"I sent them upriver to block the stream. The txipiroi requires water. We can deny it that."

"Well, I was hoping they could give us some cover. Mardok, ready to go help Frank and George?"

"Absolutely, Sire," I answered him, the blood rushing through my veins. It was about time. I slid my helmet over my head. I had enough of waiting.

"Sire," Amos interjected, "I'll follow you without hesitation, but I think this isn't the wisest course. I love Frank and George as much as you do, but there's no way we can save them. If they return to us, we'll count it as a blessing, but we cannot afford to add our bodies to theirs."

Robert stared into his eyes. "I believe you, but I can't leave them to die."

"Sire, we didn't train them to be stupid."

And sure enough, they weren't. As the horde of goblins separated Frank and George from H'gorian, they recognized the futility of the fight. They could not, even in their best of days, rescue him. And so they fled back toward the castle, the goblins on their heels.

"What think you, Amos, of giving them support in their retreat?"

"We'll leave the gate open for you."

Robert slid on his helmet and ran down the steps.

"Burke, Amos, tower!" I ordered, "Rain hell on 'em!"

"Mardok," Corwyn called, giving his sword a last look-over. "Don't get yourself killed. Meira's too young to be a widow."

"Might want to tell her that about me. I don't think she's planning on staying here."

"I go with my husband."

We unbarred the gate and ran across the fields toward our retreating Dozeners. Meira flew overhead, dashing back and forth, blazing like the sun. As we closed ranks, the goblins shielded their eyes from her sheer blinding brightness. Then Meira blasted them with jets of wind, driving their ranks back. Their stronger warriors pressed forward. The first of these were met with arrows from Mark, Seth, and Raeburn. A moment later, the deadly aim of Burke and Amos found their own marks. A clash of arms wasn't in order, though, so we retreated together when Frank and George were back in our ranks.

Meira, however, seemed to have different plans.

Meira

Meira, get back here! Corwyn called to me. I'm certain Mardok would have said the same, were he to have noticed as well. I had to find H'gorian. So upward I flew, well beyond the throwing reach of the goblins. There he was, drenching from the continual pounding of the txipiroi.

Four goblins lay around him, their throats cut. The mage was trying to escape, but my brother had him hemmed with his back to the river. A fifth goblin charged up behind him with a spear. He thrust, but H'gorian spun, snatched the spear, sliced the goblin, and hurled the spear at the mage, missing cleanly. The mage clearly wanted his staff back, but it was still stuck at the top of the stone column, a good thirty feet in the air, where the terriculum had put it.

The txipiroi fired another water spout at H'gorian. He merely reveled in it, driving the water back toward the mage, sending him sprawling into the river. It was then that I saw the river had been steadily lowering. The terriculi had successfully diverted it.

The mage screamed at the txipiroi, which obediently stood between H'gorian and himself, throwing everything it had available. H'gorian took the bait, and I wish I saw the trap before it occurred.

H'gorian ran toward the txipiroi to dispel it. He only needed to touch it. But while he moved forward, the mage slipped around behind him, took up the goblin spear H'gorian had thrown, and threw it up at his staff. The staff fell into his grasp.

"NO!" I screamed, blasting a jet of fury toward the mage.

He met it with a twirl, knocking aside the attack, then he fired several bolts of fire at me. I dodged these easily enough, but only due to range.

The river had drained to be only a thin layer of water and mud, which completely hampered H'gorian from reaching the txipiroi as it fled from him across the top of it. He mucked his way back to the shore toward the mage. Bolt after bolt he fired, which H'gorian deflected and squelched with a makeshift shield of water. Another foolish goblin drew too close, and he dispatched him with a stroke of his knife.

As he closed range, the mage began spinning his staff again, a wicked grin on his face. Lightning snapped and crackled. H'gorian drew a wall of water around himself and threw it at the mage, then charged. Several goblins ran toward him. The mage flung up his arms, tossed the water, and spun the staff overhead to drop it on my brother for a kill. But he was too late. H'gorian threw his blade mid-stride. It cut cleanly through the mage's staff arm, severing it above the elbow. The staff spun in the air, the lightening flying wildly. Four goblins, the mage, and H'gorian were struck by a massive pop of energy. All were thrown backwards.

I flew with all my might, diving for my brother, who was now laying in a heap. But the swarms of goblins were much closer, charging at his defenseless form. I launched blasts with everything I had, but I couldn't rescue him. My rage boiled; I felt hatred rise. My skin burned with fury. Dropping on them from above, I grabbed at the villains. My skin scorched the ones I touched, and they screamed in pain. The others drew their weapons against me.

I knew it was too late. Fresh silver blood tainted their blades.

And then the wind returned to me. It whispered in my ears. "Calm, my daughter." It touched me, brushed against my face. The goblins were clearly terrified of me. I could see the light of my own skin reflecting off their armor. But I would not be foolish enough to attack them all. With tears filling and stinging my eyes, I pulled back. The goblins gathered together, shielding their eyes, but still putting their weapons ahead of them. They charged as one. Behind them I saw the body of my brother, most noble of all Fae, laying still—pierced through multiple times.

Again the wind came to me. "Peace, my daughter. Be peace. Cast not your life for naught."

My throat caught still, my rage flashed in torrents. I fired a blast of hot wind, cutting through one goblin. But another took his place as they moved toward me, driving me back. They were trying to get within range to throw small axes.

I held my heart. It was hollow.

Meira, my love. Please.

Before my muscles could give way, I flew away, back to my husband.

Mardok

As Meira flew back toward us, dark clouds filled the sky where only minutes ago had been a clear day. Thunder bit at the horizon. Meira's heart and agony, stirred with rage and vengeance, were punctuated by a flash of lightening at each spasm of her body.

I stood again on the wall, waiting for her, just to hold her close, to provide her some minimal bit of comfort. I glanced at Corwyn. H'gorian was his brother, too. His face was stone.

Brother... I started. He looked at me. Deep within his eyes I could see the despair, the feeling of failure from a man who had been prevented from saving his own brother. His feelings were too deep to be called sorrow, or rage, or any other regular term — just darkness. *We still have to deal with the now,* I reminded him.

Meira stepped down next to me, and I pulled her in. Her cheeks were streaked with tears, mixing with the first drops of rain, which she buried in my chest. I felt her body shudder, and the sky flashed again. Corwyn watched the open plain as the enemy rearranged itself. Only a few hundred were left, and they were rudderless.

"Meira," Corwyn spoke, his eyes locked on the chaos. "The water has drained out from under the txipiroi. It's no longer in its domain." He turned and looked at her, and she turned her head to see his face. "It's clearly standing in the domain of the air. Call the haizea."

Her eyes narrowed and her teeth clenched. "Take the traitor," she whispered, and buried her face back into my chest. Immediately, a rush of air swirled around us, hastening off to the black, boiling clouds over the txipiori. The sky belched and seized, then twisted and curled. Tiny fingers of darkness stretched from the bottom of the swirling mass, reaching down, twisting together.

What water was left of the river the wind drove ahead of it downstream more quickly. The ground under the spirit dried as the terriculi squeezed out every bit of mud. The txipiroi swung its heads about looking all around it. It moved its legs to retreat to the water, but it was having great difficulty moving across the surface of the cracking earth.

Then over its head the dark fingers coalesced into a funnel. Amongst the flashes of lightening, I saw what seemed to be several giant eyes, entirely cloud, staring down at the txipiori. The wind drove the funnel faster and faster as it dropped from the sky toward the ground. The tornado fell over the txipiori, spitting the water of the spirit's makeshift body in every direction. It gave a screeching gasp, and then it was gone. The goblins fled, but the wind had not come to bring judgment on them. Mere seconds reduced the txipiroi to spray and mist. With the water spirit dispelled, the tornado extinguished, and the wind dissipated. Steady rain began to fall.

Meira's muffled voice came from my shirt. "Did we win?"

Robert stood there silently shaking his head. Harry put a voice to the new concern.

"More have arrived, my lady. Another thousand, perhaps more, mostly goblins. They're coming out of the forest now. They appear to have a general with them, so we can't rely on a lack of leadership." Silence. "At least the mage is dead. Your good brother H'gorian saw to that."

Meira shook.

"No, not dead," Corwyn told him. "They don't die that easily. See how the goblins have returned to his body. Goblins don't care for the dead, not even their own filthy mothers." Indeed, it appeared they had more or less bandaged the stump.

"Why aren't the humans out there helping him?" Mark asked.

"Perhaps," Corwyn answered, "because they have seen him suck the life from other humans to heal himself. As he becomes more powerful… if he ever does… then whatever living thing is nearby will be a target for him. Even the grass."

"So," Robert summed, "we still haven't won." We stood in silence, watching the army march toward the walls, still well outside the range of arrows. The trolls were back under control, this time surrounded by large goblins. This general clearly understood how to motivate these beasts.

"You know… I caught a gryffin once," Corwyn mused, "while on Ehiza."

"No, you didn't. That was Jardrik and Iona," Meira mumbled.

"Really, I did. They caught them, too, but so did I. It has a black mane. Totally different face, though."

"I thought they lived really far away," Seth commented.

"They do. He caught a wild pig."

"It was the size of an ox. And it flew."

"You launched it with a catapult."

"Still counts."

"You tied a lion's skin and fake wings to a boar. That's not a gryffin."

For some reason, I believed Meira.

"You wanna see?" Corwyn inquired, a flash of cunning crossed his face.

Meira stopped and looked at him, perplexed.

He pressed. "Let's open the Kaiola and see what comes out."

"I have no idea how to do that. That's something only Father can do."

"Didn't he tell you? He gave you the key to open it."

Meira looked at Corwyn like he had grown two heads.

"He told me. I'm stunned he didn't tell you. Didn't he say to be careful not to put a drop of your blood on the ground, for Lur itself would give up those who sleep in the Kaiola within?"

Every single face from every single human turned and stared at Corwyn and Meira.

"Corwyn," Robert attempted to remain composed. "Why didn't you mention this before?"

"King, some of the creatures inside the Kaiola are best left inside it. We don't have a way to decide what comes out. I would dare say that spilling Meira's blood all over the ground would result in uncontrollable plague on the world of men."

"But a few drops," she replied.

"It's better than what's coming otherwise," Corwyn offered. "Realistically, when those trolls break down the gates, there will be blood everywhere."

Meira looked up, "Burke, would you mind lending me an arrow?"

"Certainly." He handed one to her, which she pressed into her arm until it drew molten silver blood. It coated the tip of the arrow and shimmered briefly before tarnishing black. She handed the arrow back to Burke.

"Aim well, lad," Robert encouraged him.

"Sire, I never miss." And he didn't. The arrow screamed through the sky for several seconds before finding its mark. The largest of the goblins, a hulk the size of a young giant, took it in the eye. It crashed to the ground, nearly tripping the troll behind it. The troll yelled and kicked the goblin over thirty feet out of its way.

"Nothing happened," Burke lamented.

"Burke, I really don't like cutting myself. Could you please just put the next one into the dirt?"

"Oh, sorry, my lady." They repeated the process of coating the arrow. Burke sent it sailing. The angry troll ignored the arrow as it bit into the earth between his feet.

But he couldn't ignore the rather sudden appearance of another troll directly in front of him — one a bit larger and already far angrier than he was.

"That troll," Corwyn explained later, "was captured by Telgrin. Telgrin made him angry by letting his lunch escape and led him on a chase to where the trap was waiting inside a cave."

The larger troll screamed in the smaller troll's face, then clubbed him. The resulting brawl lasted quite some time. It had the added benefit of smashing several goblins under their tussling bodies.

The enemy's other troll didn't find his challengers particularly threatening, as only a lion and a bear appeared in front of him. The troll kicked the lion out of the way, then swung his hammer into the bear, downing it in a single hit. But now he was distracted from the castle and turned his attention on the hordes of creatures that were wreaking devastation on his masters.

Among the creatures that appeared were several wild centri and satyrs, most of them armed, a pair of gryffins, six trolls, and a slew of lesser catches—primarily animal predators. The prize appearance was a massive dog, twenty feet at least in height.

"I don't know where that bad boy came from," Corwyn remarked about the dog. "That I'm aware, giant dogs haven't been around for centuries." Of course Meira had to correct him, because the dog was actually a girl.

She seemed far less interested in fighting than in playing, but the troll didn't have the good sense to leave well enough alone. He swung his hammer again, smacking the dog, who was taller than he was, in the leg. The dog yipped and backed up, stepping on several goblins. Spears and arrows flew pointlessly into her fur until she was fully irritated. She grabbed the troll's head in her mouth and shook him until his neck broke. She dropped him dead, her slobber drenching two goblins who were trying to chop at her forelegs. Then the dog ran, scattering goblins every which direction.

The most numerous appearances by far, though, were the pixies. These were the pixies that had not managed to escape the traps they were springing. Thousands upon thousands of pixies erupted into the sky.

Pixies, while not being considered a formidable opponent, are vastly more irritating than a plague of insects. Perhaps more important for the spectator is that when pixies die, you feel even less sympathy for them.

Their tiny screeches and humming wings combined to a thunderous roar as they latched onto every shiny thing they could find. Weapons, shields, and pieces of armor were expropriated from the goblins and humans. The pixies, being miscreants by nature, then flew up into the air and randomly dropped these items back onto their heads.

The trolls were far more devastating. While goblins and trolls tend to have mutually miserable appreciation for each other, an angry troll is frightening even to his own family. They smashed and crushed their opposition without feeling or remorse. Before the battle ended, the goblins had managed to kill four of them.

The gryffins were the noblest appearance. They are a proud race, having the majesty of an eagle and the wit of a fox. These beasts immediately noted the presence of their mistress and friend, Meira.

"This is our enemy," she spoke out to them. And they provided their devastation accordingly, with high-pitched screaming roars.

"What's that?" Mark pointed to the sky. A large object was flying… perhaps falling… into the field of battle. With a lion's skin draped over it and flapping in the air as it fell, one wing torn off, a terribly loud squealing pig fell into the center of a company of men. Only six or so were killed outright. The rest scattered from the giant exploding tusker.

"I told you I caught a gryffin."

"Boar."

For the fourth or fifth time that day, chaos reigned. Wild animals and fae alike tore apart the enemy, who attempted to flee before them.

"Gryffin. Just tell father it was a gryffin."

A few hundred troops made it back to the tree line, where there was at least a bit of safety. The remaining were butchered. The pixies, so happy to be free, harassed them mercilessly. As the sounds of the enemy faded to nothing, with the remaining pair of trolls chasing them through the trees, the two gryffins settled on the wall beside us.

"Boar," Meira repeated, before addressing them. She listened carefully to their muted growls. "Yes, we can do that," Meira answered. "Corwyn, they wish to return home."

"Assuming the hebetate is either gone or dead, I certainly can."

"You mean that beastly little bat that messed up your get-us-out-of-here magic?" Ira asked, leaning against the wall.

"Yes, that thing."

"That one ate it," he pointed. "Snatched it right out of the air."

"Good boy," Meira stroked the gryffin's face. It purred.

"Might have stood a chance trying to get away if those pixies hadn't caught it and brought it to him to eat."

"Ooo… pixies can be so pesky," she smiled, still petting the gryffin. "Glad they helped."

"Yep, he ate them, too." The gryffin licked her face and snuggled.

"Goodbye, my friends," she told them. It took several seconds before she could force herself to let them go. They raised their heads and wings in salute.

Corwyn walked up to the first and pressed his hand against it, closed his eyes, and the gryffin vanished. The second flared back from the shock and settled, permitting Corwyn to do the same with him.

With my heart still aching, I walked with the men out to the fields. Corwyn was polite enough to take the slow trip with us on foot. Our first interest was in finding H'gorian. The second would be the alpha wolf. Both would be honored in the court of my father.

The pixies were busying themselves pilfering the bodies of the dead of everything metal, and they were building a massive pile. What they planned to do with that pile was anybody's guess. Likely, though, it would be irritating.

We found the site where H'gorian fell. The pillar where the mage's staff had been taken was several yards away, as were torn portions of his yellow garb. The mage, his arm, and his staff were all missing.

H'gorian was within a stone dome erected by the terriculi, who were standing by. I expressed my gratitude to them, satisfied that the encasement they made was sound and secure.

"It's fitting that we leave him here beside the river," Corwyn remarked. "If Father wishes otherwise, I'll retrieve him later."

I wept again and held onto my brother and my husband.

Mardok

After Meira and Corwyn cast a spell of protection over H'gorian's sepulcher and left instructions with the terriculi to finish the demolition of the castle, the cloudy skies opened and a steady rain fell. The fifteen of us gathered for one last time outside the gates, and we held hands.

"Blank your minds," Corwyn told us. "Imagine a snow-covered mountain in a range of others. Near the summit of this mountain is a dwelling, cut entirely from solid stone. The walls are perfectly smooth, without fracture or filling. It was made by Bakarrik himself. It is the home he made for his wife Opella, and it is where my great-grandfather was born.

"In front of the house is a fresh spring. It bubbles continuously from beneath a cherry tree which is ever blossoming, and it runs down the mountain where it splits into four rivers. It is said that this spring is the tears of Bakarrik as he mourns for his wife. Personally, I think a god's tears would be rather salty.

"My father and mother are there, mourning her death. They are there to do what the King of the Fae has done every year since the time she died — to reinforce the spells placed upon her home — to seal it and to keep out decay. For to this day Opella's body rests within those walls.

"Breathe deep, and go with me there."

We breathed… and we went.

The air was crisp, although not frozen as it should have been for such a high place. Around the encampment of High Fae the mountain was buried in ice and snow. And looking out were several other mountains—all rock and ice and snow. But here, where we were, was a garden with fresh flowers. In the center was a giant cherry tree, pink and freshly blooming. From between the roots was a spring that trickled down the slope of the mountain.

"You are all welcome in this place," Matthias nearly whispered to us. "But I ask that you speak softly, for Mount Talibakas is sacred." He was wearing a split-color cloak. On the right half, which was crimson, a cherry tree was embroidered in gold over his chest. The left half was deep blue, with an eight-point silver star. On his head was a crown I had not previously seen. Silver thread, twined like cord, had been loosely braided. At each crossing of the twine was a jewel.

"I hope you do not mind, Robert, but when I heard that your life was in danger I saw fit to bring your betrothed here to us."

He led us through the garden to a table, on which was set a wide variety of fruits and vegetables. At the table were Lilliana and Amelia, numerous other Fae all dressed in subdued vestments, and an elderly woman of much reduced stature wearing a wide variety of amulets and pendants. Amelia jumped at the sight of Robert and ran to him. They clutched tightly.

"Oh papa," Meira started. H'gorian..." she stammered.

"I know. He has gone from among us."

She cried and held on to him.

"After four hundred and thirty-seven years, H'gorian, lord of the waters, has passed from this life into the next." They and Lilliana held each other in silence, tears wetting each of them.

At the table were numerous hugs and quiet weeping as well.

It was in this quiet that the elderly lady took to her legs and approached us.

"Robert, King of Men, I bring you peace."

"I beg your deepest pardon, my lady, but I do not know you."

"I am Higridath of Bakarrik's Mountains, Empress of the Dvergr. All of the mountains that you see are mine, and many more beyond."

"So you keep all of this," Robert indicated the garden around them, "fresh and growing."

"No, this garden and the house here belong only to Bakarrik himself. They are kept by the High Fae. But my dvergr protect it from intruders. Goblins and trolls to the south and east continually threaten us. But here and anywhere this side of the Wall of Garagrinth, you are safe from them."

"Not to dispute this, my good empress, but goblins and trolls came into my kingdom. They were led by a mage. He had enough power to conjure or summon a txipiroi."

"That is not a good sign, King Robert. We were able to observe some of what happened in the battle that you fought...."

"You watched it?"

"Yes, of course. We have the Pool of Seeing." She led us down a short path away from the groomed garden. A small trickle of water wound its way beside and between the steps. At the bottom, under the shade of an unkempt willow, was a muddy pond. Wooden stools were situated around its edges. Other than the tiny trickle in and a corresponding trickle out at the far side, the surface was smooth.

The empress passed her hand over the water. Within it appeared what little remained of Governor Craddok's castle—dim and difficult to see. The fishing village could also be seen. And there was the river, now flowing again, with the sepulcher for H'gorian beside it. We could even see the pile of armor and weapons the pixies had made. "You signaled Matthias that you needed his help, but he was not able to come, even with the efforts of every Fae here. We were forced to watch from a distance.

Matthias, Lilliana, and Meira joined us.

"You saw, then, that he dealt a significant blow to the mage," Robert told Matthias.

"The mage may or may not heal from it. H'gorian was a powerful Fae. The blade he used was made within this mountain range, in a dvergr forge. It was imbued with magic by Perwish, the daughter of Telwer the healer. This mage would have to be very powerful indeed to undo the damage H'gorian did to him," Matthias explained.

"I hope so. It cost him his life," Robert stated.

"It cost H'gorian nothing," Lilliana replied. "In an instant he went from this life to the next. It did, however, cost us much. We are the ones who suffer for his departure. And for my beloved and I, this is our first child to leave us. For as many times as a son or daughter of ours has stood upon the edge of the knife, all have previously returned to us."

Robert was silent, trying to figure out how to process this.

Tears glistened in his eyes.

"Robert," Lilliana nearly whispered, "please understand that we love you, and we hold nothing against you for the loss of our son."

"I try to bring people home; I do. As soldiers we give up our lives to save lives. But no matter how hard I try, I can't rescue them all."

Lilliana embraced him. "You are a king. You weigh lives in the balance. Some you save, some you cannot. Some you sacrifice, and some you esteem above others. Do it not for yourself, but for the love of your people, and you will do right. There is not a bit more that you should ever expect of yourself. You are young, and soon you will pass from this life and find those who died beside you waiting to greet you again."

"If you don't mind me asking then…" Robert's face was perplexed. "Why then do you mourn for your mother… for Opella?" Matthias, Lilliana, and Meira all looked at each other, unsure how to answer. So Higridath did.

"Robert, the Fae do not mourn for Opella. All of their songs and chants speak about their sorrow for her disappearance. Their writings are filled with it. But that's not why they mourn. They mourn that Bakarrik abandoned the world after she died. They mourn because he won't stop mourning. He is the most powerful of the gods, but he can't have her back. And so he mourns continually. For thousands of years he has mourned, because he's selfish. And while he mourns, the people of this world suffer under the strain and burden of evil things he could destroy."

Robert looked with open mouth at the three Fae. They did

not deny it.

"Matthias, I haven't read the book you gave me yet."

"The Histories, yes."

"It's all there, isn't it?"

"Much of it, yes. And probably enough."

"I figured as much. I really hate reading."

"It's alright, my beloved," Amelia offered. "You're the king. You have servants who read for you."

A Fae with a light blue cloak stepped up to Matthias. "Father, it's time for the twelfth convocation."

In silence we followed them to the front of the stone residence. We stopped quite a distance back where the dvergr empress stopped, assuming she knew what she was doing. The Fae, including now Meira and Corwyn, who had quickly changed their clothes, stepped up to the house. They each passed a front window, looked inside, and placed two fingers to their foreheads. They sang mournful and depressing notes. Each passed twice before disbursing back into the garden.

"There are seventeen convocations, each spaced a third of a day apart," Matthias explained to Robert. "Each has a slightly different song." He looked about to each of the Dozeners. "If you men would like to return home to your wives and children, perhaps for hot food or bath, we can take you now. None of these things are here."

They looked at Robert.

"If it's the same to you, Matthias, I would like to stay,"

Robert said. But looking at his men he added, "But I certainly am not recommending it for anyone. It's been a terrible day to follow a painful fortnight, and you all deserve time off. How's a month sound?"

Bewildered looks went around.

"Okay, fine, two days. If I remember correctly, there's still a giant dog and a pair of trolls wandering around the landscape somewhere. We have to catch them before they kill anyone."

"When we're finished here, we'll look for them as well," Matthias offered.

"Yes, I'm sure that someone will want to score well for their Ehiza."

"I see my children have taught you well."

Seven of the men opted to return home, to wives and children who were excited to have them back. Amos, who was a widower, elected to stay with Robert, Amelia, and myself, as did Frank, George, and Edgar, all of whom were unmarried. Over the next two days, we did a lot of listening, very little talking, and not a small bit of reading and studying maps of the world. It was a much larger place than I had ever considered.

Epilogue

22nd of Lar Indar

Meira

"Papa, we haven't talked about the powrie yet. How did it get here?" I sat next to him at the table in Opella's garden.

"How do you think?"

"Corwyn and I posited the idea that perhaps Nahasmen had regained a body. And then the mage arrived, and we wondered if perhaps he was the hæmomancer that summoned the powrie."

My father sat and thought for well over a minute, gazing out over the mountains. The frozen rushing mountain air arrived in the garden as only a crisp breeze.

"T'xerren Nahasmen is imprisoned on his island. No, my Rae, this is not the problem we face. But clearly he still has many tendrils wandering around Lur. Where these have come from, I do not know."

He continued, "For the powrie, I see options. Either he was summoned by a mage, or by someone else. Or, perhaps the powrie wasn't summoned at all, but came by another means. Perhaps the gods have answers for us regarding this, or the centri can provide us with guidance."

"You just asked more questions than I did."

"And yet I have fewer answers. But I do know this: If we maintain the course Bakarrik set before us, we will have done our duty by him and by all of Lur."

"It would be helpful if Bakarrik would cease his mourning."

"He cannot. The gods are incapable of change or growth. They are what they are. So if he mourns, he mourns forever, until the reason for mourning is relieved. I'm afraid that in the upcoming struggle we'll be on our own again—just as your great-grandfather Keltus was."

"We're more powerful than we were then."

"Be weary of power. It's a fickle thing. Even your own weapons can easily be stolen and used against you. And this, as you know, is exactly what our enemy intends to do. We may field a large number of ours, yes, and the dvergr will be loyal to us, certainly. But there are countless others who would side with the enemy if they were commanded. Even our own brethren could be overcome, and we would have to defeat them on the field of battle. This is what we have to prevent. Long has T'xerren Nahasmen sought to inhabit one of our own."

"Has he not?" Robert sat at the table beside us.

"Not in the way he desires," Matthias answered, clearing a spot for him. He gave him a chalice and poured wine. "T'xerren Nahasmen influences agents and subjects all over the world. He possesses them in a way, yes. We call these his tendrils. But he's never fully within any of them. The dark spirit himself still roams restlessly over the barren landscape on a distant island, waiting for opportunity to inhabit anyone who draws too close to him."

"Well, if he could take possession of someone and control

him, why not just bring him to the island. Get a boat and sail."

"The island is heavily guarded by a nation of merfolk and the txipiroi they control. An agent of T'xerren Nahasmen could not penetrate those defenses without all-out war. If rumors of such a war were to reach our ears, the forces of every free nation in all of Lur would reign down on the perpetrator. I would see to that personally."

"If this is the case," Robert asked further, "then how does it create more agents off the island?"

"This I do not know. We have long sought an answer to this question. If we're able to determine the means, we could combat it. In the meantime, we remain ever vigilant."

Robert pondered further in silence. He had been doing that quite a lot since coming here.

"Papa, did you see Corwyn's gryffin?"

"Corwyn's gryffin? I thought he caught a pig."

"No, papa, it was definitely a gryffin." I left the table to find Mardok. He was near the cherry tree, talking in hushed tones with Corwyn about the library in Killallia. When they saw me, they waved me over.

"I was going to take Mardok to see the library. Would you like to come?"

"I am where my husband is."

"I was counting on it." We grasped hands and appeared in the Entrance Hall of the Sphinx Library of Killallia. As we approached the entryway, a sphinx halted us.

"Grand mistress, your enchanted bag, please." He held out his clawed hand in expectation.

"Certainly, lord. And since I'm here, I have a musical script for you to copy. You're welcome to hold it until I return." I pulled it from my bag and handed it and the bag both to him. He peered over the script carefully and smiled.

"We don't have this one. Written by D'harias Indi Gra. Dvergr have dreadful music, do they not?"

"Empress Higridath gave it to me. It's new. I believe it was inspired by his current paramour, whose beauty I understand is all in the eye of the beholder."

"Do you know her name, perhaps?" the sphinx' eyes flashed with curiosity.

"Sadly, no. The empress has more decorum than I." I smiled at him. He was dreadfully disappointed.

"We are grateful for the addition, grand mistress." The sphinx bowed and bade us to enter.

"That's new for me," Mardok commented. "Stories have nothing on seeing the actual creatures."

"Grubby knowledge mongers," Corwyn whispered. "But if you ever need to know anything, and you have gold… or somehow something they don't know…" He eyed me curiously.

"I wouldn't know where to begin," said Mardok.

"The real reason I brought you here is because Father can't overhear what I need to talk to you about."

Mardok and I both looked at him quizzically.

"You don't sound like you're setting up a prank, Corwyn," I said expectantly.

"No, not this time. I saw Malachi here yesterday."

"Oh. I thought he was dealing with…"

"The priests of Satyriasis? Yeah, that's what I thought, too. Apparently not. I was just here trying to find a good word to describe Empress Higridath. Anyway…"

"Really? That's so mean."

"What's mean?"

"She's a sweet lady."

"She smells like a sack of troll…"

"Oh, stop it. She's put out so much to protect us. Do you know how many dvergr die every year keeping back goblins from Opella's house?"

"No, I don't. How many?" He had me.

"It's a lot." I glared, warning him not to argue.

"Fine. Anyway…"

"What was it?" Mardok spoke up.

"What was what?" Corwyn seemed displeased at being interrupted a second time.

"The word you found, for the empress."

"Oh… um… Graocrat. Anyway…"

"Graocrat?" I asked. What's that?" Corwyn rolled his eyes.

"It doesn't matter. Malachi was here, too. And he wasn't here for the words. He was studying a book. I'll show you." He turned to a centaur who waited. "Brin, could you bring the text that Malachi and I were viewing yesterday?" Brin nodded and stepped through a curtain.

"I was going to ask him about the priests of Satyriasis, until I noticed what he was reading. By the way, did you see the sunset last night?"

I stared at him. He made this painful. "I'm going to kill you if you don't get to the point."

"You have to wait. Brin's bringing it. And sphinx rules clearly state that you aren't allowed to kill anyone in their library."

I glared. "They actually like me; they might make an exception." We waited.

We waited longer.

Brin reemerged with the book. I recognized it immediately.

Mardok

Brin did not hand the book to Corwyn, but rather he carried it to a large wooden table, where he placed it with great care, even reverence. Corwyn thanked him with a coin and spread his arms as though displaying a prize.

The book was completely oversized, with glyphs covering its face and spine. The cover appeared to be some sort of reptilian leather, although it wasn't clear that the book wasn't alive. In fact, it appeared to be breathing ever so slightly.

"Corwyn, that's the Mystery Writings of Barus," Meira gasped.

"Yes, I know."

"I'm sorry," I interjected, "I'm unfamiliar with this particular book."

"The Mystery Writings of Barus," my wife explained, "this book here was written by Barus back in the Second Age, we believe. This is long before humans came into being."

"It's called the mystery writings, because no one can read it," Corwyn added. "Not even Barus himself anymore."

"How's that possible?"

"Back in the Third Age," Meira answered, "Barus divided his powers, and he lost the wisdom that was required to read it."

I was baffled. "You would think that if you write something, you could read it again, whenever."

395

"That would be the normal way of doing things for mortals, yes," Corwyn said. "But gods aren't subject to the same rules that we have. In many ways they're superior. But in some crucial ways mortals are. This is one of them. When Barus gave up his powers to create the lesser gods, he lost most of who he was in the process. I'm not certain he could read any language anymore."

"The question is," Meira pondered, "How was Malachi reading it? Did he get the power from another god? Can any of the other gods still read it?"

"So you have no idea what's in the book?" I inquired.

"Not a clue," Corwyn confirmed. "It could be really bad poetry for all we know."

"Or," Meira corrected, "it might actually be important. Let me show you." She opened the cover carefully. The front page contained thousands upon thousands of glyphs, all jumbled and in no particular order. Meira took her finger and touched the page. The letters moved away, bumping and crowding each other. Then she moved her finger around, and beneath where she passed several more letters appeared. They rushed to the edge of the page and vanished.

"Interesting?" she asked.

"Definitely."

Meira flipped the page and waited. The thickness of the book grew several inches. On this new page was something completely different. The glyphs were larger now and complicated. They appeared to be written in columns from the top and bottom of the page.

"Now this is where it gets tricky," Meira said. "Obviously there's something more to the book."

"Well, yes. It grew."

"But good luck getting to any of it." She pulled on the next page to flip it, but it wouldn't budge. "And that's pretty much what we know about the Mystery Writings of Barus." She closed the book.

"What do the glyphs mean?"

"Well, individually some of them are the same as glyphs we use now. For example, on the first page I recognized the glyphs for cactus and purple. But there's no guarantee that Barus used those glyphs to means those things when he wrote it."

"We're not even certain that anyone other than Barus used that language," Corwyn explained.

"So it really is a mystery," I stated.

"Was, at least. When I arrived yesterday, Malachi was reading from the rest of the book."

"That's creepy. How?"

"He wasn't exactly in an expansive mood. But what he did tell me was this. Sometime during the last week he began to understand a bit of the language. I'm not sure how he knew; he just did. So he started reading. And amongst his research he found various forms of power and magic that would give him a means of defeating T'xerren Nahasmen—things that some of the gods know but refuse to share."

"The gods have always been like that. It's not really a

surprise."

"His words, not mine. Anyway, this knowledge can apparently make it possible for him to confront Nahasmen directly. So he's planning a frontal assault."

"That's insane," Meira told him.

"Except that he has the magic that he needs to defeat him. Well, he almost has it. He's still reading."

"What magic is this?"

"He didn't say."

"He didn't say, or you didn't ask?" Meira questioned.

"I asked. You don't think I would pass that up, do you?"

"Well," she said, "I just know that with Malachi sometimes it's safer not to ask."

"He wants us to go with him."

"Like I said, it was safer not to ask."

"Specifically, he wants Mardok and me to come. He doesn't want you within a thousand miles of the island."

"I'm not a tiny tot anymore. I think I've proved myself."

"That's the problem. You've executed three of his agents and demolished one of his armies, besides assisting in dispatching a mage. Nahasmen will see you as a prime target for possession. You're too powerful."

"Like Malachi isn't."

"I resent that. I would like to think that I'm a pretty good target, too."

I snickered. "Death to the world by laughter."

Meira laughed.

"Okay, fine, I know I'm not the most dangerous Fae the world has seen. But it's precisely my skill that Malachi wants."

"He needs a teleporter," I presumed.

"No, he needs someone who can keep his mouth shut around Father. Father can't know anything about this. He would never approve."

"Well, if Father knew that Malachi had a new form of magic available…"

"He said that he's already talked to Father about it. But Father's hard-set on his plan to simply keep Nahasmen contained. The problem is that we can't do that any longer. The renegade txipiroi is evidence enough of that."

"Father's no fool." Meira was defensive now.

"And neither is Malachi. The difference is that now Malachi knows more than Father does. And let's face it; the world's changing. Malachi is out in the thick of it every day. Father isn't."

"So what's Malachi's plan then?"

"He's working out a way to capture Nahasmen, like he has a few of the other gods."

"Malachi has captured gods?" I was stunned.

"Yes. Technically, he kills them and captures their released powers, but it's essentially the same thing. You didn't know that?" Corwyn cocked his head to the side, bewildered.

"No. That... that one's a bit of a surprise." I paused, and the puzzled look on my face gave them something to stare at for a bit before I continued. "If Malachi captures... kills gods, what's so difficult about destroying Nahasmen?"

"Well," Meira started, "Nahasmen isn't exactly like the gods. It isn't properly formed. For one, it's completely ethereal, so there's nothing to kill. It's like trying to stab a cloud. And when you kill a god, you, or someone near you, tend to acquire the powers of the god you just killed. But Nahasmen doesn't submit when someone absorbs it. It takes over the person instead. We believe it's part of the curse that was put on it. But Malachi thinks he can correct that?" she inquired of Corwyn.

"He's certain of it. Barus described how it's done. Personally, I think it explains what happened after the death of Indar."

"Well then," I stated, "victory is in our grasp."

"Yes, it is. Soon."

"We need to get back," said Meira. "The time."

"Yes, we do. Brin, we're done. Thank you." The centaur and Corwyn exchanged brief pleasantries, and then we walked to the entrance hall.

"When do we leave for the island?" I asked.

"Not yet. Malachi has to get ready. He's looking for a few things, and then we can leave."

"That sounds wonderful. To victory?" I prompted my new brother.

"To victory."

We grasped hands, looked within our minds eye at the house in which Opella still dwelt, and blinked.

About the Author

As a teenager Rebekkah Kniffen would hide in the corners of her school libraries, reading everything on the shelves — especially fantasy. The spectacular worlds opened up her imagination to the impossible. She writes from a desire to share her love of literature with the world.

Rebekkah Kniffen is a Christian, a dearly loved wife, a mother of seven, and grandmother of one (so far). She enjoys sewing renaissance costumes and works as a project manager at a Seminary in the DFW area of Texas.

www.ingramcontent.com/pod-product-compliance
Lightning Source LLC
Chambersburg PA
CBHW051000210726
48287CB00004B/1312